# Sergi

## OF BLOOD AND DREAMS
### BOOK SEVEN

KIM ALLRED

STORM COAST PUBLISHING LLC

SERGI
Of Blood and Dreams, Book 7
KIM ALLRED

Published by Storm Coast Publishing, LLC

Copyright © 2025 by Kim Allred
Cover Art by Dark City Designs

Print edition March 2025
ISBN 978-1-953832-42-9

This book is a work of fiction. Names, characters, places, incidents, and dialogue are either drawn from the author's imagination or are used fictitiously. Any resemblance to actual events or locales or persons, living or dead, is entirely coincidental and beyond the intent of the author or publisher.

Know thy self, know thy enemy. A thousand battles, a thousand victories.

*Sun Tzu*

THE SLOW DRIP of water trickled onto the hard stone floor, the endless sound echoing through the dark, dank tunnels. Lanterns, barely bright enough to ward off the lurking shadows, reflected down the wide passages that led to a maze of narrower ones and dimly reflected the aged wooden doors. Behind each one, small barren rooms carved from granite like the tunnels themselves were empty.

Except for one.

In that cell, third from the end of this particular passage, the latent sound of a harsh pounding followed by a slamming door slowly pierced the peacefulness of sleep.

The beast woke.

It took a moment for its eyes to adjust to the darkness. It was weak. Thirsty. Tremors clutched its gut, and every nerve ending sizzled as if on fire. The bone-chilling air was the only comfort, numbing most of the excruciating pain.

But nothing tortured it more than its hunger. Its ravenous need to feed.

The only peace was in slumber.

Sometime later, the vampire lifted his chin and glanced

through the dim light, confirming he was still alone. That was good.

He dropped his head, his body held upright by a four-inch steel band that stretched across his chest and bolted to the wall on either side of him. His arms were spread wide, held in place by narrow steel manacles strapped to the wall.

Even the beast wished for the hard surface to lay on.

He wasn't sure if he'd fallen asleep again, but his eyes popped open at the scratching of wood on wood as the bar that locked the door was lifted. His body tensed, preparing for the next round of torture—or worse—the tainted blood.

The door scraped along the stone floor as it was pushed open. The light from the hallway cast a long shadow of the lone figure. It scurried in, quick as a mouse.

The beast howled.

# Chapter One

*Four weeks earlier - somewhere in the Carpathian Mountains*

I unrolled from a fetal position and slowly stretched my aching muscles, stiff from the cold air. Eleven months and the chill still bothered me. Though not nearly as much as the hard surface of the stone floor, barely tolerable beneath the thin, lumpy pad.

I pushed back my unwashed hair, still expecting to feel the long, dark strands that had been sheared off when I'd first arrived. It had grown to frame my face, but even this short, it was dull and tangled. At some point, they'd chop it off again.

Accustomed to the darkness, I made my way to the bucket in the corner, lifting my knees in a highly exaggerated manner, a macabre march to start the blood flowing, grimacing as the pins and needles sensation worked its way through me. After squatting to relieve myself, I continued with my morning ritual, shuffling to a different corner to run my fingers over the scratched markings on the rock wall. I bent and picked up the small stone tucked away in an easy-to-find spot and spent several minutes scratching another mark. I ran my fingers over them as I counted and breathed a sigh, pushing back the tears I thought I'd spent months ago.

Day twenty. Bath day.

Thank god. I didn't think I could take another day of my own stink.

After performing my daily exercises, I ran a filthy finger over my teeth. It was the only way to remove the film from the evening until the daily ration of water arrived with the porridge. If I was lucky, they'd include a hardboiled egg.

Even better if they assigned me to a work detail. I hadn't been given one since my last bath day. Not after I stuck Tallon, my guard, in the neck with a fork. He didn't die—unfortunately. But he was the floor leader, and no one questioned his right to take whatever female he wanted.

Until I said no.

I'd take the twenty days locked alone in my cell to rape any day. The fear had dissipated months ago, but I wouldn't give up hope or my humanity. Not yet.

The dull whacks of the billy club on wooden doors brought me around to face mine, placing myself in the middle of the room, ready to defend myself. Or grab the breakfast tray the guard slipped through the slit in the bottom of the door.

The next few moments were a fifty-fifty chance of going either way.

When the bolt securing the door slid to the side, I braced myself. They didn't come to take me for my bath until midday. Maybe I was being assigned to a work detail.

I squinted against the glare of the light as the door burst open. When the shifter came at me, I moved as quickly as I could, but there was nowhere to run in my ten-by-ten cell. It was more my well-honed instinct not to make it easy on anyone meant to harm me.

It was useless to fight, and most of the time, I played the game and appeared weak—but not with this guard. Tallon quickly caught me and slammed me against the hard stone wall. His hand gripped my neck, holding me in place, and I tugged at his fingers as he slowly choked me, my feet dangling an inch from the floor.

His breath stank as he slowly sniffed me, his body leaning into mine. "I should throw you on your mat and take what I want. I should have done it months ago. But the Master has forbidden it. Even after you stuck me in the neck." He squeezed my breast before running his hand between my legs.

"They think they know you. That you've tamed down to a willing slave. That you only acted out because I wanted a taste of you." His lips hovered over mine, then he continued his sniffing like the good hound he was. He whispered in my ear, "But I know better. They'll have problems with you. Remember one thing, girl. The Master might have a say during the day, but he's not here during the long, cold evenings. There are ways to hurt you that will never leave a mark."

He let go. I dropped to the floor and clutched my aching throat, grateful for the chilled air I slowly sucked in as it numbed the pain.

"The Master has an assignment for you." He chuckled. "And I can't think of anyone better for the job. Now get up. You're to eat your breakfast in the common room today."

I scurried to my feet, unwilling to give him any excuse to hit me. Not that he needed one, but I wouldn't lose the opportunity to get out of my cell, even for a day.

I didn't like the sound of this new assignment, but if it kept me away from this bastard, it was enough. How simple life became when you only had one thing to worry about.

Survival.

~

TALLON LEFT me with the women attendants who stripped the ragged shift from me before they pushed me into a wooden tub of cold water. I shivered as they soaped and scrubbed me with harsh brushes until my skin turned red. At least they washed my hair.

A clean shift made of rough fabric wasn't new. It would have been scoured and bleached many times over. Old stains marred the brown fabric, giving it a mottled appearance. I gave up wondering where the stains came from long ago. Just like I'd stopped wondering if anyone would come for me, or whether they thought me dead.

The first few weeks after my capture, I'd paced my cell over and over again, fighting the claustrophobia and fear that I would never leave this hellhole. Not until I was dead. One year. Five. Longer.

Would I be the same person or forever changed? Would the self-preservation blanket I wrapped myself in morph from the terror of living in this place to fear of everything outside these barren walls? Was it possible I might escape, only to live alone, afraid of my own shadow?

I smiled as the attendants handed me the worn rubber-soled slippers. The icy air forced goose bumps to rise over my skin, and I shivered, almost laughing as they sneered at me as if I were a raging beast.

My thoughts wandered to my uncle and his words of comfort so freely given. He would stare down at me with his deep, nut-brown gaze, searching into the depths of my soul before leaning in until our foreheads touched. "You are wolf, Alexandra. Let no one take that away from you. She will protect you."

So, every morning when I woke, I spoke to my wolf. It was against the rules to shift, punishable in ways I didn't want to know. I'd heard enough as the screams echoed through the tunnels.

But sometimes, on nights when my uncle's words couldn't comfort me, I let the wolf come out. If nothing else, I slept warmly, until I heard the first slam of a wooden billy club hit the door at the end of the hall, and I shifted back.

"Come on, girl." Tallon stuck his head through the open door-way. "You're late if you want any breakfast."

I trailed behind him as we climbed the stairs from the third level to the first and traversed the passageways that were no longer made of rock but of drywall and painted a stark white. My slippers shuffled over pristine tile floors rather than rough stone. Cool filtered air streamed through vents and smelled of disinfectant rather than unwashed bodies, feces, and blood.

The cafeteria, where some of the captives were allowed to eat, was the dividing point between the cells and the labs. A thick wall of impenetrable frosted glass separated the paid lab staff from the rest of us. It wouldn't be proper to force the privileged to look upon the slaves while they ate.

It was bad enough they might have to look upon those who were deemed safe enough to work in the labs. Not that we'd ever be entrusted with anything important, but someone had to clean the rooms or—and the thought made me shiver—become a subject for the scientists' experiments.

Breakfast was a thick porridge, what I would usually get in my cell, in addition to scrambled eggs and a few slices of banana. I savored the coffee, which was surprisingly strong, and it warmed my bones.

I ate quietly at a table with six other prisoners. Talking among ourselves wasn't permitted. The only sound was the scraping of spoons as we finished our meal.

"S-473." The female's voice was monotone as she studied a tablet. After a moment, when no one responded, she lifted her head. "Shifter 473." This time her words were spoken slowly and loudly as she gazed around the room, her eyes stern and her jaw clenched.

We didn't have names—just numbers. And it took a moment to realize she was calling out the one I'd been assigned. It had been some time since I'd heard anyone use it. I was usually called *girl*, or *dog*, or some other unpleasant curse.

I raised my hand, and two male attendants grabbed my arms, pulling me from the table. I didn't struggle as they led me to the door where the female stood. She looked me over, her face a mask of indifference, then nodded.

"She'll do."

I didn't like the sound of that, and when I was led down a corridor with more white tile flooring, white walls, and white ceiling tiles, I wanted to squirm. Was I someone's next experiment?

The attendants released my arms but stayed two steps behind me as I followed the female, panic seizing my throat with every room we passed until we came to a set of double doors. The female waved her badge over a pad, and the doors slid open.

I took a step back when I saw the carnage inside, a hand flying to my mouth in a reflexive movement to keep my breakfast from returning. The attendants pushed me forward.

Blood was everywhere, mixed with lumps. A quick glance was all I needed to know the lumps were bits of flesh, some with short strands of hair still clinging to it.

The gore was on the floor, on the walls, and dripping from the ceiling. It had splashed over the stainless steel tables and counters. The scent was easy to recognize. Shifter flesh. The heat of the lamps and overhead lighting warmed the blood and intensified the stench.

Humans wouldn't smell the decaying flesh as intensely as a vampire or shifter, but it would still activate the gag reflexes, as was evidenced by the female who began breathing through her mouth.

"We need this lab spotless by tomorrow. S-272 will show you where the cleaning supplies are stored. You'll be returned to your cell once the lab is ready for the next experiment." She glanced at her tablet then nodded at the attendants, who stepped back.

If I weren't so sick at the sight of the lab, I would have smiled at how pale the attendants had become.

"S-272, come here." The female tapped the tablet against her leg.

A sound of scraping came from a far corner, and an older male shifter lifted his head, glancing around. Seeing the female, he nodded and moved out from around a counter. He wasn't very tall and was as thin as the rest of us. He walked with an exaggerated limp, but if it caused him any pain, he didn't show it. So, an old wound.

"Yes, mistress." His tone was submissive as he bowed his head. A good little shifter slave greeting his master.

"This is S-473. She'll be assisting you today." The female gave me a side glance, and I lowered my head. "If she works to your satisfaction, I'll consider her for your assistant. We've been ordered to increase the experiments."

I gave the female a quick peek. Did she notice the twitch in his shoulders, the tension now riding along his back? I didn't think so, but, as a shifter, it was possible I was the only one who would notice. For the moment, I would hold my judgment on S-272 until I spent time with him. But I would have to tread carefully.

While most of the imprisoned shifters would fight if given half the chance, some had been enslaved for too long and would defend their masters—human or vampire.

S-272 took a moment to look me over with a detached glance. "Yes, mistress."

"I know she doesn't look like much, but according to her chart, she listens and does what is asked of her. We'll see if she can appropriately handle the benefit of working outside the cells."

"Yes, mistress." He continued to nod like a bobblehead.

"I'll send someone to check your progress in two hours."

The doors slid shut, and the lock engaged.

S-272 turned to me, his blank expression never changing, but I saw a spark of interest in his gaze before he dropped his head. "Follow me."

I trailed after him, staring at the blood-soaked room. All of a sudden, stuck in my cell didn't seem so bad after all.

# Chapter Two

I was pushed into my cell, barely able to walk as I dropped onto my sleeping mat, too tired to eat the cup of congealed stew that had been left for me. After five straight days, I was utterly exhausted from cleaning the bloody aftermath of the vampires' failed experiments on shifters.

On my first day working with S-272, the only words he spoke were to tell me where the cleaning supplies and water basin were. Then he grumbled a word or two each time he assigned a new task after I completed the previous one. He could have just told me to clean one side of the lab, but for some reason, he broke the jobs down to a specific table or counter and then a narrow section of the tiled floor or wall.

He might have been testing me, or maybe he didn't think I could understand simple directions. I chalked it up to him spending too many years in service to the vampires. They had always looked down on shifters as if we were nothing more than dimwitted apes and not the intelligent, pack-oriented species we were.

On the second day, as each cleaning area grew in size, it confirmed my earlier suspicions that S-272 was testing me. The next day, the tasks returned to his careful doling out of smaller tasks, ensuring each one had been completed to his satisfaction before assigning the next one. It took the fourth day before I understood he was waiting for me to complain with frustration and sloppy work.

Today had been different.

Each of the previous days, as we cleaned up the remains of one of our own, S-272 never showed any emotion. He'd either grown cold and indifferent with time, or he'd learned to mask his emotions.

I handled it much the same way. It wasn't that I didn't care that it was shifter flesh and bits of bone I scraped off the floor or cabinets. It was easier because I had no idea who the shifters had been—no facial image to haunt my dreams and no knowledge of the life they'd led that warranted such a horrendous end. It would catch up with me, and until then, I would keep my head down and do the work.

But today, S-272 kept to himself, and I only caught his gaze twice. Both times, his eyes brimmed with unshed tears. Each time, I glanced away. And I understood. This one. This shifter, who was nothing more than a bucket of remains that were dumped into a hazardous waste receptacle, had been someone S-272 had known. Possibly cared for.

It gutted me.

I had wiped my eyes with the sleeve of my blood-stained lab coat and continued the task before me. Now, all I wanted to do was sleep and forget.

Forget where I was. Forget my new assignment. Forget all I'd left behind. Forget who I had been.

I was S-473.

~

I TENSED in weary sleep when I heard the billy club at my door. It couldn't have been more than an hour or two since I'd dropped onto my mat. I moaned when the door burst open and a bright light from a lantern shone on me.

"Get up, girl." Tallon stomped over and nudged my arm with the tip of his boot. When I didn't immediately respond, he kicked my side, forcing me to roll over and cringe in pain.

I drew in a shaky breath and threw an arm over my face as I forced my eyes to adjust to the brightness.

Sour breath coated with liquor almost made me gag as he bent close. "I don't know what you did to curry such favor, but you're being moved to fancier quarters." He ran a hand down my arm and over my hip, letting it rest there. "This might be the last time for us to get to know each other better." He rubbed my hip before sliding his hand down to my thigh, squeezing the soft flesh before moving to cup the spot between my legs. "It might be worth whatever punishment they give me."

I rolled away, but he yanked me back.

"One wrong move on your part, and it will be a long time before you see the outside of your cell again. Where you will remain under my warm regard and protection."

He was locking me into no choice at all. I could either submit for one night or suffer the threat of him coming to this cell whenever he wanted. It wasn't a choice at all, but that didn't mean I wouldn't fight him. I would have to be smarter than the last time he tried.

Rather than roll away again, I slowly sat up and pulled my thin blanket around me. I stared at him, and my gut clenched at his leer and the crazed look in his gaze. He gripped my chin.

"Now that's better. You and I can have a good time if you just cooperate."

Cooperate. That was one word for it.

He leaned in, and I closed my eyes and held my breath.

"Tallon!"

He jumped up so fast that I was knocked to the side. I yelped when his boot tromped on my ankle.

"Yes, sir."

"S-473 needs to be moved now. Find your pleasure with someone else."

While I was relieved by the statement, I worried who that someone else would be. It was bad enough, or perhaps typical, that the chain of command didn't care that females were being raped. I'd never had to worry about sexual abuse until Tallon came along. The guard before him preferred young male shifters.

I stood and wrapped the blanket tighter.

"Take her to the commissary and hand her off to the attendant who's waiting for her."

While I might have escaped his rape, Tallon had no problem squeezing my arm so tight he'd leave a bruise. Or, with his strength, crush the bone. He dragged me through the corridors and up the stairs as if I couldn't remember where the commissary was. All the prisoners visited the place every three months to receive freshly-washed clothes and a pair of slippers.

Tallon's rough treatment had nothing to do with whether I could keep up with his fast pace. His anger stemmed from his loss at brutalizing me now that I would be in a different ward. I would thank my lucky stars if they hadn't deserted me months ago. The sad truth was that a better cell didn't mean my new guard would be any less savage.

Regardless of what my new situation might become, at least I'd seen the last of Tallon—or so I hoped.

When we reached the upper floor, Tallon stopped in front of the attendant and stormed off. I didn't give him a backward glance. Instead, I turned to the slim female with a beak nose and stern, steely eyes. Rather than speak to me, she nodded toward the plastic bucket that held my new clothes. I picked it up and followed her down a different set of corridors. Whether in the rock-hewn tunnels or these sterile white halls, they all looked the same, except for the plaques that either indicated a room number or arrows pointing to a different section.

I'd only been in this area of the underground lab when I'd first been captured. I'd been on smaller missions, but this had been the first truly important one. We'd been a four-shifter team. Our mission had been to locate the lab.

*Well, we'd found it. Hurrah!*

After we'd been darted and dragged inside, my attitude, a mixture of sheer rage and fear, had put me in the disciplinary ward for several weeks before being moved to this section. I'd only been an occupant for a couple of months before I shoved a guard away from a shifter he'd been beating during a work detail. That was how I ended up down on the third level.

These cells weren't any larger than the rock-lined one I'd been living in. However, they were more civilized pens with four white walls, a small cot, and a curtained area for my waste. The doors had the same slit carved out at the bottom to provide food and water.

On a positive note, there would be more days of eating in the cafeteria, but most of my meals would still be eaten alone in my cell.

The attendant stopped in the middle of one of the shorter hallways. There were eight cells, all on one side with a plain wall on the other. My cell was the third one from where we entered the corridor. We were rarely let out in groups, so it was impossible to know who, if anyone, was in the cells next to us.

On the third level, the doors weren't locked, just barred with a wooden crossbar. These doors were more advanced and opened with a key card. Each guard had one that could open all the cell doors, but with this hi-tech facility, I assumed someone in a heavily secured communications room would have access to all the locks from a single terminal. Not that the knowledge helped me in any way. The closer one was to the labs, the more they relied on the tech to keep us safely locked up.

When the door to my new cell opened, I walked inside without prodding. Yep. Exactly as I remembered it. The mattress on the cot was as thin as the one in my old cell, but the blanket was thicker. I'd be warmer.

"Someone will be here to retrieve you in the morning at eight o'clock sharp. Make sure you've eaten and relieved yourself. You won't have another chance until your mid-day break."

I set the bucket down and pulled out the clothing, laying each article on the bed. A new shift, this time, though the fabric was still rough, it was blue—or, various shades of it. The cloth had been bleached so many times the color had become a variety of hues, but it was good enough to signify I'd be working in the labs. The slippers were similar except for a thicker sole. There was new underwear and underneath the first set was a second identical one. The last item was a white lab coat.

It made sense. It was impossible to go an entire day without smearing blood on my lab coat. The shift would be mostly protected, but I'd have a second set available while the first was being washed, which, if I remembered correctly, was every third day.

A new lab coat was provided at the end of each day after the bloodstained one was dropped in a hazardous waste receptacle. In some way, it made me sad.

At least the blood added some color to the monotone environment.

I giggled at my macabre humor.

Perhaps it was my first step into madness.

# Chapter Three

CRESSA LANGTRY TOSSED in her sleep, the dream forming in bits and pieces. Sweat broke out on her forehead, and she reached for her temple, her skin damp under her touch. She slowed her breathing, searching the room that was both foreign and familiar.

She sat at a long dining table and her eyes caught on the flickering light of flames in the centerpiece display. Her breaths slowed as she focused on one steady flame, her meditation technique calming her.

This wasn't a dreamwalk of her making. And it was too realistic to be a mere dream. Was she in some dreamwalker nightmare?

She glanced down at the sage silk dress she wore. A gold tennis bracelet scratched against her left wrist. The aromatic scent of what she knew without looking came from the remains of a roasted pheasant dinner woke a few buds of hunger.

She was tempted to take a drink from the half-empty wineglass because this wasn't a normal dreamwalk. How could a memory be so vivid, as if she had time warped back to the actual event?

Voices snapped her out of her reverie but not out of the dream. She gasped when she turned to the right.

Lorenzo Venizi leaned back in his seat at the head of the table.

*What the holy hell?*

The earlier anxiety returned. Her heart raced, and the cold hands of fear snaked through her when she couldn't rise from the chair. Okay. So, she had limited control of this dream. Was that because when she'd been on Shadow Island, she'd been mesmerized at this point?

Lorenzo's gray suit matched the hair at his temples. The vamp was a handsome male. Sophisticated, well-educated, and charming —when he wanted to be. He commanded a room and had many like-minded friends, but at the end of the day, he was nothing more than an asshole with evil intent. No better than a sleazy bounty hunter like Sorrento.

If he'd noticed her gasp when she first set eyes on him, he didn't show it. In fact, he wasn't looking at her at all.

She turned her head to follow his line of sight to find a thin man with a severely balding head. The few thin strands that remained were a dull, dusty blond. Almost transparent in the low light of the room. His equally dull brown suit hung from him as if, at one time, he'd weighed fifty pounds more and never thought to buy a new one after losing the weight. He wore glasses that perched halfway down the bridge of his nose, and she itched to push them back up.

He seemed familiar.

She tapped the table with her fork, surprised she could do that much.

"Hello."

When no one acknowledged her greeting or the tapping of the utensil, she determined she'd reached the parameters of the dream. She didn't appear to be needed for the dream to continue, so she let her gaze drift around the room as she recalled her memory of this event.

She'd only been on Shadow Island for two or three days before Lorenzo brought home a dinner guest and wanted her to attend the meal. Dinner conversation was subpar as the little man had fidgeted through most of the meal, though it hadn't been from fear of being in Lorenzo's home. They had business to discuss, and he wanted to get to it. He was almost salivating.

Lorenzo had been aggravated but finally relented once the main course was finished. When the crème brûlée and coffee were served, he placed a new linen napkin over his lap and said, "Tell me what's so important, you've squirmed all through dinner."

She remembered being bored as she played with her dessert, more interested in the coffee, and, unknowingly at the time, she'd let Pandora out to search the room for valuables. Try as she might, she'd always be a thief at heart.

At some point, the cadence of Lorenzo's tone shifted, and though she hadn't thought much of it at the time, he sat up and leaned into the table. She'd seen that look before. A long stare, his gaze unfocused, like a robot that froze as it ran multiple calculations.

What had they been talking about?

Then it flashed before her as the little man in her dream replayed part of the conversation she'd missed from her memories. He was working on a special project. Tests had been performed, but the earlier formulas hadn't provided satisfactory results. Until recently. Someone had stumbled upon a formula that performed to most of Lorenzo's specifications. They would need to perform more testing before it could be considered reliable in the field, but they were very close.

Lorenzo's entire demeanor had changed to one of extreme interest and eerie satisfaction. His focus shifted, catching her off guard as his gaze locked with hers—it was the eyes of his beast.

"Forget what you've heard, Cressa. This is of no concern to you."

She snapped awake and popped up. The earlier sweat that had dried was back. She glanced around. Devon's room.

Her breath rushed out as if she'd been holding it for hours. She looked at the empty spot next to her. Devon was gone. Her gaze slid to the drapes, where enough light leaked around the edges to signal it was morning.

What the hell had just happened?

She threw the covers off and jumped in the shower to wash the sweat away, then quickly threw on jeans and a pullover sweater. The clock reflected thirty minutes before breakfast. She had to talk to Devon.

When she reached the stairs, she stopped and changed course to her bedroom. She had time for one quick call.

$\sim$

DEVON TRELANE ROSE EARLY. He hadn't slept well. Something nagged. Something he'd overlooked. He couldn't pin it down, which only served to annoy him. Rather than having Cressa wake up to an irritated vampire, he dressed, stopped in the kitchen for a mug of coffee, and shuffled to his office, still half-asleep.

With his feet resting on the shelf behind his desk, he stared out the window at the breaking dawn as the caffeine cleared the cobwebs. It was unusual for him to be scattered, but he sensed a pending doom he hadn't felt for decades, not since before his parents' horrific deaths. A tragedy he'd been unable to foresee or prevent.

No matter how hard he tried, he couldn't shake loose what lay just beyond his grasp. After twenty minutes in a meditative state that provided no solution to his quandary, a knock at the door saved him from further useless attempts.

"Come."

The door opened to reveal Cook with a carafe of coffee and, if his nose wasn't deceiving him, a beignet.

"I'm sorry to disturb you, but I knew you'd require more coffee, and I thought a bit of sugar might help start your day." He placed the plate down along with a fork and napkin.

Devon smiled at the offering. "You've been speaking with Romero's chef."

"And I had to give up two of my most treasured recipes in exchange for her secret beignet recipe." His voice held disappointment in what he perceived as an unfair exchange, but he winked. "She promised to share another secret, but she wanted to try the recipes I gave her first. She's a tough one, but I have high hopes for many more exchanges."

Devon smiled as Cook rushed out the door. Breakfast was a busy time for him, even though most of their guests had left while the Family planned for the next stage in the House war against Venizi. Once the sugary treat and another cup of coffee were devoured, he picked up the folder that held notes from the raid on the Underwood mansion where they'd removed Cressa's mother and half-sister from under Venizi's control.

So far, Jasper, the vampire Venizi had placed in charge at Underwood's estate, had been unwilling to give them any useful information. They were, however, able to get a sample of his writing, which validated the journal Harlow had taken from Underwood's office had belonged to the vampire. More time in a cell might soften him, but Devon couldn't shake the thought that time was of the essence.

The problem was, he didn't know what could be so critical.

Devon refilled his mug and spread the contents of the folder across his desk. Most of the papers held nothing of interest. Security protocols and guard rotations that Sergi and Simone might find interesting if Devon decided to attack Lorenzo's businesses. Then his focus turned to Jasper's thin journal.

He was intrigued that a young vampire like Jasper would use pen and paper for notes rather than a tablet like most males his age would. He opened it and ran a hand over the first page. This would be his third review of the pages, and while he hadn't found anything of interest the first two times, something made him go through it again.

It wasn't a diary, nor did it retain critical notes from meetings. That information had likely been entered into a tablet or computer. The pages of the journal seemed to be nothing more than general observations of humans and brainstorming sessions—either from a meeting with his guards or his own private thoughts. The lines of script were a hodgepodge of incomplete sentences. Words and phrases that meant nothing to Devon. Perhaps they were ideas from previous missions or ones that were being planned. The various strings of information might be connected or simply random thoughts of a bored vampire. Sergi and Lucas were still reviewing them against reports from Trelane's security details.

He was closing the folder when something caught his eye. Carpathian Mountains. The name was listed by itself with a space above and a space below. A single thought or something more?

He shut the folder and, unable to think about anything else, picked up the handful of folders Sergi had left for him. The morning meeting wouldn't start for another couple of hours, so he might as well return them.

Sergi was in his office, reworking the weekly security changes. He was surprised to see Devon. "I could have come for those."

Devon dropped them on the desk and took a seat. "Not necessary. How else will I get my exercise?"

Sergi typed a few more words then closed his tablet and gave him a sour look. "It's been too long since we've trained."

"No time like the present."

Two hours later, they sprawled on the training room mats, staring at the ceiling as their sweat slowly evaporated.

"I needed that." Devon flexed his leg. "I think I pulled a hamstring."

"There's no excuse for that," Sergi grumbled.

"We need to get back to our weekly schedule."

Sergi's only response was a grunt. After centuries of their long friendship, Devon understood the non-verbal to mean it took Devon long enough to realize it.

A comfortable silence returned, and after several long minutes, Devon asked, "Have you heard any recent news about the Carpathian Mountains?"

～

SERGI STRODE in step with Devon, both eager to return to Devon's office to review the journal and the notes Sergi had put together. Devon had pushed the morning meeting to after lunch, but when they arrived at Devon's office, it wasn't empty.

Cressa paced the room, clearly upset about something. Decker, who'd driven over before receiving the text about the postponed meeting, sat on his usual stool, leaning back against the bar as he watched Cressa, an amused expression on his face.

"What's all this?" Devon asked as he dropped into his chair.

Sergi glared at Cressa. When she stuck her tongue out, he held back his smile. He wasn't sure when it started, but they began challenging each other with the pettiest of games. His fallback was the one thing he knew irritated her the most—stare blankly at her for an uncomfortable length of time before turning to his tablet.

He held a deep respect for Cressa, who he considered to be Devon's consort, but it wasn't her relationship with his friend that earned Sergi's favor. It was her loyalty and determination to never quit, like when she crawled along the training room floor and attempted to rise even when she knew she'd been beaten. She was a warrior on the battlefield. Yet, she was a human, dreamwalker or not, who was loud and pushed boundaries. She would never change, and Sergi came to terms with that. She enjoyed rattling others, so he considered it fair game to return the favor. Everyone needed a pastime.

Cressa ignored Sergi and shifted her gaze to Devon, exploding with hyper anxiety. "I remember something from when I was at Shadow Island."

Sergi shifted in his seat and waited.

Devon glanced at Decker, who shrugged. So, she hadn't shared it with the shifter. She'd been waiting for Devon. "Sit down and tell us."

She paced for another minute before finding a chair but only perched on the edge as if ready to take flight, reminding Sergi of Bella and her need to be in constant motion. Her foot tapped with the energy roiling in her, but Devon's calm tone soothed her. She blew out a long sigh, leaned back in her seat, and ran her fingers through her hair.

"It came in a dream, but it wasn't a normal dream, and it wasn't a dreamwalk. I'm not sure what it was. I was at dinner with Lorenzo and one of his business associates. If I had to guess, the vamp was a doctor or scientist of some sort." She picked at the edge of her sweater. Her fingers found a loose yarn, and she began twisting it. "I was fully aware during the dream. I could smell the leftovers from dinner and the light scent of candles. The strange thing was that I couldn't leave my seat, but I could move my arms and hands. When I called out, neither vamp seemed to hear me."

"You're sure this wasn't a dreamwalk?" Devon had leaned back and was holding the white crystal that seemed to focus him.

"No." She shrugged. "Although, I don't remember dreamwalking in a past event. Only current or future ones."

Devon turned the crystal, moving it from one hand to the next. "It makes sense you wouldn't be able to change an event that already happened. What was so important about this dinner?"

"It was the discussion between Lorenzo and this other vamp. The guy had been anxious since he arrived. I assumed it was nervousness being around Lorenzo, but the man droned on about tests and statistics that bored me at the time. I barely listened to any of it and was relieved when Lorenzo dismissed me."

Sergi met Devon's glance. They had to be thinking the same thing. Did this have something to do with the lab?

"Your subconscious must have picked up on something for

you to dream about it now." Devon gripped the crystal and leaned forward, his forehead scrunched in thought.

She heaved a sigh and let her head fall back until she stared at the ceiling. "I don't know. Now, talking about it out loud, it doesn't seem very important."

"Just tell us the first thing you remembered," Devon encouraged.

These were the moments that defined Devon's leadership skills. Sergi had seen it in his leader since their early days. Devon's willingness to slow down and make the speaker feel at ease, gently luring the information out of them. He was using the same technique with Jasper in hopes of breaking Venizi's hold over him.

"I woke to find myself at the dinner table. Dessert had just been served. I don't remember specifics, even though the vamp couldn't stop talking all through dinner. It upset Lorenzo, who kept trying to change the subject."

"He didn't want you to hear sensitive information." Sergi almost grinned at Cressa's immediate nod as she turned to him.

"Exactly. That was my thought during the dream. But I don't remember it concerning me at the time. It was just before Lorenzo excused me that the vamp mentioned something about the tests being successful, but they required time for further refinements or something to that effect. He said they were close to field tests."

"Dammit," Decker swore.

"How can we be sure this dream is accurate?" Sergi asked. "Your subconscious could be adding false information based on our discussions about the blood results from Remus's lab."

She nodded, which surprised Sergi. He expected her to be frustrated by his question. Another example of her maturity since first arriving at the manor. "At first, I was positive, then I wasn't so sure. Not until I discussed it with Colantha."

"You spoke with her about this?" Devon asked.

"While you and Sergi were in the training room. She said dreamwalkers dream about past events like any other human, but she thought my experience, especially my ability to pick up smells, sounded odd."

"When was this dinner in relation to when you first arrived on the island?" Sergi had a feeling he understood why this particular dream was different.

"Colantha asked that too. It was either the second or third night."

Devon picked up on Sergi's train of thought. "Before we tried to reach out to you."

She nodded.

"While you were under his mesmerizing." Sergi didn't fully grasp how dreamwalking worked, but at the time, Colantha had suspicions that even though Cressa had been mesmerized, it wasn't as deep or as effective as Venizi assumed. Her dreamwalker nature, though subject to mesmerizing, would eventually override the mental push from Venizi. At least enough to make her question what she was being told.

Cressa nodded again. "That's what Colantha believes. With all our current discussions focused on Lorenzo's labs, my latent memories of that meal are resurfacing. My dreamwalker nature is making them more realistic, putting me in the middle of the dream with full awareness."

Decker stood, his face a mask of anger. "If what Cressa remembers this vampire saying is true, then Venizi is close to field testing, assuming he hasn't already started. And we don't know if it's some new version of Magic Poppy or something worse. We need to find that lab."

# Chapter Four

SERGI SETTLED back in the leather armchair and rested his feet on the ottoman. He stared at the low embers in the fireplace. The weather was mild, and a fire wasn't necessary, but it reminded him of the old days when the army would gather around campfires and talk of long-ago campaigns—whether won or lost. Though most of the tales would be about the individual battles where one warrior went up against the other.

He smiled as he sipped brandy and closed his eyes. The movements in the Mozart sonata filled the room. A room that was surprisingly large for the vampire. While he preferred his office small so it wouldn't invite too many visitors, his personal room at the manor was a different story.

It was as large as Devon's, and, fortunately, didn't require permission from the Historical Society when most of the manor restorations were completed in 1940. The decor would be considered austere by most when, in actuality, it was more equivalent to a museum with artifacts he'd collected over the centuries.

The knock on the door surprised him. It was rare for anyone to intrude on another's privacy unless an emergency.

His eyes remained closed as he called out, "Come."

Maybe it was Lyra. She used to visit when she'd been ill, and he always made time for her. But she wasn't that young vampire anymore—physically or mentally.

"Sorry to bother you." Devon took a step in.

Sergi sat up. "Is there a problem?" If there had been, Devon would typically text.

"No problem." He walked farther into the room, moving from relic to relic. "I wanted a few moments to talk, and it's been some time since I've seen these." He stopped in front of an old wood-and-metal shield. It was nothing remarkable; the wood scratched and marred, the metal banding dented from battle. "My god. Is this the one you used that first day we met?"

Sergi stood and poured a brandy for Devon while pouring a second one for himself. He smiled as he handed the snifter over. "It was in storage until a couple of months ago."

"Why bring it out now?" Devon took the chair next to Sergi, and they both turned to the fire.

"Once I knew a war with Venizi was inevitable..." He shrugged. "Some of the old days came to mind. It seemed apropos."

"That was a good day."

Sergi laughed and rubbed his elbow. "That cost me twenty silver denarii."

Devon grunted, his gaze brushing over Sergi. "A fair exchange at the time." After a few minutes of silence, he turned to the fire. "Those were the days of true war. Brawn, might, and strategy."

"And yet, even without the battlefield skirmishes, we seem to leave a trail of blood wherever we go."

"It's the vampire way."

Silence returned as the two sipped their brandy and listened to a violin sonata. The fire crackled, and a cool breeze floated in from the open window.

Devon tapped on the soft leather of the armchair. "Have you read Remus's report?"

"He seems convinced Venizi's secret lab is in the Carpathian Mountains." He hadn't been pleased when he'd read it. They were rugged mountains where wild shifters roamed.

"I'll need your expertise on this one."

"Remus has lost several shifters searching those mountains. Do you believe his intel?"

Devon took his time considering the question. "What I know is that Remus doesn't like losing wolves. There's something more than wild shifters there. The question is whether it's the lab where the Poppy is coming from."

"I've already sent out some feelers, and I'm confirming what I can from his report."

"We're getting close. I can feel it."

Sergi grunted. "Like Vienna."

Devon chuckled. "That one was a bit of a surprise. I never thought Geiger had it in him to consider that strategy."

"It didn't help him in the end."

"Those were some good days."

They each reached over to clink their snifters together.

"I'll need a couple of days to complete my investigation." Sergi wouldn't skimp on a mission with such risk. "Will Remus wait that long?" The Wolf wasn't always a patient man, and after losing shifters, restraint would be hard to come by. A sentiment Sergi understood.

"He'll have to. We need a solid plan before we send anyone in. No more losses."

TWO DAYS LATER, Sergi entered Devon's office before anyone else. He reviewed the data before connecting his tablet to the display on the wall above the hearth. The map indicated an area in Romania that ran along some of the most rugged terrain in the Carpathian Mountains.

It had been centuries since he'd fought in one of the worst campaigns he could remember. The battle had been won, but both Houses had suffered heavy casualties. Not all the deaths could be attributed to the battle. The area had been rife with wild shifters, and they had taken advantage of the weakened and injured warriors.

A couple hundred years later, not much had changed. The wild shifters, according to Decker, still lived in the forests. Their numbers had declined with increased civilization, but they were dangerous and shouldn't be discounted. If that wasn't enough risk, the weather conditions, even in early fall, could be deadly.

"A difficult task for any team."

Sergi glanced at the door and nodded at Simone. "There are many caves that run through the area. Any one or more of them could have been excavated to build a lab."

"It would have taken some time and a great deal of labor. Most likely built a hundred years ago. How would they keep the local villagers quiet after all this time?"

"Many villages are probably gone, and those left are likely under Venizi's control."

Simone shrugged, not disagreeing as she dropped into her regular seat. She leaned back and stared at the screen, rubbing her right thigh. Her recent injury still plagued her, but her recent training with tai chi seemed to be helping. "A small strike force makes the best sense."

"We agree." Devon strode in with Decker behind him. "Let's give Lucas and Bella a moment to arrive and we'll get to it." Devon strode to his desk while Decker took his seat at the bar.

"Was Colantha of any help?" Simone asked.

Devon shook his head. "She's not aware of any dreamwalkers in the area. The closest ones don't have the mental power to be of use."

While they waited, Sergi received an update from one of his

contacts and made an adjustment to his data. Though interesting, the new data didn't make the mission less risky.

When Lucas arrived with Bella and Jacques behind him, Devon waited for them to take a seat before providing an overview of the mission. "As Simone suggested, we'll use a team of three."

"Not much of a strike force," Simone said. "I was thinking five to six."

"This won't be an actual strike." Sergi tapped a key, and the map zoomed in to a specific area of rugged terrain. "The mission will be to seek the lab, confirm its location, and return. The Carpathians are an unforgiving group of mountains, volcanic activity, and wild shifters. An area that Remus has been focusing on for some time. It doesn't matter how deep someone wants to hide a lab, unless you fly in supplies and resources, you need roads."

"There are places all over the world where it would be safer to fly people in and out," Lucas suggested.

"We believe, as Remus does, that this lab was created long before flight, let alone airplanes that could handle transports required to keep a lab operational." Sergi zoomed the image closer to show a group of small villages surrounded by narrow roads. "There's no doubt the lab would have been smaller at one time, but knowing Venizi, he would have planned for a long-term operation. We've suspected the lab is creating Magic Poppy, but we'd be foolish to believe that's the only thing he's developing."

"It's long been believed that the ability to change humans to halfling vampires was somewhat miraculous." Simone tapped a nail against her chin as she stared at the map. "And House Venizi was one of three Houses who were first to use the practice."

"You think Venizi's lab created a formula to hasten the change?" Lucas asked.

"I do."

"Remus first got word that shifters in this area had been disappearing from local communities for several decades." Decker held a bowl of nuts he'd taken from the bar and picked through them. "Not many. Nothing that couldn't be blamed on the wild shifters, who were known for stealing members from local packs. But the number of disappearances has increased over the last five years. Remus began sending teams in about a year ago, but they disappear."

"Killed?" Bella asked.

Decker shrugged and wiped his hands on his pants after popping a couple nuts in his mouth. "It's possible they were taken by wild shifters, killed by security teams protecting the lab, or worse."

"Subjects for experimentation?" Simone's fangs dropped when Decker nodded.

"We can't be sure, but Remus doesn't know what else to do. He doesn't want to send more wolves in until he can find a way to make it safer."

Before anyone could respond, Cressa crashed through the door.

"Oops, sorry." Cressa's face reddened, but when she glanced at Sergi, he caught the amusement in her eyes. "I just got off the phone with Harlow and Roxie."

"Excellent timing." Devon waited for her to take a seat.

Sergi, like the rest of the cadre, had noted Devon's change in his meeting style since Cressa arrived at House Trelane. Now that the two had developed an intimate relationship, Devon's approach to handling House business had become more casual. The only exception was with security.

Some Houses, like Venizi's, would see Devon's form of leadership as a weakness. Perhaps at one time, Sergi would have agreed, but when he looked at House Trelane from an unbiased viewpoint, the cadre was more cohesive. And, in his opinion, blending the teams with shifters, humans, and dreamwalkers strengthened the House, not diminished it.

Who would have thought humans as chaotic as Cressa and

Ginger could bring more stability? The answer was simple. They brought a different perspective. Though not true for all, most vampires preferred to color inside the lines.

"So, what do Harlow and Roxie have for us?" Devon asked.

Harlow, the leader of a small group of human thieves, had a knack for finding stellar members for his team. Cressa, using her street name of Pandora, had been invaluable with her skills at cracking safes. Roxie was a relatively new member after their previous hacker had double-crossed them. It turned out to be a good move as Roxie was one of the best he'd seen, and she kept up with all the latest technology. Harlow's team didn't always have the money to invest in hi-tech, but when it was required for a House mission, Devon bought the tech and let Harlow keep the items as part of their payment.

"Subcutaneous trackers." Cressa gave the two-word answer and sat back, seemingly proud of her answer. Sergi couldn't argue with the suggestion.

Devon squinted as he considered her answer. "How do they work? And how far away can we track them?"

"The tracker works off GPS. Once the tracker is placed, usually in the arm, the person can be tracked from anywhere."

"That's something Remus should have been using." Decker shook his head. "Are they easy to come by?"

Cressa glanced at Devon, and he nodded. "I can have them delivered by tomorrow."

"How many will we need?" Cressa asked.

"Three," Sergi answered. "I'll be leading the team with Rafael." He turned to Decker. "I believe Remus has made his decision."

"Carlos. He should be here tomorrow morning." Decker closed the container of nuts, stood, and set it behind the counter. "I'll be back in the morning to meet him. I have an appointment I need to get to." He nodded at Devon and squeezed Simone's shoulder on his way out.

"Cressa." Devon turned his attention back to the map. "Can Harlow and Roxie join us tomorrow to set up the trackers?"

"I believe so. I'll call him right after the meeting."

"When is the team leaving?" Simone asked.

"Tomorrow evening," Sergi responded. "Remus is providing a plane that will take us to Spain. From there, we'll fly commercial. There will be no communication once we enter Europe. We'll have burner phones, but we won't use them until it's time to call for a ride."

"This doesn't feel right." Cressa bit her nail.

"Come now, Cressa." Sergi gave her his best smile, which usually made her snappish. "You're not going to worry about me."

She stiffened and gave him a scathing look. "I'm worried about Rafael."

He grinned, but a knot formed in his gut. He was worried, too. A light shiver ran up the back of his neck. An old battle sign that told him the mission wouldn't go as planned. Tomorrow might be the last time he'd see his Family.

# Chapter Five

I COWERED in the corner of the lab, focused on a spot on the floor as the screaming increased. S-272 sat next to me, his head down as well, but his leg touched mine. After three weeks of working with him, I'd come to recognize it as his way of connecting, especially when it got bad.

The first two weeks became a ritual pattern. The blood-spattered lab was always empty of staff, and we worked amicably and quietly. He'd yet to say one word to me other than his commands or to answer questions about the assigned task. There was no idle chatter.

Then, last week, after we'd cleaned the lab, we were told to wait because it would need to be cleaned again before the end of the day. No one wanted to waste time taking us back and forth from our cells. I wasn't comfortable being forced to stay and had no idea what to expect. All I'd seen was the aftermath of blood, guts, and bits of bones.

S-272 had given me a quick glance, worry in his gaze, and maybe a bit of fear. Not for himself, but for me. He knew what was coming. When I thought back to the first time I'd entered the blood-soaked lab, S-272 had been sitting on the floor in a corner, just like we were now.

He must have seen what happened. Knew what the screams were from. That morning's porridge made a gurgling sound, and I had no doubt I'd be picking up its partially regurgitated remains before too long.

When the double doors opened, a thin female her long hair piled haphazardly on her head and wearing a white lab coat, entered. Behind the wire-rimmed glasses her eyes were sunken, the whites touched with a light shade of pink. Her cheeks were sallow. She hadn't slept well for some time. The increased workload seemed to be taking a toll. I wasn't naive enough to believe it had anything to do with the loss of shifters.

Where were they getting them all?

I stifled a weary laugh. Well, I certainly knew where they found me. And the thought sickened me when I thought of the others sent before me and those that came after.

Two steps behind her had been a scrawny dude, probably her assistant. He was what I'd call a geek. He wasn't as thin as the female, and though his skin was pasty, it appeared to be his natural coloring. His walk was more of a bounce. He was energetic, his eyes sharp with excitement.

*Great.*

Behind him were four males walking two abreast, the sleeves and pants of their uniform reflecting thick arm and thigh muscles. Most shifters would cross the street to avoid them.

In the middle of the four men was a young shifter male, maybe in his mid-twenties, dressed like the other males I'd seen—a brown pullover V-neck shirt and simple pants made of the same rough fabric as my shift and tied with a drawstring. His eyes were huge bright-blue orbs, and he stumbled every few steps. His wrists and ankles were manacled, and I smelled his anguish.

I took another look at his restraints. They weren't just metal, they were silver. Of course. That would dampen his ability to get out of the cuffs. And though rage simmered somewhere deep within him, fear was taking control.

Did some survive the experiment? If they did, it was most likely a small percentage, considering how often we cleaned. And the female administrator had let it slip one day that another two-shifter team cleaned other labs.

To ensure the shifter had little room to struggle or attempt a shift, a silver collar an inch wide and half an inch thick was placed around his neck. Two long metal poles were attached to his collar, and a guard at each end of the pole held him in place while the other two guards cut the shirt and pants from him, snipping along the seams so another shifter could sew them back together. Waste not, want not.

Once he was naked, they removed his restraints and pushed him onto a platform and against a stiff metal back wall. His arms were pulled away from his body and clamped into manacles. Additional manacles were placed around his ankles; his legs spread a foot apart. They removed the poles and collar before stepping back as a cage door closed the shifter inside the structure.

The geek assistant picked up a string of black-coated wires that had been gathered over a machine. That was the first time I paid attention to the line of machines on either side of the cage. Each wire ended with a suction cup, and reaching through the square openings in the cage door, the assistant placed them on various parts of the shifter's body.

I remembered the countless times I'd cleaned similar cords, laying them in a basin of bleach water until the blood dissipated.

After the cords had been applied, the assistant walked by each machine and turned it on. Within seconds, lights flashed, and while I couldn't read the displays from where I huddled, various bits of information popped up on the screens.

The female, who I finally pegged as one of the scientists, stood at a counter. Several items were spread out over the steel countertop—bottles with various colored liquids, small vials of what looked like blood, and other items I couldn't see from my position on the floor. I'd been so focused on the shifter, I hadn't paid attention to where the items had come from. I assumed some came from cabinets where glass doors reflected similar bottles and some from a commercial-sized refrigerator that was locked with a keypad.

She filled a syringe with a viscous dark-red substance then handed it to the assistant before picking up her tablet and moving behind a glass divider. She wouldn't want to get her nice, white lab coat spattered.

The assistant walked around the cage, and with every few steps, the geek actually licked his lips, practically wetting himself with anticipation. There wasn't anything I could do to stop him, but I promised to rip him limb from limb in my nightmares.

"Come along, Leonard. We have more after this one."

I would remember his name, if nothing else.

He finally selected a spot near the shifter's lower abdomen, somewhere near the kidneys. I didn't know if that was the only possible injection sight, or whether Leonard's preamble pacing had been an act to instill fear into the shifter. It wasn't necessary. The shifter struggled against his restraints. The whites of his eyes were enormous, and his pupils appeared dilated. A faint red glow shimmered behind the irises. His wolf had to be terrified.

The injection was administered slowly, and the shifter screamed in agony, the sound echoing around the lab. Neither the female nor the guards seemed to hear the wailing as they stared at the shifter. The cries of rage and fear didn't register with Leonard as he removed the needle, staring up at the shifter, his tongue taking another lick of his lips.

He and the guards then moved behind the glass shield.

"Make note." The female spoke out loud as she typed into the tablet. "Twenty cc of TA54 was injected into specimen 303 at nine thirty am." She glanced up to study her test subject.

Nothing happened. For five full minutes, nothing happened.

It started with sweat. A light sheen covered his face, then his entire body flushed. He struggled against the restraints, his head turning to the right and left in a rapid succession as he screamed. His hands fisted and released over and over until they remained in a tight ball. He began panting. His eyes glowed a bright red. If he shifted in his restraints, it would kill him.

Then, suddenly, the screams stopped, leaving the lab in an eerie silence except for the beep of the machines. The shifter relaxed, his head hanging low.

The female's interest piqued, and she glanced at the clock before typing furiously into her tablet.

Then a long, piercing scream came from the shifter. His head fell back against the cage, and his whole body shook as the flush that had dissipated returned. Blood leaked from his nose. His spasms increased. It seemed as if the shrieking went on forever. I leaned over to check the clock. It was nine forty-five. Fifteen minutes since his injection. The shifter's entire body was red, as if his blood was trying to escape through his skin.

Liquid ran down his leg, and it took me a moment to realize he'd urinated, unable to control his body. For a moment, I thought I saw a change in the structure of his forehead. Had his nails grown longer? One moment he was beginning to shift, then his facial features returned to normal. Did they want him to shift or prevent him from shifting? What the hell was this experiment supposed to test?

I wanted to cover my ears to block out his tormented cries. The air was thick with his fear, resignation, and the worst—his desire to die.

I dropped my head and stared at the floor. I didn't want to see what happened next. Not when I'd already seen the end result.

While I couldn't look, I had to listen. I had to stand witness to this horror show. My wolf howled with its own pain. She wanted out, and it required every bit of control to keep her in. Sweat broke out on my forehead as I struggled to stay human.

A hand gripped my arm. I didn't have to look, couldn't look, had to remain focused, but I knew it was S-272 attempting to calm me. To keep my wolf locked down.

When the shifter howled, S-272 squeezed my arm so hard I thought he'd break bone. My focus turned to him. He was strong regardless of his apparent weakened and beaten state. My wolf howled inside, and I cried with her.

When I didn't think I could take it anymore, there was a loud, spongy pop. The sound was followed by the soft, wet thuds of whatever was left of the shifter, and the return of silence.

Horror filled every cell in my body. What had been in that syringe?

Now, I sat in the same corner with S-272 by my side as we listened to another horrific death. This one was shifter 346. This was the fifth shifter who I'd heard, if not watched, implode from another failed test. I remembered each shifter's number. After the second shifter had died that first day I'd witnessed the experiments, I stole a scalpel from one of the drawers, wrapped it to protect the sharp blade, and hid it in my room. I found a spot behind my bed where I carved numbers into the drywall. Each shifter who'd died on my watch.

After we cleaned up the remains of 346 and then 294, I was returned to my room for another congealed bowl of stew. I forced down the stale roll. When the lights went out, my wolf came out. She remained on the bed, head on her paws as she watched the door.

When I woke the next morning in my human form, I made one decision. One thing I could control.

I would no longer turn away from the experiments. I would learn everything I could about what was happening here. It was most likely a useless effort, but I would no longer just participate.

*I am wolf.*

I would watch my prey and learn their weaknesses before they came for me.

*I am wolf.*

# Chapter Six

SERGI, a backpack slung over his shoulder, exited the plane and strode up the jetway into the Bucharest airport. He didn't stop to wait for Carlos. Rafael, who was first off the plane, hadn't waited either.

They would meet at the hotel. Three big men in dark clothing traveling together would draw eyes. If there were vampires in the airport monitoring arrivals, he and Rafael could blend more easily among the humans if they weren't together.

Carlos was the safest of the group. He was a rogue and, like Decker, kept in contact with Remus. He was eager to do his part, knowing that if Venizi took control of the Council, shifters' freedoms could be in jeopardy, and rogues would be the most vulnerable without protection from a pack.

Since Carlos would be the least noticeable, his first task was to rent a vehicle. Rafael grabbed the hotel shuttle while Sergi stood at the taxi stand and waited for a cab. He scratched his arm where the GPS tracker had been placed. It didn't itch, and with his vampire blood, any evidence of a scar had been erased. He couldn't feel it, but he knew it was there, and it was a bit unnerving.

He reminded himself it was for his team's safety. He wasn't sure it would be enough.

With the wait for a taxi and then the drive to the hotel, he arrived at the hotel twenty-five minutes later. It was a middle-of-the-road franchise. Nothing too fancy. Nothing subpar. Amenities included a dining room, a bar, wi-fi, and coffee pots in each room.

Each team member had their own room on different floors. His room was on the third. He placed the backpack on the dresser and removed his Dopp kit and satellite burner. He turned on the bathroom lights, scanned the accommodations, and dropped the kit on the sink.

Back in the main room, he played with the clock radio until he found a classical station and turned the volume low. He sat on the end of the bed and sent two texts with his room number and a time. Then he laid back, his feet still on the floor, as he stared at the ceiling. He slept for one hour before his internal time clock, honed from centuries of battle, woke him. There was a menu in one of the dresser drawers, and he placed an order with room service before settling into a chair at the small table.

He stared out the window while he waited.

It was moments like this that he wished he could meditate. Simone had sat with him numerous times, always providing a single candle for focus. Try as he might, his mind never calmed. She'd claimed he was too impatient, and then they would laugh since she was no more patient than him. The last time they'd practiced together, she had tapped his knee and gave him one last suggestion.

"Don't force it. If all this does is help organize your thoughts, consider it a success."

Her advice had been sound, and he followed it now, allowing his mind to wander through his past. His first memories were always of battles. It didn't matter if they'd won or lost. He thought of the vampires he'd fought with—those he'd lost contact with and those who had died on the field.

He grinned when he remembered the foolish raids he and Devon performed on their own. Those times had brought the most joy in his life. The raids were spontaneous, often after too many mugs of ale or wine, yet they rarely got caught and, even then, managed to escape. Back then, they thought they owned the world.

The minute he'd read the words *Carpathian Mountains* in Jasper's journal, he'd anticipated this day. He took the assignment, volunteering before Devon ordered him. If he didn't return, he didn't want it to be on Devon's shoulders. His friend would still consider it his fault, but with time, Devon would come to realize this mission had been his choice. No one had a better chance. Even then, his gut told him this mission would be different. Regardless of how well he knew Romania, the Carpathian Mountains, or Venizi—his greatest adversary—if he found the lab and walked away, he wouldn't be the same vampire.

If he walked away.

The knock at the door broke his reverie, and he looked through the peephole to find a male with his room service order. After the attendant placed the trays on the table, Sergi handed him a tip. Rafael and Carlos would be there soon, but he didn't wait to open the bottle of Scotch.

He'd finished his first drink when the second anticipated knock came.

Rafael strode in and immediately went to the bar before grabbing a vegetarian sandwich. "I walked the perimeter of the hotel and spent an hour in the bar. If there are any vampires close, they're in a car, though I didn't see anything suspicious."

Sergi wasn't surprised. "There aren't many strong Houses in Romania. Not anymore. The few that are left support Venizi, but I doubt they have the numbers to patrol all the transportation sites."

"That will most likely change the closer we get to our target." Rafael finished the sandwich and swallowed it down with Scotch.

Before Sergi could agree with Rafael's statement, the last expected knock came.

Carlos's hair was still damp from a shower, and he followed Rafael's path to the bar and then the food, selecting two roast beef sandwiches. "The SUV is clean of tracking devices. I expect we'll have more eyes on us once we get to Brasov."

"We should pick up the supplies we need before leaving Bucharest." Sergi wanted to be as inconspicuous as possible. Even a store run could be noticeable in Brasov.

"Agreed." Carlos devoured the sandwiches. Then he attacked the potato salad while Rafael picked at the chips. "According to the barmaid, there's a mountain supply store next to a supermarket on the edge of town. It's in the opposite direction of where we need to go, but that's probably a good thing."

Sergi strode to his backpack and pulled out several items. One was a map of Romania. They continued to eat, storing up energy as they reviewed the map.

Carlos tapped a spot. "This is the last place Remus heard from his teams before they went silent."

They all knew this. The mission had been reviewed multiple times before leaving Santiga Bay, but they went through the plan again. Then, they turned their attention to the printed satellite maps of their specific region of interest. These maps reflected roads not found on the commercial ones.

"A lab facility would require at least one road for supplies and general access for staff." Rafael ran his finger along one such road. "Most of the area is heavily forested, and there could be roads hidden beneath the dense foliage, unseen by any satellite."

Their job would be to find that single road that led to the spot where the shifters had disappeared. They would be hiking through miles of rugged terrain. It was the beginning of fall, and while the snow would be in the higher elevations, it would be cold. They would be fine, but Carlos would feel it the most.

Sergi glanced at the spot where the shifters had disappeared. He tapped the map. "There are a handful of villages around this area. We'll focus on the roads from these three hamlets and see if any lead toward the general area of the missing shifters."

When the other two nodded, they fell into general conversation, more eating, and even more drinking.

After they finished off the Scotch, Carlos and Rafael left for their rooms. When Sergi dropped into bed, that earlier doubt wouldn't go away. Instead of fighting it, he let it sink in and become part of him. It was better to know your enemy before a battle, even the internal ones.

ONCE THEY COLLECTED supplies in Bucharest, they packed into a dark, older model, nondescript SUV. The drive to Brasov took three hours, where they had agreed to stop for lunch. They drove another two hours to a remote site in a forested hillside, not too far from one of the villages. Carlos parked the SUV behind a stand of trees to keep it hidden.

Sergi laid their map on the hood of the SUV, and the three studied it and compared it to their current GPS position.

Carlos pointed to the same spot on the map he'd pointed to the day before. "This is where we received the last message from the team. Several of the teams disappeared in this area, but this location is at the base of one of the higher ridges."

"A good place to find caves." Rafael scratched his chin and shook his head. "And a good place for a trap."

"I agree." Sergi hated the position they were facing. He'd expected it. Thick forest on one side, tall cliffs on the other, and what appeared to be a single road running along the mountainside. It was one thing to be in this predicament with proper surveillance equipment and extensive intelligence.

In this instance, they were going in blind. The forest provided cover, but it also hid the enemy.

He rubbed his elbow and shrugged off the light ache. If this were any other time, he'd end the mission until he had more intel. But this wasn't any other time. It was critical they locate the lab. They weren't there to engage or infiltrate. They only required confirmation.

"You don't like this." Rafael's tone was soft but firm.

"The conditions are in their favor." Sergi smiled at him, but it was a grin of someone preparing for a battle they were likely to lose. "Let's remember the goal of this mission. Locating the lab. If we run into interference, at least one of us must return to report in." He glanced up at the sky before returning to study the map. "It's late. Let's get to this lower ridge." He tapped the spot and looked at the other males, who nodded their agreement. "We'll spend the night and then go in before dawn. It's our only advantage."

They took off with Sergi in the lead, Carlos behind him, and Rafael watching their backs. They walked single file, making as little noise as they could, moving slow and steady. Eight miles and four hours later, within the hilly, forested terrain, they made camp.

No fire was lit, and they ate cold rations they'd purchased in Bucharest. They ran a tarp between two trees to provide shelter from the wind and slept in cold-weather sleeping bags. Three shifts were quickly decided, allowing two to rest while one stood sentry. Before they moved out at four a.m., they stowed their packs behind rocks to be retrieved on their way back to their vehicle.

It was another five miles to their target location, and the terrain grew steeper. This time they moved faster, stopping occasionally to listen for movement. When they were two miles away, they changed their formation from single file to three abreast with no more than ten yards separating them.

They moved slower, constantly searching the dark. Being

vampires and a shifter, they could see well enough to navigate their path and watch for unexpected movement.

When they were within a quarter-mile of their target, Sergi stopped, and the others grouped on either side of him. He sensed someone out there. But after a long minute of scanning the trees, he couldn't discern any movement. The only sound was the chittering of early morning birds preparing for their day.

He didn't like this.

He scratched the spot on his arm where the tracker rested. They'd left the burner phones with their gear. The key to the SUV was hidden under a rock near the vehicle. Nothing was being left behind that would point to their identities, and they still had an avenue of escape.

All the things the previous shifter teams would have done. Yet, they'd disappeared.

Would the GPS tracker be enough?

He shrugged off his concerns. He'd led a long life. Longer than he'd ever thought possible, considering the number of campaigns he'd seen with Devon. He rubbed the ache in his elbow that had returned that morning. It was always worse in the colder weather.

He studied his team, and they peered back for a long moment, then they both nodded. They knew the stakes. They understood the risk. They were ready.

He moved out, and the others fell alongside, staying ten yards to either side of him. This time they also remained three steps behind.

It didn't take long before he spotted the light. He waved to the others, and they slowed but didn't stop. The light was stationary, and his heart rate ticked up a notch.

They made it to the edge of the forest, where it opened onto a paved parking lot. A single asphalted road led off to the right that most likely changed to a well-maintained dirt road several yards down the hill. Across the parking lot, against the backdrop of a cliff were roll-up doors wide enough for two semi-trucks. A set of man-sized double doors were to the right.

Something important lay beyond those doors, hidden within the mountain. Whether it was the lab or not would require more surveillance.

Before he made the decision to back away, the sound of a spring-loaded latch caught his attention seconds before he spun around. A wide panel lifted from the surface of the forest floor, creating a doorway to an underground blind. They must have walked over unseen tripwires. Four heads lifted from beneath the door.

Vampires with rifles.

Sergi didn't move, but he glanced at his teammates.

Another blind had sprung open to the right of the first. Another four vampires. Eight to three odds, and the enemy had rifles. Sergi and his team had their innate skills and daggers.

All three dropped to the ground when their supernatural hearing caught the click of safeties being released. When no bullets came, they scrambled toward the forest.

Sergi heard a single shot, but rather than the loud pop he expected, the only sound was a light whoosh. When Carlos went down, Sergi turned to Rafael, who had been the farthest from the blinds. He had reached the deeper protection of the forest when he turned back. Sergi was turning to run the other way when he heard the second shot, and something pierced his neck.

He reached up, expecting blood, but felt the light brush of fletching. He pulled out the dart, then gave Rafael a last glance. Their eyes met in acknowledgment. Rafael turned and ran. Three vampires climbed out of the blind in pursuit.

His last thought before he lost consciousness was that Rafael was quick, but the others knew the terrain. The odds of Rafael losing them were fifty-fifty at best. Then everything went fuzzy.

~

FLASHES of intermittent light broke through the darkness as Sergi fought off the drug. He and Rafael had found a couple of unsuspecting blood donors before leaving Brasov, and his vampire blood dampened the effects of whatever had been in the dart, but it wasn't easy.

Two vampires held him up by his armpits, his feet dragging behind as they made their way through a long tunnel. He fought for wakefulness if only to monitor where he was being taken, the route along the way, and anything else he could see or hear that might be useful.

There was nothing to see but rough-hewn stone walls. The only sound was the pounding of boots.

He had no sense of how far he'd been dragged before a door to his right opened, and the vampires holding him turned, shifting him sideways as they yanked him down a staircase. Bright lights and white walls greeted them at the bottom, and he was dragged across tile flooring before being turned and pulled down another staircase. Here, the light was muted, the walls once again made of stone, the air musty and cold.

With each step, it became more difficult to keep his eyes open. Random bits of information came at him.

Wooden doors.

Bars over the doors.

A soulful scream quickly silenced.

The wild smell of shifters.

Vampires.

Maybe a human.

Then the worst scents of all—fear, rage, and despair.

He lost track of the corridors as his guards turned right and then left. How they knew their way through the maze, he didn't know. His head dropped, and he didn't have the energy to lift it. His thoughts became murky, and he barely noticed when they stopped in front of a door.

A wooden bar was lifted, and the guards moved him through

the opening. After a few steps, they released him, and he hit a hard stone floor.

When the latch was dropped back in place, Sergi let the drug take him.

The only sound was the echo of dripping water.

Then nothing at all.

# Chapter Seven

I LAID on my cot and stared at the ceiling. Breakfast had come and gone, another bowl of porridge, but this time a hard-boiled egg had come with it. They were late in taking me to my assignment.

Two days had passed since the last experiment, and we'd been given other tasks, cleaning smaller labs and offices. S-272 said the experiments had been put on hold. After the last horrific shifter death, S-272 talked more frequently. It was always in whispers and always with his head down. Security cameras were in every room, regardless of size. When we entered a room for the first time, S-272 would slowly point his chin in the location of the camera.

I kept my head down and asked, "Do you know why the tests are on hold?" Maybe they'd run out of shifters.

"From what little I've heard, I believe they're reworking their formulas again."

I shivered. "How often does that happen?"

He rinsed out a rag then took his bucket to the sink, pouring out the dirty water and replenishing it with fresh water and cleanser. I sprayed disinfectant on a counter and wiped it, slowing my efforts as I waited for him to respond.

He wiped a lower cabinet, his motions thorough as he moved

the rag up and down. "It depends on results. Sometimes they go through twenty or so subjects, sometimes only five or six before pausing the tests."

I shuddered at how many shifters had been killed. Horrific actions hidden from the world of the supernatural. "Do you know where they get the shifters?"

He slid the bucket away, and I slid next to him, cleaning the cabinets above the counter.

"The wilder ones are local to the area. I believe they transport others from various places. Isn't that how you came to be here?"

I almost shook my head but stopped before the camera could pick up the motion. My skin crawled. How far were they going to kidnap shifters? "No. I was sent here to find the lab. I was captured outside the facility."

I glanced down in time to see the look of shock on S-272.

"Who was looking for the lab?"

I didn't think S-272 was a mole for the vampires, but I wasn't willing to test that theory. Trust didn't come easy in this place.

"A friend who wants to shut this place down."

They worked in silence after that. It wasn't until after our short lunch break that S-272 spoke again.

"Do you think they will send others?"

I would have said yes when I'd first been captured, but that had been some time ago. I considered the experiments. What if others had been sent? Family. Friends. Others from my pack. Were they here now? Beaten and possibly chained in their cells? Or were they the bits and pieces of flesh I'd been picking up for the last three weeks.

"I don't know."

We didn't talk after that. What else was there to say?

I spent most of my working day memorizing each room. The layout, the location of the cameras, the labels on the cabinets and drawers that identified their contents, and anything that was left on the counters. Their organizational skills were top-notch, but they were foolish to give the shifters too much information. Maybe they didn't think we could read.

What I wanted to see were the contents of the refrigeration units. Each lab and office had one. Commercial-sized units in the labs and apartment-sized for the offices. All of them had keypads. Some of the staff, who'd been in the labs while we cleaned, had been lazy. I caught the first couple of numbers from one vampire and a couple other numbers here and there until I was positive what the five-digit code was. The only problem was that every refrigeration unit was in direct line of sight to the cameras.

I shook off the information I'd been gathering, which only left questions and reinserted my initial worry.

Why hadn't anyone come for me this morning?

Had they noticed me talking to S-272? It might be nothing more than using the other shifter team to share the workload since the experiments were on hold. And if I didn't think of something else, I'd drive myself into worst-case scenarios. Instead of going down that tortured path, I returned to reviewing everything I'd learned, starting with the main labs and working my way down the list.

Then I considered the overall lab operations. I'd once seen a map of the facility in one of the offices. I couldn't look at it very long, always concerned about the cameras, but enough to get a bird's eye view of the maze of tunnels and the direction of the exits, as if that would ever be needed.

A wolf could hope.

The place was run by vampires. I'd seen a couple of humans, but there must be more. Vampires would eventually require blood. They might be taking it from bags but why not from their workers? They couldn't take it from the shifters. All pups learned early on that vampires didn't like shifter blood. It wasn't palatable and didn't provide the necessary nutrients. That was something at least.

It was an hour later when the lock on my door released. The

same key card seemed to work on all the doors, and the lab workers and guards appeared to hold the same clearance. It could be anyone on the other side.

I sat up as the door opened but didn't move from the bed. They didn't like us close to the door, and I wasn't going to take a chance on a beating. I also didn't want to lose my work detail.

The guard waved me out as if he was in a hurry, and I was tardy. He didn't say anything as he led me past the stairs leading to the first floor where the labs were located. Instead, he led me down the stairs to the third floor, where the walls and cells were made of stone. Was I being sent back to my old cell? Back to Tallon and the threat of abuse?

At the bottom of the stairs, a female waited. Not my normal handler. She was taller than me, thin as a rail, and had a pinched face. Her gray eyes matched the color of her hair which had been gathered in a tight bun.

In addition to a second guard, a young male stood next to her. He was a pretty boy, tussled brown curls cut short, average build, and while he held his head high, his gaze seemed unfocused or perhaps just uncaring. He wore a lab coat, so I assumed vampire, but he might have been human.

The female—there seemed to be a lot of them in charge—spoke to her assistant as if I wasn't there. Of course, shifters weren't supposed to be very smart. I'd play along if it meant they'd talk freely in front of me.

"It's bad enough the experiments are on hold for another week, especially when it seemed we were so close," she grumbled, her tone snappish. "Now I have to waste my time reassigning these shifters to keep them occupied." Her irritation appeared to grow as her lips thinned, her focus on her tablet as she swiped and typed.

"Why aren't they just kept in their cells?" The assistant had a deep, melodic voice. I wanted to punch his face in.

"We're running low on the docile ones. Until a new shipment

arrives, we need to use the ones we've trained. You know how long it takes to get them to understand basic commands."

Okay. I'd like to punch her too. Another shipment. Like we were nothing more than cattle. My wolf whined to be released. Pushed to rip out both their throats, but with the two guards nearby, that would be foolish.

*Wait, wolf. Patience.*

"Shifter S-473. I see you've worked in the labs for almost a month without any trouble. For now, you'll clean the detention cells and guard's quarters on this level during your morning shift. After lunch, you'll go back to the labs. For some reason, the staff prefers your method of cleaning." She stared at me, a sneer on her face until it turned into a tight grin. "You must have been a house slave before coming here."

It was all I could do to swallow my fury and keep my expression blank. Or could she see that I wanted to bash her face in?

"She must have been a problem if she was transferred here."

"It's more likely they got a good price for her. The unruly ones are usually marked for experiments."

I bit my tongue. I wasn't sure what was worse. Her belief that I had been a slave, something that had been outlawed over two centuries ago, or that they were marking us for experiments. Would I have been marked as a test subject if I'd continued to rage at my keepers? Yet, they hadn't tagged me after I'd stuck Tallon in the neck with a fork. Either way, the thought was sobering.

The female nodded at the guard who'd been standing next to her. "Make sure all the animals are either out of their cells or fully restrained before she's allowed to enter. There'll be hell to pay if we lose a decent cleaner."

"Yes, ma'am." The guard gripped my upper arm and led me to the far end of the hallway, toward the guard's quarters.

I shivered at the cold air and wrinkled my nose at the stink. Had it gotten worse down here, or had I never noticed when I lived in these cells?

"I'm Dallas, and you'll be brought down to report to me at the guard's station each morning." He released my arm when we entered the guard's quarters.

I nodded. I wasn't sure if his name was a given name or a nickname. What I did know was that he was a shifter. He must have been here a long time, like Tallon, to be trusted as a guard. So, not a friend.

"My understanding is that you're a good worker, so I'll show you your duties over the next couple of days. Then you'll be expected to work on your own. You've lived down here before, so you should remember that guards walk the corridors. One misstep and you'll find yourself back in one of these cells marked as a test subject."

He gave me a long look. His jaw was firm in his once handsome face. A scar ran from his left forehead across his face to the right side of his chin. However he'd gotten it, something or someone had stopped him from shifting, otherwise a shift would have prevented the scarring. His lips were set in a scowl, but when I met his gaze, something in his bright green eyes gave me pause. He was either sizing me up or perhaps looking for something else. An ally?

Interesting. But his threat still hung in the air. I lowered my gaze and nodded. "I understand."

I walked behind him as he gave me the tour.

"Each level has quarters for the guards. They include private rooms, a cafeteria, lounge, and game room." This side of level three had white walls and tiled floors rather than the rough-hewn stone that encompassed the rest of the level. He opened one of the private rooms. It was surprisingly spacious and included a single bed, wider and longer than the cots in the cells, and the mattress was thicker, a galley kitchen, a dining table and chairs, and an entertainment center with a small sofa.

"The bathrooms and showers are communal." Dallas stopped

at one. "There are two in the quarter's area and two bathrooms without showers in the cell area."

He showed me the storage closet where the cleaning supplies and linen were stored. The cleaning of the guard's room included removing the used sheets and providing clean ones. The guards made their own beds. I was responsible for removing the trash and replacing the wastebasket liners, but the guards were expected to do their own sweeping and dusting. That was something. Otherwise, they'd need a full-time maid to thoroughly clean all the rooms.

However, once we started through the rooms, only twelve of the twenty available rooms were occupied. Twelve guards for how many prisoners? I'd soon find out. I stored away the information, along with the discovery of a security room and armory, both requiring key cards.

The quarters took two hours to clean while Dallas explained the routine. It would be faster once I was on my own.

The detention cells were just as I remembered them. Cold, dank, and held nothing more than a thin pallet on the floor and a bucket for waste. In this area, I was assigned a cart. It held a large tub where I dumped the buckets of shifter waste. After scraping out any remaining food in a second container, the bowls and trays were stacked on two top racks. The third container held fresh water to refill the one plastic tumbler each shifter was allowed.

"The shifters are rotated through here frequently. When a cell becomes available, you'll need to sweep it out and replace the pallet."

The used pallets were set on the bottom rack of the cart. The cleaned pallets were on the middle shelf. It made sense to change out the pallets. They wouldn't want to spend time dealing with pest control. That was why all shifters were bathed every twenty-one days. They must have determined that was the longest they could go before lice or other infestations occurred.

Before we went into the first cell, Dallas pulled me aside.

"We currently have twenty-two shifters in this area. There are six main corridors and various side tunnels. Before you start on a new hallway, a guard will check each room to ensure the shifter has been restrained. Don't dawdle in the rooms. Once you're done with a corridor, you need to check with the guard in the next corridor to ensure the cells are safe." Again with the strange look in his eyes. "Do you understand the importance of that?"

I met his gaze, searching to understand what I saw—concern, warning, or information that I wasn't sure what to do with. All I said was, "Yes."

# Chapter Eight

"YOU'RE WORRIED."

Sergi glanced over his shoulder when the soft tones of his mother's voice reached him then turned back to stare at the Family's orchard. He stood on the balcony, just outside the dining hall, still in his battle armor.

"Father isn't listening to reason." His anger rose, and he took a deep breath, not wanting to take it out on his mother. She'd tried to talk sense into the old male more times than he had. But Father was the House leader, a weak male who depended far too much on the grace of their allied Houses and was easily swayed by false promises.

"He's only doing what he thinks best to save our ancestors' land."

"Why do you do this? Protect him when you know he's wrong."

Her hand was warm when she placed it in his. "Because he's the House leader not just my husband."

"He cares more for land than he does his Family. You're outnumbered, and House Meinstein will show no mercy."

"Your Father believes House Braun will send warriors."

Sergi shook his head. "House Braun is battling on another front and any army he can send is days away. House Meinstein will be here by the morrow." He turned around and took her hand. "Please. Take Lizet and Greta and leave for Linz. If by some miracle the House isn't taken, you can return when it's safe."

She looked up at him, sorrow in her gaze. After a long moment, she turned to view the same landscape he'd been staring at for the last hour, thinking of another way out. When her hand slipped from his, he knew it was no use.

"It would shame him. It would show disrespect in his time of need."

Sergi took a step back. "Is his pride worth the life of Lizet and Greta? Worth your life with this foolishness?"

He saw the pain in her eyes. She was caught in the middle like so many others. Unable to consider their own welfare over Father's.

"Can't you stay and help?" Her voice cracked, already knowing the answer.

"I'm not in Father's army, remember? He traded me to another House. My commitment is to my new leader. I only came here as a last resort to change Father's mind." He paused, gripping her hand again though she tried to pull it away. "And if that didn't work, to give you an option to save yourselves."

When she tugged on her hand again, he released it. Then, without another word, he stormed out. He wasn't giving up. There was still one last option.

The icy water woke him from his dream.

He shook his head, and the pain that had been forgotten in sleep returned tenfold. The multiple wounds he'd suffered healed slower than they had the day before. He wasn't sure which was worse—being a prisoner in the lab or locked in the memory of mistakes he could never change.

They were both hell.

"Sorry to wake you." The vampire grinned with even, white

teeth, the tip of his fangs showing. He rubbed his stomach. "I'm on my way to breakfast but wanted to stop in to say good morning." He gripped Sergi's hair and pulled back until they stared into each other's eyes. "This is only day three. The blood you most likely gorged yourself with before coming here won't heal your wounds for long. In fact, when I return later for our next session, we'll be moving on to phase two. I have a special treat for you. Until then, go back to sleep or ponder how you will die here. Whatever makes you feel better."

Sergi held the vampire's stare. They'd wondered what had happened to this male, where he had gone. Now he had his answer.

Boris Gheata was alive and well in Venizi's underground lab.

SOMETIME LATER, Sergi woke and glanced around the dank-smelling cell. He'd nodded off again, but this time he hadn't dreamed, and he was grateful to avoid those dark memories. His stomach grumbled. Three days without food or blood.

He'd gone longer, so he wasn't worried yet. With how long he'd been alive and the number of battles and infiltrations that had gone wrong, this was far from the first time he'd been captured and tortured. Though the last time had been long ago, the body remembers. It remembers the pain, and it remembers the quest for survival.

When he'd first woke in his cell, and the drug had worn off, he'd found himself in restraints. His legs and arms were numb, and the silver band across his chest burned.

If his captors planned on leaving him like this, there would be no hope for escape unless someone unlocked the restraints or Devon massed a rescue. The second was more likely, but small teams wouldn't work. A full attack force would be needed. Devon would consider it, but unless Rafael survived, he'd be working under the same insufficient intel that had plagued Sergi's team. He had to believe that Rafael's wit, training, and penchant for being unpredictable would give him the advantage over three vampires.

He glanced at his arm and wondered if the tracker was still there. They could have discovered it and cut it out while he was drugged. His arm would have healed before he woke. Even so, Devon would know his last location.

On the first day, they'd mostly left him alone. He was given water, though most had dribbled onto his chest. What he'd assumed to be late that same day, the door burst open to show the outline of someone. Even with the weak light from the hallway, it was easy to tell it was a male. He stood as tall and wide as the doorway. He didn't enter. He watched for several long minutes. If his performance was meant to intimidate, it wouldn't work.

The effectiveness of breaking someone didn't come from the size of the opponent. It came in the form of both physical and mental torture. And though he had no idea who this male was, this interrogator would understand Sergi's resolve and would do whatever it took to break it.

The second day a different male started the torture. He was thick with muscle but not near the size of the first male he'd seen. This male wore loose sweat-style pants made of a rough fabric and no shirt. When he turned his back to roll out a leather-wrapped bundle, the heavy scarring was easily visible in the light of a single lantern only used for the torture sessions and cleanup. The male had been whipped many times by someone who understood torture.

When the tools within the bundle were revealed, Sergi focused his mind elsewhere and ignored the male. Until he stepped in front of Sergi. One whiff was all it took.

A shifter.

He'd laughed at the time. It made sense. In most cases, shifters and vampires didn't get along. Then he understood. This male's scars had been from a vampire, and Sergi was a payment of sorts.

The session had been long and painful. His breathing

increased as he held in the pain as his face reddened and spittle flew, but he'd only screamed once. In the end, the session was nothing. Mostly cuts to make him bleed, removing as much blood as they could to weaken him and bring on the beast.

They would have to work harder. And when the big male he'd seen in the doorway arrived on the third day and revealed himself to be Gheata, Sergi had known the worst was yet to come.

~

I MUST BE HONEST. There wasn't any reason to be scared of other shifters, but it wasn't like we all knew each other and had some secret handshake that made us all simpatico. The shifters on level three were here because they couldn't be tamed. Yet, they were shifters. My people. Other wolves who were only trying to survive.

But S-272's words came back to me. The vampires had been known to capture wildlings from the nearby forest. Wolves who were more beast than man and had no regard for the more civilized shifters. So, when I stepped into the first cell, my eyes darted around the room, searching for the shifter. After a few seconds, while my eyes adjusted to the darkness, I found him in the corner.

He wore a thick collar around his neck, and a heavy chain ran from it to a metal ring bolted into the floor. The chain wasn't long, only permitting the shifter to move a couple feet from where he huddled, his legs pulled into his chest. The bucket was on the other side of the ten-by-ten cell. The dinner tray lay close to the door, the bowl empty except for the plastic spoon.

The shifter kept his eyes on me, as I did him, while I picked up the bucket with one hand, uncaring of the atrocious scent of bodily waste, and picked up the tray with the other. I scurried out as quickly as possible, emptying the bucket and placing the bowl and tray on their appropriate racks. Once I refilled the tumbler and set it next to the door, I backed out of the cell. Before I took the last step through the doorway, the shifter, his eyes wild with fear, his scent filled with anger, he caught my gaze and held it.

I had no reason to do it, but I smiled at him and gave him a brief nod.

Then he did something I hadn't expected. He made the slightest of nods that barely registered, and the guard, who stood outside the door, wouldn't have seen it.

But I knew it for what it was. He hadn't given up. Wouldn't give up until his last dying breath. He was ready to fight.

I moved through the rest of the cells with practiced motions. The task was too simple to dawdle. In each cell, with every shifter, I smelled the same anger, and the fear in their eyes turned to fire. It was as if they weren't chained to a wall like some backyard mutt who'd been forgotten. They only waited for the word to be given.

But how long before they were nothing but another failed experiment?

Once the last door was closed, I counted the trays again. Twenty-one. One more cell to go. But when I glanced around, there weren't any more cells in this corridor. I turned to Dallas.

"I thought you said there were now twenty-two cells to clean."

Dallas gave me a long look. "The last prisoner is two corridors over." When he seemed satisfied by whatever he saw in my eyes, most likely irritation combined with a general sadness that had crept over me, he waved for me to follow.

One more cell, then lunch. The bland food would at least restore my energy for a long afternoon in the labs.

I pushed the cart, which had grown heavy with the weight of the shifter's waste, down the long hallway as I followed Dallas, his club out and ready for anything—or anyone. With each corridor we passed, I glanced both directions. No guards could be seen. All was quiet.

At the last intersection, Dallas turned to the right and led me past several empty cells, the wooden bars used to lock in a prisoner lay on the floor. With the turnover of shifters, it made it easier for the guards to know if there was a shifter inside without having to look, which meant opening the door. Always a security risk.

This hallway was darker than the others with only one lantern burning in front of the barred door. The sound of dripping water was a gentle tap on the stones. It could either be soothing or maddening, depending on one's state of mind. I glanced behind me, knowing no one was there, but for some reason, I was creeped out.

Dallas lifted the bar, opened the door, and stepped inside. After a quick glance around, he backed out. "You don't want to linger in this cell. There isn't a bucket or tray. You only need to take out the trash."

I stared at him for a moment, unsure why this cell was different and not liking it. I'd heard rumors of interrogation rooms where a vampire the size of a gorilla, who I'd once seen in the cafeteria, handled special cases.

Was this one of those cases?

I swallowed the lump in my throat as I moved inside. This cell was unlike the others. A dim lantern lit the interior, but it wasn't bright enough to chase the shadows from the corners.

A workbench sat along the wall to my left. It was nothing more than a wooden table two feet wide and eight feet long. An old, stained leather cloth stretched across the top with a line of tools spread across it. More precisely, instruments of torture. I swallowed hard. Just when I didn't think I could see any more horrors.

A mug sat on the end of the table, but I wasn't sure if I should refill it since it wasn't the normal plastic tumbler. I took two tentative steps and peered inside, then picked it up and sloshed the remains before pouring some on the ground. It ran clear. I brought the cup to my nose. No scent. It had to be water.

I took it back to the cart, emptied what was left, and refilled it. When I placed the mug on the table, I jumped at the light sound of movement.

I spun around.

How could I have missed him?

I took a step closer, barely able to see him in the dim light. A naked male was strapped to the wall by a wide metal band that crossed over his chest. His arms were spread wide, his wrists manacled to the wall. His legs were free, but his feet barely touched the ground.

His eyes were closed, but that didn't mean he was sleeping. With the way his body hung against the metal bands, he didn't appear awake. When I considered the instruments on the workbench and the blood stains that covered his body, he most likely passed out.

I took another two steps and noticed a small puddle of blood on the floor.

That was weird.

I studied his body. He was well-muscled with thick arms and thighs. His ridged stomach was lean. He was a fighter, or maybe he was one of those males who spent all his free time in a gym.

The dried blood stains reflected several trails that ran from his chest, stomach, and sides.

But why weren't there any wounds?

I blinked and took another step closer. My legs shook, and I didn't realize I was holding my breath until my brain forced me to breathe deeply.

And then I caught the scent.

No. It couldn't be.

Vampire.

THE FOLLOWING DAY, I replaced the tumbler of water in the last of the twenty-one cells when a soul-wrenching scream echoed through the corridors. No one had to tell me where that scream had come from, and the thought sent shivers through me, knowing that was my last stop.

I gave the shifter a weak smile. It was obvious he'd heard the scream. Of course, he had, but instead of curling into himself, he nodded at me like the others had. In a single day, the shifters had been prepared for my visit, and while they remained guarded, I sensed the first kernel of change. The scent of hope. The thought depressed me. I was the last one to offer them hope.

I closed the cell door and replaced the bar.

I glanced down the hall but the guard who'd been there earlier was gone. Dallas wasn't around either. He'd met me when I arrived on the third level with my guard and walked with me to the guard's quarters, but I hadn't seen him since. And rather than a different guard stationed at each of the main corridors, there was only one who checked the cells before allowing me to clean. Now that one had disappeared. It seemed I was considered harmless, and they'd lost interest. More the fools them.

I was also surprised that I hadn't run into Tallon or that one of the guards would try to push me into an empty cell. For some reason, I appeared to be off-limits. The only thing that made sense was that I wasn't just a prisoner—I was a worker. Right. I was special. I should be happy with the situation and focus on my job, but something had shifted. I didn't know what, but when I glanced back down the last corridor, I knew exactly what had changed.

The new prisoner. The vampire.

Why would they be torturing one of their own?

Something my uncle had once told me niggled in the back of my mind, but it was elusive. I'd remember eventually. The decision at this single point in my life was whether to go to that cell on my own or skip it for the day.

But they'd know. Someone was down there with the vampire. Why else would he have screamed? Maybe I'd be lucky and could refill the water and be done.

I pushed the cart down the corridor to the end, suddenly noticing the squeaky wheel. It did that when the cart became heavier with waste.

When I reached the last hallway, I paused. There was a guard standing outside the last cell. He leaned against the wall, his beefy arms crossed over his chest, one knee bent with his boot resting on the wall behind him. Was he enjoying the show?

I considered backing up, but before I could put my thoughts into action, the guard waved me forward.

"Get down here, girl. We've been waiting for you."

His gruff voice pricked at my wolf. Had they continued torturing the vampire while they'd waited for me? It shouldn't have bothered me. It was just a vampire. Yet, that nugget of memory I couldn't recall made me wince with guilt, and I pushed my cart forward.

I ignored the sneer from the guard when I reached the door and tentatively peered in.

"What are you waiting for?" A large male dropped a bloody dagger on the table and wiped his hands on a rag. "Get in here and clean this up."

I didn't want to look at the male pinned to the wall, but it was beyond my power not to. He was a bloody mess with dozens of cuts. A couple of them must have been deep because blood still dripped on the floor. He wasn't healing quickly. They weren't giving him blood. The cuts were more than just inflicting pain, they were draining him. They wanted him weak.

I glared at the male, who I now recognized. He was the gorilla they used for their special interrogations. I shouldn't have been surprised. I glanced down at the bloody floor where it pooled and congealed.

"I can't clean this."

When I didn't move, he growled. "Don't you clean the labs?"

"Yes, but I don't have the right supplies for this. The only thing on my cart is water. I don't have the proper rags, buckets, or disinfectant."

He stared at me, and I dropped my gaze, waiting to see if he'd hit me, send me back to my cell, or provide the supplies I requested. It wasn't like I hadn't been cleaning up blood for the last few weeks, but I wasn't going to do it without the proper supplies.

"Check with Dallas and get her the supplies she needs." He stepped close and yanked my head back by my hair.

I tried not to look, but it was impossible with the way he held me in place. It took every ounce of strength to hold the wolf at bay and give this vampire my most submissive glance. "I'm told I can trust you."

I didn't respond. What could I say to that? Sure, you can trust me. Just don't turn your back while all those shiny instruments are within my reach. I don't know why he was torturing one of his own, but I could see everything I needed to know about this vampire by his soulless eyes.

He shoved me away, and I stumbled and fell to the ground, unable to miss the edge of the pooling blood. Great. Now the prisoner's blood was all over my shift.

"Start with the trash and refill the mug." His laugh sounded a little crazy. Then he threw the rag he'd been wiping his hands with at me. "And you can use this to get started."

The rag landed a few feet from me, and I crawled over to pick it up.

"I want the floor spotless and the instruments gleaming for my afternoon session." He strode next to me. I kept my head down, staring at the floor, waiting for him to hit me, so all I saw were his thick-soled boots. "Don't disappoint me."

Then he strode out, and I released my breath as his boots faded down the corridor. When I heard him turn the corner, I whispered, "Fuck you."

It was silly, but it made me feel better.

Clutching the rag, I stared up at the vampire on the wall. Only one of his wounds still dripped blood, but the rest had stopped. Some appeared to have healed but others had formed crusty scars. I'd been right. His body couldn't heal as fast as it should. They were starving him.

Stop it. His fate doesn't concern you.

When the guard returned with the supplies, I stood and rubbed my head where my hair still tingled from being pulled. I picked up the trash basket and the mug and returned to the cart. I checked over the items the guard had dropped by the cart and nodded. "These will do."

"So happy they meet with your approval. I'll be back in an hour to check your work." Then he strode away.

My body relaxed now that I was alone to work. I used the allotted time cleaning and disinfecting the floor, then turned my attention to the instruments, where bits of flesh still clung to them.

The vampire never moved during the entire time I'd been there, but after I dumped the last bucket of bloody water and sprayed the instruments with disinfectant, I glanced up at him one last time.

His head was still lowered to his chest, but his eyes flashed open and caught mine. I took a step back, not expecting the look in his gaze. Even in his current state, he must know I was a shifter. And after such a severe torture session, I was expecting to see anger, disgust, or fear.

I saw none of that. Rather than clouded in pain, his eyes were clear. They were a deep brown, warm and gentle. They reached into my soul without judgment or hate.

"I'm sorry." His voice was raspy. Then his eyes closed, and his head dropped lower. He'd passed out.

My wolf whined.

"Hush," I told it. I rushed out and stacked the rest of the cleaning supplies on my cart just as the guard rounded the corner.

I waited the few minutes it took him to review the room and bar the door behind him.

"Gheata will be pleased," he said. "Make sure you keep it that way. We don't have the resources to watch you every minute. Now, let's go. They're waiting for you in the labs."

His words echoed in my ears. They didn't have the resources. What did that mean? Was that why there didn't seem to be as many guards today? And if they were waiting for me in the labs, then I missed lunch. I didn't think I could eat anyway after cleaning all the blood.

I should have focused on what his words revealed, but as I followed him, pushing the heavy cart over the rough stone floor, all I could think about were the words the vampire said. "I'm sorry."

Why would he be sorry for me?

My wolf whined again, and this time, I didn't bother to hush her.

# Chapter Nine

DEVON HURRIED down the hall buttoning his shirt. He ran a hand through his tousled hair as he stormed into his office.

"Give me the basics."

Bella glanced up from where she'd pulled a chair up to his desk to use her laptop. She pressed a button, and the display over the fireplace lit up. Jacques finished an espresso and handed it to him as he dropped onto the couch.

He took two long sips, needing the caffeine to clear the cobwebs. He'd only been down an hour when Bella alerted him of a change in their monitoring of Sergi's team. The single red dot pulsed on the screen just south of Brasov.

Two days ago, he'd watched this same screen as two dots disappeared and another moved away from its original position. Its movement was erratic, and, at the time, what was left of his shrinking cadre had agreed that the single remaining dot was on the run.

With Sergi in Romania, Simone on a short research mission, and Lucas at Oasis, Bella and Jacques, by extension, were the only remaining cadre at the mansion. Cressa and Decker were currently taking their own well-deserved downtime.

Ever since they noted the slow movements of the dots in the general vicinity of the expected lab, which had been an indication that the team was on foot, they'd been monitoring the situation 24/7. There was no indication of who the red dots belonged to, and as worried as he was about each of his three-member team, his chest tightened at the thought Sergi might have been lost.

Decker kept Remus updated every hour, even though The Wolf had been provided his own access to monitor the team. Each team member carried a burner phone, but if they were being chased, they wouldn't use it until they were in a secure location.

"We received a call from Rafael about ten minutes ago."

Devon's chest clamped tighter. "Play it back."

After a minute, the recording started.

"This is home station. Report." Bella's voice answered the special line that had been established for the mission. She followed standard protocol. Under no circumstance were names or locations revealed unless necessary.

"This is Team Beta." Rafael's voice was calm and clear. "Target was achieved but guarded by two underground blinds. Team Alpha and Charlie were taken. I've been followed for the last two days but am now clear. Tails have been eliminated."

They had decided not to identify how many team members had been sent, so if anyone was somehow listening, all they would know was that three teams had been sent and not that each team only had one member.

"Roger, Beta. Teams Alpha and Charlie are dark. I repeat, Alpha and Charlie are dark."

A moment passed before Rafael responded. "Alpha and Charlie were taken alive. I believe they were darted. Not sure of current status."

"What is your location?"

"Three miles south of Brasov."

"Are you safe?"

"Yes."

"Contact in one hour."

The line went dead.

Bella brought her laptop over and sat in the chair next to the couch. "What do you think?"

Devon stared at the map. Rafael thought Sergi and Carlos had been taken alive, yet their responders had gone dark right after Rafael had run. The team understood the importance of delivering word back to home base. Rafael had accomplished that.

Devon gave Bella the only response he could give. "We know where the facility is. What we don't know is why they took Sergi and Carlos alive."

"They hoped to get intel on who sent them." Jacques seemed assured of his response as he studied the display.

Devon nodded. "But would they need both or just one? Had the shifters Remus sent been killed or captured for some other reason?" He finished the espresso and turned to Jacques. "Can you have Cook send in coffee and something to eat? Bella, wake up Decker and Cressa."

After they left, he pulled out his cell phone and called Remus, who answered before the first ring.

"What have you heard?" Remus's voice was almost as neutral as Rafael's, but Devon caught the slight edge.

"Rafael just checked in. He confirmed the location. Sergi and Carlos were taken, but we're not sure of their status."

"Why did it take two days to hear something?"

"Rafael has been on the run. He didn't say how many were following, but they've been eliminated. We don't have any further information, but he'll be calling back in about forty minutes."

"Interesting. What does Decker think?"

"He doesn't know yet. I've sent someone to wake him and Cressa. They'll be available for Rafael's next check-in."

"Are you recording?"

"Yes. I'll have Bella send Rafael's initial contact."

"Don't bother. I'm having my car pulled around, but I doubt I'll make it for the next check-in."

"I'll notify the gate."

When Remus hung up, Devon considered why the trackers went dead. They shouldn't go offline if the subject were dead, which gave him hope. Had the trackers been found? If so, what made them think to look for them?

"What's up?" Decker stormed into the room with Cressa and Bella a few steps behind. "Bella said Rafael reported in."

Once everyone had settled and Jacques returned with two urns of coffee and a large plate of appetizers, Devon glanced at his watch. Three o'clock in the afternoon. Their personal schedules were disjointed with the constant surveillance, the guessing, and the worry.

"Bella, replay Rafael's call." Devon waited and watched the team as the call between Rafael and Bella plaid out. When it ended, he said, "Remus is on his way. While we wait, any thoughts on why Sergi's and Carlos's trackers went dark?"

"I spoke with Roxie before I crashed." Cressa pushed back her tangled hair. The dark circles told him how worried she was for Sergi. She was concerned for the others, but she had a strange relationship with the head of his security—close at times, irritating each other the next. They held great respect for each other, tormenting aside. "We assumed the lab would be underground. It's possible minerals in the ground could be creating interference, or the lab security is using some type of blocking technology."

No one else had a better answer and agreed it made sense.

"So we keep monitoring." Devon didn't like it, but at least they had the location. The first phase was completed, but the next phase had become more difficult.

Bella changed the screen on the display to show a closeup of the location where they lost the signals, but before she could go into detail, the anticipated call came in.

Bella answered. "Home station. Report."

"It's Team Beta. I'm at the same location, which is secure."

"Can you provide more intel on the target?"

"The terrain is difficult. Wild wolves, possibly shifters, are in the area, but they're staying away. We came in from the west. A single road dead ends at a parking lot. Wide, rollup doors carved into the mountainside. One set of double doors. Nothing else outside. If there are cameras, they weren't easy to spot in the dark. We were pulling back when two underground blinds opened up behind us. I was the farthest one back, and didn't get a good look inside, but it appeared to be at least three vampires in the first one. I was already turning to run when the second one opened. Team Alpha and Charlie were hit with darts. Alpha signaled to run."

"It was the correct call, Beta. We needed confirmation, and now we have it." Bella glanced at Devon, who nodded for her to continue. "Are you injured?"

"Nothing that hasn't already healed."

"Can you find your way to Madrid?"

"I'm staying put."

Bella glanced at Devon again.

With Aramburu's assistance, Devon had arranged for a safe house in Madrid to support both phases of their mission, assuming team members could make it there. He'd also contacted Philipe Renaud, who agreed to call the Family in France for a temporary stayover. Rafael's refusal to leave while his teammates had been captured was understandable.

"If he's in a secure place where he can dig in for a couple of days, he can wait for us."

"Roger, Beta. Dig in and maintain four-hour check-ins."

"Got it. Roger out."

The line went dead seconds before a short rap on the door drew everyone's attention. The office door swung open, and Remus, duffel bag in one hand, stood in the doorway.

Devon glanced at the clock on the wall. Remus had made record time getting there. If he didn't know better, he'd wonder if

Remus had shifted and ran all the way. "Bella, have Greta prepare Remus a room."

∾

DEVON WANDERED THE HALLWAYS, searching for Remus. Greta said he'd left his room, but she didn't know where he'd gone. Devon had just come from a shower with his mental faculties fully awake.

After the meeting, he'd followed Cressa back to her room, where she fell across the bed, eager to go back to sleep. He'd laid next to her until her eyelashes fluttered in troubled sleep. She would have to work through her emotions on her own. It wasn't easy observing a mission without an ability to help, especially when one of their own was in peril.

Not wanting to wake her, he'd left for his room. After a twenty-minute nap followed by the shower, it was time to revise phase two.

He stopped in the kitchen and grabbed a cup of coffee from the ever-full urn.

Cook turned from this dinner preparations. "You have good timing. I just refreshed the coffee." He turned back to whatever he was marinating. Devon couldn't see what was in the pan.

"You don't happen to know where Remus is, do you?" Devon took a long swallow and closed his eyes. He could feel the caffeine stimulating his senses. It wasn't a physical thing but a mental one. Or perhaps both because he was fairly certain he was addicted to the stuff.

"He's in the library."

Devon opened his eyes and gazed at his chef. "I should probably have asked this decades ago, but how do you know everything that happens in this house?"

Cook wiped his hands on a towel and set a bowl aside before turning to Devon. His eyes were lit with humor. "I can't tell you the number of vampires that come to the kitchen throughout the day. Something to drink, something to eat, or requesting a particular meal." He placed a fist on his hip. "Do you think I allow anyone to leave without repaying me with information?"

Devon chuckled and shook his head before draining the cup. "And how did you know where Remus is?"

He winked. "Letty just took him a tea service."

"Of course."

Devon was still smiling when he strode to the library with a full mug of coffee in his hand.

Remus was in the far corner where Devon had found him once before, sitting in his mother's favorite spot. The Wolf was reading something on his tablet. Papers were scattered around it, the tea service a few inches away. He picked up his cup, his eyes focused on the tablet as he took a sip.

"We could have provided you office space." Devon took a seat across from him.

Remus leaned back with his cup of tea and assessed the room. "This is an excellent library. It provides a sense of comfort even in times like these. I believe you said it was your mother's favorite as well."

Devon reviewed the room, remembering one of the last times he'd seen his mother in this exact spot. "She used to say she preferred the solarium. Despite her words to the contrary, she enjoyed the sunshine, always modifying the blinds for her guests' comfort. Yet, Father and I always found her here at this table. I think she told everyone she preferred the solarium so they'd look there and why she ensured this table couldn't be seen from the doorway. You had to have a true desire to find her."

"Why didn't she just keep an office in her room?"

"She did. It's my personal office now, but, like her, I use it sparingly because I believe, as my parents did, that a House leader should always be available. She considered it true for the mistress of the House, though she saw no reason to be easily found."

Remus chuckled. "I never met your mother, and I'm sorry I never had the opportunity."

"She often questioned Guildford's wisdom to reach out to the shifters, but she would have welcomed you with hospitality."

A small smile surfaced as Remus studied his tea. "That was over a hundred years ago. It's only been in the last few decades that partnerships between our two races have progressed so quickly."

"Far too long in the making, and now we're at a tipping point."

"What if this lab doesn't hold the secrets we believe they're hiding?"

Devon studied the shifter. It wasn't like him to be pessimistic. Perhaps it was nothing more than having come so far for so long, and they were now on the brink of a major discovery. Fear was a reasonable reaction, but he believed Remus's fear came from something else. He had to be thinking of the shifters he'd sent. Could they still be alive?

Maybe fear should be riding his shoulder, too. At the moment, he was distracted with concern for his friend rather than what might or might not be in the lab.

"If they have nothing to hide, then why build an underground lab in the Carpathian Mountains? It would have cost Venizi a great deal of money for infrastructure, logistics, security, and resources. And why the unusual hidden defenses, then dart intruders rather than just kill them?"

"Do you plan on going on the recovery mission?" Remus didn't drop his gaze with his sudden change of direction. He seemed to be testing Devon's resolve.

He shrugged. "I only have two available cadre. Lucas is needed at Oasis." It wasn't much of an answer.

"You could send Bella and Jacques."

"I am. We need strong leaders for a full infiltration. Just like you're making a decision on whether to send Elijah and Braden."

"You're planning this as if it were a battle campaign." Remus blinked, the only motion on his expressionless face. If he hadn't been convinced how far Devon was willing to go to get to the truth, that moment had just arrived.

"That's exactly what this is. Or, perhaps I should say the precursor. We sent scouts, and now it's time to get them back. This is the time to discover what Venizi has been up to all these years. And if necessary, tear it all down."

"You haven't answered my question."

Devon glanced down at the mug. The coffee had grown cold, but he took a drink before turning to Remus. "I owe it to him."

Remus nodded. "And I owe it to the many I've sent that never returned."

Devon stared at Remus. There was no doubt of The Wolf's conviction. There wasn't any way he was going to sit this one out. He returned the nod.

"We leave tomorrow at midnight."

DEVON FOUND Cressa in her room. She was sitting on the window seat looking down at the garden, which meant she was in one of her pensive moods.

"I thought you'd be sleeping." He stepped next to her and glanced down to see what might be holding her interest. There was no one down there, just the garden, the sycamore tree, and his parents' graves. When she didn't respond, he gently rubbed her shoulders and waited for her to collect her thoughts.

"What do you think your father would have made of all of this?"

Her question surprised him. He could give her a flippant answer, but she was working through difficult emotions, and he wouldn't belittle them. He scooted onto the bench behind her and wrapped his arms around her as he stared at the headstones.

"That's difficult to say. If he'd made it home with the *De første dage,* events would have played out very differently. I don't know if he would have taken it to the Council. He might have waited for more evidence. but the science of the time wouldn't have been able to decipher the differences in the blood. The fertility problems had only recently been confirmed. And chances are, Lorenzo could have easily found another way to kill them."

"It's weird how fate plays a hand in everything. He provided the first lead, but so many other things had to happen to get where we are today."

"You mean like having a dreamwalker drop into my lap?"

She leaned into him. "He had Hamilton but not Colantha, who we needed to interpret the last half of the book."

"You know it's pointless to wonder about what-ifs."

She placed a hand over his. "You're going to Romania and leaving me here."

At least he didn't have to be the one to bring it up. "I need Bella and Jacques with me, and I need to know the House will be safe in my absence."

"A duty that falls to Lyra, not me."

"Lyra can handle the business operations, but she'll require a strong head of security."

"You have plenty of vampires to support that. And what about Decker?" Her tone was even, all emotions held in, but he sensed her building excitement. She hadn't expected to be placed in charge of security.

"I have many vampires who can lead squads, but I need someone who can strategize with all our teams. Decker will provide access to the shifters and maintain stability with the rogues we currently have on staff. You also have Harlow."

She snorted.

"We need his connection with Roxie, but he isn't the fool he wants people to think he is. He's a resource for you."

Her scent changed. She was pleased.

"I still think I should be going."

He brushed back her hair and kissed her temple. This was her last-ditch effort to appear stubbornly resistant and a little whiny. He hugged her tight. "If Venizi discovers we've breached the lab, he could send trouble your way. Don't hesitate to stay in sync with Lucas. He can reach out to other Houses for support."

She pulled away and turned to face him. Fear filled her gaze, and he couldn't remember the last time he saw it. She didn't show it often. Maybe it was when they were on Shadow Island surrounded by Venizi's men with both of them too injured to fight, let alone escape. There had been dread in her gaze then, but it had been for him. That was what he saw now. Her concern wasn't for herself or even the House, but for him.

"If they capture you..."

He placed a finger on her lips to stop her. "We have a strong team, more intel than Remus had before, and Rafael can walk us straight to the door."

"You need to get through the door."

He grinned. "That won't be a problem." When her brow lifted, he added, "We're taking explosives."

She snorted. "Don't tell me. Friends in all the right places?"

"Something like that."

He slipped off the bench, and she squealed when he picked her up, slung her over his shoulder, and slapped her rump.

"Hey." She squirmed. Not in an attempt to get down but to find a more comfortable position.

His grin widened when she punched his backside.

Before they reached the bathroom door, she tapped his ass again. "Stop. Go by the dresser." When he turned, she said, "Not that one, the other one."

When he noted what was on the other dresser, he laughed. He stopped long enough for her to grab the bottle of wine and two wineglasses. He was going to miss her.

# Chapter Ten

SERGI STORMED through a path of vampires drenched in blood, dodging them as he swung his sword. He connected several times but whether it was someone's neck, arm, or their armored chest, he didn't know. His vision had narrowed to a single objective, everything else nothing but a blur. The castle was within reach, but the number of warriors increased the closer he got.

He stopped and surveyed the battlefield, hoping to find a better way through. He caught the movement at the last second and ducked. The blade missed his head by inches, close enough for him to hear its hum above the grunts of men and the clash of steel.

Sweat ran down his face and stung his eyes, and he'd almost given up hope when he remembered the cellars. They were on the west side of the castle. Not many would know of the small side door except the workers and the kids he played with when he was young. The battle was focused on the main entrance, the two forces evenly matched.

He cut across the field, skirting the edge of the fighting. Once he was clear, he ran along the southwest side of the castle and hoped no one followed. He should have come sooner. He'd begged the leader of his House to let him return home. Not to fight, but to get to his mother and sisters to safety.

His House leader was at odds with Sergi's father. He worried that Sergi's presence at the battle, should he be recognized, would appear as if their Houses were aligned. And the old male was unwilling to put his Family at odds with House Meinstein.

In a fit of fear and guilt, Sergi had made a decision that changed his life forever. When the rest of the guard was asleep, he slipped out, taking one of the horses. It was a long ride to the place of his birth, taking all night and most of the following morning. When he crested the last ridge, his heart clenched.

He'd been too late.

The two armies were fully engaged, and the enemy had reached the gates.

He wouldn't be able to return to his House after this. His leader was a hard and unforgiving male, and Sergi would be beheaded as a traitor. But nothing mattered more than the safety of his mother and sisters.

He reached the cellar door and shook his head. His father had stopped working the orchard some time ago if the cellar door was half-hidden behind overgrown hedges. He sliced at the branches, then yanked open the door, revealing a dark passageway. He raced down it, his heart thundering with fear.

There was still hope.

He took the steep stairs two at a time but slowed when he heard fighting in the main hallway. At the door, he peered to his right. Several of his father's guards, their armor smeared with blood, battled to hold the line. If the enemy had reached this deep into the castle, they were sure to be on the upper floors.

The hall was clear to his left, and he ran, turning down hall after hall until he reached the back staircase. He hadn't seen a single person as he ran—no servants, no Family members, no guards. It didn't ease the panic in his gut.

When he reached the second floor, his heart sank. Three

bloodied bodies lay on the floor. One was a guard, the other two were young females. He stopped and pulled their hair away.

No. His heart twisted as he stared at his sisters' attendants.

He didn't hesitate, not caring who he came across. He held his sword high as he raced to the end of the hallway where the double doors were open. Blood smeared the stone floor, but he heard nothing from inside.

He raced in, slipping on pockets of pooling blood but somehow staying upright. At first, everything seemed in order until he reached the other side of the spacious bedchamber, where arched doorways led to the terrace. His steps faltered, and he reached for the wall as a sob broke from him.

Three females lay on the terrace. Blood soaked their gowns, which had been drawn up their thighs. Whoever had done this had assaulted them. His sisters had barely been of age. He wanted to shut his eyes. Wanted to drop to the floor, pull them to him, and beg their forgiveness.

His honor wouldn't allow it.

He forced his legs to move him toward the heads that had been separated from their bodies. There was no question what he'd find. He knew by the way their hair was braided with the jeweled bands. But he had to look. He had his duty and refused to look away.

But when he saw their faces—the bruising and the fear—he broke.

He fell to his knees, dropping his sword as he placed his hands on their lifeless bodies. What had they ever done to deserve this? They had been kind, working with the sick, and supplying food for the hungry. That was the real reason they'd stayed behind. Not because Father had demanded it, but to help the servants.

When Sergi had fought with his mother and walked out, he told himself Meinstein would take them as hostages. But he knew better. He should have forced them to go with him, even if he had to drag them out of the castle.

He didn't notice the tears that fell, dripping off his chin and falling into congealing blood. He didn't notice anything until he heard a sword pulled from its sheath.

His hand inched toward the sword that lay at his side. When the boot steps grew closer, he grasped it. Before the person behind him could take another step, he was up, twisting and swinging the sword into a defensive position as he assessed the situation.

A single male, two inches taller with blond hair hanging to his shoulders and bulging muscles, smiled at him as he lifted his sword.

"So, the son returns." Felix was the muscle for Meinstein. He was a despicable male, just like his leader. The male leaned to his right to look behind Sergi, where his mother and sisters lay. Felix chuckled. "I have to say, they didn't go down easy." He licked his lips. "But at least I got a taste of them before I took their defiant heads."

Sergi didn't wait. He leaped at the male. And he was merciless. Rage at the male's words fueled his strikes. He could have been lying to get a rise out of Sergi. Though he believed the male's boasting, it wouldn't have mattered either way.

Felix defended himself the best he could, but the only thing driving him was his will to live. Sergi didn't care if he died. This went beyond life. This was pure, heated vengeance. Strike after strike. Blow after blow. He drove the male back. And when he grew tired, images of earlier times pierced his rage-filled attacks. His sisters laughing in the orchard each time Sergi jumped to reach the exact apples they wanted. His smiling mother, blushing when he brought her favorite flower whenever he came for a visit.

When Felix's movements slowed, Sergi kicked out, hit the male in the chest, and sent him sprawling. The male hit the floor hard, and within a single breath, Sergi towered over him, knocking the blade from his hand and planting his boot on Felix's throat.

"Why? What did they do to deserve such dishonor?"

When Felix's only response was a cruel smile, Sergi brought his blade down, the point ripping into the male's chest, just above his armor and inches from his neck. Blood spurted from the male's mouth, and his smile turned to a pain-filled grimace.

"Why?" Sergi shouted.

"It was on orders. If your father wasn't here, I was to kill his bitch and whore daughters."

His father wasn't there? Sergi pressed down on Felix's throat, ignoring the blood that trickled out of the male's mouth.

The male gurgled a laugh. "You didn't know? He ran with his cadre. He left his entire Family behind. Your House is a disgrace. You were such a disappointment that your Father traded his only son rather than keep him as an heir."

Sergi closed his eyes. He didn't want to believe the words, though he didn't doubt them. And it grieved him to know his traitorous father's blood filled his own veins.

He stepped back and brought the blade down, severing Felix's head from his body. If nothing else, the male looked him in the eye the entire time.

His attempt to save his mother and sisters had been for naught. He'd raced from his House and became a rogue, and in the end, he hadn't been able to save them.

A piercing stab made him cry out. It was unexpected.

His eyes flashed open to the unforgiving eyes of his tormentor.

Gheata smiled. At least the savage interrogator had pulled him from his nightmare.

And when the next stab of the dagger was shoved into his kidney, he laughed.

GHEATA PACED a tight path in the confines of the cell. Sergi hadn't spoken a word since his capture, and his interrogator was showing signs of agitation. He tried to remember how many days ago that had been. Long enough it seemed that the loss of blood had decreased his body's ability to heal quickly. Sleep was his only means to conserve energy.

His beast scratched at its barrier, pushing to be released. If he thought he could control the beast, he'd unleash it for the most brutal part of the interrogations. In his weakened state, and with the beast's rage, Sergi didn't think he'd be able to rein it back.

"Perhaps we need to start from the beginning." Gheata locked his hands behind his back as he strode back and forth. His gaze focused on the path of his boots as he considered the situation.

Gheata was a cleaner. What some called a fixer. He came in at the end of a mission with carte blanch to handle unforeseen problems. That didn't make him a useful interrogator. Whoever ran this place, or perhaps it was Venizi himself, thought size mattered for a successful interrogation. But torture rarely worked. At least not by itself. Mind games were more likely to render a favorable outcome. And to this point, it appeared to be a skill Gheata hadn't mastered.

"I don't need to know your true purpose," Gheata said as he stopped at the table of torture instruments. He selected a scalpel and lifted it for inspection as if he could see its gleaming edge in the dim light. "You were searching for the lab with the intention to infiltrate. Perhaps with the intention to steal our formulas or find information to use for blackmail."

He laid the scalpel down and returned to his pacing. "At first, I thought you were sent by one of Venizi's competitors. Now, I'm not so sure." He stopped in front of Sergi, who refused to meet his torturer's gaze.

Gheata pulled Sergi's head back by his hair, his eyes glowing an intense yellow. "Tell me who sent you." Spittle formed at the corners of his mouth. His frustration had to be unbearable. If he let his captive lose too much blood, he could force Sergi's beast out with only one thought—to feed. Worst case, he'd be left with a dead vampire. That might be the eventual outcome, but the male's determined gaze told Sergi one thing.

They weren't ready to let him die.

Gheata dropped Sergi's head. He returned to his pacing and spent the next minutes calming his own beast, the glow leaving his eyes. "Let's try something simple. Your name. Surely that isn't so difficult to share."

They were too early in the game for Sergi to discern if Gheata had switched to mental interrogation. Providing his name sounded like a simple request, but there was power in a name, and he was unwilling to hand that over to Gheata. All he had to do was check the House rosters for anyone with Sergi's name. He would search the largest ones first and would quickly discover that his name matched one of Devon's cadre. He'd been surprised no one had taken a picture to send to Venizi. Maybe they had, and they were waiting for orders.

A motion at the door made Gheata turn around. "You're early, girl."

"Sorry, sir," the guard said. "She's actually a few minutes late, and the lab is asking when she'll be done here."

Gheata struck fast and hard, slamming a fist into Sergi's gut. It was unexpected, and he blew out a large breath of air as he winced from the pain. Not from the blow but from the open wounds that were still bleeding.

He seared Sergi with a glare and stormed to the door, where he paused and glared down at the female who cleaned the cell. "Feed him and clean him up. I want his skin fresh to start again tomorrow."

"You won't be back this afternoon, sir?" the guard asked.

"No. I'm involved in another project that will require my attention for the next few afternoons. We need to make these morning sessions more meaningful. I'm not ready to lose him to his beast quite yet."

Sergi would have laughed but didn't need any more punches.

He'd learned more today than Gheata did, and it validated Devon's quest to find this lab. Something important was going on here.

He would only be interrogated in the mornings, at least for a few days, and they were going to feed him. This all worked in Sergi's favor. And the odds improved if Rafael had gotten away.

Devon would come. He had to hold on.

# Chapter Eleven

I FELL BACK as the male bruiser shoved his way out the door, glaring at me as if I were the one who'd interrupted his torture session. The eerie yellow glow in his eyes made his scowl all the more menacing. The interrogation must not be going well, and while that piqued my interest, I was more curious about the special project.

I couldn't see him helping in the labs. He appeared to be nothing more than a bruiser with no finesse when it came to interrogation. Not that I was an expert, but I'd seen my uncle use masterful techniques that delved into a prisoner's psyche, which provided faster results and typically less mess than torture.

The guard strode into the room, and I pushed the hulking vampire from my thoughts. I picked up a bucket of water and rags but stopped when I stepped through the doorway. The guard squatted in front of a cooler I hadn't noticed before. They must have brought it this morning.

I stepped closer, my eyes glued to the cooler as the guard opened it. Several vials of blood lay in soft padding. He selected two and, in no particular hurry, strolled to the vampire. He stuffed one vial in his shirt pocket and popped the top off the other.

Lifting the prisoner's head by his hair, the guard poured the blood into his mouth, and the vampire drank what had to be nothing but a morsel to him. His tongue darted out to capture every drop. The motion was repeated with the second vial.

The prisoner had been eager, not caring what the guard thought of him. The meager amount of blood couldn't possibly sustain him, but it might heal his wounds. I shuddered. All it did was give the bruiser a new canvas of skin to carve into.

Once the empty vials were dropped into the cooler, the guard turned to me.

"You'll need to clean the prisoner and the room. Be quick about it. I'll be back in thirty minutes to take you back to the lab."

They wanted me to clean the prisoner? I gulped and glanced down at the bucket, the rags clenched in my fists, and a light sheen of sweat glistened on my arms. I straightened as my wolf paced. He was pinned to the wall like a moth in a display case. I could do this.

There wasn't much blood on the floor, and I quickly cleaned it so I wouldn't stomp around in it. Once that was completed, and I'd emptied the trash and replaced the mug of water, barely ten minutes had passed.

The cooler sat next to the trash can. I glanced at the open door and listened. All quiet. Unable to stop my curiosity, I squatted and opened the cooler. It was empty except for a six-pack of vials, and after today, two were empty. I picked up one of the used ones. The label identified it as H-12 followed by a date. The blood was three days old, if I trusted the calendar in the guards' breakroom.

Did the H mean human? It made sense. Vampires could drink shifter blood, but they got little for the effort—a brief spark of energy but no usable nutrients. Several humans worked in the lab area and probably other areas as well. Were these vials from the staff, or did they bring it in from someplace else?

I'd procrastinated long enough. Best to get it done. I replaced the vial and shut the lid. The bucket had already been emptied, so I added water and grabbed a clean rag.

I shuffled to within a foot of the prisoner. His head hung motionless. I dipped the rag, and my first thought was to just quickly rub the dried blood off. Until I lifted the rag, eager to be finished, and pressed it to his shoulder.

I couldn't do it.

The first time I'd been cut, it left an indelible mark. With three deep cuts that, even after a couple shifts, required several sutures, and a throbbing pain that lasted for days, it was a memory that never left, never got old. These wounds were fresh, raw, and sensitive.

I couldn't make him feel worse.

I didn't know this vampire. Why should I care?

But I did. And I couldn't explain why.

I held the rag over the cut until the crusty, dried blood softened, then I gently brushed it away. A few of the wounds began to bleed, and I applied extra pressure, waiting for his vampiric blood to close it. I worked until all the wounds were clean. His body was still marred with blood, and, moving gingerly around the wounds, I washed off the last remnants.

His skin was warmer than I expected, and though I kept watch for any eye movement, I tensed in anticipation of him waking. When a couple minutes passed, and he still slept, I traced a finger over the dark tattoos. They were a mass of swirling lines and unknown symbols that made me think tribal, though which culture, I didn't know. Perhaps they were from some ancient vampiric language. Tattoos were rare on vampires because of their ability to quickly heal, and I was curious how these had remained. It must have been a painful process.

I was so focused on one particular symbol as I repeatedly traced the lines that I stopped paying attention to the vampire. A muscle flexed under my hand, and my gaze flashed to his eyes.

Warm, chestnut-colored eyes stared back at me. I couldn't look away, and I couldn't read them. They weren't blank, angry, fearful, or pained. And they should be pained.

"Thank you." His voice was gruff from disuse. If he never spoke to the interrogator, there wasn't anyone else for him to talk to, and he'd been in this cell for days.

I opened my mouth to respond but wasn't sure how to. I couldn't tear myself away from eyes that held me.

The sound of boots on stone snapped me out of the moment. I nodded and then dropped to the floor to clean the last specks of bloody water off the floor. I was lugging the bucket back to the cart when the guard entered the room.

He glanced around, striding by the table, and then to the prisoner. When turned to me, he grunted.

I supposed that meant he couldn't find anything to complain about.

"Dump the bucket and let's go. You won't be getting lunch today since you're late, and the lab's team leader is waiting for you."

When he turned to glance back at the prisoner, I did the same thing, but the vampire's head hung limply. For some reason, I didn't think he was asleep, and instead, was listening to every word.

WHEN I ENTERED Lab Two where I'd witnessed the shifter experiments, I stopped. All the cabinet doors and drawers were open. S-272 was pulling out equipment, beakers, jars of who knew what, and racks of vials, some filled with various colored liquids, most of them empty. They were sorted into various groups on the countertops.

A female lab assistant rushed over and grabbed my arm like I was a toddler, dragging me to the commercial-sized refrigerator.

"I was expecting you an hour ago."

Honestly, if they were going to continue assigning me to multiple jobs, they needed better coordination with scheduling. I didn't bother responding because she would either ignore me or slap me, which wouldn't have been the first time, and I wasn't in the mood for either.

For some reason, all I could focus on was the whispered "thank you" from the vampire. After days of torture and limited feedings, I hadn't expected his skin to be so warm.

"Are you listening to me?"

I glanced up at the female, taking a long whiff and determining she was human. Her throat was so enticing, and my wolf urged me to take a bite. I sighed. I'd have to shift for that delicious snack, then shift back to clean up the blood just before they put a bullet in my head or stuck me in one of their silver cages so they could shoot their experimental serums in me.

It was all I could do to hold in my hysteric laughter. Then S-272 was next to me, and he nodded at the assistant.

"She understands the task." He held his head down as he always did. His voice wasn't patronizing but calm and even.

The female stared at S-272, and her lips formed words, but she paused. She glared at me as she nodded. "See that she does, or you'll be the one punished for her sloppiness."

The female stormed out, and it wasn't until then I realized my body was shaking.

"Are you alright?" S-272 kept his head down as he spoke to me. He was always aware of the cameras.

I blew out a breath. "Yeah. It's been a rough morning." I followed him as he opened the refrigerator doors that had been left unlocked. "What's going on?"

"They're restarting the experiments soon. They want everything cleaned from top to bottom, including all the equipment."

His words slammed into me like a rollercoaster on its downward trajectory. More experimenting on shifters, killing them without a second thought.

"The vials are labeled with colored dots. Anything with a yellow dot is to be removed and tossed in the red container for hazardous waste removal. Everything else is to be wiped down and pushed toward the back to wait for new vials."

He turned toward me when I didn't respond. All I could do was stare at the contents of the refrigeration unit. Dozens of vials. Most appeared to be blood, but others were filled with a variety of colored liquids, similar to those stored in the cabinets, though they must be different if some had to be refrigerated. They were all labeled.

"S-473. Do you understand?"

"My name is Alexandra. Alex. And I understand."

I stepped forward and took out the first rack of vials. Each rack held ten vials, and these were filled with a thick, purple substance. The labels were marked with a blue dot. I set them on the counter to the right of the fridge and picked up the next one. This one held vials of light green with a yellow dot. I placed them on the counter to the left.

My motions were slow and methodical. And at first, I didn't hear S-272.

"S-473, are you alright?"

I think I nodded, but wasn't sure.

"Alex, are you alright?"

I stopped, a rack of dark-orange vials with green dots still in my hands. I glanced over at S-272 with my head lowered like his. "I'll be okay."

He pulled out a rack as if he was instructing me on the task. "You don't look okay. Why were you late?"

I set the rack on the counter to the right and pulled out a rack of blood. I took a moment to check the label. It was marked H-9 with a date and a yellow dot. The date was five days ago.

I set it on the counter to the left. "Did you know they have a vampire prisoner on level three?"

I'd never shared that information with him, but it was possible he might have overheard it from someone else. The assistants

98

tended to talk freely as if we weren't there. We were nothing to them after all, except a future experiment test case.

"Are you sure?" He sounded surprised.

"I clean his cell every day, and they torture him. They have him strapped to the wall so he can't move." My hands shook as I retrieved another rack of blood labeled the same as the previous one. "They made me wash the blood off him today."

"Is he one of the guards?"

"I don't think so. It sounds like they captured him outside the building. Another vampire is interrogating him, and he keeps asking who sent him. The prisoner won't speak. He won't even give them a name."

But he had spoken. To me. A shifter. He had to know I was a shifter. Not that he'd said anything of value. At least, nothing that would have been important to the interrogator. But somehow, it had meant something to me. A vampire had thanked a shifter.

I shook my head to dispel the memory. He was probably hoping I'd feel sorry for him and do something foolish like try to help him.

"Are you sure he came from outside the building?"

I gave a light shrug as I pulled out another rack of orange vials with green dots. "That's what it sounded like. Why?"

"I need to go back to the cabinets. You seem to understand the task."

I understood. He didn't want anyone who might be watching the monitors to think we were together longer than we should be.

Only taking a moment to stretch, I glanced up at the cameras. I knew where they were, but I wanted to confirm their position in relation to where I stood and the location of the red hazardous waste tub. The tall container was only a couple feet away and in clear view of the cameras.

After removing all the vials from the fridge, I stepped back. There were twenty-one racks of vials with yellow dots. I grabbed two rags, doubled them up, and cleaned out the shelves in the fridge, mentally reviewing the crazy thoughts pressing on me.

Of the twenty-one racks of vials, twelve of them appeared to contain human blood, if my interpretation of the labels was accurate. If memory served, human blood lasted a few weeks when refrigerated. I wasn't sure how long it was viable if not stored in a cool environment.

Once the shelves were clean, I laid the rags next to the racks of vials requiring disposal while I put the others back in the fridge, ensuring they were on the correct shelves and pushed to the back as requested.

Then I turned to the vials to be tossed, keeping my back to the camera.

I closed my eyes. This was crazy. It was a huge risk, and the penalty would most likely be lethal.

My uncle might question the actions I was about to take, but I had to know why the vampire was being held prisoner. The hopeful eyes of the shifters chained in their cells haunted me. If the vampire had been caught outside the building, he'd been there for a reason. The lab was too remote for it to have been a hiker who got lost—certainly not a vampire hiker. Then why had he been out there?

I kept my back to the camera as I separated the two rags, leaving each one open on the counter. The first step was to follow the order I'd been given. I removed four of the colored vials from their rack and made a show of dumping them in the waste container. I repeated the action a few more times until half the racks were empty.

The next step was easy enough. I removed nine vials labeled H-9 and placed them on one of the rags. I rolled up the rag, folding it so the vials were wrapped tightly together to prevent breaking, then tucked in the ends.

Another deep breath. This wasn't crazy. This was insane.

I grabbed a few vials and made three short trips to the waste container until all the racks were empty. Without a glance at the camera, though I seriously wanted to take a peek, I dragged the container toward the counter and to my left. I turned to the right and stuffed the empty rag in the pocket of the lab coat while I stuffed the package of vials in the left. The container should have blocked the camera's view of my left side, but it was a risk.

There was one blind spot S-272 had pointed out to me the second day we worked together. It was in the same place in both of the larger labs where the experiments took place. I picked up the container, holding it tight against me, and moved toward the hazardous waste receptacles on the other side of the lab.

I slowed as I reached the blind spot, and taking two more steps, I stopped and dropped the container, allowing it to tip on its side. This time I did look for the cameras, and I couldn't see either one. I pulled the vials out of my pocket and pulled up my shift, stuffing the package under the waistband of my underwear. I gave the box a slight kick, then stumbled into view of the cameras as I picked up the container. It seemed dramatic, but I hoped if anyone had been watching, all they saw was me stumbling over my feet and dropping the waste bin.

Shaking off the nerves, I shoved the container in the receptacle and returned to the area where S-272 worked. If he'd noticed anything, he didn't mention it. For the next two hours, I moved slowly, occasionally rubbing up against a counter to push the package back in place and managing to complete my tasks within the allotted timeframe. I was cleaning off the last counter when the assistant came in.

"S-473. Come here."

I jumped, startled. Had they already discovered my theft? My hands shook, and I slowed my breaths in a vain attempt to calm my nerves.

"Now, girl."

With my hands in my pockets, hoping the package would stay where I put it, I shuffled toward the female.

"I spoke with your morning guard. I didn't realize they'd assigned you additional tasks without informing us. It's obvious you're a bit slower this afternoon, though you did manage to get your tasks completed. However, this won't do for our new schedules.

"Starting tomorrow, you will no longer be cleaning the guard's room, though you will be required to clean the cells. That should give you a half hour to eat." She glanced over at S-272.

"S-272. You will both be working in Lab One tomorrow. The same routine." She turned and spoke to the two guards who'd stepped up behind her. "Return them to their cells. They can eat there this evening."

I tossed my lab coat in the bin outside the lab and followed the guard, consciously aware of the package slipping toward my left leg. I scratched while pushing it up, taking the longest walk of my life down the stairs and to my cell.

When the guard opened the door to my cell, he grabbed my arm.

I didn't move.

"Are you feeling ill? Do you need a healer?"

His question wasn't out of concern for me. The entire facility was in constant fear of illnesses and contagions from the filthy shifters.

"I'm just tired." I glanced up at him. Whatever he saw in my expression seemed to put him at ease, and he let me go.

When the door closed and locked behind me, I dropped to the floor and sucked in a huge breath. What the hell was I planning on doing with nine vials of human blood?

The deeper question was one I wasn't ready to analyze.

Yet it wouldn't go away. Every time I closed my eyes, he was there.

The vampire's warm gaze, and his rough words of thanks weren't enough to put my neck on the line. Yet, I couldn't come up with a viable reason why he'd been outside the facility, if that was truly where they'd captured him. And I refused to get my hopes up. He had to stay alive long enough to tell me.

Though what made me think a vampire, who'd been strapped to a wall and had little chance of escape, could be of benefit to the shifters, I had no idea. Rather than continue to ponder something I couldn't answer with the limited information I had, I allowed my wolf to take over and trusted she would protect me for one night.

## Chapter Twelve

SERGI FELL in and out of wakefulness. The last session with Gheata had been brutal, but he'd managed to give him nothing—not even his name. His body was beyond hunger, though they continued to feed him small amounts of blood after each interrogation. The only possible reason was to extend the sessions and prevent the beast from rising to the point where gaining any further information would be useless.

His bones ached. This wasn't the first time he'd been in such tight constraints. For interrogation, it was critical for the more dangerous vampires, even when a captor thought them too weak. But never had his bones ached so deeply. It only served as validation of a far worse fate. He'd suspected his condition for some time and hoped he'd been wrong. It would be years, possibly decades, before the blood disease that inflicted so many took its toll, but he could no longer deny the evidence.

The only current option was either sleep or force his body into a meditative state. Since he lacked the practice for proper meditation, he focused his mind elsewhere. He was a man of simple tastes with few exceptions—a finely aged Scotch, a sharply honed sword of Damascus steel, and the artifacts he'd collected over the centuries. They were nothing but small souvenirs he'd saved after a battle or raid.

He'd never understood why a warrior like him would save them. Over time, he suspected he would someday want a physical connection to his long memories. Perhaps more endearing for someone who lived as long as a vampire.

He mentally strolled through his storage unit in Santiga Bay. He'd never paid attention to how much he'd stored away until he'd seen Simone's room in the manor after her brain injury. She also preferred a simple life, but the art she'd collected reminded him of his own stash. And when he considered modifying his bedroom decor, of all his cherished objects, one stood out over all the others —the dented and stained remnants of a shield.

He pictured the leather, wood, and steel armor that saved his life more than he could count, but that hadn't been why he'd saved it. And it was that image he held onto as the beast let him sleep.

SERGI IGNORED the group of men as they prepared for another skirmish within the ranks. He was churlish after his meeting with the Captain of the Guard. He'd been doing this for too long— dealing with brash hotheads who thought they knew everything.

Although, to be fair, he'd been that young warrior at one time. After he'd become a rogue, he'd traveled from House to House, picking up work where he could. He'd been brash, daring, and filled with rage. He'd let down those he cared for the most, and though it hadn't been his fault, the guilt was never far away. And he took it out on the world around him.

Those days had made him a better fighter, had honed his skills as a warrior, and had earned him trust among the men when he'd face the enemy with a fierceness that couldn't be contained.

Then one day, he found a House that hit a chord deep within him. There were plenty of Houses worth fighting for, and though he didn't agree with everything his new leader believed, something he couldn't name made him stay and pledge his loyalty. Yet, that flame of anger held by his beast had never gone out, and it rose that day after meeting with the Captain of the Guard.

He marched back to his unit, irritated as he shucked off his mantle and grumbled. "As if Agar's orders aren't enough to contend with, now I've been given a new whelp to train."

The men grunted, but a few glanced around when Sergi mentioned the whelp was the young son of their House leader. A son most had never seen since he'd left for continued education in the Far East. Sergi had seen enough sons of leaders who pranced into battle believing their House name made them resilient—untouchable. He'd seen many of them fall or crawl back to their Father.

He was still complaining about his new assignment as he sharpened his dagger when a stranger walked into the guard's tent. He wore common battle gear but no insignia. No colors to show who he fought for.

Sergi gave him a quick perusal, then ignored him, returning to his dagger. New warriors were always joining the House.

"You think you can take the Master's whelp in a fight?" the stranger asked.

"You think anyone in this battalion couldn't take someone who's nothing but a pup?" Sergi threw back. He had no time for this. "The only education he should be getting is on the field."

"Were you calling the Master's son a dog?"

The men's eyes shifted as they looked from the stranger to Sergi, and even through his irritation, he took note of it. Sergi might be a warrior at heart, but he played politics better than most, and he tempered his tone.

"I only meant that he's young. From what I hear, barely over a hundred years."

"And he's taken no credit for the battles he's won."

Sergi chuckled at that. "So they say."

"I wager he could take you in a fight." The stranger picked up a lance, checked its length, then hefted it to test its weight. After giving the tip a closer inspection, he tossed it into a heap on the floor.

"Twenty pieces says you're wrong." Sergi stood to his full height, the muscles in his arms and chest pulsing with eagerness to fight.

The stranger dipped his hand into a pocket beneath his armor and pulled out a handful of coins, tossing several on the table and pocketing the rest.

Sergi glanced at them before reassessing the stranger. He wasn't as large or muscled as Sergi, and though something didn't feel right, he'd gone too far to back down. Not now.

He pulled coins out of his pocket and tossed them on top of the others. The men murmured, excitement growing at the pending fight.

Sergi led the stranger out of the tent and onto the training field. Though both men wore their weapons, two pages followed closely with training swords. The two vampires took their places on the field, stared at the wooden swords, and then at each other. They ignored the pages and pulled their steel swords as they circled each other.

Warriors began to form a ring around them, and those who'd been training dropped their wooden swords and joined them, their voices rising in cheers of encouragement.

The two males continued to circle each other, each male studying the other. Sergi had to admit, he was impressed by what he saw. The male moved easily, his feet light and not giving away any sign of which foot he would lead with. Sergi grinned. This would be an even match, and his beast rattled its cage, ready for battle.

Tired of the slow dance, Sergi lunged. His challenger didn't feign as expected but charged. Their swords clashed, echoing through the valley and over the yells of the crowd.

Sergi twisted as he came out of the lunge to find the other male ready with his sword raised as he came at him. Sergi dropped and rolled, coming up fast to block the strike and then delivered one of his own. It was blocked.

The male was quick on his feet, only giving away his direction as he moved to strike. Sergi had to admit his admiration was growing, but he never lessened his blows. When the male came at him before he was ready, he raised his shield and felt the power of the strike but managed to maintain his balance.

He changed tactics and went after the challenger with a continuous series of attacks until the other male was forced to use his own shield. It brought the two of them close, and before Sergi anticipated it, the male kicked Sergi, landing a blow to his stomach that sent him reeling backward.

He landed on his back but immediately rolled as the sword came down where his head had been.

With each blow he landed, the other repaid in kind. The chanting of the men grew as they began to take sides. No doubt the betting was heavy as the two continued to fight, neither giving any quarter.

It wasn't until Sergi's blade frayed the leather strap of the male's armor that he caught sight of the emblem on his tunic. This was no errant warrior testing Agar's men. This was the whelp he'd so arrogantly called out—the Master's son.

This fight was no longer a mere challenge, no matter the coins that lay on the table in the war tent. He'd slandered the House leader's son, and this had become a different fight indeed.

If he was going down, he wouldn't make it easy. Sergi might have nothing left—the House of his birth gone, his family gone. But he had his honor. And no one could take that away.

The fight continued for another ten minutes until both males were drenched in sweat, and blood marred their bodies. Sergi had taken blood that morning, and his cuts healed quickly, except for one along his left arm that had cut almost to the bone.

The deep lash across his thigh ached, but the skin had closed over.

The blood and gashes didn't bother him, but he'd grown fatigued. His opponent's movements had also slowed, but Sergi wouldn't outlast him. And he'd rather take the honorable way out.

He dropped to one knee, laying his sword and shield at the vampire's feet. He bowed his head, knowing after seeing the blood drip down the male's arm and left leg that it was his leader's right to have him put to death for the injury, even in this mock battle.

"I give you my life," Sergi said.

The male stared down at him for several minutes. "Why do you give me your life?"

He was confused by the question, then shrugged as he looked up into crystal blue eyes. "For the grievous injury I've caused the Master's son."

He dropped his head. There should be murmuring from the men, but the silence was so complete one could hear a grasshopper move through the grass.

"I'm told you came from House Lennox a few months ago."

Sergi nodded. "As a rogue."

"So, you might not have learned that we don't punish others for simply trying to best those of higher rank."

"No, Master."

The male clucked his tongue. "I'm no Master, and you don't want my Father hearing you saying that." His tone was one of humor, and Sergi glanced up at the male's next words.

"You might have heard of the pending House war between Beaumont and Vaughn. My Father has no wish to move his army against Vaughn, yet he understands the consequences should they win. House Beaumont has called for our support, and while our Father won't risk the House by sending men, he's given me leave to create my own army."

When Sergi couldn't hide his interest or curiosity, the male grinned.

"My Father has also given leave for me to take five members of his army as seed for my own. I want you to be my Captain of the Guard. Will you accept this role and ride into battle at my side?"

Sergi's blood soared at the thought, but he squinted at the male. "Why would you ask me of all vampires after I challenged you?"

"It's because you challenged me." He touched his arm where Sergi's blade had sliced a long opening. "And you have moves I've never seen before." He stretched out his hand. "Will you join me and fight alongside the son of House Trelane?"

He would never forget that moment, all those centuries ago, when he took Devon's hand. The warriors who had formed a ring around them to watch the fight had cheered. He smiled and choked out a laugh then grimaced at the pain it created.

When the door to his cell burst open, Sergi lifted his head and stared into Gheata's victorious eyes that glowed a bright yellow. The interrogator was no longer interested in making Sergi talk.

He'd given his life to Devon that day on the training field, and nothing had changed since that moment. He would still give his life for his House.

Gheata smiled as he lifted a syringe. Sergi wanted to close his eyes against whatever was to come next, but he never wavered as he watched the male stride forward and plunge the needle into his neck.

## Chapter Thirteen

DEVON DROPPED his duffel by the front door and strode to his office. Their expanded team had spent most of the day gathering data and reviewing reports. Rafael continued to check in at four-hour intervals, but his status hadn't changed.

Bella had been monitoring the red dot on the map that represented Rafael's GPS monitor since his first report. Earlier in the day, she'd been sullen when she reported the other red dots were still dark. Devon had squeezed her shoulder.

"The dot doesn't tell us whether he's alive or dead. They either found it or something is blocking the signal."

She nodded in agreement, but her voice was thick when she replied. "If they took them into the mountain, there could be any number of materials blocking the signal."

"Exactly."

Though she'd said the necessary words, her spirits hadn't risen, and he'd known not to push her. Bella handled crises better when she kept busy and stayed on task. And, in doing so, she'd found another lead.

When Devon joined the group in his office, he was a bit shocked at seeing it transformed into a command center of sorts.

The teams had broken into groups—mission preparation, tactical for the assault, and the exit strategy.

Bella led mission preparation, and when the group settled to provide their updates, she hit a key on the remote control, and a face appeared on the wall display. The man was ordinary with a ruddy face, curly black hair that appeared disheveled, and dark, heavy brows behind black-rimmed glasses. His lips were thin and, at the time of the photo, seemed pinched.

Before Bella could provide her report, there was a sharp intake of breath from Cressa.

Devon turned to her. "What's wrong?"

"I know that man."

Bella, who thought better on her feet, moved to stand in front of Cressa. "How? I was lucky to find him just a couple of hours ago."

"Who is he?" Remus stared at the photo before glancing at Decker, who sat next to him at the bar, but Decker shrugged, as clueless as everyone else.

Bella was going to answer but looked to Cressa instead.

It took a moment for Cressa to realize they expected her to know, but she shook her head. "I don't know his name, or more likely, I hadn't paid attention. Lorenzo might have mentioned it or assumed I didn't need to know. He was the vamp Lorenzo invited to dinner while I was on the island and still under his influence." When no one responded, and Bella crossed her arms over her chest, she continued. "He was some type of scientist and was excited about some new formula he thought would be ready for field testing soon. Lorenzo's mood changed after that, but I was sent back to my room before anything else was said."

"This was the memory you recently relived." Devon wasn't sure if he should be concerned about the timing of Cressa's dream and Bella finding the man's pictures hours before the team was set to leave. This all assumed that the man's discussion with Lorenzo involved the lab they'd been searching for.

Cressa seemed stunned herself. "Yes. Maybe it was all the talk about finding the lab and that memory finally surfaced from my subconscious. I don't know."

Bella stared at Cressa for a long moment, but whether she was waiting for more or simply digesting what she'd heard, Devon didn't know. It only lasted a minute before she turned back to the wall display and pointed at the photo. "This is Dr. Garner Krasinski. I've been watching the video feeds Remus was kind enough to provide of visitors going to Shadow Island."

"For what period of time?" Lucas asked. He'd driven over from Oasis with Ginger and a security motorcade for a couple of days to help the team prepare for the mission.

"For the last six months."

"That must have been exciting to watch." Ginger turned red when the team glanced at her, but then everyone chuckled.

"You have no idea," Bella replied, bringing the conversation back to her. "The feeds come from several cameras of the parking lot, so I caught this guy arriving in a limo. He appeared a bit scattered when Lorenzo's security led him to one of the go-fast boats. He hunched over when he walked, kept looking back at the limo, and held his briefcase under his arm and tight to his chest. He seemed like he wanted to be anywhere else and was terrified someone might take the case.

"After the first couple hours of watching, only certain people appeared important enough to take over on the go-fast boats rather than the ferry, but it was his actions that made me dig further. Let's just say I called in a debt and was able to run his face through a face-recognition program and found his passport photo. I assumed he was likely vampire, so I ran his name through the House rosters and got a hit." She glanced around, but it was more theatrics than anything. The room was glued to her every word. "Dr. Krasinski works for House Larkin, who we know owns the lab that has been studying the fertility issues for Lorenzo and the Council. He spends most of his time outside the US and his passport stamps reflect travel between Bucharest and San Francisco by way of London. He comes to the US at least once every three months."

"To report on the lab work," Lucas suggested.

"Most likely."

"So what does this give us?" Decker asked.

"A direct connection between this vampire, House Larkin, and Lorenzo." Devon considered if it gave them anything else. "It also puts the good doctor in Romania. The question is, where is he now? Though I assume he's locked up in his lab." Devon considered their options. "Send a copy of the photo to Remus to share with the shifters on the docks."

"If he shows up, do you want us to intercede?" Remus asked.

Devon nodded. "On his return to the airport."

Remus nodded with a grim smile.

"This doesn't help us get into the mountain," Lucas said.

"No." Bella changed the display to show the location of where the red dots disappeared. The next shot was of a single-lane dirt road that disappeared in and out of the dense forest canopy. "We backtracked this road to a small village. The road appears to only run between the lab and village, with no other connecting roads. There are a few small trails, most likely created by hikers, horses, or motorcycles."

"It would be dangerous to use the road," Lucas said. "But it would be worth checking out the town."

"Agreed." Bella turned to the team. "However, if we have a three-member team on motorcycles with all-weather camping gear and hunting bows, they would look like hunters if intercepted. The plan isn't to reach the parking lot but to build a defense parameter about a mile from the entrance.

"I want Rafael to relocate to the village and monitor the road for a day or two. He could provide some valuable intel on how often it's used and what type of vehicles are going in and coming out. That would still give him time to meet us at the first checkpoint." She turned to Devon. "I've asked Rafael his confidence rating on whether he could do this without being noticed. He believes the risk is low." She winked at Harlow. "It appears he's learned a trick or two from Jamal. He can stay under the radar, and we can monitor his movement." She paused and glanced at the room before turning a concerned gaze to Devon. "And to be honest, I think he's a bit stir-crazy. We should put him to use."

"What about the motorcycles?" Devon asked.

"Rafael believes he can have them waiting for us."

"Alright. Rafael has a go. What about the entrance?"

"Two teams would be best." Bella changed the screen to show a parking lot in a forest with various red, blue, and yellow marks drawn over it. "Based on Rafael's input, this is the best software rendering of the parking lot we could put together. These red circles are where the underground blinds are. We don't know if there are more security measures in place, but from what Rafael reported, these seemed efficient enough to capture a small group of infiltrators. The yellow line is a best guess on perimeter security. There are a lot of woods. It's possible, since the lab has been there for over a century, that they've had time to build a solid defense grid."

"You don't sound like you believe that." Lucas, as Devon had expected, was becoming a well-rounded cadre member. His specialty wasn't security, but he had a knack for it, which was a reason he and Ginger had survived the hunt for the *De første dage*.

Bella shrugged. "The satellite images and Rafael's report tell us this is rough terrain. The facility is in a mountain which means the underground blinds were created with explosives. If they had additional underground security outside this yellow line..." she pointed to it. "The landscape around it would be vastly different than the old-growth forest. If they hung cameras or other monitoring devices, the wild shifters would eventually dismantle them. The team believes there's an underground tunnel that leads from inside the mountain to these blinds. When an alarm is triggered, they send a security team through the tunnel to the blinds. They could send as many guards as needed for any type of incursion."

"But this is just a guess," Remus said.

"Yes. The only other option is for the security team to rush out of the building and jump into the blinds. It's possible they might keep security details down there 24/7, but an underground tunnel makes more sense."

"And if they used explosives for the blind," Decker added, "it's easy enough to blast a tunnel."

"Let's prepare for both options." Devon stared at the screen. "With only one way into the facility, we only have to worry about one access point and possibly the blinds. On the other hand, that also means the lab's security team only has one point to focus their defense.

"This is why the plan includes a second team. We know they're using tranquilizers, so the first team will be fully covered with a mesh suit designed for shark divers. It should prevent any dart from piercing it. The second team will be heavily armed. We're not taking prisoners."

Bella glanced around the room, but no one seemed to have a problem with Devon's kill order.

"How are you getting in?" Lucas asked. "Rafael might not have spotted them, but there must be other security measures at the doors."

Bella grinned and pointed at the blue circles on the display that identified two oversized roll-up doors and a separate double-door entry. "We'll blast the doors open. As far as additional security, we'll have to make those decisions on the ground. We might have to wait for the first team to get darted and see what they do. Then we go in Level One infiltration."

Lucas whistled. "And I'm going to miss it all."

Devon chuckled, but his gaze settled on Remus. "This is a discovery and rescue mission. But we'll be prepared for a full take-down if necessary."

Harlow shook his head and threw back a shot of whiskey he'd poured when they started the meeting. He scowled at the burn. "You don't have nearly the numbers to overtake whatever security they have in that building."

Devon leaned back, happy with the plan. "It's not always about the numbers."

"No." Remus shared a wolfy grin. "Sometimes it's all about luck."

DEVON FOLLOWED Remus and Decker out of the office, but as he stepped into the hall, Cressa grabbed his hand and dragged him away from the others. She turned into the library, shutting and locking the door behind them.

"What's all this about?" Devon asked. The team would be gathering in the foyer, preparing to leave for the private airfield.

"You haven't said goodbye, and I don't want to do it in front of everyone."

He grinned. "My mistake."

She wrapped her arms around him and laid her head against his chest. "Did you make a decision on whether you're landing in Hungary or Romania?"

"I only considered Hungary because I thought we'd be flying commercial. Remus preferred to take his own plane, and Jacques found the perfect spot to land in Romania. This helps with logistics, and we'll only have to deal with customs and not a border crossing. Once we're dropped off, the plane will fly to a private airport and wait for retrieval."

"And everyone has their GPS trackers?"

He pulled away and tapped his forearm. "Roxie tested them earlier today. We're good."

"And you have your satellite burner?"

He muffled a chuckle. She was being a mother hen, but he

understood her fear. Rafael had survived, but they'd lost two in the process, though he was working under the premise that Sergi and Carlos were still alive. Remus had lost many more.

This mission was risky and dangerous, but he'd be damned if he'd leave Sergi without personally attempting a rescue—and hoped it wouldn't be a recovery. "Each team member has one." He tapped his chest, where he kept the phone in his pocket.

"Bring him home." Her eyes shimmered, and he lowered his head.

There wasn't anything he could do to prevent her worry. He could tell her not to obsess over watching their red dots because she would simply nod in agreement and then do the exact opposite. No reason to waste words.

His kiss was long and deep, and her response went right to his soul.

When they broke apart, she ran a hand over his cheek, her tears now breaching her defenses.

"You come home. You bring everyone home. And find the evidence we need."

"Remember to use Decker wherever you can. Don't be worried about calling in extra resources if necessary. Venizi shouldn't know we're gone, but once we breach the lab..."

She placed a finger over his lips. "He'll think he has an opening. He doesn't. You have nothing to worry about here."

They kissed one last time, and then he wiped away her tears. "Time for your game face."

She grinned as she rubbed her eyes. "Let's get this done."

## Chapter Fourteen

*WHAT HAD I BEEN THINKING?*

I hadn't left my bed since returning to my room the previous night, and now I leaned against the wall, knees pulled to my chest, and stared at the door. I'd barely slept the last two nights. All I could think about were the two rag-wrapped packages tucked under the far corner of the slim mattress. The only thing saving me was that, like on level three, each prisoner was responsible for keeping their cells clean except for the waste bucket and receiving fresh water.

The day before, I'd been assigned, along with S-272, the extensive cleaning of the second lab. It had been similar to the previous day. All cabinets, drawers, and the refrigeration unit had been cleared out, and once again, I'd taken more vials of blood that were to be tossed.

S-272 had seen me tuck the package into my lab coat, but he'd quickly turned away. I questioned whether I should have taken it out of the lab, but I'd begun to trust S-272, who wouldn't share his name, though he'd begun using mine when we were alone.

I couldn't put a defining point on why I trusted him, but as I considered it in the silence of my cell, I believed it came down to his eyes. Eyes that still held a fire deep within. Eyes that, when I'd first met him, seemed lost but now flickered with hope.

The day before, when I was on the third level, and before taking the second package of vials, something had changed with the vampire prisoner. The torture had stopped, but the guard expected his cell cleaned. The mug had been empty, and after refilling it, I noticed the cooler with blood vials was still under the table.

The guard hadn't bothered to stay, and after I cleaned the floor, I dusted off the table where the sharp instruments still lay. I was tempted to take one of the knives, but it wouldn't go unnoticed.

The waste bin had only one item in it—a syringe. The label identified it as MP-32 with a date of a month ago. They must have dosed the vampire with something. Perhaps some new drug that could induce him to talk or some other pharmaceutical form of torture. My gut twisted at another thought. Not a form of torture but an experiment. Though there wasn't much difference. Would I come down here one day and find nothing more than pieces of flesh and bone?

The vampire had been quiet, as he always was. His head hung down, and a muscle occasionally twitched. I ran a warm towel over him, still fascinated by his tattoos and his muscles. He was a warrior or had been long ago. It was impossible to tell how old a vampire was, but the same could be said of most shifters, though most of us didn't live nearly as long.

I was wiping his body dry when he lifted his head.

I fell back a step. His gaze glowed red with the beast. Something I'd seen often enough as a captive, but then his gaze quickly returned to the warm brown I'd expected to see.

"I'm sorry." His voice was rougher than before.

I stared into his eyes. "I'm not afraid of you, vampire."

He watched me for a long moment, and I could have sworn I

caught a slight grin. It might have been a grimace of pain, but the fine lines at the corner of his eyes crinkled. "You should be."

Then I laughed. It was short, and I couldn't believe it had come from me. I placed a finger on his chin. "I'm not the one mounted on the wall."

His gaze turned hard. Not mean but serious. "We're both trapped here." His head dropped. He'd expended too much energy.

I tossed the rags in a bucket, locked his cell door, and pushed the cart back to the elevator, where I waited five minutes before the guard arrived to take me to the labs.

After all the vampire had been through in a few short days, he still showed resilience. I doubt he'd given them any information. So, why had they stopped the torture? It had something to do with the empty syringe. I couldn't think of any other answer.

The syringe had been empty but a thick, red substance had settled at the bottom. After seeing all the vials while deep cleaning the labs, none had been labeled MP-32. The consistency was the same as blood, but the MP made no sense.

I'd considered asking S-272 if he understood the labels, but there had been too many staff members in the lab, and I didn't want to risk a vampire overhearing us.

I glanced at the far corner of my mattress. I wasn't sure what to do about the blood vials or why I'd taken them. The safest thing to do would be to take two or three at a time and drop them in a third-level waste bin.

Before I could make a decision, the bang of the billy clubs snapped me to attention. When the door was thrown wide, I cringed. Did they suspect something?

"S-473. Hurry up. You're eating in the cafeteria this morning."

The guard stared at me as I scrambled from the bed. I slipped on my shoes and followed him, relieved my secret was still safe. S-272 was sitting at a corner table with two other shifters. He kept his head low as he gulped the porridge. It was rare to see him in the cafeteria, but I didn't get to eat there often, so maybe they only let one of us eat there at a time.

His gaze caught mine as he dropped his tray on the wash racks then turned to meet the guard who would take him to the lab. I don't know what I read in that glance—worry, irritation, fear?

After breakfast, I was led down to level three. Dallas, the guard who'd given me a tour on my first work day waited for me. I hadn't seen him since that day. Had something changed?

"S-473. The guards have been given new rotations, and we won't have time to babysit you anymore." His eyes were kind. Unusual for the guards, or was something happening I wasn't going to like? "Based on your work in the lab and down here, the Master believes you can be trusted to work on your own. Someone will still bring you down each morning, but you'll be responsible for collecting and preparing your cart before your duties. Most of the prisoners have been moved upstairs in preparation for the next round of experiments. Those who remain will be secured during your cleaning schedule. You'll be given two hours for your tasks, and a guard will be waiting at the stairs to escort you to the labs." He gave me a long stare. "Don't disappoint me."

Then he turned and was gone. They trusted me?

I thought of the vials of blood under my mattress and smiled.

SERGI WOKE when the door opened. He'd been lost in memories again, but they were better described as nightmares. He suspected it had something to do with Gheata's earlier visit and a second injection of what he'd been told was Magic Poppy.

"They tell me you'll start feeling the changes after the second dose." Gheata's macabre smile didn't get a reaction out of Sergi, at least not a visible one.

Gheata paced in front of him, his eyes shifting to the table of torture instruments, and Sergi was curious why he didn't pick one up and start carving. They continued to feed him a daily vial of blood, but he didn't understand why after injecting him with Magic Poppy. And why stop the torture?

Gheata's hands flexed into fists. He wanted to inflict pain but had been told no. Maybe they wanted to see what the Poppy would do without adding additional pain.

There was one thing that would give Gheata his satisfaction. Sergi had already begun to feel the effects from the first injection. His beast, already irritated by the restraints, was doing its own pacing, pausing only long enough for it to howl with hunger. Maybe that was the answer. They wanted to bring out the beast without the emotions typically required to evoke it. Or maybe he was already losing part of himself.

He chuckled, which made Gheata turn, his face inches from Sergi's.

"What do you find so funny?"

Sergi smiled. If he had contracted the rare blood disease, what did it matter if his beast took over? Wouldn't that be a better end for a warrior than wasting away day by day for decades? Gheata would understand. Instead, Sergi dropped his head, unwilling to play his game.

Once he'd fallen asleep, the nightmares came again. This time he relived Devon's readdiction to Magic Poppy after Boretsky's murder. Was that how he'd end up? Trapped in his beast form, forever changed. Would he even recognize his friends? What was the end game? A mindless beast always hunting.

When the door opened, he remained still, feigning sleep. He recognized the soft shuffle of feet seconds before her scent washed over him. The shifter. He sensed her fear, anger, and the briefest sweet whiff of her wild nature.

He lifted his head. He hadn't heard the guard. She was alone.

She glanced his way once then ignored him as she dusted off the table. After she replaced the mug of water, she looked over her shoulder, appeared satisfied they were alone, and opened the cooler. She gave a slight nod. He wasn't sure why, except to confirm the decreasing number of vials. She closed the cooler, picked up the waste bin, and stared into it. She reached in and pulled out the syringe Gheata had thrown out. She studied it, then turned her gaze to him.

He caught her eyes. They were hazel. She was too far away for him to have determined that in the shallow light, but he remembered from her last visit when she'd stood inches from him after washing off his body.

She stepped closer, and it didn't escape his notice that her steps weren't tentative as they had been in the past. Her curiosity had been piqued, and she showed him the syringe.

"Do you know what was in this? It has a different label description."

A different label description. Had he heard that correctly? Different than what? Maybe she was talking about the blood vials in the cooler.

He never took his eyes from hers, and she never turned away. There was a fierceness in her he'd only caught quick moments of before.

"Magic Poppy." The beast raged at his words, and he used every ounce of strength to silence it. Each time he had to suppress, it became more difficult.

Her forehead scrunched at his words. "I've heard of that." She paced in front of him, her gaze going to the door again. She turned her head as if listening. Sergi didn't hear anything, and she must not have either. She stared at the label on the syringe then snapped her fingers.

"This is the drug that makes vampires go crazy." She spun around to face him, her eyes wide. Yes. Hazel eyes ringed with a smoky blue circle. He slowly nodded, and she squinted, little lines forming over her nose. "But why?" She went back to pacing. "Unless they're trying to control you through your beast the same way they're trying to control shifters. Maybe."

Control shifters? Is that what they've been doing here? It seemed Venizi had his fingers in many pots. But it made sense. An army of mind-controlled vampires and shifters. He wasn't sure it was enough to crush the humans, but what other reason was there?

"Is there a cure for this?" She held up the syringe.

"I don't know. I think this is a different formula than what I've seen before." His voice was ragged, and he dropped his head, unable to hold it up.

She looked at the label again. "Magic Poppy. That must be what the MP on the label means. It's the same dose they gave you yesterday."

She was a smart one. But what game was she playing? She tossed the syringe in the trash and left to empty it. Once she placed the bin back in its spot, she strode to him.

"Why are you here?"

Was this a trick? Did Gheata send her? Had their experiments worked and this female was a test?

Her expression was encouraging, but after a moment, she grinned. "You think their Master sent me. I understand. But I could say the same of you. Purposely sacrificing yourself for the common good. Try to find troublemakers within the shifter slaves." She shrugged. "I suppose it's too late to do anything about it now. There are shifters who work for our captors. I used to hate them until I witnessed the experiments. Some would do anything not to be a test subject."

Her face paled in some memory, and when she looked up at him, her anger was palpable. "I have another question for you, vampire. Are you someone who can help us, or will you be our ultimate ruin?"

She shuffled to the door. Before she closed it, he croaked, "Blood Poppy."

She turned back to him.

"I don't know if it's a cure, but Blood Poppy might work."

She studied him, and without responding, she walked out.

When the bar locked in place, he tried to sleep. When the beast pushed to be set free, he found peace in hazel-colored eyes.

AFTER STOWING the cart in the closet, I followed the guard to the cafeteria. It hadn't been that long since breakfast, but I wouldn't complain about extra food, especially since I'd missed lunch the last two days.

I sat at a table filled with shifters, but with the rule of no talking we might as well be sitting at tables for one. Today, I was grateful for the rule because my mind whirled with the few statements the vampire had shared with me.

Was he a spy for the Master? Would a vampire be willing to go through the amount of torture he'd endured in the hopes of getting information from me? It was crafty, but based on my experience living in this hellhole, it seemed overkill. All they had to do was threaten us with an injection of their serum and most shifters would tell them whatever they wanted to know. Even if we knew we'd end up in that silver cage anyway, there was always a chance of living one more day.

I'd know soon enough whether my last encounter with the vampire had been a well-laid trap.

Magic Poppy. My uncle had mentioned it before and considered it a major threat to shifters. Vampires, their beasts raging out of control would not only be a danger to shifters but to humans as well. Though, I'd never heard of Blood Poppy. The vampire seemed to think it was a cure for Magic Poppy. Had the Blood Poppy been created as an antidote?

I thought back to the vials from the refrigeration units. H appeared to symbolize human blood. The MP was now confirmed as Magic Poppy. All the other labels started with an S, which I assumed were the drugs being given to the shifters in the experiments.

Maybe the Blood Poppy didn't need to be refrigerated. Each lab had at least one locked cabinet, but S-272 had cleaned those.

When they called for S-473, I dumped the remains of my lunch, placed my tray on the rack, and followed a different guard to the labs. However, instead of going to the main labs, we stopped at a supply closet.

"You'll need the cart." He stepped aside and waited patiently for me to step into the closet, review the items on the cart, then push it out to follow him down a hallway with multiple rooms.

These were smaller, private labs for the various scientists and lab assistants. From what S-272 had shared during our short chats, these labs were where the formulas were created and tested before being used on live subjects. While I'd been aware of them, I'd never been in any of them.

The guard, who'd stood close enough to determine he was a vampire, was chattier than the others. "The next phase of testing has been pushed another day, and the shifter that usually cleaned these rooms is no longer available." I didn't dare ask why that was. "Until we can train a suitable replacement, and while the labs you're typically assigned to are in standby mode, you'll clean these labs."

He slid a keycard over the panel to open the door to the first lab. Stainless steel cabinets ran along two sides of the room, a round six-person conference table was in one corner, and a desk covered with files and books was in another. Beakers, racks of vials, Petri dishes, and a computer currently in standby mode covered the top of an island positioned between the counters.

"Dr. Lister is at lunch. You have twenty minutes to clean the office. Don't touch the counter where he has important research underway. It will be noticed, and the punishment for such an act is severe. Do you understand?"

The scientist was at lunch. That made sense. When I noticed theguard staring daggers at me, I responded, "Yes."

His forehead scrunched, his eyes narrowed, and his lips thinned as he assessed me, as if he didn't understand how someone so slow could be allowed to work in the labs. I ignored him and stepped outside the room to grab the basket of cleaning supplies from the cart. His glare followed my every move as I removed a rag and bottle of disinfectant spray and began cleaning the cabinet doors and empty counters.

After a couple of minutes, he growled, "I'll return in twenty minutes to take you to the next lab."

He didn't seem any happier when he returned to find me waiting at the cart. "Why are you standing there? Was there something missing from your cart?"

"I'm finished with this lab." I kept my expression blank but grinned when he left to prowl through the room.

When he returned with no complaints, I pushed my cart to the next room. He'd barely swiped the card before walking away, his mumbled words barely audible. "I'll be back in fifteen minutes."

The only disparity among the individual labs was how clean or messy a particular scientist was. Other than whatever research or tests they were performing, everything else was the same from lab to lab. Besides the general layout, two security cameras were positioned at each end of the room, and an apartment-sized refrigerator and a single cabinet were next to the cabinets on the lab side, both requiring a keyed combination. What were the chances the codes were the same as the main labs?

I didn't touch the top of the island counter where the staff appeared to do most of their work, but I peeked at the files and specimens as I swept the room.

All of the rooms had racks of vials with an S on the labels. These were the shifter formulas they were perfecting. Though what result they strived for continued to be a mystery. Only one of the labs had a rack of files with an H on the label. They must be working on something that either required human blood, or they were testing the effects of their formulas on it. Somehow, that idea was as horrifying as what they were doing with the shifters.

Maybe the rack of vials was nothing more than the scientist's mid-afternoon snack. I stifled a macabre laugh at the possibility, then lowered my head so the guard wouldn't see it as he led me to the next lab. When it appeared I'd finished the last one, I was turning my cart around when he stopped me.

"I was going to leave this corner office for tomorrow, but you're ahead of schedule, and I just received notification that the director is coming back early. It would be best to clean his office before his arrival."

He opened the door to a room befitting a CEO. If the building hadn't been inside a mountain, there would have been floor-to-ceiling windows to show off an amazing view. And it appeared the director was a scientist as well as an administrator.

The room had been divided into two equal parts. On the left was a replica of the smaller labs, including a locked refrigerator and cabinet.

On the right was the administrative side. A massive desk with two visitor chairs, a row of dark oak filing cabinets, two bookcases stuffed with books, ledgers, and stacks of files that appeared to have been stuffed in any open crevice. A dull gray couch with two matching side chairs was against the only open wall. The painting above the area was monochrome in various shades of brown and reminded me of similar impersonal works in corporate offices and hotels.

Between both sections was a rectangular oak table that seated eight. It seemed to represent both a separation between the two sides of the office and a connection that tied them together.

"The director didn't have time to complete his current work so, like the other labs, refrain from cleaning the island. You have a full hour for this office. Make it sparkle, girl."

I placed the cleaning supplies on an available counter and took a moment to survey the room as if I were planning where to start. There were two security cameras, which surprised me for the director's office. Were they concerned about unwarranted visitors, or was no one trusted—not the staff or the director?

Like in the other labs, I scanned the director's experiment as I swept. My gut lurched when I noted the labels on the racked vials. There were five vials. One was labeled MP, one was labeled with an S, one was labeled with a V, and two were labeled with BP.

BP...Blood Poppy? If the vampire hadn't mentioned it, I might have questioned what the initials meant but wouldn't have given the vial a second look.

MP was the Magic Poppy, the S a shifter formula, and I suspected the V was a vial of vampire blood. I didn't have time to read the paperwork in the open file folder, but with the number of printouts spread across the counter filled with rows of numbers, graphs, and grids, he'd been documenting a great deal of data. What kind of data, I couldn't tell.

When I completed the lab area, I dusted the file cabinets, the coffee table, and the bookcases. The director wasn't a neat man. His desk was covered with more files, books, science magazines, and what appeared to be several days of mail that had been dumped on top of everything.

I glanced at the door and listened for voices or boots. Not hearing anything and guessing I had another ten minutes before the guard returned, I searched the desk for anything of interest as I wiped a clean rag over everything. While the desk was messy, it didn't mean the guy didn't know where everything was. I'd known a few shifters with similar organizational skills. One guy, a good friend of my uncle's, could find a single sheet of paper in a mess like the director's without blinking an eye.

I was taking a second deeper look, keeping my back to the single camera with a view of the desk, when my fingers touched something unexpected under a file folder. I pulled the object out and blinked. A vial of a thick, red substance.

My heartbeat ratcheted up as I read the label. BP-43. The date was from the previous week.

Why wasn't the vial locked up? The director had either been lazy, distracted, or had merely forgotten about it. Without a second thought, I palmed it, gave the edges of the desk a final wipe, then stuck the vial in my lab coat along with the rag.

I stood back, turning in a circle as if I was checking for anything I might have missed in my cleaning, then picked up the bucket of supplies and carried them to the cart.

My heart was racing, and I sucked in a few breaths, forcing a calm I didn't feel.

I couldn't let the guard pick up on my anxiety. The only good news was that he wasn't anywhere to be seen. I leaned against the cart, and in a flash, I moved the vial from the pocket to under my shift as I had with the others I'd pilfered from the labs.

The guard returned five minutes later, and by then, I'd had time to settle my nerves and consider my actions. There were too many questions and not nearly enough information to connect the dots. But one thing was clear.

While I hadn't decided on whether I could trust him, the vampire pinned to the wall was the only one who could provide answers.

## Chapter Fifteen

DEVON STOOD at the door of the plane and scanned the area. The sun was out, but the air was cool. The customs agents had processed the plane quickly, and he assumed some money had exchanged hands. He stepped down to the tarmac and strode to the two vans that waited for them.

The team followed him, taking their duffels to the back of the vans where they would be stored for travel. Although the jet belonged to Remus, its ownership and tail registration were listed under a private corporation that was mired within dozens of false companies. If anyone were interested, it would take days to uncover the true owner.

The team consisted of ten vampires and ten shifters, including Devon and Remus. Rafael added one more to the count. He wasn't sure if it would be enough. Their plans depended on there being more scientists and lab workers than guards, but he'd brought extra toys to even the playing field.

"We're clear to go." Remus dropped his duffel next to the pile. "The plane will stay at a field south of Timisoara until they get the call to retrieve us."

"So far so good." Devon waved Bella over from where she was

monitoring the duffels packed into the second van. "Have you contacted Rafael?"

She glanced around the tarmac then waved at one of the shifters and pointed to the first van. "He's on his way to Deva. The road to the lab had been quiet until last night. A supply truck went up, but it hadn't returned before he left."

"Was it a cargo van or something larger?" Remus asked.

"It was a cargo van," she answered.

"Could be anything." Devon checked his satellite phone.

"Or more guards." Remus finished for him.

"Increased security?" Bella asked the question, but her attention was focused on the extra supplies being loaded into the vans.

Devon understood. "Because they caught a vampire along with a shifter."

Remus nodded.

"That makes sense." Bella paused to answer a question from a team member, then said, "It's possible other vampires might have wandered too close, but my guess is that Sergi has been their first vampire intruder. If that's true, they have to be concerned that someone might come for him."

"He was captured over a week ago." Devon shrugged off the concern. If there had been more than one cargo van, he might have been more worried. "If they had concerns about their security, they would have done something before now."

Remus, who had also checked for messages, pocketed his burner phone. "At this point, it's all speculation. Maybe Rafael can tell us more when we get to our first checkpoint. Either way, we planned for this."

They agreed, and once everyone was in the vans, they settled in for the two-hour drive to Deva. It was late afternoon, and while the team broke into general conversation, Devon pulled out his phone. Bella would have checked in with the manor once they'd touched down, but he wanted to speak with Cressa. It would be her first day as head of security.

It could be an overwhelming job for anyone's first few days, regardless of how long they'd been there. Cressa kept up with the security protocols, but she bored easily with the fine nuances Simone and Sergi added to the daily updates for the manor, Oasis, and both safe houses.

She answered on the first ring. "Devon? Is everything alright?"

He chuckled. She sounded a bit frazzled. "Everything is fine. We just arrived, and we're in the vans heading for Deva."

"Oh, thank god. I thought maybe something happened since Bella checked in."

"Which was only twenty minutes ago."

"Exactly. What if someone attacked right after she hung up?"

He grinned but held back his laugh. "How's your first day going?"

Her growl was low, but he heard how tired she was, and it wasn't yet noon in California. "I don't know how Sergi keeps up with all of this. It's not just updating, reviewing, and communicating the protocols, but everyone has a million questions. I've never seen Sergi break a sweat with this, and thank the stars he keeps immaculate records." She was silent a moment. "Don't you dare tell him I said any of that."

This time, he did laugh. "I won't say a word, but I'll give you one secret if you're not already doing it. Delegate."

He heard her heavy sigh. "I know that, but why don't they call their team leads?"

"Sometimes, the team leads haven't read the updates yet. Other times, the team leads aren't available, and, in either scenario, the guards tend to be impatient and don't like to wait. But I think the reason you're getting more calls than Sergi is because the guards like you and want to talk to you."

"Oh. I didn't realize that." She went silent for a moment. "Alright. I don't mind helping them at least once, then I'll direct them back to their team lead. Thank you."

He would have hugged her had he been there. She made it

sound like she was helping, which she was, but the truth was more that she didn't want to hurt their feelings and felt guilty she didn't know most of them. "No problem. How are you otherwise?"

"Worried about you. Worried about Sergi and Carlos."

"We'll get them back. We're going to go dark soon. No communication except for emergencies. I wanted to call before that happened."

"I know you're in the van, so I'll make this easy on you. I love you, and I miss you. You take care of yourself, and if I have to come find you? Well, no one will like it if I show up."

"We'll make sure that doesn't happen. And for everything you said before that—me too."

"See you soon." She hung up. Not surprising since he heard the tears in her voice, reminding him just how dangerous this mission was.

"Is everything alright with Cressa?" Remus didn't bother hiding a grin when he asked the question.

"She's fine and wishes us well."

They fell into talk about the old days, the advancement of weapons, and how they both preferred hand-to-hand, or in Remus's case, hand-to-fang combat over anything else.

As the afternoon waned toward dusk, the two fell silent, each experiencing the burden of the mission and what they would discover. Remus had lost many to secure the location of this facility, and Devon understood the pain of sending others to their deaths.

How did one put the life of one male over dozens of others? Sergi wasn't just his friend, he had been a companion for centuries. He'd saved Devon's life countless times. And while Sergi never wanted to be a House leader, his value to a House was immeasurable.

If it hadn't been for the GPS trackers and Rafael's survival, they wouldn't have the slim advantage they had. They'd find Sergi and Carlos and, with any luck, maybe Remus's other shifters.

When they reached Deva and the team stepped out of the van, Remus held Devon back.

"I have a request."

Devon studied him, understanding whatever was coming was difficult for the shifter, but he could see The Wolf behind the haunted eyes, ready to fight—ready to die if need be.

"Anything." Devon wasn't sure what he was promising, but at this juncture, he didn't see how he could deny the male who'd gotten Devon farther than he thought possible in his personal crusade.

"Whether we win or fail, I need this to be seen as a raid by the shifters."

The request shocked Devon. "Are you sure you want that kind of heat from Venizi? He won't take an attack instigated by shifters lightly, especially when we take what we came for."

Remus laughed. "You know we're going to do more than take the evidence we need. Our plan is to dismantle their entire infrastructure. Besides, if the heat is on us, Venizi won't suspect you have the information he's been hiding from the Council, assuming they don't already know about it."

"No shifter will be safe."

Remus's laugh was filled with contempt. "No shifter is safe. This is how we live our lives each day. But I've put all the packs on high alert. They know we're in Romania and they know why." He gave Devon a rueful smile. "Don't take this the wrong way, but we need a win against vampires. The shifters I sent need a win."

Devon considered the statement and the ramifications. Shifters were smart. They knew there was a divide among the vampires—those willing to work with shifters and those who hunted them. Trust had to be shared on both sides. There would always be shifters with a distaste for vampires. Cato, the recluse shifter who'd been a slave to Venizi for most of his life, was one of those, though he had provided critical information toward the successful raid of

Shadow Island. Minds could be swayed through success. And that built trust.

Devon held out his hand, and Remus took it. "This mission will be a success, and the credit will fall to you. You have my word."

～

DEVON FOLLOWED Remus out of the van and surveyed the area. Rafael had found a quiet location at an isolated, run-down inn on the far edge of the village. It was run by an older couple who were barely scraping by, and currently, the motel had no other guests.

Rafael had been getting by with English, but the couple was more comfortable with Romanian, and Remus was fluent enough to ease the couple's minds. He advised them they were on a mission to find a friend lost in the Carpathian Mountains. They became more helpful when Remus handed them a couple stacks of Romanian leu that would last them for some time.

Before he walked the property, he found Rafael, who was carrying gear from the van to the inn.

He shook the male's hand. "Thank you for following orders and escaping. I know it feels as if you failed the team, but your ability to get word to us gives us the upper hand in this mission."

Rafael ducked his head. "It wasn't easy to run away."

Devon nodded. "It never is, but there are times when it's the only solution. And I've had to do it more than once in my life. This was necessary."

Rafael lifted his head to give Devon his eyes. "We'll get them back."

Devon grabbed his shoulder and squeezed. "Yes, we will. And you've done a great deal toward that success."

Rafael walked away with a confident stride. Satisfied, Devon strolled the inn with Remus.

The inn had twelve rooms. There was a bungalow next door

that Devon assumed belonged to the older couple. The closest buildings were a block away and hidden behind trees.

The rooms barely fit a bed, shower, and sink, but there was running water. A single meeting room had been turned into a spacious storage closet. There was enough room to use it as a dual command center and extra sleeping area. Their equipment had been brought in, and the weapons and ammunition were being divided among the defined teams.

When it was time to settle into their planning session, four of Remus's team members shifted into wolves to secure the area.

The older couple, who cooked a meal for them even after being told it wasn't necessary, became a wealth of information. They reviewed the team's map and advised on which areas to avoid. Of course, the area where the lab was situated was one of those places.

"Many go missing in that area," the old man told Remus, who then translated to Devon. The problem wasn't the mountain but the wild creatures. The old man wasn't stupid. He glanced at the duffels, and his last words before leaving the room were succinct. "You'll need decent weapons to survive."

Remus agreed there were an equal amount of wild wolves to wild shifters in the area, but the team determined most of the disappearances were more likely from those who wandered too close to the lab. But the warnings about wild shifters weren't taken lightly. They were intelligent and ruthless and would have to be taken down if they got too close.

The plan for their attack on the facility was simple.

Team One, which consisted of one male vampire and one female shifter, would be stationed in the village as a couple preparing for a three-day hike into the mountains. They would monitor the dirt road that led to the labs. The road was concealed behind a warehouse, but Rafael had found a tiny cafe with a clear view of the area. They would remain in contact with Teams Two and Four.

Team Two, a three-member team of two shifters and one

vampire, would travel up the mountain on dirt bikes. Their task was to prevent traffic from leaving or entering the area. They carried C4 with remote detonators and would set the trap a mile from the facility before Teams Three and Four reached their destination on foot.

Team Three had the most dangerous part of the mission. They would be the bait. It would be a four-member team with two shifters and two vampires. The team would wear mesh diving suits over their clothing so they could be removed once the darts were no longer a threat. The suits were too bulky to wear for the entire mission. Their goal was to trigger the alarm to open the blinds, allowing Team Four, the remaining twelve members, to overtake the guards, gain computer access, and take out the exterior security cameras, leaving the interior security teams blind to the size of their force.

Once the security team in the blinds was eliminated, and assuming there was a tunnel to the main lab, Teams Three and Four would reorganize into the preplanned eight-member teams. Team Three would enter the lab through the tunnel, and since they would be blind to what might be waiting for them, they would take most of the smoke grenades Devon was able to procure.

Team Four would blast the exterior doors with C4. Once inside, communication via wireless earbuds would be critical as the teams located and seized the command center, giving them control of communications and security.

Only then would the team move through the lab. Scientists and lab assistants would be safely secured so long as they didn't pose a threat; otherwise, they would be eliminated. It was harsh, but Devon knew all too well how much damage a single individual could create, especially if they were able to send information out of the mountain.

They reviewed the plan three times before the members were divided into their initial teams to go over their gear. Then they slept, waking early to find a large breakfast waiting for them. The four wolves returned to their human forms, ate heartily, then crashed in the van for the ride to the village.

Devon glanced out the window as they left Deva. Old passions stirred. At one point in his long life, he'd wondered if the call of his ancestors and the excitement of battle would dull with time. He'd heard the roar of his blood and sensed the rise of the beast during the raid at Shadow Island and when they'd infiltrated Underwood's home to retrieve Cressa's mother and sister.

Remus nudged his shoulder. His grin was wide. "Do you feel it? The promise of victory."

The last bits of worry drained from Devon, and he shouted, "To victory!"

His heart filled with pride when the van—filled with vampires and shifters on their first true mission as a team—shouted as one.

"To victory!"

## Chapter Sixteen

THE FOLLOWING DAY, before the guard came for me, I stuffed four vials of blood and the vial of Blood Poppy under the waistband of my underwear. Once I was on level three, I pulled the cart out of the storage closet and moved slowly around it, ensuring the necessary supplies had been loaded. The guard, one I hadn't seen before, turned his back to speak with another guard, and I jumped on the opportunity to stuff the vials into the middle of a stack of rags.

When he turned back to me, he growled, "There's a change in the cells. There are three more males. They're wilder than most but don't worry, they've been chained to the wall like the others. Be quick about your business."

I nodded, still wondering where they were getting so many shifters. He led me down a row of cells I hadn't cleaned before. Like the other cells on this level, the doors didn't have keycards, and instead of one wooden beam barring the door, there were three.

Before the guard left, he gave me a malicious grin. "Try not to get yourself ripped apart." Then he strolled down the hall, banging the doors to the other cells with only intimidation in mind. An abusive tactic. I glanced at the rags with the vials hidden among them. If I got caught, I could be back in one of these cells and added to the list of test subjects.

I took a deep breath and shook off the thought. I'd gone too far at this point. It would be safer to give the blood to the vampire and then toss the empty vials out with the garbage. I lifted the three bars away from the first door, wanting to get this over so I could spend more time with the vampire. If my uncle could hear me, he'd wonder if I'd lost my mind.

I opened the door of the first cell slowly, not convinced the guards had chained the shifters. This guard didn't seem trustworthy, but I didn't have to worry. The shifter, a young, wiry kid, was curled up in a fetal position and didn't move the entire five minutes I was there. The second shifter, about the same age as the previous kid, was shorter and heavier. He sat in the corner, knees pulled up to his chest. He didn't move either, but his eyes followed my every move.

"I know you must be scared." I wanted to ask if he was friends with the other male but decided to wait a day. "I'm also a shifter. I've been here for a few months, just trying to stay alive. Never give up."

I don't know why I shared that last thought. Did I still believe that? I'd been on the verge of accepting my fate after witnessing the horrific experiments.

Until the day they chained a vampire.

I'd opened the third cell door and had taken two steps inside when the shifter stood. He was chained and appeared more coherent than the first two. I immediately raised my hands to calm him.

"I'm also a shifter. I'm just here to..." I stared at the shifter and blinked.

He stood motionless. Staring. Then he spoke. "Alex?"

"Carlos?" Without a thought, I ran to him and grabbed his arms. "What are you doing here?"

"I could say the same of you." He pulled me in for a hug. "We all thought you were dead."

Tears sprung to my eyes. "Even my uncle?"

His smile was sad. "I think he still holds out hope, but with each day that passes..."

He couldn't finish, and I could barely see beyond my blurred vision.

"What's happening here?" He gratefully changed the subject.

"Horrible experiments." I sat on the floor next to him, taking in his bruises and cuts inflicted by the guards' welcoming committee. His expression, happy I was alive yet sad to see me in this place, changed as I explained everything I'd witnessed. Maybe I shouldn't have said anything. His eyes, shimmering with the light glow of his wolf, reflected his anger and a touch of fear.

And I was scared for him. "How did they capture you?"

"We were sent to find the lab, just like you'd been."

I scoffed. "Then you were sent on a fool's mission."

"There were two vampires with me. Have you seen them?"

I jumped up and almost tripped over the mattress. What was he saying? "You came with vampires?"

He nodded. "Your uncle is working with them." He shook his head at what must have been my look of dismay. "These vampires are different. They're fighting as much for us as they are themselves. Have you seen them?"

Shifters and vampires working together? And my uncle agreed with this? He had mentioned something about testing a business partnership with a vampire House. It must have developed into something more than I'd realized. I was never one for politics and considered my uncle's dream of shifters and vampires working together nothing more than a fantasy. But then again, I had more of a grudge against vampires than my uncle.

"Alex, have you seen vampire prisoners?"

He'd also stood, and I glanced up. "Just one."

He considered my answer. "Maybe Rafael got away. If he did,

143

they'll send in a larger team." He scratched at the iron cuff around his wrist. "If he didn't, we might be on our own for longer than I'd hoped. Sergi can help."

"Who's Sergi?"

"He's the vampire prisoner. He's cadre."

I stepped back, my eyes darted around the cell, unable to focus. This just kept getting better. The vampire was cadre. Now, it all made sense. His refusal to speak. The anger and frustration he created in the interrogator. His willingness to endure the torture. He was on our side? I sensed he was different. But still.

"How do you know we can trust him?"

Carlos tilted his head and studied me. "I understand your distrust. But much has happened in the months you've been gone."

That was an understatement.

"Your uncle trusts this House implicitly. As do I."

That rocked me. While Carlos didn't hold anger toward vampires as I did, he had his own reasons to mistrust them. To hear him say these things now, well, I wasn't sure what to make of it.

Or did I?

When I'd first seen the vampire—Sergi—strapped to the wall, I'd been curious why they would torture one of their own. He'd been defiant from the start. And after all he'd been through, he hadn't given up. Maybe there was a faction of vampires who didn't see us as an inferior race. Had he been kind to me because he didn't see me as something less? Or was it a ploy?

Carlos wouldn't lie. Not about my uncle. Not about this vampire.

"What can I do?" I asked.

"You need to free him. Free me."

I shook my head. "That's impossible."

His words were low and even. "Nothing is impossible when the truth is on your side."

My gaze shot to his, and it was impossible not to see the sincerity. My uncle's words.

I glanced at the door. I'd been here too long.

"I need to go. I have more cells to clean before they come for me." I changed out the water and dumped the waste bucket.

Before leaving, I placed a hand on his cheek. I didn't know what I could do, but I would not allow my friend to be an experiment. Not if I could help it.

Besides, if I hadn't already planned on helping the vampire, why did I have four vials of blood and one of Blood Poppy hidden in the cleaning rags?

"I need some time to replay everything you've told me. My schedule sometimes changes, but I currently clean the cells on this level every morning. With any luck, I'll be back tomorrow. I only have one piece of advice. Stay wild. From what I hear, they usually prefer their test subjects broken."

He nodded. "Trust him, Alex. We might not be able to wait for the calvary."

THE DOOR SCRAPED against the stone floor, and the light from the hallway cast the long shadow of a lone figure. Sergi struggled to push the beast down, but it was harder each time. The Magic Poppy was stronger than he'd anticipated. He watched the female, her steps tentative, but she drew closer as her eyes darted from him to his restraints and back again.

He howled—deep and long. A lonely sound filled with rage and sorrow.

Instead of taking a step back in fear, she took a step forward. He wanted her to go away. His beast was taking over, and the last thing he wanted to do was harm her.

"You shouldn't be here. I'm not safe to be around." He

sounded as if he'd been running for miles without a drop of water to quench his thirst.

Rather than heed his warning, she took another step. "Because of the injections?"

He nodded.

She stepped close enough for him to pick up her scent. No fear. Curiosity if he had to guess. "I have to admit, that howl was pretty fierce."

"The Magic Poppy is forcing the beast to rise. It's hungry."

She studied him. "Your name is Sergi."

He tensed, his eyes narrowing with concern. How could she know that?

She tilted her head as she continued to study him. "I won't tell anyone. I just came from Carlos's cell. He told me."

"You know him?" He grimaced as an excruciating pain jolted through him.

She nodded then turned to the table, keeping her back to him. He watched with his own growing fascination as she reached under her shift and pulled something out. She laid a small wrapped package on the table and opened it up to reveal several vials.

"This is labeled with an H." She held up the vial, and he focused on it, but he couldn't see it clearly enough to confirm what the label said. "It's the same naming convention as the labels on the vials in the cooler." She waved the vial at him. "Will it help?"

"I'm not sure if it's enough, but it might take the edge off."

"I brought four vials. They're dated from a week ago. I have more hidden in my cell, but I have to be careful."

She stepped closer, and her gaze shifted to his shoulder. When he glanced down, he wondered if it was the patterns in his tattoo that caught her attention. It wasn't the first time he'd seen her interest in them. He could still feel the path her finger had taken when she followed the curves and lines of his ink when she thought he was sleeping.

She opened the vial and, tipping his chin up, poured the entire contents into his mouth. It was warm and stale but would still have the nutrients his body needed. He'd drunk worse to stay alive.

Once the last vial was empty, the beast settled. It wouldn't be for long, but it was a reprieve.

"You're face has changed." She stroked his cheek then, seeming to realize what she'd done, stepped back. "Sorry."

"It's the Magic Poppy. It forces the physical changes of the beast."

"You mentioned something about Blood Poppy. Would that help?"

Devon and Remus had thought Blood Poppy was the major ingredient in Magic Poppy, yet only a small amount had shown up in the test results. No one understood why. According to Colantha, Blood Poppy was the source of life for vampires. Without it, fertility rates had dropped, and rare blood disorders were on the rise. She'd also warned of the Blood Poppy's addictive component.

Devon's addiction to Magic Poppy had been hard to shake. Colantha admitted Blood Poppy was used in her special juice that healed the psychic strain in dreamwalkers. The juice was addictive, and its use was monitored closely. Was the Blood Poppy, albeit used in small quantities, what made the Magic Poppy so addictive? They might have added an additional habit-forming ingredient since the Blood Poppy was considered rare.

There might be other reasons for the low quantity of Blood Poppy used. It might be potent enough in small doses to be sufficient for the end product. Or, perhaps, adding Blood Poppy past a certain amount negated the effects of the other ingredients in Magic Poppy, countering its effectiveness.

That left the question of whether the Blood Poppy would help his current dilemma or make it worse.

Desperate times.

"At this point, it couldn't hurt."

She walked to the table and picked up the last vial. "This is labeled BP, so it's only a guess that it's Blood Poppy."

"I'll risk it."

She glanced toward the door. "Did you hear something?" She closed her fist around the vial and ran to the door, carrying the waste bin, and peeked out. Then she disappeared into the hallway but returned after a few seconds and set the emptied bin next to the table. "We don't have much time. They'll come looking for me soon if I'm not at the stairs."

She opened the vial. "You're sure about this?"

He was caught in her worried gaze. The smoky blue ring around her hazel eyes was more pronounced today. Was it impacted by emotions?

He nodded, and he kept his eyes on her as she poured the thick liquid on his tongue, waiting patiently for the last drop to leave the glass tube. She shoved the vial in her pocket.

"Before you go, tell me the layout of the place. Do you know where the command center is?"

She hesitated as she considered his request. Was it because she didn't want to tell him or because she didn't know? Then it all came out.

"You're on level three. If you go left out of this hallway, make the first two rights to take you to the stairs. Level two is where most of the prisoners are held. On this level, wooden bars are used to lock the doors, but on the upper levels, they use keycards. I think the same one opens all of them.

"There are guards' quarters on each level. The labs are on the first floor, along with the cafeteria and the living quarters for the lab staff. I only go where the guards take me, which is either to this level or the labs." She paused and tapped a finger on her chin. "There are signs on the walls, and if I remember correctly, security and the command center are in the opposite direction from the labs."

He nodded. "Do you know where Gheata sleeps?"

When she looked confused, he added, "He's the one who's been interrogating me."

"You know him?"

"In a way."

"But he doesn't know you?"

He shook his head. "He's never seen me before. I thought he would have checked the House rosters, but he hasn't shown any indication that he knows who I am."

Boots echoed in the hall, and her eyes widened. This time, they reflected fear.

"Tell them I made a mess, and you had to clean it up. They won't check."

"I'll try to bring more blood tomorrow." As the boots got closer, she asked, "Do you think Rafael got away?"

He wasn't surprised by her question. If she'd spoken with Carlos, he'd be wondering the same thing. He wouldn't lie to her. "He's capable, but I'd say it's a fifty-fifty chance. We can't wait."

She nodded and turned as the guard entered, and she lowered her head, her tone turning submissive. "I'm sorry I'm late. I hadn't been expecting the new shifters, and then this prisoner had made a horrible mess. It won't happen again."

The guard glanced at Sergi and then at her. "Just get moving. You'll be late for the labs. The experiments start in an hour."

She gave Sergi a terrified glance then scurried from the room.

Once the door was closed and bolted, he closed his eyes but didn't sleep. He reviewed the information she'd shared. And though he couldn't be sure, he thought a tingle had gone through his system after drinking the Blood Poppy. It tasted good. Better than human blood.

Unsure how much it would help, and while he still had his faculties, he went over the facility's layout again and formulated a plan.

# Chapter Seventeen

I WAS ALLOWED a quick lunch before the experiments started, but I picked at it, preferring an empty stomach in case I threw up. The guard led me down familiar hallways, but this time, I paid attention to the hallway signs.

I'd been right. There were signs conveniently placed for the staff to find their way through the maze of hallways. They probably didn't think most shifters could read. It was more likely they considered the guards and their threats of severe punishment enough. They had been until now.

My skin prickled when I walked past other shifters. I'd sensed it in the cafeteria. It might have been my imagination, but this was the first inkling I'd had since arriving that rescue was possible. And if not rescue, then the ability to fight back.

Under the noses of our guards, small whispers between shifters had begun. The word of a vampire chained on level three was no longer a secret. Perhaps they'd heard it from the guards, but the shifters had found a way to communicate—a necessary first step for any rebellion.

I snorted. Rebellion. The idea seemed daunting. But Sergi hadn't thought so.

The first signage we came across were arrows pointing to the medical treatment office, an area for the staff's medical emergencies, various conference rooms, and the staff quarters. When we reached the end of the hallway, the sign indicated the labs to the right and, to the left, the security offices and command center.

I'd never paid attention to the signs but must have subconsciously stored the information since what I'd given Sergi regarding the facility's layout had been correct. The signs changed as we moved deeper into the building, providing directions for the various labs. This was the area I'd become familiar with.

When I entered the main lab, I immediately caught S-272's eyes. It was the easiest way to assess the mood of the staff. He gave no head nod or facial expression, but I caught a glimpse of a red glow that left as quickly as it came. His wolf was near the surface. Something had provoked him.

Two lab technicians worked on the metal cage that held shifters in place for their injections, stringing monitoring cables through the openings. Across the lab, three others were busy at their stations, their eyes glued to their screens as they typed, pausing only long enough to jot down information.

S-272 stocked the cleaning supply closet, and though he kept his head down, I caught his side glances directed at the lab staff. The guard pushed me to a counter with boxes of medical supplies that included first aid items, bottles with names I'd never heard of, and other items I'd seen in my pack's medical unit, like tranquilizers, pain medications, syringes, and needles.

I finished the task of storing the supplies as the lead scientist strode in with her entourage. They scurried like rats to their stations, whispering among themselves with excitement. I glanced at S-272, who'd also noticed the unusual behavior. It wasn't that they hadn't whispered before, but never with such emotion.

A guard stepped next to me and pushed me toward the corner of the lab as another one forced S-272 into the same area. We sat with our backs to the wall without further instruction. It was the same routine with each experiment. We would wait, forced to watch until it was time for cleanup.

I startled when S-272 nudged my arm. After glancing at the others in the room to confirm they were occupied, I looked down. His fist opened to reveal a vial. I didn't have time to read the label, but I grabbed it, and keeping an eye on the guards, I slowly brought my knees to my chest, allowing easier access to slip the vial into the familiar place under my shift.

"Can you feel the difference in the shifters?" S-272 asked.

I lowered my head and said, "I'm hearing whispers."

"There's a rumor that the vampire prisoner was sent on a rescue mission."

I didn't shake my head, though I almost did. "He was sent to locate the lab. I spoke to a shifter who was sent with him. One of their team members might have gotten away."

We sat in silence for several minutes before S-272 spoke.

"That explains the rumors of an uprising."

An uprising? That matched my earlier thoughts, and I connected the dots on how the shifters were communicating. I wasn't the only shifter going into cells to clean, and the guards didn't watch as closely as they once had. They'd grown complacent. It would be slow and tedious, taking a few days to communicate a plan, but one by one, each shifter would only have to be told which day to be ready.

"What did you give me?" My curiosity couldn't wait until I returned to my cell. I wanted to know what I was carrying to determine the risk of being caught. I could always dump it before I left the lab.

"The lab assistants talk freely around me. This morning, they were working on something extremely addictive to vampires. I assumed it would be bad for them, but the assistants were tempted to try it. On its own, it's supposed to revitalize a vampire. The vial is labeled BP-X."

When he mentioned something addictive to vampires, I

assumed it was Magic Poppy. Yet, the label identified it as Blood Poppy. The X in the label name must reference a newer variation. The question was, modified in what way? If the lab assistants were willing to try it, it couldn't be bad.

"Will it help?" S-272 asked.

"Maybe. I found a vial labeled BP without the X. The vampire seemed eager to try it. I'll know tomorrow if it had any effect against the drugs they're injecting him with."

"There's something else I need to share with you."

We fell silent when one of the guards strolled over. His grin was ugly as he sneered down at us. "It won't be long now. Wait till you see what's going to happen. We'll be making better shifters." He nudged my legs that I had lowered to the ground. "Ones that won't talk back." He laughed. "Now you just remain where you are like good little doggies."

He strode back and bumped fists with the other guard.

S-272's eyes glowed, and I laid a hand on his arm until his eyes returned to normal. It took him a moment to settle enough to speak, but his skin sizzled with energy. "There's a secret back door out of the facility. It's on the third level in the mechanical room."

"How do you know this?"

"I learned of it early on while listening to the guards. It was used when the labs were expanded."

"And no one has tried to use it?"

"The old road doesn't exist anymore. The area is rife with wild shifters, and it's a long walk through thick forest and dangerous terrain to any village."

"It would be impossible to get everyone out that way."

"Not for one or two with the stamina to survive."

Before I could respond, a window at the back wall that I hadn't noticed before slowly illuminated to reveal a group of six people. I recognized one of the female scientists and her two assistants. There was a male, the only one wearing an open lab coat over a suit, who seemed to be dictating something to a young female. I wondered if he was the director, or what the guards and staff referred to as Master. A cold dread ran over me when I saw the muscled male behind him. I would never forget his face or his nasty leer. The interrogator. The one Sergi had called Gheata.

Then the door leading to the hallway opened, and four guards strolled in with a shifter between them. His feet were bare and shackled, and his only clothing were loose fitting pants all the male prisoners wore. He appeared resigned to his fate or perhaps they fed him a sedative in his food.

I closed my eyes and mentally prepared myself for the carnage to follow.

I THOUGHT I knew what to expect.

I'd been witness to a handful of experiments on shifters that left only bits and pieces of them behind. Someday I would have to face that trauma and know it represented only a fraction of the shifters who'd been unlucky enough to find themselves trapped in this facility. And that it happened because they'd been seen as less.

S-272 and I sat shoulder to shoulder, our arms touching. A mutual need to remind ourselves who we were. This time was different. These scientists believed they'd achieved a breakthrough, and it terrified me. S-272's energy was tangible, and I wasn't sure if it was from fear or anger. If he felt as I did—it was both. I was both horrified by what was to come and angered by their excitement at using another sentient being for their games.

The shifter fought being put in the cage. If they had drugged him beforehand, it wasn't very effective. But he was no match for four vampires, who removed his restraints before shoving him in the cage, stretching his arms wide, and latching the door with an audible click that seemed to echo through the lab.

He continued to thrash, as ineffectual as it was, and his eyes darted around, seeking any assistance he could find until they lit on

S-272 and me. My chin lifted as we held his gaze, refusing to turn away from his plight. Neither of us would show weakness at what was to come. It was the only solidarity we could provide.

With his eyes locked on us. He understood his fate, and for some reason, perhaps the simple knowledge he wasn't alone, he calmed and showed the last of his inner strength.

"Let's get on with it." The words came from the director, who appeared irritated and anxious, his hands never stopping as they fussed with his tie. He tugged at his lab coat before stuffing his hands in his pockets then quickly pulling them out. In. Out. In. Out. He finally found a pen in one of the pockets and twirled it in his fingers as a lab assistant picked up a syringe.

I wasn't surprised to see Leonard, the sadistic assistant from the earlier experiments, as he held up the syringe so everyone could see it as he gave it a dramatic flick with his finger. The syringe was filled with a thick, bright pink liquid, and even from where I sat, I could see it ended with a long, large bore needle.

The female scientist standing next to the director tapped her hands along her leg. "It has to be given intramuscular, either in the bicep or the thigh."

Leonard glanced at her, nodded, then moved toward the shifter. He bent as if going for the thigh, but the shifter moved his leg out of reach. The assistant stepped back, his expression one of irritation. He shrugged and went for the bicep, which was restrained in the arm clamps.

I questioned why Leonard had moved toward the leg first, and the only explanation I could come up with was that it would have hurt more in the thigh than the arm. The vampire was truly an evil male.

He jabbed the needle in, and the shifter jumped at the assault. Leonard waited a beat, a nasty grin on his face, before his thumb slowly pushed the toxic cocktail into the shifter. At first, the shifter remained calm, but then he began to scream. Throughout the entire long minute it took for Leonard to continue pushing the serum into the shifter, the screaming never stopped, even after the assistant removed the needle and stepped back.

I glanced at the people in the booth, who were smiling and nodding their heads. All except Gheata, who watched expressionless. Were they happy with the screaming, or did the continuing shrill wailing mean this was the outcome they'd hoped for?

I wanted to cover my ears so I couldn't hear the painful sounds, the screams turning to howls. S-272 leaned into me. His earlier energy radiated through me, and I sat straighter while we watched in horror as the shifter began to morph.

He wouldn't be able to shift properly in his current position. He might not explode like the others, but the way he was positioned in the cage wasn't feasible for the structure of a wolf. It would kill him.

The first things that changed were his hands. Thick fur erupted on his knuckles, then the fingers and over his hands, and then up his arms to his elbows. His muscles bulked, and his fingernails changed to razor-sharp claws—long, thick, and deadly. Not the same as a wolf, but close. Thick hair covered his feet, his toenails changed to match the lethal claws on his hands, and his soles thickened into pads that were better for gripping the ground.

The howling continued as the male's face turned next. A snout grew where his mouth was before his whole head turned into a wolf. Drool ran from his fangs as the shifter struggled in pain. His ears became pointed but remained without fur, leaving them with an eerie human appearance.

The howling ceased as the transformation appeared to stop.

His legs, arms, and torso remained in the form of a human male.

I turned to S-272, who was as shocked as I was.

When I turned back to the room, Leonard pumped a raised fist, and everyone behind the window were smiling and shaking hands. Except for Gheata. He stood like a statue, the only change in his expression was the slight squinting of his eyes. Then it came. The slow grin of satisfaction.

They had somehow managed to stop the transformation. When I forced my gaze to the shifter, my stomach twisted.

He was terrified.

He was aware of what had happened but couldn't shift back. Was he stuck like that? Maybe when the drug wore off he'd return to his full human form. Or maybe that wasn't the end goal.

"Well done, team," the female scientist said. "Phase one is complete. Please record the final measurements, then we'll proceed to phase two."

The group behind the window began talking among themselves, ignoring the lab assistants as they reviewed their monitors and typed at their keyboards. The guards faced the wolfman, whose eyes skittered around the room, once more landing on mine.

I nodded to him, trying to keep calm for his sake. He tried to hold it together, but his gaze moved from mine as he searched for a way out. His body shuddered and strained as if he was attempting to shift back but finding the ability taken from him.

"We can't allow this to happen." S-272 spat the whispered words. "You need to find a way to free the vampire and get out. Find someone who can stop this."

"What if the door isn't there anymore?"

Before he could respond, the lab assistant spoke. "We're ready."

The group behind the window turned back to the lab, their expressions, still uplifted, turned serious as they readied for the next phase.

The female scientist scanned her team. "This is a momentous occasion. Let's see it through." She nodded at Leonard, who now held a second syringe. This one was a clear light green. "Begin phase two. This injection can go anywhere but to speed up the results, let's try closer to the head."

Leonard grinned and turned toward the wolfman, whose huge eyes pleaded for release. Without pause, he jammed the needle into the wolfman's neck. This time the injection was quick and for several minutes nothing happened.

No one seemed concerned, as if they knew this one would take longer.

The wolfman's gaze fell on me again, and it was filled with a hopeless sadness as his body relaxed. His gaze changed from terror and sadness to nothing but a blank expression. He was still alive based on the rise and fall of his chest, but he'd either been sedated or they'd somehow cut off his emotions.

"Put the collar on," the female scientist ordered.

Leonard picked up a thin nylon collar with a small black box that had been threaded onto it. It looked like a dog collar used to control barking or inappropriate behavior.

Deep anger filled me with silent rage.

Leonard didn't seem as brave as before and handed the collar to one of the guards. That was the first time I noticed the smaller cage door that allowed access above the waist.

The wolfman remained still as the guard fitted the collar around his neck. He was stepping back to close the door when the female scientist said, "Let's keep it open."

The guard looked at her, nodded, then stepped back.

She removed a cylindrical black box, aimed it toward the wolfman and pressed a button. The reaction was instantaneous. The wolfman snarled and pulled at his restraints. His eyes were no longer blank but filled with rage and, based on knowing my own wolf, hunger. His hands flexed and unflexed, unable to form a fist because of the long nails but wanting to strike at something. Anything.

When the button was hit a second time, the snarling instantly stopped. The wolfman's body relaxed and the dull expression returned.

The female scientist smiled and turned toward the director. "Phase two is complete. We have success."

The director's expression changed from his earlier anxious state to all smiles, as if a great pressure had been lifted.

"We have several more tests to perform before we move to field experiments," the female scientist continued. "I'd like to turn five more so we have a good working group for the next stage of trials."

The director rubbed his hands together. "Yes. Yes. As many as you want, but I want field trials ready in two weeks." He kept nodding, his smile wide as he stared at his creation. "This is excellent. Our Master will be quite happy about this."

The words hit like a sledgehammer to the gut. I was trying to understand what this all meant, but his words about the Master stopped all other thinking. The director wasn't the Master. If not him, then who, and were they somewhere in the facility or someplace else?

Two weeks before field experiments. This had to be stopped.

The discussions between those behind the window and those in the lab continued. The remote control was passed around so others could turn it on and off as if it wasn't some evil game.

Through it all, Gheata stood and watched the wolfman. The grin was still there as he slowly nodded. He seemed eager to see Frankenstein's monster unleashed.

I rubbed a hand along my waist, feeling the bump of the vial. What could one vampire do against this? What would happen to those left behind if the vampire escaped?

"This has to stop." My words were nothing more than a whisper.

"You can't worry about the rest of us. We're all doomed. But you have the ability to save the rest of the shifters."

What would my uncle do?

It was a stupid question.

Protect the species—at all costs.

# Chapter Eighteen

I STARED at an irregular brown stain on the wall. It had faded over time, and the guards hadn't bothered to paint over it, probably tired of buying white paint. I'd been staring at it for hours. I called upon my wolf, but only enough to ignite the red glow.

Shifters had excellent eyesight in the dark, but it could be heightened through our wolf. I couldn't hold the wolf in that state for long—close to awakening but not enough to shift. Tonight, my rage lay too close to the surface, and it was a struggle to keep her at bay.

She wanted to come out. She wanted to hunt. She wanted to taste blood.

So, I focused on the stain. There were several like it on the walls of my cell, but this one was at eye level when I sat on the bed, my back to the wall. During long days when I had no work assignment, I'd study it like a Rorschach test, counting how many different objects I could create from the image.

Not tonight. Though my gaze was locked on the shape, I saw it for what it was. Blood. Shifter blood.

When I walked into the main lab that first time to find it painted red with shifter blood, flesh, and bone, I didn't think anything could be worse. I said it again when I witnessed the experiment firsthand, watched as drugs were injected into them that resulted in their implosion, and then forced to clean it up. I still had no idea what they could have given them to make that happen.

But today was worse.

A shifter had been forced into a partial change and locked there. Incapable of speech, and unable to give his wolf any rest. It was a painful position to be in. Not just physically but mentally. We might be able to retain our thoughts and awareness during a shift, but it was co-mingled with the wolf.

Hard to explain to someone who'd never gone through it, but what they'd forced on that shifter was worse than death. I'd been grateful when he received the second shot of who knew what. To see the fear and pain in his eyes dulled as his body relaxed. He was no longer aware, and, in this situation, it was the best outcome any shifter could hope for.

Was there an antidote?

I snorted into the darkness.

Why would they want to save a shifter? They wouldn't want to waste the time and resources to create an antidote. A shifter wasn't worth it.

I dropped my gaze to my hand and opened my fist. The vial labeled BP-X lay in my hand. Would Sergi drink it? There were still fourteen vials of human blood under my mattress.

I closed my fist and strode to the corner where I kept my spare shift and underwear.

We were running out of time.

But I had a plan. It was a horrible plan.

Yet, this was the best time. The staff were ecstatic with the results of the last experiment. They would be distracted. They wouldn't see it coming.

I began ripping my shift into long strips.

Tomorrow would be my salvation or my death.

*Tomorrow the wolf comes out.*

~

SERGI WOKE from a strange and difficult dream. If he'd thought reliving his mother's and sisters' deaths had been gut-wrenching, this one had reopened a gash in his heart he didn't think could ever be repaired.

He hadn't thought of Ines in decades. He'd been close to death on many occasions and had never experienced such realistic dreams. Even though they'd begun soon after his torture had started, they'd become more palpable after the first dose of Magic Poppy.

The beast was growing stronger, and maybe it had forced the memories he thought he'd locked away, far from his reach. Whatever the reason, the sight of Ines, standing in the light of the rising sun, was as clear as if he were standing in the room next to her.

She arranged the colorful silks around her shoulders. Her hair, black as onyx, hung in soft curls, the tips skimming along the small of her back. A soft breeze blew in from the desert, rustling the tips of the silk scarf she pulled over her head.

When she turned toward him, his heart thumped loudly at the thought of running his hands over her skin, soft as satin and warm as the desert sand. He felt the touch of her fingers as they played across his shoulders then reached below his tunic to stir his manhood. He remembered the previous evening when they'd tumbled into bed, her legs wrapped around his hips. She'd urged him on with words of love and screams of pleasure as she trembled from her release.

They were to leave in two days before House El Farah's army reached the city battlements. He would take her back to House Trelane where she would be safe. After their lovemaking the night before, she'd spoken of a spring wedding, and they'd laughed as they discussed names for their children.

His heart had been full.

"You should stay here where it's safe." He didn't feel comfortable letting her go alone when battle drew near. "Can't Carmen go to the market for you?"

She slipped on her sandals then brushed her fingers under his chin as she strolled by. "Carmen has other duties this morning. Besides, there's a new vendor with exotic oils from the Far East." She stepped up to him and ran her hands over his shoulders, tracing a finger over his tattoos as one hand slipped down his leg.

He caught it and brought it to his lips. "If you give me a few minutes, I can go with you."

"No." Her tone was harsh, and then she smiled. "I want to buy you a surprise. It won't be a surprise if you're with me."

"Then let me send one of the men with you. El Farah's men could have reached the city by now."

She laughed, her voice melodic, and it sent a shiver over him. "You worry too much. It will take another few days before they even think of coming here." She stepped back and tied a pouch around her waist before pulling a sheer caftan over her shoulders. "I'll only be an hour, maybe a bit more."

She strolled to him, wrapping her arms around his waist as she tilted her head back. Her half-lidded eyes were sultry, and she slowly licked her bottom lip. He crushed her tighter, his lips brushing hers as he ran a tongue over that same lip before pushing past it to taste the sweetness within. She purred as she tugged him closer, her hand running through his hair.

The kiss didn't last long enough.

She pulled back and pinched his chin. "Go back to bed and wait for me." Her grin was infectious. "You'll never guess my surprise."

He was still smiling as she sailed out of the room, her caftan flowing behind her.

With thoughts of the previous evening still on his mind, he did as she asked and stripped off his tunic. She'd left a cup of his favorite Moroccan coffee, and he took the cup to bed and enjoyed the exotic scents drifting in through the window as he savored the brew.

It wasn't long after he set the cup aside and nestled under the silk sheets that his lids grew heavy. A smile was on his lips as thoughts of Ines' return and their impending joining lulled him to sleep.

The loud bang of the outer door being thrown open pulled him from sleep. He jumped up but teetered as the floor swayed beneath him. For a second, he couldn't remember where he was until he caught Ines's spicy scent. He took a step but stumbled, his legs refusing to follow his command.

He fell against the wall as the room erupted with men in armor. His wits came back to him, but his legs moved as if he were wading in a pool of honey. He turned to where he always laid his sword, but it wasn't there.

It wouldn't have mattered.

Six armored vampires surrounded him. Someone kicked his legs out from behind, and he dropped to his knees. Unable to lift his lethargic arm in time, another male slammed a fist into the side of his head, and he toppled over. He was dragged from the room and down the wide staircase before being tossed onto the stone floor of the foyer.

His head pounded. Not just from the slam to it, but from something more insidious. He'd been drugged. His only sustenance that morning had been the coffee Ines made for him.

He refused to believe she would have betrayed him. Could Carmen be involved?

"Finally." A gruff voice pierced the dull ache in his head. "Sergi. Do you know how long I've been looking for you?"

Sergi wasn't able to push himself up, but he managed to open an eye. Worn leather boots stood inches from his face. He recognized the voice.

Yousef El Farah. How had he found him so quickly?

The vampire squatted down and shoved Sergi until he rolled to his side. He opened his eyes to glare up at El Farah. "Such a sad affair to find House Trelane's Captain of the Guard unprepared. You grow lax between the legs of a woman." El Farah chuckled. "Let's see what the crows make of you." He gripped Sergi's hair and yanked his head back. "But before I hang you from the walls of my castle, we shall spend a little quality time together. We have much to discuss."

He stood and kicked Sergi in the stomach. The next one would have broken his jaw if he hadn't turned his head at the last minute. But the kick was enough to descend him into darkness.

He'd woken, chained to a wall, and endured two days of torture before the castle was stormed. Two of his guards had found him. His only thoughts during his captivity were of Ines and whether she'd gotten away.

When he stumbled out of the dungeon of the castle and into the harsh sunlit courtyard, he found satisfaction in seeing El Farah on his knees along with his cadre. Devon paced in front of them, a bloody sword at his side.

Devon turned when he heard Sergi approach, his guards directly behind him in case he stumbled, but he refused to show weakness. When the two met, Devon laid a hand on his shoulder and gave him a long, appraising look.

"Are you alright?"

"I'll be fine." Sergi's throat was raw, the words thick on his lips.

"I thought you might want to do the honor." Devon held out his sword.

He mustered the strength to take the sword and swung it once, chest level, to test its heft. He would need both arms to lift it any higher.

El Farah glared at him, hatred shining in his eyes, his head held high. He had to give the vampire credit. He wasn't a weak man. Just not a smart one.

"I guess you won't be seeing the crows peck out my eyes after all." Sergi wanted to lean against the sword, but he held it loosely in his right hand.

"If not me, then someone else. And if you continue to fight for House Trelane, I'm sure it will be soon."

"Any last words?"

El Farah spit at his feet. Fair enough. Sergi lifted the sword with both hands, but before he had time to swing it, a scream shattered the silence.

He glanced up and dropped the sword to his side when he saw Ines being held back by two guards. Her hands were bound in front of her. He expected to see gratefulness at finding him alive, but instead, her eyes flashed with hatred.

He took a step back. "Ines?"

"You filthy pig. Leave Yousef alone. Just leave us and go back to your home."

Her words stung.

El Farah laughed. "At least I have the privilege of seeing this moment." He gave Sergi a pitiful look. "Didn't she tell you?" Sergi wanted to knock the smirk off his face. "Ines and I have been betrothed since childhood. I wasn't originally in favor of her seducing you, but then, the quarry was too difficult to pass up." He shook his head. "Though, to be honest, I'd expected more information than she was able to gather while opening her legs to you." His laugh grew louder as Ines continued to yell obscenities at Sergi.

Memories of that morning, bits and pieces he'd refused to contemplate, could no longer be ignored. Carmen had nothing to do with it. He'd drunk the coffee Ines had made. Her desire to shop without him, wanting him to wait for her in bed. The feeling of being drugged.

Anger burned deep, not only from her betrayal but by what a fool he'd been.

Without warning, and with all his rage spurring him, he lifted the sword with one strong arm, spun around, and sliced through El Farah's throat, some sick satisfaction releasing a knot in his chest as the male's head toppled from his shoulders.

Ines's screams rebounded in his head.

Sergi dropped the sword and walked out of the courtyard. He'd walked for miles, and it was several hours before Devon tracked him down.

He'd stopped by a river and had fallen to his knees on the soft grass. Some time passed before he heard the soft tread of footsteps. He knew it was Devon without looking.

Devon stopped behind him, not bothering to sit or kneel. "She's the one who's been leaking information about our army's location." His hand rested on Sergi's shoulder, and though he tensed, he didn't move away.

"I was a fool."

"Then I was as well." When Sergi didn't respond, Devon added, "I saw the way she looked at you, even when you didn't notice. I would have sworn it was love." He hesitated, then finished. "We discovered that she'd done this before with House El Jilali. I'm sorry, Sergi."

"Is she gone?"

"I took care of it myself."

He hung his head. They could have assigned her to a different House, but a repeat spy, especially an angry one, couldn't be trusted not to do it again. Male or female, a traitor could never be left alive.

Devon walked away, and it was four days before Sergi returned to the city to find him and the army waiting for him. They never mentioned her name again. And Sergi never let another female that close to his heart.

The kick to his upper thigh woke him, unaware he'd fallen back to sleep as he recalled the nightmare. A pair of glowing yellow eyes glared at him.

*Gheata.*

Sergi roared.

Gheata smiled for the first time. "Finally. The beast has been released."

# Chapter Nineteen

THE NEXT MORNING, I was grateful they delivered breakfast in my cell. I wasn't fit to be around shifters, knowing what I knew of the latest experiment. I imagined sitting at one of the tables, staring through the frosted glass at our keepers on the other side as a pack of wolves descended on them. Mostly, I didn't want anyone to see the anger brewing inside. I was usually good at maintaining a blank expression, especially after eleven months—or had it been a year now?—playing my role as a subservient slave. I didn't think I could hold it in anymore.

I'd eaten the porridge quickly, then laid out the long belt made from the strips of my extra shift. I had spare material that I'd ripped into smaller pieces to wrap the individual vials to prevent them from making noise or breaking. I stared at the fourteen vials of blood and the single vial of BP-X. If that didn't give Sergi a boost, I wasn't sure what else I could do.

I wrapped each vial and tucked them into the long makeshift pocket I'd created by doubling the material in the belt. Once the vials seemed secure, I tied the belt around my waist, then slipped my shift on. It felt snug, but to be sure, I moved around, bending, stretching, and then walking. The material had loosened, and I re-tightened it then tested my movements again.

Better.

I sat on the bed and waited for the guard to take me to level three. Within minutes, the jitters began. What if they decided to keep me locked up today? No. Breakfast had arrived less than thirty minutes ago. I sucked in a long, deep breath before slowly releasing it, attempting to stop the pacing of my wolf, and I continued the exercise until she quieted.

When the billy club hit my door I jumped but remained sitting on the corner of my bed with my head down. The door creaked open, and I glanced up, surprised to see Dallas from level three.

"Come, girl. You have a busy day ahead of you." He backed up, the billy club clutched to his chest.

I stood, wondering why he'd come upstairs rather than meet me on level three. Alarm bells went off in my head, but I pushed them aside. I wanted to ask, and while he might have answered, I decided to appear sullen. It wasn't difficult. After bearing witness to yesterday's experiment, it would be expected.

My nerves rattled as we walked through the halls, and I didn't relax until we descended the stairs to the third level.

"We're short-staffed today due to training. Follow your normal routine and don't stray. Do you understand?"

They were still short-staffed? That made me curious, but I nodded as the last of my anxiety drained away. My plan was back on track. I rushed my cleaning of the cells, eager to check on Carlos.

He wasn't in his cell.

It didn't mean anything. They must have moved him to level two, but as I pushed the cart down the hall toward Sergi's cell, the anxiety returned. It wasn't the good kind—the restlessness that hit just before a difficult assignment. The jumpiness that even though I was more than prepared, the butterflies remained to focus me.

This was the disquiet that spoke of something gone wrong.

The feeling of doubt doubled when I reached the last hallway and found Sergi's cell door open. Had they taken him somewhere, too? Oh god, my plan was crumbling by the minute. I should have made a decision sooner. Taken the chance.

When I grew closer, I heard a low growl, followed by a howl, and then the sound of flesh on flesh. I sighed with relief and held in a hysterical laugh. He wasn't gone. He was getting his morning beating.

I stopped the cart and peered in.

Gheata punched Sergi in the kidneys, and I took a step back.

It wasn't Sergi anymore. It was his beast.

I'd once seen a vampire who'd completely lost his mind to his beast. His body had morphed into something unrecognizable. He'd been almost seven feet tall, even with his hunched back. His head was misshapen, and his hands were nothing more than vicious claws. Two other vampires—Eliminators—had put him down.

I recalled what my uncle had said. The vampire had been drugged with something and had become too dangerous to save. Or it had been simpler to take him down and pretend it never happened. Had that incident been from Magic Poppy? I hadn't heard the term before Sergi named it, so maybe my uncle hadn't known.

Sergi hadn't completely morphed into that state, but his face had changed. It was still him, but his forehead had thickened, forcing his brows lower. His fingernails were long, more claw-like, and he howled again. His eyes burned a bright red as if he'd been spawned in hell.

Gheata appeared gleeful as he punched Sergi in the ribs. "This is more like it. Let it all go. Bring out the beast."

The beatings were making Sergi's beast angry, forcing it to push past what defenses Sergi had built to keep it down. It didn't matter now. The beast was winning.

I panicked. This had to stop, but how? If I had one of those billy clubs, I'd show Gheata a thing or two about beatings.

All I had was my cart, and I rammed it into the doorway. It wasn't much, but I hoped to get Gheata's attention. Not that I wanted the asshole to start beating me, but a distraction was in order.

It worked. Gheata turned his gaze on me, and I stepped back, almost tripping over my clumsy slippers.

"What do you want, girl?" At first, it was apparent I'd surprised him. Then recognition hit, and he stood straighter, turning his back to the beast. He rubbed his fist, then pulled a rag from the table and wiped the blood off his hands. He'd reopened a deep gash in Sergi's side that hadn't completely healed.

He stormed toward me, and I took another step back before he shoved the bloody rag at me. "I want this cell spotless. The director wants to see our new beast, and he doesn't like to step in blood."

I nodded, keeping my head low.

He didn't move, and I waited, tensing in case he decided to hit me after all. But all he said was, "God, I can't wait to get out of this dump."

He brushed past me, his shoulder hitting me with enough force to knock me off-balance. I remained standing and glared at his back until he rounded the corner and was gone.

I stepped inside the cell. Drool ran down Sergi's chin, and he chafed against the metal bands. Had his beast loosened them? When the beast lunged again, I focused on the bolts holding the bands in place. Had they moved?

I swallowed and took several more steps, staying an arm's reach away. The beast glared at me, and I almost peed myself when it roared, his fangs fully extended.

I was too late. Sergi was gone. The beast had won.

~

ONCE GHEATA LEFT, Sergi struggled to pull the beast back, but the beast, starved and filled with rage, fought back. When the female stepped through the doorway and approached, the beast howled once more, then something strange happened.

The beast lifted its head and sniffed the air. It whined, and Sergi, who was sweating with the effort to pull it back, was shocked by the sudden change. Bit by bit, the beast calmed and settled back, allowing Sergi to regain full control.

The hunger still clawed at them, and if he didn't feed soon, not even this shifter would be enough to soothe the beast.

In his hundreds of years, he'd been the only one with the ability to satisfy his beast. Yet this female had done the impossible simply by walking into the room. Maybe she brought more blood. He followed her movements as she cleaned his blood from the floor, dusted the table of torture instruments, and dumped the waste bin.

Every few seconds, her eyes flicked to him, but not in fear. If anything, it seemed like curiosity. Interesting.

Once she'd replaced the water, she moved toward him, her steps tentative, and her steady gaze never left his body. He flinched when she touched the gash where Gheata had sliced him. It had been one of Gheata's techniques to anger Sergi, or more accurately, to encourage the beast to come out.

Sergi could have kept the beast at bay, but Gheata had to believe him weak. And while it had been the right move, the beast had been more powerful than Sergi expected. When the physical change began, he wasn't sure he could pull the beast back.

He would have eventually won, but the female saved him the energy it would have required. He grimaced when she touched a bruise along his ribs, but when her fingers moved over his tattoos, his skin tingled. Her fingers were warm, soft, and light as a dove's feather and triggered shivers along his skin.

"You need more blood." She turned away and rushed to the doorway. Satisfied they were alone, she walked to a corner and pulled up her shift, revealing long, lean legs. There had been muscle there at one time.

"How long have you been here?"

She spun around, a makeshift belt hung from her hand, and her shift settled over her knees. "You can talk." She took a step closer. "And you're eyes are clear."

"The beast has settled." He heaved a heavy breath. "Gheata had to believe his potion was working. It's a struggle to keep my beast quiet, but the blood and Blood Poppy you gave me seems to be helping. But the hunger will eventually do what the Magic Poppy hasn't been able to."

"Let's see what we can do about that." She laid the belt on the table and unwrapped it. His eyes widened as he watched her pull out one vial, then another, and another until there were fourteen vials on the table. Then she placed a fifteenth one off to the side. "It's been a year since I was sent to find the lab."

"What?"

"How long I've been here."

"A year without shifting?"

She picked up a vial and strode to him. "We're not allowed to shift, and it comes with severe punishment if we do." She shrugged. "The cells don't have cameras, so the guards don't know what we do at night." She gave him a quirk of a smile. "I only do it once a week, sometimes less, sometimes more, depending on the need." She opened the vial. "Now, open up."

He opened his mouth and closed his eyes as the drops of blood fell on his tongue. She had to stand on tiptoes as he leaned his head back so he wouldn't lose a drop. It was stale but not too old to have lost critical nutrients. He needed fresh blood, but this would do for now.

All but one of the vials had been emptied, and she wrapped them in her belt and took them to her cart, most likely hiding them in the trash. Would she be able to get more?

When she returned, she picked up the last vial. "A trusted

friend gave me this. From what he overheard, this should revitalize you. I was suspicious, but my friend tells me a couple of lab assistants were tempted to try it." She shrugged and brought it to him. "This is labeled BP-X. I don't know what the X means, and it wasn't on the first vial I gave you." She held up the vial so he could see the label. There was a date behind the name, but it meant little to him since he'd lost track of how long he'd been captive.

"How old?"

"A little over a week. This has obviously been modified, but I don't know how. And I have no idea what this might do with the Magic Poppy already in your system. This could help you, make you worse, or possibly kill you." She looked up at him. "This has to be your decision."

At first glance, her expression was one of doubt. He looked past it to the worry in her eyes. For a split second, he caught a blush of the tell-tale sign of a shifter's red-eyed glow. Something else bothered her. "Tell me what's happening."

Tears instantly erupted, and she blinked rapidly, trying to keep them at bay, but a few slipped past her defenses. Her lips tightened while her eyes darted around the cell. Like a teapot blowing off steam, the words tumbled out—a new experiment, a shifter partially morphed, unable to talk or shift back, his temperament dulled by drugs, the ability to force him into a snarling rage. The shifter probably lost forever to the drugs.

Sergi considered her story. A shifter physically changed, and their behavior controlled by the push of a button. A vampire addicted to Magic Poppy until they could no longer control their beast. He was beginning to see a pattern.

When her tears dried, she gripped his arm. "I can't let it happen again. I won't be able to hold back my wolf."

Without hesitation, he said, "Give me the Blood Poppy." When she looked doubtful, he gave her part of his plan that was coming together as they spoke. "When the beast battled for control, I felt the metal band give. If you can use one of those instruments to pry the bolts loose, I can do the rest. The question is what to do once I'm free. Were you able to confirm where the command center is?"

"Yes. It's where I told you, but there's something else you need to know." She told him about the hidden back door. "It's on this level. All you have to do is go through it."

A back door. That was unexpected, but it shouldn't have been. The door might not have been used in decades, but Venizi always had an escape route.

"Oh, I almost forgot. The guard said they were short on staff. Something about training, but they've been light on guards for the last couple of days."

"We won't have a better opportunity. But I need that Blood Poppy." He nodded toward her hand.

She hesitated, then opened the vial and poured it on his tongue, ensuring not a drop was wasted. "I'll have to hurry. The guard will come for me if I'm not at the stairs on time." She found a metal tool with a thin, sharp edge at the tip. He flinched, remembering Gheata's creative use for it. She wedged it under the bolt that held the band in place. She pried it several times before moving to the next one. With each loosened bolt, he felt a gentle release.

"That's enough. Do the ones holding my arms."

"Are you sure?"

When all he did was give her a grim smile, she didn't hesitate. She was working on the second to last bolt when boots echoed in the hall, growing close.

Her eyes widened, and she raced to the table to dust off the end of the tool. She laid it in the exact position she'd found it, then picked up the mug of water and stepped toward the door. As the boots drew close, she spun around and slowly walked back to the table as if she was just bringing it back with fresh water.

"What's taking so long?" The guard stepped in, and she jumped at his words.

If she had faked the response, she was good. Sergi had noticed over the last few days how intelligent she was, how quick she worked the bolts, and how courageous to have stolen and hidden the vials. She must be one of Remus's best warriors, maybe from one of the local packs. He would do whatever he could to return her home.

A tremor in her voice was accentuated with her bowed head. "I'm sorry. There was more blood than I was expecting."

The guard studied Sergi, who had lowered his head to watch the male through his lashes.

The male's gaze focused on the new cuts in Sergi's body, and he nodded. "Finish up. I'll be at the stairs."

He turned away as Alex picked up an already-emptied waste bin. The guard had walked away, but she carried it to the door, peered out, then disappeared. She was probably dumping the vial she'd hidden in her fist.

When she returned, she gave the room a last look, then turned to him. "If you can get free, get to the door. There are wild shifters out there, so you have to be careful." She paused and appeared to want to say something, but he sensed she'd changed her mind on what she'd been about to say. "Get away from this place and find us help."

Before he could ask what she was going to do, she gave him a last glance. "And my name is Alex."

Then she was gone.

# Chapter Twenty

DEVON STARED at his satellite phone while the team unpacked the gear from the vans.

"You've been staring at that for some time, my friend." Remus dropped into the seat next to him. "Are you expecting his locator to suddenly show up?"

Devon ran a hand through his hair and looked out the window at the tiny village, though he wasn't really seeing it. His mind was a hundred years in the past, remembering some ill-advised mission he'd talked his friend into. "You never know. Sergi never gives up."

Remus grunted. "A pit bull. I sensed it in him the first time we met." He studied his hands before meeting Devon's eyes. "We have to be ready for anything. Everything."

He shook off the past and turned away from the village. "How long have you known Carlos?"

Remus chuckled. "Since he was a pup. He was always the one slipping out in the evenings, curious about everything. He never showed fear and was always the first to step up."

They sat in silence, thinking about their males and their fate— alive or dead.

Devon shook off the tension that had been riding him since they left Deva. "Let's go find them."

They jumped out of the van and picked up their duffels.

Devon stuck his head back into the van to speak to the driver. "Stay alert. They might not have anyone watching from town but assume they do."

"I'll keep you posted, boss."

Devon closed the door and tapped it twice with his fist then stood back as the van slowly moved away, heading for a garage on the other side of town. The drivers would remain with the vans to ensure they weren't tampered with.

Three miles before they reached the village, they'd stopped at a gas station where Rafael had arranged for the motorcycles. Devon and Remus gave the three team members their final instructions and watched them head off into the woods. The team would take small trails until they were a mile in, then cross to the road leading to the lab. Team One was officially in play.

Now that the vans were out of the way, it was time to ensure the rest of the team wasn't being watched.

Once the vans were out of sight, Devon turned to find Remus in deep conversation with a local man. He found a spot on a rock wall to wait and surveyed the area, searching for anyone who showed interest in their group who might be a vampire. There were several people eyeing them, but none he would suspect of being vampire, but that didn't mean there weren't eyes on them from inside one of the several buildings surrounding them.

Ten minutes later, Remus shook the man's hand and met Devon at the wall.

"Is he going to be trouble?" Devon asked.

Remus shook his head. "I don't think so. He's the mayor and wanted to complain about the vehicles that use the road that goes up the mountain. And, of course, was worried about the size of our party. The village have enough problems with some of the men, vampires I assume, who come to town."

"That makes sense."

"Apparently, the government disregards his concerns."

"Which means someone in the government is being paid off." Devon wasn't surprised.

Remus rubbed his chin. "It would be necessary to keep the lab a secret all these decades."

"There's a small House not far from Brasov that's tied to House Larkin. I imagine many of the government officials are vampire."

"Does this impact our mission?" Remus asked.

"No. Bella would have raised it earlier if she considered them a threat."

Rafael ran up to them. "Everyone has settled in. We have three rooms, and the money we gave the innkeeper has calmed any concerns he had. He'll also contact a restaurant to bring us dinner."

"Let's get inside." Devon stood and stretched his back as he gave a final scan of the area. "I want to check on the House and see if they've picked up any chatter."

The inn was two stories and had a couple dozen rooms, but most were empty. From what Rafael told them, the other rooms were rented by local villagers. Their three rooms were adjoined at one end of the first floor.

Devon found Bella in the room by the exit door. She huddled over her seat at a round table and sipped from a mug as she scrolled through her tablet. The room was filled with everyone's gear that had been sorted into two piles.

His nose led him to the counter in a tiny kitchenette, where a fresh pot of coffee waited. After rubbing the dust out of a mug, he poured a cup and sat across from her.

"Team Two left for their inn." Bella pointed to a paper map on the table. "The inn is the one circled in blue, and the cafe where they'll spend most of their time monitoring the road is circled in yellow. The garage is the green one, and this inn is red."

Devon gave the map a quick scan, familiarizing himself with the town. "Anything from home?"

She nodded. "The city safe house has been quiet." She gave him a pleased grin. "I think Lorenzo's thinking twice about disturbing the local street gang. The coastal safe house also appears quiet. It's more difficult to do drive-bys on a dead-end street. But there has been activity at the front gates to Oasis as well as the manor."

When her pleased grin turned to one that was more wicked, he asked, "What?"

She turned when Remus set a mug on the table and took the last chair. "Excellent timing. Lucas has two shifters patrolling the front gates to Oasis, and after a couple passes from an unknown vehicle, the wolves made their presence known. The cars haven't returned. When the manor started seeing several unknown cars making frequent visits, Decker sent four wolves to the main gate. Those vehicles haven't been back either. Cressa put the security teams on level three alert, and she's working with Decker and Lucas in preparation for a level two."

Devon shifted his gaze to Remus. "Were the shifters at the gates your idea?"

He shrugged. "I merely suggested to Decker there wasn't any reason to hide our involvement. We lost the element of surprise with the raid on Shadow Island and the attack at Oasis."

"Perhaps it's time to start adding more shifters to the safe houses, the manor, and Oasis." Devon grimaced as he took another swallow of the coffee before pushing it away. "Having a handful of shifters is helpful, but if Lorenzo comes full force, we'll be outnumbered."

Remus nodded. "We have to be careful not to leave the packs without their own defenses, but smaller packs could take refuge with the larger packs until we return. That will free up wolves to increase your security."

Devon nodded. "Bella, send a note to Cressa. Have Decker

contact Braden and Elijah." He stopped and glanced at Remus, who nodded his consent. "Have them start working on an updated security plan to support Remus's suggestion. Let Decker take the lead on what works best for the shifters."

Bella didn't waste time sending the message.

"Where are the rest of the team?" Devon asked.

"They're doubling up in the other two rooms."

"Except for the four shifters I've assigned to patrol the inn." Remus pulled over the map and gave it a quick scan.

"Should I send a couple of the vampires to help?" Bella asked.

Remus shook his head. "Let the wolves handle it. They'll be less conspicuous."

"Agreed." Devon looked at his watch. "I'd like to move out at midnight. If we keep a fast pace, we should arrive at the lab by midday."

"Are you still confident that's the best time to infiltrate?" Remus asked.

"Up to now, the teams have all gone in at night, which has probably kept the facility's security on alert for more early morning visitors. I doubt they'd be expecting a raid in the middle of the afternoon."

"Then we stick with our plan." Remus's gaze flicked to the window. "Let's get some rest before dinner."

Bella rose. "Take the beds. I need to check on a few more things."

The two males took a bed as Rafael came in and dropped to the floor near the gear, his body turned on his side. The male had been working hard, and he wouldn't stop until they found Sergi and Carlos. There wasn't anything more Devon could say to reduce Rafael's survivor guilt. He had to work it out on his own.

Devon stared at the ceiling and ran through the planned mission one more time before letting his thoughts turn to Cressa and their time on the south coast of Spain. He didn't know how

SERGI

long he'd slept when shouts woke him. It was dark, but he didn't waste time to glance at his watch as he flew through the door.

Several team members raced ahead of him toward the front of the inn, where they took up defensive positions. Devon didn't stop until he found Remus, who was kneeling over one of the wolves. It was lying on its side, panting heavily.

"What's happening?" He asked.

Remus stood. "Four vampires attacked. I don't think they were expecting wolves. We took down three, but one male took off toward the woods."

"How long ago?"

"Only a few minutes."

"Have we sent anyone after him?"

Bella rushed over. "I was getting ready to send a vampire and a shifter. We were able to save one for questioning."

Devon checked his boot to ensure he still had a dagger on him. "I'll go."

Remus began stripping. "I'll follow as soon as I shift."

Then Devon was off, racing in the direction Remus had pointed. Although it was dark, Devon easily found a trail and assumed the vampire would take an easy path until he put some distance between him and the village. Once he felt safe, he'd veer off to confuse anyone trailing him.

The vampire had to be caught before he reached the lab. They couldn't lose the element of surprise. He wasn't sure where these four vampires had come from, and he hoped Bella would get something out of the one they kept alive.

Devon ran some distance before spotting a small deer trail. He stopped and listened. The snapping of twigs came from the right. The same direction the deer trail headed, and Devon took the path at a dead run. He'd traveled a quarter of a mile before a wolf sprang from the woods.

The massive wolf stopped in the path. His coat was a dark sable, and it looked as if someone had dipped his ears and tail in a pot of black ink. His eyes changed from a fiery, red glow to dark brown.

Remus.

This was the first time Devon had met his wolf. The red glow returned to the wolf's eyes, and he raced off into the woods. When Devon followed, Remus stopped and tossed his snout to the right.

Devon understood, and he raced back to the path to continue his pursuit. Remus would flank the vampire.

If compared from a human perspective, one would expect a younger vampire to be faster than an ancient. The fact was, in most cases, the opposite was true. He would agree that many of the aristocrats couldn't keep a long and fast pace. He snorted. Most could be taken down in the first mile. But vampires born in Houses built from the old days, when war was an ever-present danger, the older one was, the more deadly they were.

Venizi was right when he'd said the vampire race had become too complacent. The larger Houses kept a well-trained security team and cadre, but the smaller Houses had become dependent on the stronger Houses for safety. Over the years, there were fewer Houses training their people as House Trelane and House Venizi did. And without continued training and testing of skills, their Houses would remain weak.

The difference between Trelane and Venizi was that Lorenzo wanted to old days of war, where vampires were the dominant species. Devon envisioned a world where vampires, shifters, and dreamwalkers formed an alliance, not to take over humanity but to live as true equals, maintaining a sustainable balance.

The bottom line was that while Devon was a few minutes behind the vampire, he'd eventually overtake him. The only question was how far he'd have to run to catch him.

The answer came sooner than he expected when the vampire he'd been chasing came racing toward him. If he was shocked to see Devon, the terror in his gaze overrode any concern.

"Wolf. There's a wolf coming."

184

Before the vampire reached Devon, he fell face-first into the ground.

That wasn't the best way to describe it. He was trampled to the ground by the wolf who now stood on the vampire's back, his fangs gripping the vampire's neck. He shook the vampire a few times until the male went limp.

Remus stayed on the vampire, but he lifted his head and looked toward Devon. Blood dripped from the wolf's fangs, but Remus would stop if Devon asked. He considered the situation. Bella said they'd saved one, so they didn't necessarily need this one.

Devon waved Remus off and squatted next to the vampire. He slapped the male's face until he woke.

"Don't move. I'm going to ask you a question. How did you find us?"

When he didn't respond, Devon said, "Alright. If that's your choice, I'll let the wolf finish you."

"No. No." The male gulped air. "We come to town every other day to check in with our lookout."

"And who is that?"

When he didn't respond, Remus placed his front paws on the male's back.

The vampire visibly shook, and the scent of urine made Devon's nose twitch. "It's a guy that works at the garage. He saw your vans pulling in."

"The owner?"

"No. One of the mechanics is a vampire."

"So you decided to take us down?"

"We didn't know who you were other than vampires running with filthy shifters. There's only one response for that." When the vampire realized what he said, the shaking increased along with a bit of whining. "It's what we're taught. Anyone willing to work with shifters is no better than them. You're..." He seemed to search for the right word, then spit out, "You're an enabler."

Devon didn't have a response to that. He let the silence grow until nothing could be heard but the occasional hoot, the rustling of a small creature scurrying past, and the labored breathing of the wolf. Drops of bloody drool fell on the vampire's bare neck, and he began to struggle again.

"Please, let me go. I'll go straight to Bucharest and fly back to the States."

"What House are you from?"

It took a moment before he rasped out, "Larkin."

It would've been too easy for it to have been Venizi. Devon stood and nodded to Remus. "I'll meet you back at the inn."

He turned and jogged back the way he'd come. The screaming followed him for only a minute before it stopped.

They'd found the mole. He'd let Bella take care of him and the one they'd saved once she was done with her questions.

He grinned. This had been the first time he'd hunted with Remus. Whatever tension he'd been holding in was gone. Those old feelings of going to battle returned, along with the scent of victory.

## Chapter Twenty-One

WHEN I ARRIVED at the stairs after leaving Sergi, my head was down, deep in thought. The guard waiting for me slapped his billy club against his leg but didn't say anything, assuming I was being submissive. There might have been a slight pause that I barely registered before he turned for the stairs.

Sergi thought he could bust through the loose bolts. Either way, the guards would eventually discover the door had been left unlocked, the wooden beam lying undamaged on the floor. They might consider one of the guards had helped Sergi, but I would be their first suspect. Until then, I had to focus on my work and not give them any reason to question me.

After I was handed off to a lab assistant, I followed him to the same lab as the previous day. My gut wrenched having to witness another shifter have their humanity stripped away. Where was that other shifter now? The last S-272 and I had seen of him, they'd switched the dog collar, for lack of a better name, with a metal one. The guards had attached two long metal poles to it and had walked him out of the lab.

No one knew what to expect from this new creature—half man, half shifter.

The second I shuffled into the lab, S-272 waved me over. I'd seen him sad, stoic, angry, but never distressed. But as I grew closer, it wasn't difficult to catch the whiff of anger boiling under the surface. I wasn't sure if the appearance of worry was a facade to hide his rage or if it was the cause of it.

I scanned the room. No guards were present, only the eight lab staff. The lead scientist hadn't arrived yet, and the windowed room where the director had watched yesterday's experiment was dark.

S-272 led me to the storage room and pulled out a bucket. "They're modifying the serum." S-272 handed me the bottle of cleanser.

"Why? They seemed pleased with yesterday's results." I opened the bottle and poured a small amount into the bucket.

"They had a problem subduing him. They're not sure what set him off. He was being kept in one of the security cells on this floor and appeared calm. Sometime later, when a guard slid a tray of food in, the shifter grabbed the man's arm and tried to pull him through the slit."

"Oh my god." The opening in the door was only tall and wide enough to slip a food tray in. I had a bad feeling where this was going, but I asked anyway. "What happened?"

"The shifter ripped the guard's arm off. Even with all the screaming and the cameras, the guard bled out before help arrived."

I cringed at the thought but couldn't muster up remorse for the dead guard. Not after all the shifters who'd been tortured and killed. "What happened to the shifter?"

"They terminated him."

That bothered me. Yes, he had been genetically changed, but that didn't mean it couldn't be reversed. I wasn't a scientist and didn't know that for sure, but had anybody even tried?

"How do you know this?"

"They asked me to clean the lab where they performed the autopsy."

He didn't have to say anymore. The staff ignored us. We were such good little doggies.

I lifted the bucket into a sink and filled it with water. How much longer could we allow this to go on?

We had cleaned the floors and were working on the cabinets when S-272 asked, "What of the vampire prisoner?"

I told him of his torture and the Magic Poppy. "From what Sergi, that's the vampire's name, has told me, the drug is highly addictive and meant to force his beast out."

S-272 paled. "Is that what the blood was for?"

I glanced at the lab assistants, who were too busy with their noses in their computers to care about us. "What do you mean?"

He quietly snorted. "You think I didn't see you steal blood vials from the lab?"

Well, damn. I thought he might have seen me, but he'd never said anything. "I thought it might help him fight the drug."

"Did it?"

I shrugged and sprayed a countertop then wiped it down. "Sergi seemed to think so, especially with the vial of Blood Poppy you gave me.

"This Blood Poppy will cure him?"

"Enough to calm the beast." I didn't want to mention the beast appeared to settle when he'd caught my scent, which was before Sergi drank the Blood Poppy. I wasn't sure what to make of that myself.

"Did you tell him about the door?"

"Yes." When I hesitated as if I had something more to say, he grabbed my wrist.

"This isn't a game."

Whatever I was going to say next flew out the proverbial window. My eyes widened at his touch.

He'd never touched me before, other than our arms or legs occasionally connecting as we watched the experiments. He might have grabbed my sleeve, but never a skin-on-skin touch. Now I knew why. I'd misunderstood the energy I'd felt, believing it to stem from his anger or horror.

Did the guards know? That didn't seem possible with the responsibilities S-272 had been given, or did they believe they'd broken him?

Yet, I hadn't sensed it until now. His simple touch sent unmistakable tingles through me that called to my wolf, and there was no other explanation.

S-272 was an Alpha.

ALEX. Was that short for something? Alexandra, perhaps? Protector of men, as some remembered the meaning behind the name. It was fitting.

After she left, Sergi closed his eyes and relished the aftertaste of the Blood Poppy. Now he understood the internal battle Devon faced when dosed with the Magic Poppy, and Cressa's recovery time when she'd drunk Colantha's juice. And neither had proven to have much Blood Poppy in it.

He didn't know if the volume in the two vials Alex had given him was more than what was typically used when blended in other concoctions. All he was aware of was the extra vigor that coursed through him as the Blood Poppy interacted with his blood. The BP-X she'd given him had tasted more alluring than the first vial. More potent. He wanted more of it, and he hoped the addictive properties would wear off long before his energy did.

First things first.

He flexed the muscles in his arms and fisted and unfisted his hands several times. Rather than trying to free one arm at a time, he tightened his muscles and, straining against the metal band across his chest, pulled his arms away from the wall. After a few seconds, he stopped. The bolts had loosened. One more time, maybe two, and his arms would be free.

He relaxed his muscles and glanced at the door, listening for the guard. The only noise came from the constant drips of water he'd been listening to since the first time he woke in the cell. He bunched his muscles again and strained as he pulled on his arms. After a brief attempt, he stopped. He jiggled the bands, doing his best to loosen the bolts more before making his third attempt.

With a huge intake of breath, he flexed and pulled. His face grew hot and was most assuredly red from effort as spittle flew from his mouth. Without warning, and with the last of his breath leaving his lungs, the bolts fell away, and his arms dropped to his sides.

He leaned his head against the wall and breathed out a slow breath, allowing his muscles to relax. If he had the time, he'd rest longer, but that wasn't an option. The guard and Gheata only visited in the mornings, but earlier, Gheata had mentioned the director wanting to pay him a visit, which sounded like this after-noon. While he'd like to meet the director, this wasn't the time or place.

He repositioned what little footing he had and pressed his hands on the wall as he pushed his body forward. There was a slight give but nothing more. He changed tactics, and though it was a bit awkward, he fingered the bolts, working them back and forth until he was able to pull them out of the wall. There was still one bolt remaining when he ripped the band from the wall and threw it across the room.

Once he was free, he fell to the ground. His legs cramped, and he grimaced as he fought through it. Once the cramps had eased, he bent each leg until he had control of motion and was able to flex his feet and wiggle his toes.

He used the wall to stand and leaned against it as he considered his next move. He couldn't escape through the back door Alex told him about without taking evidence with him. And he had to find Carlos, who was supposed to be on this same level. She'd told him the doors on this level were only locked with wood beams, so it shouldn't be difficult to extricate him.

Before he made the attempt to break out, he stopped at the table and drank the water in one long gulp. He wiped his mouth and checked the cooler. Only two vials of blood left, but they'd have to do until he found something fresher. While the blood settled, he stared at the torture instruments spread across the table. He'd like to take them all, but he was currently naked, so no pockets. He grabbed two daggers and faced the door.

He shook out his arms and called on the beast. It was dangerous with the beast so close to the surface, but he had little choice.

He took several steps back and, leading with his left shoulder, stormed the door. Wood shattered, and he flew through it and, unable to stop his momentum, slammed into the stone wall. He shook his head, surprised he was able to burst through the wood beam on the first try.

When he glanced down the hallway to see if anyone was coming, he understood why he'd broken through the door so easily. The beam lay on the floor next to the open doorway. Alex hadn't barred the door.

He grinned in appreciation. If he hadn't escaped from his cell, she would likely have gotten a beating for her carelessness. She was more daring than he'd thought. A true warrior. Her name more fitting with each courageous action she revealed.

He pushed to his feet and gave his body a quick once over. A few cuts and scrapes from splinters, but nothing else was damaged. With daggers still gripped in his fists, he raced to the end of the hallway.

Alex mentioned the guard's quarters were on the far side of this level. Her guard had suggested she wouldn't get her lunch when she'd been late with the cleaning. That meant it was lunchtime, and most of the guards should be on break. He required clothing, so he had to take the risk. While he could resist cold weather, he wasn't going to traverse the Carpathian Mountains naked.

He strolled by the cells. Most of the doors weren't barred. The wood beams lay useless on the floor. Others had bars across the doors, reflecting prisoners inside. He moved passed them, wanting to keep his escape unknown for as long as possible. When the walls changed from stone to drywall, he slowed and peered around the first corner.

Two guards, one laughing at whatever the other one said, were headed in his direction. He raced back the way he'd come and ducked into the first unbarred cell he came to. He closed the door and leaned against it.

He heard the stomping of boots, but they stopped a few feet from the cell he was hiding in.

"Let me check these cells, then we can get lunch."

One pair of boots continued on, and he heard the slam of something hitting the door. A billy club, like the one the guard who came with Gheata gripped tightly while Sergi was tortured. Not as deadly or incapacitating as a dagger, but it was a worthy weapon.

The guards should pass by him, assuming the roaming guard didn't check his cell with a broken door lying in pieces across the floor. It was two hallways away, and all the cells in between had been empty. With any luck, this was a lazy guard.

Within a few minutes, the guard returned. "We're good. I hear they're having roast beef and mashed potatoes."

The other guard chuckled. "A new shipment must have arrived. That must be where the other guards went."

"Thank the gods, we didn't get that duty."

They laughed as they continued on, passing the cell he was in without a pause. Sergi hadn't passed stairs or an elevator so the guards must be heading for a different hallway. A couple of minutes ticked by before he felt it safe enough to move.

He returned to the hallway where he'd first seen the guards

and, not hearing anyone else, checked the first door he came to and found it unlocked. Rather than using stealth, he charged in, quickly scanning the room, prepared for a fight, but it was empty.

A simple bunk room he'd seen before. They were similar to the security rooms House Trelane provided at the safe houses. The occupant kept the place orderly with minimal decor. A bed, a table with two chairs, a dresser, and a desk with another chair. There was a counter with a sink and a small single-serve coffee maker. A compact fridge fit between the counter and the wall.

He opened the dresser and found a pair of pants. He held them up. The guards who'd come to his cell had been about his size. Most of them would be big men with lots of muscle.

He slipped on the pants, which fit well enough, and pulled out a shirt. The sleeves were an inch too short, but the shoulders fit. He found socks and a pair of boots that were too tight. He left the shoes and, peering into the hall, ran to the next room.

It was also unoccupied, and the boots fit. He tied them and glanced around for other weapons. Nothing. He found an empty weapons belt, probably a spare, and slid the daggers in before leaving the room.

It was deathly quiet in the hallways, and he could only assume the guards were at lunch or on assignment on a different level.

His next task was to search for the door Alex told him about. He found it faster than he expected, even if it had been buried behind shelving. It must have been decades since it had last been opened, and it required the closest thing to a prybar he could find to muscle it open.

Cold air blasted him in the face as he stared at a dark tunnel. He raced down it, a slight breeze blowing in, and when he turned a corner, light reflected the rough stone walls. The tunnel made another two turns before he found the exit. There was no door, and vegetation had grown over the opening. He pushed through it and scanned the forest beyond. It was a way out.

Without another thought, he ran back into the building and

shut the door. He had a few tasks to take care of before he left. And he wouldn't leave Alex behind. The thought had popped into his head, and he didn't question it. She'd dared her own life to save his. He wouldn't leave her to whatever his escape would cost her.

Other emotions bubbled up and were instantly squashed, but the memory of her warm fingers as they traced his tattoos heated his skin. The heinous experiments she described and the image of someone leading her to one of the metal cages as another test subject made his blood boil. And she'd said the experiments were continuing. How many would die before Devon mounted a rescue?

He wouldn't consider escaping without Alex, but he wasn't sure of the best way to protect the rest of the shifters until Devon arrived. Then a crazy thought came to him. Something Carlos could assist with. The least he could do, after all, was give them a fighting chance.

He retraced his steps to the first of the barred cells. The wooden beam lifted easily, and Sergi dropped it next to the door. He opened it slowly, unsure how the shifter would react to seeing him dressed as a guard.

The shifter was curled up in a corner. His clothing was filthy and mottled with stains. He kept his head lowered but lifted it enough to see who'd entered. Sergi held his hands out. "You might not believe this, but I'm a friend. I've been sent by Remus, The Wolf, to help you escape."

Nothing changed in the shifter's posture until he heard mention of The Wolf. His head lifted higher, but when he got a better view of Sergi and noted the guard attire, his body curled tighter, and he shook his head.

"Look. We don't have much time. Yes. I'm vampire. I'm cadre sent on a mission to discover what's been happening in the lab." When mistrust shined clearly in the shifter's gaze, he added, "I was also a captive." He opened his shirt to show the recent scars that to his surprise looked better than they did an hour ago. His evidence didn't appear as convincing as it once had. "Alex—you might know her as S-473—helped me escape."

The shifter's eyes widened at the mention of Alex, or more correctly, by her assigned number.

"We have little time, and I need help letting the other shifters out. It would be faster if they saw a fellow shifter opening the door. I can't promise that you'll survive, but do you want to die in one of their experiments or die fighting for your freedom?"

That did the trick.

The shifter pushed himself up and took a few steps. "Some of them will be chained in their rooms."

Sergi swore under his breath. "I assume the guards have the keys."

The shifter nodded and stood a little straighter. "Yes. But some of these shifters are wilder than most."

Sergi grinned, letting the tips of his fangs show. "All the better, assuming they won't attack you."

"There's a room where they keep their weapons. I think the keys are there." He glanced at the floor, then shrugged. "At least, I saw a board with keys on it. They might work on the chains."

"Is it on this level?"

He nodded.

"Show me. Then we'll let the others out."

Sergi followed the shifter toward the guards' quarters. He turned right when they reached the corridor where Sergi had turned left in his search for clothing. The shifter stopped at the second door with a nameplate that read security.

The shifter waited to ensure Sergi was behind him before he opened the door on a surprised guard, who was watching a video feed. Before he could get out of his chair, Sergi shoved the shifter aside and grabbed the guard. He quickly stabbed the vampire three times in the kidneys with one of his stolen daggers. The vampire went limp and fell to the ground.

By the time Sergi turned around, the shifter shook a set of

keys in the air. Sergi checked the pockets of the guard and found another set of keys and a keycard he stuffed in his pocket. They compared the two sets of keys and determined they were identical.

Before they left, the shifter tied the guard's legs and wrists while Sergi scanned the video feed. There was row after row of cells. They all had keycard entries, and rather than stone, the walls and floor were a bright white. This must be the second floor. In one of the monitors, a guard walked down one of the aisles and slammed a billy club into a door. He passed two doors before bashing the billy club into the third door. It was a form of intimidation, reminding the captives of who had control, as if they could forget.

They left the room, and Sergi took the lead. The second door on the right provided what he was looking for—the armory. He grabbed a shoulder harness and transferred his daggers to it, then added a couple more. He tossed the weapons belt he'd been wearing to the side, but when he turned to leave, he spotted several billy clubs leaning against the far corner of the room. He picked one up. He preferred daggers, but a club to the head would work just as well.

"Do you want one?" He raised the billy club.

The shifter grinned, and Sergi handed him one before they rushed out of the room, shutting the door behind them.

Sergi led them to a closed cell door, and the shifter opened it. This shifter was chained to the wall, and he glared at them. His gaze turned to confusion when the shifter in prisoner garb ran toward him.

"Be calm. I'm here to release you. It's time to fight."

The shifter looked past his rescuer to stare at Sergi.

"I'm cadre and a friend to shifters."

While there was distrust in the shifter's gaze, the fact he was being released softened his expression. When the shifter managed to stand, Sergi handed him the second set of keys.

The first shifter looked at him. "You might need them if you're going to the second level."

Sergi shook his head. "If I do, I'll find another guard." Sergi considered whether he should continue with the plan to find Alex and the evidence Devon needed or stay to search the cells for Carlos. "I was captured with a shifter by the name of Carlos. I was told he was in one of the cells on this level. When you find him, ask him to assist with organizing your group. Do you understand?"

Both shifters, who hadn't appeared strong enough to battle a guard, even in their wolf form, stood straighter, their chins lifted high. A red glow appeared in their eyes. Nothing but a glimmer at first, but as they considered what was at stake, the glow brightened into a look Sergi knew well—a beast full of rage and seeking vengeance.

Any doubt of their ability fled. "Get everyone out of the cells, clear the floor, and set up perimeters. I'll start releasing the shifters on the next level."

He shook their hands, but before he took two steps, alarms blared through the hallways.

# Chapter Twenty-Two

I STARED AT S-272. The recognition in my gaze would be enough to tell him I felt his Alpha power. How had they managed to capture an Alpha? There were only two ways I knew of—someone betrayed him, or he gave himself up to save others. But now that I'd seen the number of shifters brought through the facility, they might have ambushed him, not knowing he was Alpha. He'd been able to keep his secret, waiting for an opportune time to fight back.

His touch told me it was time.

"Why don't we wait for Sergi to mount a rescue?" I glanced at the lab assistants, but they were lost in their individual tasks, ignoring us and each other as they prepared for the next test subject.

"The guards are short-staffed. I've discovered they've sent a third of the garrison to retrieve more shifters."

Garrison. I hadn't heard that term in a long time. It was a word my uncle used in sharing stories of battles so old they grew larger and more fantastical in the retelling. This Alpha had been around for some time. This was no place for him to be.

S-272 must have thought I was ignoring him because he bent

low and whispered in my ear. The soft rumble of his commanding voice made my wolf whine. "How many more shifters have to die before you remember who you are?"

His words reverberated. My wolf was eager, scratching to be let loose, and as much as I'd been prepared to fight, I pushed back. "The only way an attack would work is if we release the shifters. It would take too much time to go door to door, or someone would have to take over the command center. That's a suicide mission. They must have more than one guard working in there." But that had been exactly what Sergi had been planning when he'd asked where the command center was located.

"We only need to let out a few shifters, and they can get the others out. The keycards can be easily taken from the staff."

I shook my head as I moved to another set of cabinets, needing time to consider his words. Hadn't I already put myself at risk by helping Sergi escape his restraints? I'd even left the bar off his door. Rage had fueled my need to help Sergi, and I didn't want to see another shifter succumb to the tests, yet I held back.

Then it hit me. The reason S-272 wanted to attack now.

I brought the bucket to the sink to rinse it out, waiting for S-272 to finish his task before meeting me to do the same thing. I meant to keep my voice calm, but my words flew out as if I were scolding an errant child.

"You want to set up a diversion to give Sergi more time to escape. That's suicidal."

S-272 grinned. His smile took my breath away with how it changed his appearance. For the first time, I noticed the laugh lines around his eyes. He'd been a happy shifter once upon a time. Now, with no hope of ever seeing his pack or family again, he was willing to lay down his life to give Sergi enough time to disappear.

I blinked back the sharp sting of oncoming tears. S-272's earlier question echoed in my head, but this time in my uncle's voice. "How many more wolves must die?"

Apparently, a few more if we wanted to end the lab's existence.

I nodded my acquiescence, knowing he'd select the time and place once he determined our best advantage.

Before either of us could speak another word, the doors to the lab opened, and the lead female scientist, who'd been behind the window yesterday, strode in. At some point in our back and forth, the lab assistants had stopped their work. They had formed a line, and two of them each held a syringe—one with the thick pink solution and the other a dark green. The original formula had been a lighter green. The injection that had dulled the shifter's gaze. The shot that had erased who he'd been. This serum must be their updated version.

Behind the scientist, the shifter and his guard entourage followed. The shifter was restrained at his wrists and legs with the same silver manacles others had worn. He kept his head down, his hair dirty and matted. His bare chest was blood spattered, and a long open wound oozed a bloody liquid. He'd fought before they'd beat him down and subdued him.

He shuffled in with a limp, but it was impossible to tell if the injury was old or new. They pushed him in front of the metal cage, and when a guard squatted down to remove the cuffs that bound his ankles, the shifter lifted his head.

His gaze quickly scanned the room until his eyes lit on me, then slid to S-272.

My hand flew to my mouth as a soft cry escaped.

*No.*

Carlos.

~

THE WAVE of power washed over me before I understood what was happening. I didn't know if S-272 had known Carlos was the next experiment or if any shifter would do, but for this to be successful, S-272 would need someone with the will to fight and, if necessary, die.

A second wave flowed over me, and I heard a powerful command. "Shift."

I had no choice.

For a brief second, I glanced at Carlos, who'd been prepared for the moment. He kicked the guard at his feet, pushing him into another guard. He lifted his arms up, and with the power of his Beta blood, he yanked the silver handcuffs apart.

My shift came quickly as bones cracked and elongated, my form morphing as my wolf pushed my human shape aside. If I'd been alone, it would have taken ten long minutes to change, but with the command of an Alpha, it occurred instantaneously. It was a genetic defense mechanism for times of war. Otherwise, the enemy could easily vanquish us during a shift.

By the time I was on all fours and adjusting to my furry body, Carlos, a sleek, tan-colored wolf with rust-colored ears, attacked the guards who'd brought him in. I turned my head to see S-272, a massive gray wolf who'd obviously lost muscle but was still scary as hell, chasing down the lab assistants.

While most of the lab staff were vampires, they appeared to have no battle training as they scurried for a place to hide. They would be easy prey for S-272, so I turned my attention to the four guards Carlos was holding off.

One was down, but I didn't know for how long. The other three had cornered Carlos, or so they thought. I'd fought alongside Carlos once before. He was a slippery wolf. Three was no match for him, but then I noticed Tallon. I'd been so focused on the shifter I hadn't paid attention to the guards.

I didn't think. I took two long strides and leaped on Tallon's back, knocking him down. I wasted little time going for the shifter's neck. I didn't understand why he hadn't changed with the Alpha's command. Maybe he'd been an earlier experiment, and they found a way to block his ability to shift. The fact he might have been a test subject didn't sway my rage as I ripped into him. It didn't excuse his actions afterward—the after-hours beatings and rapes.

My wolf howled before stripping another piece of flesh and tossing it aside. Tallon kicked and strained and almost made it to his knees before I bit the underside of his bicep. He howled, and I waited for him to shift. He didn't. My only disappointment when he finally stopped fighting was that he didn't know it had been me who killed him.

I turned to assist with the other two guards, but S-272 beat me to it. I glanced over to the four remaining lab assistants, who cowered in a corner, their bodies visibly shaking. The lead scientist and the other assistant lay in bloody puddles.

S-272 had dealt with a great deal of loss during his time as a prisoner. His rage had grown day by day, and his wolf showed no mercy. It seemed odd that he allowed four to live, but the mess he'd left on the floor seemed enough punishment for those experiencing mental breakdowns in the corner.

When I turned to look at the Alpha, he was transitioning back to human. Carlos, a Beta with no desire to lead but fought like a demon possessed, had finished his shift. My wolf was stubborn and wanted to hunt for more prey. It required S-272 touching my shoulder and whispering "shift" before she relinquished herself to me.

I stared down at the pile of clothes. There hadn't been time to remove them before the shift, and now they were ripped and bloody.

"There are clean lab coats in one of the cabinets," I said, unsure what else to do as the three of us stood naked and bloody. "If the guards behind the cameras are paying attention, they'll see what happened and send more guards."

"We go as is." S-272 ripped the keycards off the shaking lab staff. "We'll need to shift again. Grab the keycards and clubs from the guards. We need to get to the second floor."

When Carlos opened the doors, the alarms went off.

# Chapter Twenty-Three

TEAMS Three and Four left the village just after midnight. Bella received a message from Team Two, who'd left on motorcycles earlier that day, that the C4 was in place, and they were watching the road from makeshift blinds with the motorcycles well hidden.

Devon wanted to take the hike up the mountain slowly. Based on their plans for a mid-day strike, they had plenty of time, and their ability to remain unobserved until they reached the parking lot was imperative.

Remus walked with him at the back of the teams, his mood pensive. "Do you believe Sergi and Carlos to still be alive?"

"I always do until proven otherwise." He gave Remus a side glance. "What of the shifters you've sent over the last year?"

Remus's brows knit together. He must have been thinking of them when he'd asked his original question. As leaders, their job was to always show strength and remain positive, especially with the Family or packs. Even if internally, they struggled with their own doubts.

In times like these, Devon had his cadre to share his concerns, and Remus had his Beta. It wasn't lost on Devon that, for this mission, and with Bella too focused on logistics, the two leaders only had each other to confide their concerns.

Remus's tone was contemplative. "Every day I think of each shifter I sent in search of this lab. I don't know if any of them made it as far as Carlos, though I suspect for some, the wild shifters proved to be too formidable. I don't know if what we uncover today will provide those answers, but if some were indeed captured, I have to believe some survived."

Devon stopped to face Remus. "Then let's hope we find the evidence we need. If we've lost shifters, we need to ensure their deaths will have been a noble sacrifice."

Remus laid a hand on Devon's shoulder. "Each step we take is for a noble cause. And I fear we'll lose more before this is all finished."

Devon, who had similar concerns, simply nodded and returned to the hike. There would be more losses to come, and possibly many more if he didn't find something solid that could be blamed on Venizi. The Council didn't take kindly to any form of slander, especially from a censured Council member.

An hour before dawn, Bella, who led the team up the mountain, made her way back to Devon. "Team One reported two cargo vans heading for the lab."

Remus was the first to respond. "Perhaps send four from our team to help Team Two, just in case. They can return once the situation is secured."

"Agreed." Devon hated to split the teams, but Remus was right. There was no telling what was in the vans. The last thing they needed was more guards being brought in. "Send two vampires and two shifters."

Devon called for a break while they waited for news. Even though he expected it, he jumped when an explosion interrupted the early chorus of birds as it echoed through the trees. Everyone turned toward the sound but held their positions. It didn't take long before a ping came from Bella's phone.

She answered it immediately. "Report." Within a few seconds, she responded. "Hold the line. Don't let anyone get past you. We're on our way."

When she turned to Devon, her expression was stone-cold hard. "The team is greatly outnumbered."

"Move out," Devon yelled, and they all raced for the road, which was a quarter mile away to their east.

With the rough terrain, it took five minutes to reach the road and then follow it to where Team Two had set the charges. Remus and the shifters had dropped their packs and morphed into wolves almost instantaneously with Remus's powerful magic. Remus's wolf let out a loud howl as they ran, which sent shivers along Devon's skin. Thank the heavens the shifters were on their side.

When they reached the cargo vans, the back door of one had been slid open. It was empty. He didn't have to run far before he saw the guards. Too many for the seven team members trying to hold them from getting past their line. Four wolves flanked the fighting to join what remained of Team Two while the remaining members of Teams Three and Four approached from behind, squeezing the guards between them.

Devon found one of his vampires leaning against a tree.

The vampire gasped for air. "I think there are shifters in the back of the other truck." He was severely injured, and with no healer or fresh blood source, Devon wasn't sure he'd make it.

Bella, who'd also ran up to check on the vampire met Devon's gaze with rage flashing in the dark yellow glow of her eyes. He nodded, and she was gone in a flash.

Devon turned to survey the situation, it was easy to see they were outnumbered, but the guards' fighting skills weren't anything special. The only reason they'd been effective was sheer volume.

The wolves wasted no time. They killed quickly before moving on, not bothering to howl or take relish in their kill.

Devon's vampires had already engaged the enemy, most fighting two or three at a time. This was bad. He couldn't afford to lose team members if they had any hope of infiltrating the facility. He spotted a vampire holding off four guards and losing ground.

He didn't have his sword, but he could do enough damage with his daggers. The wolves could finish the job. He swept in and grabbed one of the unsuspecting guards by the neck and stabbed him in the kidneys until he dropped, shoving him against one of the other guards.

The male lost his footing as he tried to catch the guard or step out of his way, it was difficult to tell which. It didn't matter because Devon was on him in a flash.

His rage was so violent, he didn't bother with a dagger and went for the vampire's throat. Fangs sank deep, and he ripped the flesh as he brought his dagger in for a strike to the heart. With any luck, the guard would bleed out if a wolf didn't finish him first.

The fight was bloody as Devon's team slowly beat back the guards over mounds of dirt and rock where the road had been decimated by the C4. Devon, now heavily engaged, lost track of who was winning or who was in trouble.

The rage he'd seen in Bella's gaze focused his own. His only mission at this exact moment was to take down as many guards as possible. He was so micro-focused that he was shocked when he was pushed aside as he closed in on a guard who'd sliced a shifter along its side, its fur stained red.

Devon didn't have time to turn toward the danger and grimaced when a dagger pierced his side before the guard was trampled by shifters. Not one or two, but as he glanced around, there were a dozen or more shifters than they'd brought on the mission. Then he saw Bella, running behind them with Remus's wolf at her side.

She'd made it to the back of the trucks and had released the captured shifters. After that, the battle was over quickly, but not without losses.

Remus's wolf let out a long, eerie howl that quieted the landscape. Not a single bird could be heard.

Devon dropped onto a log covered in moss to check his wound. There was blood, but not as much as he'd feared. The blade had caught his hip bone. It would take a few minutes for his body to heal, and he took the time to calm his beast.

Bella found him, staring at nothing in particular. "We lost two vampires and two shifters. Many are injured, but most can heal on their own. One vampire and two shifters are severely wounded. I don't think they'll make it without blood." When Devon didn't speak, she continued, "On a positive note, we've gained shifters. Remus has two shifters getting a count, including who they are and where they're from."

She waited, allowing Devon to digest the information and consider how this incident had changed their mission. They had been ahead of schedule before the explosion. It was likely at least one guard sent a message to the facility. They could be gathering guards to assist. But would they know Devon's team was aware of the blinds? Maybe they planned on waiting for the invading force to come to them, especially if they didn't hear back from their guards. They would have no way of knowing how many they would be battling. When he'd turned it over and over, he came to the same decision. Not much of their plan had changed. Bella was right. They might have lost some, but gained many more, assuming these new shifters could fight.

"Give the minimum blood required to heal the least wounded. Take half of what's left of our reserve and give to the three critically injured. We'll check their status in an hour."

"Yes, boss." She strode away. Bella was always better off with tasks to perform during emotional crises. She was still raging, and knowing his cadre as well as he did, that rage would hold until well after they infiltrated the labs.

He returned to reviewing their plan. Why would Venizi be trucking in shifters? Cressa's strange dream about a dinner on Lorenzo's island came to mind. The stranger at the table, who they suspected was someone from the lab, had mentioned experiments.

Was that what they were doing here? Not just creating drugs and serums but running live experiments?

If that were true, that might explain what happened to Remus's shifters. Once again, they sacrificed the most. He considered his options but required Remus's report before he could discuss changes in the plan. And of course, determine how many vampires could return to the mission after receiving bagged blood from the supply they'd brought with them.

He was so deep in thought, he knew someone sat next to him, but it took several minutes before he realized it was Remus.

When The Wolf seemed convinced that Devon was aware of him, he shared his report. "We were lucky to have only lost the four we did. I was able to get the worst of the injured wolves to shift a couple of times. The others were able to shift on their own. They should all be ready to continue in the next hour or two. I think your injured vampires will survive once they receive blood." When Devon merely nodded, Remus added, "Rafael fought as if he had a score to settle."

"More like guilt he needed to shake off."

Remus snorted as he moved to settle on the ground, leaning against the log, his face tilted up to the morning sun that barely reached the tips of the trees. "We were able to save two guards. And while this unforeseen event seems somewhat of a setback, it seems luck, or perhaps fate, is still on our side."

"Tell me most of the guards were from the lab and not new ones coming in."

"Not most. They were all from the lab. Apparently, their director doesn't trust outsiders. His decision to gather up more shifters didn't give their security team enough time to vet new guards."

"So, security at the labs has been compromised. How badly depends on the number of guards they had to start with."

"They've lost a third of their force."

Devon stared down at Remus, who was still focused on the

sky. His grin was slow in coming. "You were right. It is proving to be our lucky day. Who were the shifters from the trucks?"

Remus's head lifted, and when he turned his gaze to Devon, his eyes glowed a bright red. "They were taken from various packs. Some from Europe and some from the States. They were taken to a holding facility until they could be flown here."

"How many are willing to help us?"

Remus's eyes turned back to their natural brown color, and though he grinned, the sight of his fangs made The Wolf appear more frightening than comforting. "All of them."

Devon couldn't help his own smile, and to provide some male dominance behavior that Cressa would disapprove of, he included his own fangs. He didn't know if he should take it as a challenge that Remus simply chuckled. He let it go for the good humor it was and advised Remus of his updated plan.

"We'll give everyone a two-hour rest, then assign teams once we determine the healthiest from our previously planned strike team. At this point, and with the additional numbers, the rest of the team can take the road. The only problem is how close they can get before they're seen from any security cameras."

"I can have four shifters creep up through the forest and watch for our strike teams. Once the blind is taken, they can call up the rest of the team."

"That sounds like a plan." Devon stood and stretched. "I'm going to check on the wounded and try to get a few minutes sleep." He rubbed his stomach. "I miss Cook's food."

"He was good to make rations for us. Though they don't come close to a steak cooked bloody rare."

Devon chuckled. "Most dried food doesn't taste good. It's fortunate with our quick mission he didn't have to salt it too much."

He'd taken a few steps before Remus said, "You couldn't have known about the trucks. We only expected a possible supply truck, and no one could have anticipated the number of guards assigned to the cargo."

"We were already at risk of being noticed by the size of the team from the start." He turned back to Remus, his expression grim. "The mission has changed. We're not just infiltrating to grab evidence. We're taking the whole facility."

# Chapter Twenty-Four

WHEN THE ALARMS SOUNDED, I followed S-272 and Carlos as we broke into a run for the stairs. Several steps from reaching the door that S-272 held open, I stopped. Sergi needed evidence, and once the guards arrived, we'd be cut off from this level. I wasn't sure why they weren't already running down the corridors with rifles.

"Alex," S-272 urged. "We need to go. Once the shifters are released, we'll have the numbers to take over level two." His eyes darted to Carlos, who nodded. Had they agreed on some plan? When did they have time to talk? "We'll either hold the perimeter until help arrives, or we'll die like shifters."

Ah. That was one thing about shifters. When humans spoke about the fight or flight response, it always amused us. We didn't have a flight response.

I sensed his urgency, but I held my ground.

"I can't." What the hell was I doing? Evidence. It wasn't just Sergi that needed it. Once the vampires regained control, they'd continue their experiments. If they were forced to move, they'd rebuild a lab someplace else and start over. I couldn't let that happen. "We need evidence. Somebody has to be told what's happening here, but no one will believe us without proof."

Based on his expression, S-272 was about to argue, but Carlos stepped toward me. "She's right. We should be able to hold out until Devon arrives, but those running this place won't risk the discovery. They'll destroy all the evidence, and we can't let them do that. We need that proof. I'll go with her."

"No." I shook my head, my anxiety rising. "There's no time, and you don't know your way around the labs. I know exactly where to go to find what we need. Just let whoever's guarding the stairway know to let me through in case I can't shift before coming down."

Carlos stood back and waited for S-272 to make a decision.

"Be quick. Get yourself a lab coat so you look like one of them. And don't get caught." He looked at me, assessing, and though he might not like the choice I made, my backbone strengthened at the approval in his gaze. My wolf pranced at the unspoken praise.

Then, without a word, he turned and raced down the stairs.

Carlos's last glance was quite different, and I wasn't sure what I saw—regret, concern, support? It was hard to tell. I handed him the keycards I'd grabbed from the assistants, and he squeezed my arm before chasing after S-272, closing the door behind him.

I ran for the director's office but only made it past two doors before footsteps echoed down the hall. It sounded like they were running. I glanced around, searching for someplace to hide. The first door I tried was locked. Damn. I rushed to the second one, a storage closet, and stepped inside, closing the door to the barest inch. The vampires might be too far away to hear the lock engage, but I wasn't willing to take the chance.

My heart pounded in my ears, and I forced deeper breaths until my pulse slowed. I had to pull myself together. This was a mission. It might have been delayed a year, but the task I'd been assigned was happening. I had to act like the warrior I'd been trained to be. I could do this.

The words sounded good, but I couldn't stop the anxiety creeping over me when the footsteps drew near. Whoever it was never slowed, and once they were past the storage closet, I eased the door open and sighed with relief. Two lab techs were running to a safe location, which should be back to their rooms. It was something I'd overheard at the women's baths when I'd first arrived. One of the staff workers was new to the facility, and another female was answering questions about a possible raid, though one had never happened in the hundred years the lab had been in service.

If I remembered the conversation correctly, standard protocol for when the alarms sounded was to return to their room and lock the door. If they couldn't get to their room, there were several rooms on each level considered secure panic rooms—if they could make it to one.

Before leaving the storage closet, I listened for anyone else who might be out there. Another lab tech appeared but turned down a different hallway. I had to find clothing. A nude woman walking around the lab would certainly draw suspicions from anyone monitoring a security camera.

I continued down the hall toward the director's office and slipped into one of the smaller labs similar to the ones I'd cleaned before. This one was no different and was thankfully empty of staff.

I searched through the cabinets, feeling time ticking away. There had to be something to wear. I'd seen spare clothes in other labs in case of a mishap, and the second to the last cabinet finally rewarded my efforts. I slipped on a pair of scrub pants, a loose-fitting shirt, and a fresh lab coat. I'd kept a keycard and clipped it to the lapel.

I ran my fingers through my hair. It had been a couple of days since my last bathing privilege, one of the perks of working on level one. The staff didn't like the stink of unwashed shifters. Once again, I slowly opened the door in time to see two staff rushing toward me.

I would have panicked, but they looked terrified, their eyes huge behind their glasses.

"Get to your room," the male yelled as he rushed by.

The female behind him said nothing, but her quick glance my way said it all. It was everyone for themselves. I grinned. The odds were still against us, but not having to fight the staff worked in our favor.

I was passing the second main lab where some of the experiments had been held and stopped. The director's office would have the evidence Sergi needed, but what about all the vials? What if he was still trapped on level three? It wouldn't take long to grab a few samples.

I used the keycard to open the doors but only made it a few steps when the familiar click of nails on hard surface made me turn around. Three wolves stood at the doorway, their eyes alert. When they saw me, their hackles rose, and I lifted my hands.

"I'm shifter S-473. I'm searching for evidence. You need to be on level two. That's where we're making our stand."

Their raised fur lowered, but they were cautious as they drew closer, noses lifted in the air, trying to catch my scent. I'd have to let them get a lot closer. The smell of disinfectant in the labs made it difficult for shifters to get a good scent.

Once they were within a couple of feet of me, their tails wagged as one licked my hand.

When I tried to shoo them away, they stood their ground.

"Fine. But once I find what I need in here, you need to get below. We need your help holding the lower levels and can't afford to lose you to the guards."

Before I could return to my task, two guards slid to a stop at the doorway. *Unbelievable.* They lifted their rifles, but there wasn't enough distance between them and us, and the wolves didn't hesitate. They raced to meet the guards, and I caught the fear in the guards' eyes.

They managed to each get a shot off. One went wide as I ducked behind the closest counter. One of the wolves yelped and fell on their side, but then it was up. A small trickle of blood marred its coat, but it was probably nothing more than a flesh wound.

The guards never got another shot.

I blocked out their screams and focused on my mission. If the staff changed the codes, this would all be for naught, but I typed in the numbers I'd memorized. I grinned when the light turned green, and the door popped open.

I pulled out several trays from the shelves and placed them on the counter. The first tray of vials held human blood. I set it and another aside and checked other trays until I found vials marked with an S, which I believed to be an earlier version of the shifter serum.

The next step was to check the locked cabinet near the fridge. Bingo.

A tray of vials marked with MP—Magic Poppy—sat front and center. They probably kept it handy for Gheata in case he wanted to give Sergi another dose. I pulled it out and looked for the last item Sergi would need. My gut wrenched when the other vials had labels that didn't follow the same naming convention, and I didn't have time to speculate what they might be. On the top shelf, pushed toward the back, was a single tray of Blood Poppy. And not just any Blood Poppy, but the ones marked BP-X. I didn't know why they kept it stored in the back, but considering how addictive Sergi said it was, perhaps the lab techs thought, "Out of sight, out of mind."

I brought the trays over to where I'd put the other trays aside, then grabbed towels from the storage cabinet. I decided to take three vials each of the Magic Poppy, the Blood Poppy, and the shifter serum. Not knowing how much blood Sergi might need, I decided to take a dozen vials of the human blood. I wouldn't be able to carry more than that.

I tightly wrapped the vials so they wouldn't jostle and break, then wrapped them again, creating two bundles. They barely fit into the pockets of my lab coat.

I was on my way out when I heard a whimper. I spun around. The sound was coming from behind the island. I peered over the top and found a man huddled in the corner of two cabinets. He wore a lab coat, and that was all I needed to know as I raced around the island.

When he lifted his head, I grinned. I recognized that face, though his expression was filled with terror rather than his normal arrogance.

"Well, hello, Leonard."

He screamed, "I was only doing my job."

A hundred different responses raced through my head. None of them mattered. I'd seen the excited anticipation each time a shifter was led into the room. His glee as he walked around them, caged like an animal, as he decided the most painful spot to inject their poison.

I'd spent many nights thinking of ways to kill him. I turned toward the doorway as I heard the tell-tale sound of nails and low growls. Their muzzles were stained with blood from the guards.

Their eyes glowed with the bright crimson of rage and blood lust.

This wasn't my kill.

I grabbed the collar of Leonard's lab coat and dragged him out of the corner to the center of the lab. I snatched his keycard and tossed it on the ground by the wolves.

I faced them, and their eyes locked with mine.

"He's all yours."

I turned and walked away, ignoring Leonard's pleas for mercy. I never looked back as his cries turned to whimpers, more shouts of pleas, and then screams of agony as he was ripped apart.

I smiled with satisfaction as I broke into a run.

∾

WHEN THE ALARMS RANG, Sergi encouraged the two freed shifters to follow his orders to free the other shifters and secure the third level before the guards came. His instinct was to race directly to level one, but someone had to get all the shifters out of their cells. He would have to trust that Alex could protect herself.

Five minutes later, he continued to work his way down the hall on level two, stopping at each door to open it. Many of the cells were empty, but there were too many that weren't. When he found a shifter inside, he went through his practiced speech.

"I'm Sergi. Cadre for House Trelane and your liberator. Come out and join your pack. We're taking this facility."

He waited long enough to ensure the shifter heard, but he didn't wait while they made their choice whether to join or remain in their cell. He simply moved to the next one and ignored his internal clock that said he was losing his opportunity to find evidence. When he reached the end of the hall, he turned back to find six wolves who'd left their cells. They lifted their snouts to catch his scent.

"We need to flush out any guards who might be down here." He pointed down a hallway to their left. "The guards' quarters should be that way. I'll open some more cells, but it wouldn't hurt to find more keycards."

A thin brown wolf with matted fur yipped, and the four raced away in the direction Sergi had pointed.

He opened a few more cells, his mind elsewhere. If Alex had made it down to the second level, he hadn't seen her. If she'd been in wolf form, she would have made herself known. He might have missed her, but he worried she was still on the upper level.

Where he needed to be.

He reached the end of the hallway and decided he'd released

enough shifters to get the rest out on their own. He tossed his keycard to one of the shifters who hadn't morphed into his wolf. He grabbed it, nodded, and ran for the next hallway.

Sergi, free to accomplish his own goal, jogged in the opposite direction, circling back to the stairs. He wasn't expecting the two naked males striding toward him. He didn't know the one on the right, but he recognized the other one.

"Carlos. It's good to see you. I thought you were on level three." Sergi shook his hand.

"And shouldn't you be on your way to contact Devon?" Carlos noticed Sergi eyeing the other shifter and said, "Sergi, this is S-272. He's an Alpha who's been here a long time."

"So, this is Sergi who I've heard so much about. You can call me Cadfael. Though in here, as I'm sure you've figured out, they call us by numbers." He shook Sergi's hand. "But Carlos is right. Did you not find the door?"

Sergi studied the old shifter, and though the face didn't register, his name did. "Are you the same Cadfael from the Buckholt uprising?"

The shifter smiled. "You heard the stories?"

Sergi scratched his chin and matched the shifter's grin. "I might have been in Monmouth about the same time."

Cadfael assessed Sergi as if altering his original perception of the vampire. "Alex was right about you. I can sense it even without knowing about your mission. But you can't stay. This all depends on you getting word out."

Sergi nodded. "Agreed. But I can't leave without evidence. The House running this operation won't risk information getting out. They'll make every attempt to destroy it."

Cadfael wasn't pleased but couldn't argue. "I can send a couple wolves with you."

Sergi shook his head. "It won't be necessary." He tapped his shoulder harness. "I do better with daggers."

"Of that, I have no doubt. We'll continue to consolidate a defense once we have everyone out."

The old shifter took a step before Sergi stepped into his path.

"Where's Alex?"

Cadfael studied him for another minute as if he'd missed something with his last perusal. His expression gave nothing away, but Sergi caught a bit of mischief in the shifter's steady gaze. "She's still on the first floor. She's looking for evidence, too."

"I need to get up there. They're probably sending guards in small groups to clear rooms."

Cadfael gave him that odd look for another moment, then nodded. "If you insist on delaying your departure, I have a small request before you search for Alex."

# Chapter Twenty-Five

THE SOUND of pounding boots grew closer, and though I wasn't far from the director's office, it wasn't worth the risk, and I slipped into another room. I expected a lab, but instead of test tubes, microscopes, and a laptop running data, this room was filled with filing cabinets.

Curious about what might be in the files in this day of databases, I opened a couple to find reams of notes that appeared to be the results of various experiments. Most of the handwritten notes were unreadable, with scientific terminology and acronyms I didn't understand.

The information was useless. While it might be readable by more knowledgeable people, Sergi couldn't walk through the Carpathians with a backpack of paper files. I might not be able to understand the files, but I did note the date—1947. I scanned files in several cabinets. The dates were scattered, but I didn't find anything later than the 1990s. This room held the data on everything they'd done in this facility from its conception up until computers. I guess they'd never gotten around to converting them.

The hallway had grown quiet. Thankfully, someone had shut off the alarms. I raced past a few offices before running into the director's office, surprised the door was open. But if he had been in the office, I doubt he thought of anything more than getting to the command center or a panic room.

Before I shut the door, I heard a distant shot followed by howls. Not just one wolf but several. They might have been the ones who delivered justice to Leonard. There would be a great deal of atonement being served today.

I leaned against the closed door and scanned the room. It was messier than the last time I'd been here. I ignored the lab side. It was obvious the director was dabbling with something, but I had enough samples. And his written notes, even recent ones, wouldn't be enough.

What I needed were files like the documents I'd just reviewed in the file room. Data that identified all the experiments being run and their purpose—their end game.

I slid into the director's desk chair and snorted. The vampire must have been too terrorized by the alarms to do anything but run for safety. He seemed the twitchy type. He didn't even take the few seconds required to shut down his laptop.

All the better for me. No password required. I wasn't a computer geek, but I knew my way around them. The best place to start was the files directory. There were hundreds of folders, most with nondescript names. I kept glancing at the door, concerned the guards would start going room by room to search for lab staff and shifters.

My knee bounced as I scrolled up and down the list of folders and, once again, had to force myself to breathe and calm down. I moved the mouse to the top of the folders, and rather than quickly scan, I read each folder name out loud, letting it sink in. I almost laughed when my cursor fell on a folder marked BPX.

I opened the folder and found numerous files that consisted of dozens of spreadsheets and data tables. This was what I needed. What Sergi needed. He might be long gone now and, with any luck, was racing down the mountain to contact his House. It would be days before someone came, but if I could save the data, there was a chance I could keep it safe until help arrived.

I searched for a USB drive, but the desk was so messy it was like searching for a specific seashell on a mile-long beach. Every drawer was like the junk drawer everyone had at home. There weren't any in the center desk drawer, and after searching the drawers on the right, I found several in a box at the back of a drawer on the left side.

I grabbed one, and after three attempts because my hand wouldn't stop shaking, I pushed the drive into the slot. When the contents of the drive popped up, there was already a folder on it. It was labeled SMP, with the last active date from a month ago. The ticking clock in my head said to ignore it, but my gut said something else.

I clicked on the folder to open it, and a knot gripped my stomach as my wolf scratched to be let out. To hunt. To kill. I didn't have to scan the list of files to know what they were about. Several of them clearly stated "shifter" in the file name.

I closed the folder and started transferring the BPX file. There would be plenty of time to review the SMP files once it was in safe hands. I groaned when the pop-up message showed five minutes to complete. It was an estimate and might finish sooner. Was luck still on my side? When my bouncing leg increased its rhythm, I jumped up to work off my pent-up energy.

I had finished my second long pace across the room, stopping to check the transfer status at each turn, when the door opened. I swung around, expecting to see one or two guards, but it was a single male that filled the doorway.

My heart hammered at the sight of him, and I took a step back. I should have hidden under the desk while waiting, not paraded around, knowing guards were roaming the halls. The male took two steps inside before stopping to scan the room. His sinister smile was enough to make my insides melt.

Gheata. The torturer.

Once he was satisfied we were alone, he walked toward me as I moved away, taking one step for each of his until my back touched the corner of the desk. I didn't dare look at the computer. Not that it mattered anymore. I could shift, but it would take too long. Even though the power of the Alpha ran through me, which reduced the time to shift, the male staring me down wasn't some lab tech with illusions of bravery.

This was a stone-cold killer.

"Where are you going, little wolf?" The male's tone was menacing but held a hint of humor. His head tilted to the side as he considered me. "I know you."

He took another step but stopped, quite aware that he blocked my exit. He'd left the door open, but any wolves that had been on this floor should have evacuated to the second floor once they'd completed their search for other shifters.

S-272 and Carlos would know I hadn't made it back to the second floor, but they wouldn't sacrifice the pack. The odds would be against them. It didn't matter who my uncle was. They would only mount a rescue if there were a reasonable probability of success. The stakes were too high. The shifter race was in jeopardy.

"You're the little wolf who cleaned the cells." His expression turned hard. "You cleaned the traitor's cell."

I assumed the traitor was meant to be Sergi.

"Why are you here, little wolf? Why would you be on this level at all?"

I considered the question. Maybe I could talk my way into a holding cell. At least I'd be alive, but for how long?

"I clean the labs." I kept my head lowered and my voice small. Let him think I'm weak.

He nodded. "I remember now. Level three in the morning and labs in the afternoon. But why would you be here in the director's office?"

That was a good question, but at least we agreed there was a reason for me to be on this level.

"When the alarms went off, I ran like everyone else. I didn't know where to go that would be safe." I barely whispered my response, knowing he would still hear it, but with my wolf snarling at him, I wasn't sure I could pull off shaky and intimidated. I should have been terrified by this male who had a good foot in height over me, but my survivor's instinct wouldn't be smothered.

Not this time.

He chuckled. "Well, it looks like this room wasn't the safe harbor you were seeking." His eyes roamed over me, and lust filled his eyes. Really? The shifters were uprising, and he thought now would be a good time for rape?

Maybe he'd just drag me to a cell for later, once he stopped the wolves. I pushed his threat aside, though it gave me one opening. I backed up until the desk was between him and me. I glanced down long enough to see the file transfer had finished. Now, all I had to do was grab it without him seeing. Yeah. No problem.

I scanned the desk for a weapon and spotted exactly what I needed. He'd easily dodge it, but it might get his eyes off me for long enough. When he took a step toward me, I grabbed the brass award sitting on the corner of the desk. I had no idea what it was for, only caring that the object, not much bigger than a softball, was hefty enough.

I threw it, aiming for his head, and while he easily ducked it, he took his eyes off me to watch its trajectory. I grabbed the USB and stuffed it in my pocket, underneath the bulky package of vials.

He moved faster than I expected for someone of his size, even if he was a vampire. He came at me from the left, and I waited until he rounded the corner of the desk before I raced for the door. I was halfway to it before he grabbed my lab coat and yanked me toward him.

I screamed as he swung me around and pushed me until my back hit the edge of the desk. He leaned his body into mine.

"Where did you think you could run to, little wolf?" He bent and sniffed me. "Did you know the smell of fear invigorates me? And yours will make this so much better."

Great. Not just a vampire, but one with a freaky kink. When he moved to position himself between my legs, I did what any self-respecting female would do—I kneed him in his junk.

My wolf was riding the surface, eager to shift, and the power she gave me made the slam to his privates hard enough to make him step back, howling with rage. I was sure to pay for that, but for now, it was a sweet moment.

I shoved him back and took three steps to the door before he caught the damn lab coat again and hauled me back. With my feet still stable beneath me, instead of fighting his pull, I forced myself backward and slammed into him and followed it with a stomp on his instep.

His curse showered hot breath on my cheek before his grip on me loosened, but once again, he grabbed me with another hand, and this time, he threw me against the desk, bending me over the top of it.

Something stabbed my cheek as my head landed on the desk. I dragged my hands over the desk as if trying to gain my footing but searching for anything to fight back with. He only had one hand on the desk, his body pinning me to it, while his other hand fumbled for his zipper.

My fingers grasped something slick and pointy. A letter opener by the feel of it.

He pulled my hair back as I continued to struggle. "The more you fight, the angrier I get. I'll still get my pleasure whether you have broken bones or not."

Maybe, but I wasn't going down without a fight. I gripped the letter opener and, with one quick thrust, slammed it into the vampire's hand.

He howled with rage and, with a forceful yank, pulled me away from the desk and tossed me across the room. I hit the side of the island with enough force I heard glass rattle, and something heavy hit the floor. My back screamed with pain, and I crawled away, trying to get distance between us while getting my feet underneath me.

He was on top of me before I gained a foot. I twisted to face him, hoping to find an opening, but he pulled me up by my hair and slammed a fist into the side of my head. I went limp from the pain. He grabbed my arm, pulled me up, and threw me again. This time, I hit the bookcase, and it knocked the wind out of me.

He went for my hair again, and I tensed, letting my body sag. It wasn't difficult. Pain radiated from every part of my body, and my vision blurred. He managed to grip a handful of hair and half-lifted me, but his hand suddenly released me, and not expecting it, my head hit the floor.

I only had a moment to see another guard pulling him off me before everything went dark.

# Chapter Twenty-Six

SERGI GAWKED AT CADFAEL. "I'm not sure what I was expecting, but a request for my opinion on battle tactics wasn't one of them. Especially from a battle-tested Alpha."

Carlos's brows lifted, but like the eager group of shifters who surrounded them, he said nothing.

Cadfael chuckled. "You give me more credit for that long-ago uprising, but I have to admit, it's been some time since I've had to worry about such things. Besides, who better to offer options on holding vampires at bay than another vampire."

Sergi bowed his head, but he couldn't help but be pleased. "I'd be honored." He shifted his stance so while he was responding to Cadfael, any shifters within a ten-foot radius would be able to hear. They hovered about in both human and wolf form, milling about in small groups or racing up and down the halls, haunted shadows buried deep in their eyes. Some probably hadn't been out of their cells for months. A look he was well-versed with from memories he kept locked away. But they all had one thing in common—a fierce glow in their gaze. They wouldn't go down easy.

He refocused on Cadfael. "How many shifters do you have?"

Cadfael considered the question. "Forty-six have reported in, but a few came out of their cells as wolves and haven't shifted, so the count is a handful more than that. I haven't used my full Alpha powers yet. I thought I'd give them time to settle on their own."

Sergi nodded. Though they might not shift back to human for days, they could still help the cause. For now, the group's first concern would be preventing the guards from infiltrating this level. The guards would be armed with tranquilizers and live rounds. "Alex said there were two staircases and one elevator?"

"That's right. And the back door on level three. We currently have twelve shifters holding positions at the other staircase and the elevator."

"Do we need to worry about the guards gaining access to level three without going past your perimeters on this level?"

"We don't believe so."

Sergi grunted. The last thing they needed were guards flanking them from below. "You might want those wolves who refuse to shift to spend their time running around level three."

"I think two are already down there." Cadfael pointed at Carlos. "Can you round up the others?"

"I'll take care of it. I also wanted to add that I've checked both armories. There weren't a lot of weapons, but we have several handguns, ten rifles, and about a dozen automatics."

"What about ammo or explosives?" Sergi asked.

"There's plenty of ammo, but that depends on what the guards will do. I didn't see any explosives. There are plenty of knives, but the shifters prefer to fight as wolves."

Sergi considered the information. "I agree the shifters in their wolf form is an advantage, but I suggest a mix of wolves and shifters with weapons to protect the access points. My other concern is that they might want to starve you out. Most of you haven't eaten well as it is. I believe there are small cafeterias on levels two and three. You might want to have someone responsible for rationing."

Cadfael nodded as Sergi gave his opinions. "I agree. Carlos, I'll ask you to find someone to take charge of the food and water inventory. But our first priority should be to focus on our perimeters. The elevator will be our weakest point. There's a limit to how many guards can fit, but they'll be better armed and could have tear gas or smoke bombs."

Sergi nodded along with Cadfael. "The guards could use similar methods at the stairs."

Cadfael considered his point as he tugged on an ear, his eyes glowing a soft red. "What we need are blockades at each entrance."

"Use whatever you can find to block specific corridors at those locations. Force them to go where you want them to go."

"Set up an ambush." Carlos grinned. "We need the shifters who know these corridors the best."

If Rafael had escaped, Devon should be on his way with a rescue team, but Sergi couldn't take that chance. Devon would be prepared, but it would still take several days to get a team to Romania. "You should plan to hold off the guards for at least two weeks."

Cadfael shook his head this time, his expression grim. "It will take you several days to find a town where you can contact your House leader."

"I'm not new to the Carpathians. I've fought many battles here over the centuries. I also studied the geography before coming here."

"And we have our trackers," Carlos chimed in.

"Trackers?" Cadfael asked.

Sergi pointed to a spot just above his left wrist. "Carlos and I were implanted with GPS trackers. We also had a third team member. I don't know if he made it out alive. Either way, Devon will already be planning a rescue. He knows Carlos and I have been in one position for too long, but he won't know why. He might think we're dead, or—" He glanced up and waved his arm to emphasize the entire facility. "Something is blocking our transmitters, and he'll want to know why our signal stopped."

"If that's the case—" Carlos looked at Cadfael, "—once Sergi is outside the facility, his tracker should work again, and they'll know there was a dead zone between where he went in and where he came out."

Cadfael nodded, his expression brightening. "And they'll suspect the lab is between the two signals."

"That's my belief." Sergi felt time starting to press in on him. He still had one objective, then he caught himself. He had two objectives, and the thought startled him.

His primary mission had shifted once he'd been captured. Now that he was inside, he had to find some piece of evidence. If the director thought the facility was compromised, they could destroy all evidence and restart somewhere else. He couldn't leave without an attempt.

Then there was Alex. Still somewhere on level one, perhaps trapped. Maybe dead. And when the thought hit him, his chest tightened. She'd saved him. Had endangered her own welfare to help him. He knew she saw him as the shifter's one way out, but that didn't matter. He couldn't betray her belief in him by running away.

He looked at Cadfael, who, along with Carlos, was already issuing commands to other shifters.

Cadfael turned to him. "It's time for you to get to the back door. Your House leader might attempt an approach from that side if he sees your signal. There are no roads, and the terrain is difficult. It will take longer for them to arrive."

Sergi shook his head and couldn't help but give the shifter a wicked grin. "Coming through the back door isn't Devon's usual style. Besides, as I've already told you, my mission isn't complete without finding evidence for the Council." He hesitated, then added, "And Alex is still missing. I can't leave without getting her to safety."

Cadfael's face was grim. "They'll have guards positioned at the stairs and elevators, just like us."

"We can use the air vents," Carlos suggested. When Sergi and Cadfael looked at him, he shrugged, but his cheeks reddened, and he shrugged. "I watch a lot of movies."

"You'll want to find an air vent in the guards' quarters. You'll be closer to the labs," Cadfael offered.

"What about the director's office?" Sergi asked.

"Try a vent near the guards' community room. That should get you close."

Sergi nodded. "Alright." He started to walk away.

Cadfael touched his arm. "We'll need a sign that it's you coming back down the vent."

"Trust me. You'll know it's me."

Carlos waved to one of the shifters, who moved through the handful of others with an armored vest, an automatic weapon, and a handgun. "These won't protect you from tranquilizer darts, but my guess is you'll run into some guards walking the halls."

Sergi put on the vest without question but refused the weapons. He tapped the daggers tucked inside his harness. "I expect the guards have relied on their weapons for too long. I'll be fine with my daggers."

It wouldn't be the first time he'd gotten through a group of vampires, and while he suspected most had some martial arts training, he didn't think they'd be as skilled as he was. Except for one. One he hoped to find during his collection of evidence.

Before leaving, he gave Carlos one order. "If I'm not back in one hour, you'll need to use the back door. You won't have to go far, but I suggest staying outside for at least thirty minutes. Bella should pick up your signal by then."

Carlos nodded. "Agreed."

With a quick nod to Cadfael, Sergi turned and ran for the guards' common room.

When he arrived, there were several shifters inside, and they'd divided the room between a break room and a makeshift medical unit. A couple wolves had been injured fighting the guards who'd been on this level. He ignored them as he studied the vent in the middle of the ceiling.

When he began moving a table underneath it, a shifter stopped him.

"What are you doing, vampire?" The shifter was tall and, if he had to guess, had once been a large, muscular male, but he'd been here for some time, and most of his muscle mass was gone. It was a wonder that any of them could still shift.

"I'm going up to level one." He didn't want to get into this conversation.

"We need Cadfael's approval first."

"I just left him at the main staircase, and we agreed on the plan. I'm not going to waste time explaining it to you."

"How do we know you're not joining their forces?"

"Would it matter? What can I tell them? How many shifters are down here? How many are building defenses? Don't you think they'd already know that?"

"You're the prisoner from level three," another shifter said.

He nodded. "Would it help if I said I was going up to search for Alex?" When they stared at him without recognition, he shook his head. "You might know her as shifter S-473."

Not all recognized her given number, but several did. A female shifter pushed through the men. "How do you know S-473?"

She looked in bad shape. Her eyes were hollowed out, and he didn't have to question the torment she'd lived through.

"She's the one who released me."

The shifters stared at each other then pitched in as they pulled the table into position.

Sergi jumped on the table and studied the vent.

"I need a chair and something to release these screws."

Someone lifted a chair onto the table, and the first shifter who'd questioned him dug into his pocket and handed him a small Swiss Army Knife. "I found this in one of the guard's rooms."

Sergi took it and, within a minute, had the screws removed and the vent opened. It wasn't a large opening, but he'd fit.

He bent down to return the knife, but the shifter refused.

"We're still searching the rooms and lockers for weapons and tools. You might need that later."

"I'm planning on coming back this way, but be prepared in case it's not me."

"How will we know?"

He grinned as he had with Cadfael. "You'll know."

He lifted himself into the vent and, after glancing left, crawled in the opposite direction. He traversed the vent, moving quickly until he came to a cross-section with a vertical vent coming up from the third level and stretching up to the first. This vent was wider than the one he'd been crawling through, which would make it easier for his large frame.

He pulled himself out of the horizontal vent until he was able to sit up, using his forearms and upper shoulders to prevent him from slipping downward. This was the tricky part, but it wasn't the first time he'd had to shimmy up something.

Taking a deep breath, he released it and, applying pressure on the vertical shaft, slowly moved his body upward. Once his knees cleared the horizontal vent, he was able to use his feet to leverage his body and push up to begin his ascent.

He chuckled as he slowly rose, remembering being in a similar position with Devon. It had been centuries earlier, and they'd sneaked into the castle of an enemy House to steal documents. He'd questioned Devon why he was going on the mission rather than assigning someone else.

"Don't you trust your warriors?" Sergi had asked.

"Of course I do." Devon had growled his response, but it hadn't shaken Sergi. The first few years as Devon's Captain of the Guard, he braced himself for a punch that never came. Over those years, he watched Devon, learning everything he could about his new general.

Devon was young, though truth be told, he wasn't that much younger than Sergi. But Sergi had fought more battles and was more seasoned. Yet, over time, Devon proved to be intelligent, strategic, daring, and worthy of leadership. He was also head-strong, and while he listened to his commanders, he couldn't always override his emotions, though, with time, he learned to control them.

Devon was also one of the few generals Sergi had served under who also led with compassion and understanding, which made him a stronger leader. One who made others loyal to him, not out of fear but with the confidence he instilled in them.

Sergi squinted at Devon. "Did your Father request you do this yourself?"

Devon turned away from him and picked up a clay pitcher, pouring wine into two brass cups. He slammed one of the cups on the table in front of Sergi, who lifted a brow.

"Father asked that I send the most reliable. Males who had the best chance of not getting caught."

"I can think of several off the top of my head. Yet, you chose yourself and me." When Devon didn't respond, Sergi's eyes narrowed. "I can understand why you chose me, so tell me the rest. Who else do you have to confide in?"

Devon's eyes glowed with the icy blue of his beast. That didn't scare Sergi, either. "Maybe I want to do something more than sit in this damn chair and give orders."

Sergi held it for as long as he could before he burst out laughing. The memory made Sergi chuckle again as he glanced down the shaft. He could see the junction below, and when he looked up, his target was within sight.

Their escape from the castle required descending a stone shaft with a drop a lot farther down than the two floors he'd fall if he lost traction. He reached the junction, and with a slight twist of his body, he was once again moving along the air shaft, searching for the first vent opening.

When he reached it, he tilted his head to get an idea of where he was. There was a room to his left, and he was just able to read the number on the plaque—134. He moved quickly toward the next vent, repeating his actions to find a room number—142. He wasn't sure whether that meant he was getting closer to the director's office, but he noted that he hadn't seen or heard anyone in the hallway. He passed two more vents, and at the third one, he did the one thing that was sure to alert anyone close. He punched through the vent cover.

It hit the floor with a metallic sound that reverberated through the corridor. He jumped down and landed in a crouch, pulling out his daggers as he scanned both directions. The only sound was a soft shuffle from the door to his left.

Curious, he opened the door, prepared to engage a guard. Instead, the lab, no bigger than a bedroom, appeared empty. Except for the tip of a shoe that bounced up and down. Not a guard. A terrified staff member.

He glanced over the island counter. Two sets of horror-stricken eyes stared up at him. He put a finger to his lips to keep them quiet. Their fear faded, and he assumed the guard's uniform had something to do with it.

It could be a fatal mistake to assume he was on their side simply because of his clothing. But he wasn't here as their judge, jury, or executioner as long as they didn't interfere with his plans.

"Stay here, but stay farther back in the corner. I saw the tip of your shoe. Can't you lock the door?"

"We didn't think we had time." The female said, her voice a tremor. Then she looked sheepish. "Then we were too scared to move."

He sighed. "Lock it behind me. The halls seem clear, but it's best you stay here until told otherwise."

When they both nodded, he left, shutting the door behind him. Another thought urged him to reopen the door, almost smacking into the female.

"To be honest, this is only my second day on the job. I was told to check the rooms all the way to the director's office, but I'm not sure where that is."

Her face brightened, seemingly eager to help. "Oh, you're almost there. The door is just past the next hallway."

He nodded. "Now lock it and just remain quiet." He pulled the door closed and continued down the hall in the direction he'd already been heading. His actions with the two lab members didn't follow his normal behavior. Any other time, he would have barked an order to stay put and stay quiet. Or he might have ignored the bouncing foot and shut the door.

There was no doubt they were doing bad things here, but how much did the staff know? Could some of the staff be unaware of the facility's true purpose? His leaving them without saying a word would have been sufficient, but he'd taken the time to go in, and what? Ease their minds? All he did was ensure they remained quiet. Then he returned to ask for directions. *Gah!* It was obvious he'd lost his senses.

Then he cursed when he realized why he'd done it.

Cressa.

Simone had warned him that working so closely with humans would change them. Change the House. He'd sneered at the time, and yet, she'd been right. Cressa's influence on the House had changed them all. Devon the most. And he grimaced with the truth—House Trelane was a better House because of it. A House to lead vampire society into the future.

He found the entire situation irritating, though a slight grin touched his lips. Devon had never been happier since the day Cressa had entered the manor. She'd also saved him from his own beast and had proven her loyalty over and over again. But Sergi would be damned if he'd show her any gratitude. It would only embarrass them both. Most wouldn't understand, but their constant bickering was their way of paying respect to the other.

He was two doors away from the open double doors at the end

of the hall when he heard the yelps and the shattering of wood. He'd have heard it sooner if he hadn't been wallowing over emotions better off ignored.

He ran the rest of the way in time to watch Gheata throw a female against a bookcase. In a short period of time, he'd come to know her thick, ebony hair by sight alone.

Alex.

When Gheata reached for her hair, a growl rose in Sergi's throat. In two long strides, he released the beast.

# Chapter Twenty-Seven

SERGI GRABBED Gheata by the scruff of his shirt and yanked him off Alex. The powerful force, fueled by rage, was enough to slam Gheata into the counter. The male hadn't been expecting it, and he shook his head before glancing up. He sneered at Sergi, but he didn't have time to react.

Sergi glimpsed Alex, slowly rising to her feet. She pressed a hand to her head and teetered but managed to stand. Thankful she was alright, his focus returned to Gheata, who had risen to his knees. Sergi grabbed his shirt in one hand, his belt in the other, and threw the interrogator across the room, where he crashed into the desk.

Gheata didn't stay down and quickly settled into a defensive posture. His face was red, his eyes narrowed into slits, but he was enjoying this. "I should have known it was you."

Sergi shrugged. "Up to now, it hasn't been a fair fight."

"It wasn't meant to be." Gheata flew at Sergi, his fists coming fast, and Sergi blocked most of them while getting in a few punches of his own.

They broke apart and circled each other. Sergi caught a glimpse of Alex behind Gheata. She'd backed into the far corner of the lab and gripped some type of weapon. When he turned his attention back to Gheata, the male grinned.

"Your little wolf slut somehow managed to set you free. I told the director he was too lenient with the slaves. Was giving them too much responsibility. They should have been manacled with just enough chains to accomplish their tasks like the good little doggies they are. But he didn't want to upset the scientists. There's nothing I hate more than weak vampires." His laugh was filled with vitriol. "Except for shifters."

"You talk too much." Sergi dove at him, and though Gheata's punches connected, Sergi barely felt them. The beast shook them off, and it was growing tired of the game. Concerned guards might show up, Sergi pulled a dagger and sliced across Gheata's belly. A streak of crimson followed in its path.

Gheata never looked down. "Now's who's cheating."

"I simply thought it was time for my own interrogation." Sergi advanced and blocked Gheata's fist but misjudged him when Gheata stepped back and landed a solid kick to Sergi's midsection.

He flew backward and slammed into the table, knocking over chairs, but miraculously stayed on his feet. The distance between them gave him an edge as Gheata charged. Sergi spun and delivered a high kick that connected with Gheata's jaw.

Before Gheata could react, he stepped in and swung out with a dagger, slicing Gheata's bicep. In a flash, he pulled out his second dagger and sliced upward, catching flesh as Gheata pushed away from Sergi.

Sergi twirled his daggers as the two vampires circled each other. The pain radiating from his chest didn't bother him. It fed the beast, stoking its anger and cries for revenge. And for the first time, there was a flicker of uncertainty in Gheata's eyes.

And Sergi struck.

I PUSHED AGAINST THE DARKNESS, my wolf whining, forcing me back to consciousness. The danger still existed. I opened my eyes, focusing on a chair leg, then the chair, until my eyesight cleared. And the previous minutes returned in a rush. A guard had pulled Gheata off me.

A body flew by, and it took me another few seconds before the guard came into view. But it wasn't a guard.

Sergi.

Mixed feelings roiled in my head and gut. The first was irritation that Sergi hadn't left to get help. Then gratitude as a strange warmth filtered through me. If he had left, I'd be dead—or worse.

Not that this outcome was assured, but the red glow in Sergi's gaze didn't scare me. It gave me hope. I scrambled to my feet, not wanting to be a casualty in their battle, but I teetered when I stood, my equilibrium off balance, and grabbed the bookshelf I'd been slammed against for support.

Punches and kicks were flying at incredible speeds, and I forced my limbs to work as I edged around the room, moving toward the safety of the lab area. I kept my eye on the battle as I searched the drawers and cabinets for a weapon. Anything I could use for defense. The third drawer revealed a pair of scissors, and I grabbed them. I inched my way to a corner behind the island and watched the battle escalate.

I considered releasing my wolf, but I didn't want to take off the lab coat with its pockets filled with the evidence Sergi had most likely come searching for. Worry gripped me when I realized the vials could be broken. I'd wrapped them well, but I hadn't planned on being tossed around the room. I checked both pockets, and nothing felt wet. My fingers scraped the USB drive, and relief grounded me.

Sergi kicked Gheata in the stomach, and as the interrogator doubled over, Sergi raced in and stabbed him in the kidney.

Gheata roared but didn't go down, and when he turned to grab Sergi, he was waiting for it. He spun and delivered a roundhouse kick that clocked Gheata on the chin and, unfortunately, sent him flying in my direction.

When he slammed into me, I pushed him with one hand, then remembered the scissors in the other, and I jammed them into his gut. When he stepped away, glancing down at his wound, I ducked in and stabbed again. I'd aimed for the kidney, but the scissors hit bone.

He stepped back and was lifting his fist to me when he was yanked back. Sergi stabbed him again and again. Gheata bent over to block the blows, giving Sergi an opening. He kneed Gheata in the chin, and Gheata flew backward.

The big male wasn't finished, but his fighting style changed from attack to survival mode. His beast was no match for the beast in Sergi. A slight physical change had enveloped Sergi's brows and forehead. The red glow of his gaze was intense, and my wolf yipped with excitement at the sight of this predator.

Gheata stood, but when he took a step back, he slipped in a puddle of his own blood. The next move came so quickly I wasn't sure Gheata saw it coming.

Sergi planted a dagger in Gheata's right eye, and he convulsed, his body temporarily out of his control. Sergi didn't waste a moment as he stabbed a second dagger into his neck.

Sergi stood over Gheata, whose head lolled back, his rage evident in his one good eye.

Blood spurted from Gheata's mouth when he asked, "Who are you?"

Sergi stared down at him, his eyes still glowing, but his facial structure was back to normal. His grin was menacing as he considered the question. Or maybe he waited for Gheata to focus on him since his head continued to roll from side to side.

The blade in Gheata's eye must have severed something in his brain that controlled motor function. His hands twitched, and one leg spasmed. With enough time, he would heal, but I doubted he'd get the time he needed. And Gheata knew it.

"I'm Sergi. Cadre to House Trelane. I'll be sure to let your Master know you died well."

Gheata's single eye widened at the words, obviously surprised, but then he nodded and grinned, his teeth and the tips of his fangs smeared red with blood.

"I suspected Trelane had something to do with this. I should have known you were cadre."

"Yes. You should have."

Then Sergi pulled his dagger out of Gheata's eye with a sickening wet sound and sliced it across Gheata's neck. He swung his other hand down, the dagger cutting deep. One swipe from the right and then one from the left. He did it again and again until Gheata's body went limp.

I wanted to turn away, but my wolf refused. The scent of blood invigorated her. Hell, she wanted to shove Sergi aside so she could get a mouthful of flesh. I could almost taste the blood pouring onto the ground.

This was Sergi's kill. He'd endured the pain. The torture. And he didn't stop until Gheata's head rolled away.

SERGI STEPPED BACK, his breathing ragged as he stared down at Gheata's body while he settled his beast. Satisfied with the outcome, he wiped his daggers on Gheata's clothing before sliding them into the shoulder harness.

He turned and searched for Alex. She was in the corner, the bloody scissors still raised in her fist. He couldn't decipher her expression, but she didn't appear frightened. Perhaps unbelieving or maybe in shock, and he wondered if she was aware that her gaze glowed red with her wolf.

Her breaths were erratic until she sucked in a long, deep one and met his eyes. Then she grinned. "I guess he had that coming."

Sergi laughed. It was a deep guffaw as if he hadn't expressed his humor that grandly in decades. In some regard, finding joy had been spotty at best. House Trelane had many dark moments during those years. The weight of House Leader had been heavy, and Sergi had remained a stoic friend—helping Devon through addiction, the censure of his Council seat, and taking the responsibility of caring for Lyra, who'd attached herself to him as a loyal companion. He would do anything to make his friend's life easier. And during that time, he hadn't once thought of his own comforts, happy enough to ensure the House remained secure.

Somehow, this mission, even through the torture, had made him feel more alive than he had since before the tragic murder of Devon's parents. When he wiped his eyes, he noticed Alex had also been laughing, but then she straightened, reality settling in.

"There could be guards coming." She didn't move. No fear, · but something else was in her gaze, and it required more strength than he imagined to glance away.

He scanned the office, finally seeing the lab and remembering why he'd come here. "I need to find evidence of what's been happening here."

He caught the slight change in her expression, unsure if it was sadness or disappointment. Had she hoped he'd come for her?

She shook herself as if settling the wolf that had shown in her eyes. "I think I have what you need." She pulled out a rag from both pockets along with a USB drive. "I have several vials of human blood and three vials each of what should be Magic Poppy, Blood Poppy X, and one of the shifter serums. Assuming, of course, they didn't break while Gheata tossed me around."

"Let me see."

While she unwrapped the rag, he asked, "What's on the drive?"

"There's a folder named SMP that has something to do with shifters, and I found another folder labeled BPX, which was the name on the last Blood Poppy vial you took."

That vial, which they both assumed was some variation of Blood Poppy still coursed through him. His reflexes were faster than normal, even after the torture, and his senses heightened. Right now, Sergi felt as if he could take on several guards and never break a sweat.

"That's good. Did you find anything on Magic Poppy?"

"I didn't have time. I was transferring the last folder when Gheata came in. I barely had time to grab it before he noticed."

Alex opened the rag and tapped the vials of human blood. Sergi took them and immediately began swallowing them.

"Do you need all of them now? You seem to be doing well enough."

When he drank the last vial, he tossed it on the counter. "Human blood has different nutrients than Blood Poppy. I have more energy and strength for the moment, but I haven't eaten in some time, and the Blood Poppy masks my body's true weakness."

"Should we grab more before leaving this level?"

"No. That was enough for what I have left to do. Let's go."

Sergi led the way down the hall, but rather than going directly to the vent he'd used to drop down, he opened doors, searching for easier access to the ventilation system.

"What are you looking for?"

When he opened the next door, he ushered her in. "This." He pointed up.

"All the rooms have one."

"Yes, but not all of them have one right over the counter."

She nodded, climbed onto the counter, and studied the vent. "I need something to use like a Phillips-head screwdriver."

Sergi shook his head. "I was going to take care of that."

She snapped her fingers at him. "But I got here first. Do you have something or not? Maybe there's something in one of the drawers."

He reached into his pocket and handed her the Swiss Army Knife.

She grinned. "Don't tell me. They send vampires to Boy Scout camps." She opened the knife to the right tool and began removing screws.

"We're on a time crunch here."

"Females are excellent at multitasking."

"I don't remember you being so obstinate before."

"I'm not. I just don't have to play the submissive anymore."

He considered her as she expertly removed the screws and then the vent cover. "Did you tell me you were sent here to find the lab?"

"Yeah. A four-member team sent by The Wolf."

"And you were darted."

"Yep. Do you want me to go first or just follow?" She folded the knife and handed it back to him. She gave him a mischievous grin. "You do remember the way back, right?"

He returned her smile without answering and leaped onto the counter. "Are you claustrophobic?"

"No."

He studied her face which was now serious. "The shaft is easy enough to traverse, but we'll have to go down a level. You'll need to be able to control your downward movement."

"No problem. Let's go." When he continued to study her, she clucked her tongue. "Today, vampire. This wasn't my first mission." Her voice lowered. "No matter how it turned out."

He didn't have a response to that, but he understood the emotions boiling in her. Had any of her team survived? He shook it off and pulled himself into the vent then moved forward to wait. Once Alex was inside, he led her back to the shaft, where he positioned himself to move downward. He lowered himself to leave her just enough room to fit in above him. He wanted to stay close in case she fell.

He shouldn't have bothered and was impressed by how quickly she'd positioned herself to use her legs and back to control her downward movement. She'd either trained for these conditions, or her missions were more creative than he would have expected. What other types of missions were shifters sent on? He'd have to ask Remus once they were back. And he had no doubt they'd survive—they'd come too far.

The move into the second level shaft went smooth and soon they were back to where he started. The vent was still open, and as was expected, there was a welcoming party waiting for them.

"Call out before you drop down." Sergi didn't recognize the voice. "And know that we'll start shooting if you drop anything other than yourself."

"It's Sergi. I have Alex, Shifter S-473, with me."

"Is that so? How do we know that?"

"While I admit, the vampire has a nice ass, I'd just as soon get the hell out of here."

There were several snickers and then, "Come on down. Slowly."

Sergi moved beyond the vent so Alex could go first. She didn't question it and was quick to jump down. Once she was out, he backed up.

She had that mischievous spark in her gaze as she stared up at him. "Come on. It's safe."

When he dropped to the floor, he quickly looked around at the ten shifters. Half were in their wolf form, while the others held various weapons. A male with an automatic pointed it to the floor and held his hand out to Sergi.

"Thank you for bringing her back."

"Where's Cadfael and Carlos?"

The shifter looked grim. "They're holding off an incursion at the staircase near the elevator."

"I don't know if anyone will realize we used the vents before help arrives. I wasn't able to salvage the covers."

The shifter nodded. "Our concern is that they might stop airflow to the lower levels."

"It's a possibility. I need to leave so I can call for an infiltration team, but I want to see Cadfael first."

"Jason will take you." He nodded to one of the wolves.

The wolf trotted to the door and waited.

He and Alex ran behind the wolf, who didn't slow as he traversed the corridors until they came to a blockade where a dozen shifters waited.

Cadfael, now dressed, turned on their approach. His shoulders relaxed, and his expression brightened when he spotted Alex. "Thank the heavens." The two embraced.

"I assume you're Cadfael," Alex said as she brushed at her eye.

He nodded. "And it's a pleasure to be able to say that again."

"They've already tried breaking through?"

Cadfael nodded. "Yes, but they didn't stay long when they realized the gas they dropped dissipated before reaching us. When the first three guards were shot, and the wolves finished them, they discovered they required a better plan." He turned to Sergi. "You need to go now."

Sergi nodded. "I'm on my way, but I didn't want to go before checking in. If it becomes too dangerous to hold this level, get everyone down to the third level. In fact, it probably wouldn't hurt to move some of your supplies down there, just in case. If they turn off the air, the back door will be your only source. And if necessary, you can leave that way. I know some of the shifters don't have the stamina for the journey, but it might be necessary."

Cadfael laid a hand on his shoulder. "A military man through and through. I appreciate your support."

Sergi copied the gesture by placing a hand on the Alpha's shoulder. "Stay alive. It's time for everyone to go home."

Cadfael glanced at Alex. "I only have one request. Take Alex with you."

Sergi shook his head. "It's too dangerous with the wild shifters."

"Which is exactly why you need me."

He turned, surprised by her siding with Cadfael. His dealings with Cressa and Ginger should have prepared him for this. He wanted to argue and had a few sentiments he was wise enough not to share. It didn't have anything to do with her being female. He wouldn't have questioned the request had it been Simone or Bella, but he knew their abilities. They trained together and knew each other's strengths and weaknesses.

Alex might have appeared weak, hiding behind the submissive female persona. but she'd risked everything to help him. He'd be a fool not to consider someone Remus was willing to send on a dangerous mission. And while he understood shifter behaviors, it might come in handy to have a wolf by his side.

He turned to Carlos, who'd been silently watching. "What about you?"

Carlos shook his head. "They need all the help they can get. I'll wait for backup."

He nodded and shook both his and Cadfael's hands before turning to Alex. "You need a change of clothes before we go unless you plan on remaining in your wolf form."

She nodded then hugged Carlos and Cadfael. "You better both be alive when we return." Then, not waiting for Sergi, she raced down the hall toward the guards' quarters.

With a quick nod to the shifters, Sergi ran after her, but she surprised him when she slowed at the stairs that went down to the third level. She stopped long enough to see he followed then disappeared down them.

She was going to the guards' quarters on the third level. It made sense since they would be leaving that way. He jogged behind her until she ducked into a supply room.

"There should be extra uniforms, maybe a jacket or two." She laid the lab coat aside and immediately got naked before pulling on a guard's uniform.

He should have looked away, but it was impossible not to take note of her lean, muscular frame. A year as a prisoner, and she'd been able to retain some of her muscle tone. Most likely a perk from her wolf. She rolled up the bottom of the pants and used a belt to cinch the waistline. She put on two shirts and grabbed a coat that wouldn't provide any protection against the cold but was at least waterproof.

She tried on several boots until she found a pair that appeared to fit once she'd pulled on two pairs of thick socks. She stomped around the room, getting comfortable in the boots and clothing. "This will do."

While she'd been dressing, Sergi found a backpack and stuffed it with supplies. A couple cans of food, nutrition bars, a can opener, two flashlights, and an emergency survival kit. One of several on the shelf. The last items to be stored were four bottles of water.

"Ready?" he asked.

She nodded and followed him out the door and down the hall to the mechanical room. The shelving was where he'd left it, pushed aside several feet from the hidden door. He didn't stop as he pulled it open, the cold air blasting his face. He didn't look back, sensing Alex was only two steps behind him as they followed the bends of the tunnel, the bright sunlight urging them on the farther they progressed.

When he reached the end of the tunnel, he slowed as he stepped up to peer out at the forested landscape. A few patches of snow remained at the base of trees where the sun couldn't reach it.

Alex stepped up next to him, and she lifted her head and sniffed the air.

"Anything out there?" he asked.

"Not for the moment."

Sergi scanned the perimeter one last time then stepped outside with Alex behind him. It didn't take long to find a deer trail heading down the mountain, and he increased his speed to a jog.

After a few minutes, he stopped to check on Alex, and though she was right behind him, tears ran down her face.

"Are you alright?" he asked.

She nodded and gave him a small smile. "It's just been a long time since I've seen the sky."

# Chapter Twenty-Eight

DEVON CHECKED HIS WATCH. The two hours he'd given the team was almost up, so he gathered his backpack and stacked it with the others next to one of the cargo vans. They would go in with minimal gear.

He walked through the now larger team, ensuring the readiness of those who'd been severely injured in the last battle. After confirming the vampires were ready, he reviewed the shifters and paused at the last one. The shifter was an older man with a full head of gray hair and a face that held few wrinkles. His eyes were a sharp blue, almost as light as Devon's, and belied his age. They were clear, focused, and reflected determination. Devon also noted that the male was leaning on his left leg, making his right leg appear shorter.

"You're not fully healed." Devon's tone was calm and steady as he studied the shifter's expression.

The old shifter grinned, revealing strikingly white teeth, and there was a general sense of merriment about him. "An old injury from many battles ago." His accent was British, most likely from around London.

"You were in one of the cargo vans."

He nodded. "Caught me coming out of my favorite pub just after closing. Must have been four or five of them, but they darted me, and I woke caged in some warehouse with other shifters. I don't know where it was, but I can tell you it was a good six hours to get here."

Devon's brow lifted. "Interesting." Six hours would cover many miles, but it would depend on their speed and whether any border crossings were involved. If he assumed a speed that wouldn't attract police and no borders, the warehouse could be four hundred miles away. But Devon didn't think it was that far, and he would guess one border crossing. Either way, it put the building in Europe and not the UK.

They must capture an easy target, move them to a central facility, then once they have their specific target number of shifters, they transport them all here. If they were gathering them one at a time from all over, no one would be aware of the connection between missing shifters from around the globe, let alone connect the dots as to why.

"If you're wondering if I can pull my own weight..." the old man ventured. "I can assure you the only reason I was injured earlier was because I'd been clubbed during our last stop."

"Why was that?"

His grin slipped easily back in place. "I might have been causing a bit of a rebellion inside the van."

Devon chuckled. "Making it impossible for the guards to determine if everyone had broken their restraints and could rush them when they opened the door. The director would probably be unhappy if his cargo were killed."

"Exactly." His smile faded, and he shook his head. "But they called my bluff. I only had a few out of their restraints before they opened the door. They beat us all, but they knew I was the one who riled them up." He rubbed his right leg as if it were an affectation as much as something that bothered him. "They aggravated my old injury. The shift helped." He met Devon's eyes. "I'm not a hundred percent, but I can still fight."

Devon held his gaze for a long minute. He didn't doubt the shifter. Remus, who stood behind him remained quiet, giving Devon the final decision. The fact he didn't say anything was enough for Devon.

"Then let's see this done, and then we'll get you home."

The shifter stood straighter and never lost his smile.

Devon turned to Remus and Bella. "Let's move the teams out."

He'd let the two of them rearrange the teams to fit everyone's best skills. He'd found a quiet place to review the plan. They had a larger force now, but the guards would know they were coming. But after mulling over it, he discussed it with Rafael, Bella, and Remus, and, with a few minor modifications, decided to leave the plan as is. The only difference would be who was on which team.

The initial breach consisted of Team Three as the bait, and Team Four would take the blind and gain computer access. No changes were made to that plan. Once successful, Team Three would regroup into a larger force, assuming there was a tunnel to the main facility. Team Four would include the remaining team members and would blow the doors and move in.

With the addition of the unexpected shifters, two additional teams were added. Team Five would be the first team to move out and consisted of four shifters in wolf form. They would approach the parking lot from both sides of the road, running through the forest for cover. Their mission was to alert Team Six once Team Three was darted.

Remus gave this last group their choice of whether to stay in human form or wolf. The group quickly determined that two-thirds would shift while the rest would remain in human form for the initial charge.

Team Six moved out next, led by a Beta who'd been captured

in Frankfurt. They would stop a quarter mile short of the parking lot. Once they heard a howl of all clear from Team Five, they'd race in and help infiltrate the building.

Team Three was the next to move up the mountain, and Devon nodded to Rafael, who led them farther west of the road, using the same path he'd taken with Sergi and Carlos. Team Four, the last group, stayed several hundred yards behind. Four of the shifters in this group morphed into their wolf forms and split into two groups, running to the left and right of Devon. The entire team moved quickly and quietly and didn't stop until they reached a point where the parking lot and building could be seen from the woods.

Remus gave a low whistle, and the four wolves positioned themselves just behind where the underground blinds should be. Devon waited five minutes to see if the wolves triggered any alarms.

When they didn't, Devon, Rafael, and Beckham, a shifter in human form, continued on while Remus took control of the remaining team with Bella beside him.

Devon pulled at the collar of his mesh suit and noted that Rafael and Beckham were also fidgeting with their own suits. No one wanted a dart to hit flesh. The last thing any of them wanted was to be tranquilized and miss the battle.

This was the trickiest part of the plan—getting the guards to believe they'd been darted. If they showed any resilience against the darts, the guards in the blinds might open fire instead, which wouldn't kill Devon or Rafael, though they might be out of commission without blood from their supply. It would definitely kill Beckham.

Devon, with Rafael and Beckham spreading out on either side of him, slowly approached the parking lot. He scanned the area where the blinds were hidden and, now that he knew where they were, easily identified the faint lines. They would be near impossible to see in the dark.

The question Devon had worried about was whether they had

changed their security protocols when Rafael escaped. And what other surprises waited inside now that they'd received a call that the cargo vans had been attacked? Too late now for any misgivings. This was still the best plan.

He continued, moving slowly and stealthily, as any team would do. They were two hours behind their original schedule, and the guards must be curious why a team would attempt something so foolish in the late afternoon. Maybe they would forget the tranquilizers and just shoot them.

He was halfway to the doors, blocking out all the ways this could go wrong when he felt something hit his neck. He hadn't heard the blind open, but he turned back as he reached for his neck, and saw the tips of the rifles as the blind continued to rise. He managed a quick glance at Rafael, who was already on his way to the ground. Devon struggled, attempting to take another step as he turned to Beckham, who, wide-eyed, had a hand to his neck. Then the shifter fell a few seconds before Devon collapsed to his knees, and his body dropped to the ground.

His head was turned toward Beckham, whose eyes were closed. The shifter was on his side, his back to the blind. His left hand twitched then fisted into a peace sign. He was okay.

A lone howl echoed through the trees as boots hit the pavement. Devon assumed they were guards on their way to confirm the three intruders were down.

They never reached Devon before the teams attacked.

DEVON HAD BEEN EXPECTING the howls to increase, but the cries for blood from his vampires surprised him. The team knew what was at stake—gaining evidence to fight Venizi. In that split-second moment, the realization hit him that the team wasn't just fighting for the mission but for themselves. Rafael for his guilt at leaving his team behind, Bella's worry for Sergi and her deep hatred of Venizi, and Remus for the shifters who'd sacrificed themselves in the search for the lab.

They weren't alone. He'd lay down his life for his Family, but he had to admit that his relationship with Sergi went deeper than with the rest of his cadre. Sergi had spent centuries with House Trelane defending Devon with his life, first as the Captain of the Guard, then as his personal bodyguard, and then as cadre. They'd been at each other's side in too many battles to count and endless missions. He was more than a friend—he was a brother.

Devon rolled to his side and sprung into a squat, readying for the guards, but they were already down, and he stood. Two were dead, and the rest were in restraints. Two dozen wolves raced around the parking lot, sniffing the ground, getting a sense of who and what they were seeking.

Bella stood next to the open blind, talking to someone inside. Rafael, assigned to infiltrate through what was hopefully a tunnel, was up and running toward her. Remus whispered something to Bella then jogged over. His face was grim for the battle yet to come, and the anticipation explained the gleam in his eyes.

Remus held out his hand, which Devon shook. "I know this might be premature, but this went better than expected."

"I assume there weren't many guards in the blinds."

"Only a handful, and they gave up easily." He turned to one of the dead a few feet away. "Well, most of them did."

A shout came from the doors to the building as Team Four placed the C4.

"The team didn't waste any time." Devon shouldn't have expected any less. The wolves had split into two groups, waiting for the doors to open.

"The shifters are eager. They have a score to settle."

Devon's attention was drawn back to the blinds when two wolves ran over and jumped in. After a few seconds, two more followed.

"I assume there was a tunnel after all?"

Remus chuckled. "Bella has excellent insight. She'd been the first to consider a tunnel and refused to believe anything else. Rafael is reviewing the security system to see what's waiting for us in the command center."

"So, which is it, old friend: the tunnel or the front door?"

Remus grinned. "You know me. I always prefer a grand entrance."

Devon shook his head. "I wouldn't expect anything less."

Devon gave last-minute instructions to Bella with Remus's additional guidance on how best to use the recently kidnapped shifters.

"They're angry. They'll want to be the first in. Use that rage, but be careful. These wolves are all strangers to each other. Use my wolves as a barrier."

Devon and Remus left her to her tasks and strode across the parking lot toward a group waiting outside the blast radius.

Beckham stood at the far end of the building with a remote control in his hand. He glanced at Remus first and then at Devon.

When Devon nodded, Beckham grinned and yelled, "Fire in the hole!"

The doors blasted outward, and team members scattered as pieces of metal flew across the lot. Debris and rock fell as if the sky had sent it. Before the dust settled, gunfire erupted from inside, and the entry team waited until they could see figures dashing around the garage before returning fire while wolves raced in, their bodies low to the ground. When the sound of screaming started, Devon strode toward the gap in the mountain where the double-wide doors used to be, Remus by his side. Two wolves raced in, and Devon pulled his daggers as he bent low to enter.

When he heard the "all clear," he straightened, confused.

Remus, who followed him in, stopped next to him. "I was expecting more of a welcome."

Beckham, who'd been the first to run in, raced toward them from somewhere deeper in the facility. "They've combined their forces at the command center and barricaded the other hallways. We're setting up in one of the conference rooms."

Devon cursed. "They're holding us off until they can destroy documentation of everything they've been doing here."

Remus growled. "Now we know what they've been up to while waiting for us."

DEVON AND REMUS found Bella in a conference room around the corner from a hallway that led to the command center. Several team members sat in the hallway, their heads leaning against the wall as they waited for new orders.

"The blockades are almost cleared." Bella stood over a table, studying a map.

"Already?" Devon asked.

"The teams had excess energy they needed to burn off. The barricades confirm they were waiting for us, but even with the two hours we gave them, they were sloppy."

Remus grunted. "We caught them shorthanded, and they weren't prepared."

"All to our advantage." Bella pointed to the map. "We found this in one of the vehicles in the garage, and we're having copies made. The facility has three levels. We're on level one where security, housing for the staff, and the labs are located."

She frowned, and Devon prepared himself for bad news. "Levels two and three are cells. One of the captured guards admitted they keep the shifters in them until they're needed for experiments."

Remus's howl was followed by a punch through the wall. Bella waited for the dust from the drywall to settle before she continued as if his outburst was an everyday occurrence.

"There's one elevator and two staircases, and we believe guards are stationed at all of them." She grinned at Remus, who only growled in response. "Oh, I think you'll like this." She gave Devon a quick grin. "The shifters mounted an uprising. They've taken control of the two lower levels, supposedly led by a vampire, who was one of the prisoners."

"Sergi?" Devon asked.

"I assumed so, except..." She pulled out her satellite phone. "A red dot has appeared on our map. It appears to be coming from somewhere on the other side of the facility."

Devon pulled out his phone, and Remus looked over his shoulder.

Remus ran a hand through his hair. "There's only one signal."

"Is it inside or outside the facility? Maybe there's a back door." Devon wasn't sure what was going on, but an uprising wasn't what he'd expected. He glanced at Remus, understanding what he was going through, knowing shifters were being held for experiments, but unable to do anything for him until their mission was complete.

"This might be something." Bella pointed to an area on the third level. "There's nothing specific on the map, but most of the engineering and mechanical rooms tend to be in the basement, or in this case, the third level. It wouldn't be surprising to have a door there when the facility was being built. The only ones who can tell us for sure are the shifters. We need to get control of the command center and remove the guards blocking the entrances."

"Agreed." Devon had to find evidence before it was all destroyed. "Continue to work on that. I need access to the labs."

Bella tapped a spot on the map. "You should be able to get through to this hallway by now." She trailed her finger from the conference room to the hallway that led to the labs. "Be careful. There could be guards anywhere."

"I'll take a small team. Me and two others. You'll need the rest to secure the facility." Devon turned to Remus. "I assume you'll want to lead the effort to clear the entrances at the stairs and elevator."

Before Remus could answer, Rafael rushed into the room.

"We broke through to the command center. They've set a self-destruct for the facility. I have one of our guys working on it, but he doesn't think he can override it in time."

Devon's gut clenched. "How long?"

"One hour."

# Chapter Twenty-Nine

SERGI STOOD next to a pool of water large enough to bathe in, but he didn't like the steam rising off it. When Alex squatted as if she would drink, he yanked her back so quickly she fell on her backside and glared up at him.

"I just wanted to see if it was drinkable."

"You don't have to get that close to know it isn't. Look at the vegetation around it." He pointed to the brown leaves and grasses that encircled the pool. "It might be drinkable, and it was only the heat that killed the grasses. The other possibility is acidic water created by gases, toxic enough to burn the flesh off you. There will be more pools that are safe enough to refill our water bottles and warm enough to bathe."

She stood and brushed off her backside, still irritated but no longer glaring at him. "How do you know so much? Are you from this area?"

He shook his head. "I've fought many battles in the Carpathians. This area is rife with volcanic activity, which creates these pools."

He moved on, following trails that led in the general direction of a village he remembered seeing on the map of the area. A map he'd studied for hours preparing for this mission.

"How long will it take us to get to a town?"

"Two or three days. This side of the mountain is more treacherous, and I doubt we'll find a direct trail. We might find a logging road, but I didn't see any on the map. Our first task is to find a cave where we can stay the night. It's almost dusk, and we don't want to be out in the open."

A half-hour later, they found a living room-sized cave tall enough to stand in. Sergi checked for any evidence a wild animal might have been using it but didn't find anything to be concerned about.

"I'll find some wood so we can start a fire." He dropped the backpack in the center of the cave.

"Don't we need something to start it with?"

Sergi pointed to the pack. "I grabbed a few supplies. There should be a lighter in there."

"A vampire who thinks ahead."

He gave her a quick grin. "We're not all savages. I'll be back soon."

She looked like she wanted to say something but didn't. Instead, she squatted next to the backpack and started rummaging through it.

Sergi walked farther than he wanted before finding branches and wood dry enough to start a fire. When he returned, he found the cave empty except for the backpack and a few things Alex had pulled out. Then he spotted her clothes lying in a pile. She'd shifted.

He dropped the firewood and considered following her. He didn't remember seeing any wolf prints by the entrance, but he'd been focused on the interior of the cave. And if he was honest, he needed food. A growl from his stomach, or was it his beast, validated his thoughts. At least he'd found a few nutrition bars and a small container of nuts.

He decided he'd give her wolf time to stretch its legs before worrying about her. But if she wasn't back in a half hour, he'd have to search for her. He didn't even know what her wolf looked like.

He started a fire, and as he watched it catch on the twigs and branches, his thoughts turned to Devon. It had been a week, maybe more, since he'd been captured, and Devon would have acted once the team's transmitters showed no movement. The question was whether he would send a large enough force to make a difference. When small footsteps interrupted his thoughts, he grabbed a dagger and jumped up.

A wolf, the size of a mastiff but thinner, stood in the entrance, a dead rabbit in its mouth. It stared at Sergi, and when he made no move, it walked to the fire and dropped the rabbit. Once it was in the light of the now blazing fire, he could make out its coloring. Mostly white with strips of brown, black, and gray running through it. A striking color.

The wolf continued to stare at him, and he said the only thing he could think of. "Thank you."

Then it yipped and raced from the cave.

Alex was on the hunt. He grinned as he picked up the rabbit and, with his dagger already in hand, began to skin it. He would have preferred something with more meat, but beggars and all.

The wolf brought three more rabbits before Alex shifted back to her human form. He didn't mean to stare at her naked-ness, but he couldn't help but appreciate what sleek muscles she'd been able to retain after a year of near starvation and little activity.

That wasn't the entire reason he couldn't look away, though he knew how rude it was. But he wasn't currently in control. His beast had a soft spot for the shifter. He brushed it off as nothing more than gratitude for a life saved. It was impossible to know where he'd be now if Gheata had gotten another dose of the modified Magic Poppy in him.

She'd been staring at him as well, and a slight smile curved her lips before she turned away and slipped on her clothes. "I think that second rabbit is done cooking."

That broke his stare, and he removed it from the spit he'd made as she handed him the next one he'd skinned to be placed on the fire.

She sat near him and took the cooked rabbit he offered her, while he picked up the first one he'd laid on a stone near the fire to keep warm. "You shouldn't have waited to eat that. It's been some time since I've had to cook rabbit over a fire. The one thing I can remember is that it doesn't taste as good cold. And you need something to eat."

"It's still warm enough, and the same goes for you. How long has it been since you've eaten meat?"

"It's been a while. They gave us porridge for breakfast with an occasional egg. For dinner, and lunch when they were generous, we got stew that was more vegetable than meat."

"It's easier to handle shifters when they aren't fed meat."

She ripped a piece of flesh from the rabbit and ate it greedily. Then she quickly swallowed a second piece, and before he ate half of his, she tossed the bones into the fire. She licked her fingers as she watched him eat, then grinned.

"You're right. I needed that. It was all I could do to stop the wolf from eating them raw."

He grimaced. "It's been a long time since I had to do that. It wasn't pleasant."

"So, how old are you?" She poked at the cooking rabbit and what little fat there was sparked a sizzle when it hit the flames.

"I thought it wasn't polite to ask," he teased.

"That's a human thing. Or are vampires more sensitive than I've been told."

"Who said we're sensitive?" A spark of indignation came out of nowhere.

She grinned. "I think you just did."

He laughed and shook his head as he dumped the bones from

his rabbit in the fire. He flexed his shoulders, and a light pain nagged. He ignored it. "Sometime before the Middle Ages."

She stared at him for the longest moment, and he turned his focus to the cooking rabbit.

"The oldest vampire I met was born during the Napoleonic war. I thought he was ancient until my uncle told me he was just reaching his prime."

Sergi leaned back on his hands and stretched out his legs, his body warm from the fire. "I know a few vampires, barely over a hundred, who would question that statement. Like many of the young, they haven't grasped the full weight of longevity." He considered his words. "I think it depends on which House they come from and whether they've been around true ancients. The smaller Houses don't view it the same as the larger ones."

"And how did you feel when you were barely over a hundred?" Her grin showed a playful side that he found endearing.

He laughed. "Like a young stud who knew everything and challenged everyone."

She laughed as if she expected his answer. "When did you become wise?"

He considered the last few days bound to a wall and the memories the torture had produced. A past he hadn't thought about in a long time, except for his brief discussion with Devon before he'd left on this mission. Maybe that was why it was so easy to select one moment over all his other memories.

"The first time I met Devon Trelane." He shook his head as Alex pulled the cooked rabbit from the spit and put the last one over the fire. "He was barely a hundred and I not much older. I didn't know who he was at first, caught up in my own anger as I disparaged the House leader's son who was to take charge of the army."

She nodded as she ripped several pieces of flesh from the rabbit before leaning over to hand him the rest. "Was it because this son showed no skill for war or that he was too young?"

He swallowed a bite and shrugged as he pulled another piece from the bone. "At the time, both. So I bet this stranger, whom I assumed to be part of the young whelp's command, to a fight."

Alex grinned as if she knew where the story was going, and she scooted closer.

He told her of battling the warrior, who had been an equal match, before he realized he was fighting the Master's son. When he told her of throwing his shield and sword down before falling to his knees, she laughed with delight, and he couldn't help but grin. When he felt his face flush, he blamed it on the fire.

When her laughter died, her expression turned serious, her brows lowered as she considered his story. "You've been with this House ever since?"

"Yes. I was Captain of the Guard for many centuries before the title became obsolete with industrialization and fewer wars of any consequence, at least to vampires. Then I became Devon's body-guard and eventually cadre when his parents were killed by Venizi, and he became House leader."

He watched her as little lines formed above her nose. He suspected she was mulling over his words, and when she spoke, he was pleased he'd read her correctly.

"I thought it was possible for a House leader to grant someone they find worthy a House of their own, or did I misunderstand that?"

"You're correct." He was surprised by how much she knew about vampires. He imagined to young shifters it was considered Vampire 101—know your enemy. "It's rarely done these days but was considered a reward for bravery in battle in defense of the House. Devon offered it to me once, but I turned it down."

"Why wouldn't you want your own House?" Once the question was asked, she lowered her head. "I'm sorry. That was rude." She played with the sleeve of the lab coat she'd put back on.

"It's a fair question considering how long I've been with House Trelane." She lifted her head, and he shrugged. "You're thinking of it from a pack perspective, and if that was all it was, perhaps I would have reconsidered. Vampire politics and law are a quagmire of corruption. For a vampire born to a House leader, they're trained from a young age to someday run the House. I have no desire to be that type of vampire. I understand the politics and how to maneuver around them, but I prefer to serve. Devon gives me more opportunities to lead than I desire."

"What you actually mean is that you've grown comfortable."

He growled and focused on the cooking rabbit, but all she did was smile. She had a beautiful smile. In fact, she had several types, and he already knew the differences. A shy smile when she'd trailed her fingers over his tattoos when she thought him asleep. A smile that was pure joy when she'd seen that Cadfael and Carlos were safe. A knowing smile when she didn't believe a thing he said. And the smile she gave him now. It was close to the one that said he spoke bullshit, but this one added an extra layer. One that said she was challenging him and his beliefs, and when she proved she was right, he'd see himself for the fool he was.

His first instinct was to react with irritation as he did when Cressa challenged him. Until he realized that with Alex, he welcomed the challenge. After staring at her for a few minutes, he gave her a devilish grin. "Perhaps we'll have to put your theory to the test."

Her laugh was lusty as she pulled the last rabbit off the spit. "So, tell me, vampire, since you know the Carpathians so well, what perils will we face before reaching civilization?"

He didn't believe for one moment that she'd given up. Her change of topic was merely a ruse. She'd wait for a more opportune time to tease him further. He reached over to take his share of the rabbit, which was larger than the last. "The only true threat is the wild shifters, but there are bears and wolves in the area. We'll want to stick to deer trails, but you'll want to keep your wolf close to the surface. We should be able to make a lot of ground tomorrow, assuming the weather remains mild, but we'll be spending at least one more night in the woods."

She nodded. "Maybe you can find one of those warm pools." She sniffed her armpit. "I could use a bath."

To see her naked again wouldn't be a bad thing, and he grinned. His cheeks hurt from how much he'd smiled since meeting her. "I'll see what I can do about that."

## Chapter Thirty

DEVON GLANCED around the director's office at the broken furniture and debris littering the floor. There had been a vicious fight, and while some of the damage could be blamed on the aftermath of purposeful destruction, not all of it could. The fresh scent of blood drew his attention to the lab side of the room.

Remus flipped through files, magazines, and books that remained on the desk, tossing the discards to the floor once he'd searched through them. Devon had assumed Remus would go with the team to remove the guards at the stairs, but he sent Beckham, preferring to help search for evidence.

"Let me know if it was a vampire kill or shifter." Remus picked up the remaining pieces of a laptop. "They did a good job on this. The hard drive looks damaged, but we should have it checked anyway." He poked around the desk and then the floor before lifting a letter opener. He eyed it curiously. "This has dried blood on it." He pried the hard drive from the laptop and pocketed it.

Devon glanced down at the body and then over at its head two feet away. He used the toe of his boot to turn it so he could see the face. "Well, I'll be damned. This is where Venizi stashed him."

"Who?"

"Boris Gheata. He's the vampire who killed Boretsky, knocked me out, and injected me with Magic Poppy."

Remus stepped over the detritus of the office to stand next to Devon. He stared down at the head. "No bite marks, but it could have been a shifter."

Devon grinned. "I don't think so. I recognize the method of killing."

"Sergi?"

Devon chuckled, and it turned into a laugh. "Yes. Thank the gods, Sergi was alive not that long ago."

Remus tapped him on the shoulder. "We only have another thirty minutes. We should ensure all the shifters are getting out. I'd like to see if any of my wolves survived."

He didn't mean the wolves that came with them on the mission. Remus wanted to know if Carlos and any of the previous shifters he'd sent remained alive. Devon didn't blame him. If there were vampires being held captive, Devon's first thoughts would be to his Family.

"There's nothing to keep us here. With all the other labs ransacked and blood vials destroyed we're lucky to have found one salvageable vial of Magic Poppy. Maybe we can find something off the hard drive."

Devon gave Gheata's remains one last look, then turned and jogged after Remus. When they arrived at the closest staircase, only a handful of shifters were coming up. One of the shifters from their original team was quickly directing them down the hallway, where additional team members waited for them.

Devon called Bella on the burner. "What's the status?"

"It didn't take long to disarm the guards. There weren't many of them. Most of the shifters are out, as well as the lab staff. We haven't found the director. He's either dead, holed up in one of the panic rooms we can't open, or the staff is protecting him. We'll find out soon enough.

"We put the guards in the back of a cargo van that was parked in the garage. It's been moved several hundred yards down the road. It would be best to have everyone out of the building in the next ten minutes. We don't know what type of explosives are being used to destroy the facility."

"We're at the second staircase. We'll follow the last ones out."

When Bella didn't respond for a moment, he prepared for her to argue with him for remaining behind. She only said, "Roger that," then hung up.

Devon turned in time to see Remus hugging one of the shifters. When he stepped back, Devon sighed with relief.

Carlos had survived.

An older shifter followed behind, and when he stopped to speak with Remus, Devon thought for a moment The Wolf might collapse, but he straightened with Carlos's help.

Devon raced over. "What's happened?"

When Remus couldn't get any words out, which was odd for him, Carlos shook his head, and Devon didn't push. The Wolf had gotten some unexpected news, but Devon couldn't tell if it was good or bad.

"He'll be alright. We were the last of the shifters." Carlos pushed them toward the exit. "This is Cadfael, an Alpha who's been a captive for years."

Devon shook the shifter's hand. "I'm Devon." He directed his next question to Carlos. "Do you know where Sergi is? His tracker showed up a couple of hours ago on the other side of this mountain. If he'd been with the shifters, Bella would have told me."

"We weren't sure if Rafael survived or how soon you'd send a larger team. There's a back door out of the building."

Two team members moved behind them to push them faster until they were all jogging toward the exit.

Carlos continued to speak as he and Remus helped Cadfael move faster. "Sergi and one of the shifters escaped earlier."

Carlos glanced at Remus, who, against Cadfael's protest, lifted the Alpha, and they all ran. By Devon's watch, they had time, but he sensed the team members' growing urgency.

Bella waited at the blown-out doorway he and Remus had come through, though most of the shifters were being moved through the garage, which had a wider exit route.

Once they were out, they continued across the parking lot and stopped by a Range Rover parked on the side of the road, close to the cargo van that housed the guards.

Devon surveyed the operation. Dozens of vampires, and he sensed a few humans, in lab coats or plain clothing were being led down the road, all restrained with their hands in front of them.

"Where did you get all the restraints?" Devon asked. "We didn't bring that many."

"Rafael found a box of them in one of the supply closets." Bella looked around and, spotting Carlos, lifted her brows. "Where's Sergi?" Her tone told him she wouldn't be happy with bad news.

"You were right. Carlos said Sergi and another shifter escaped out the back."

"Alex."

Devon turned when Remus joined them. "Who?"

"Alex." He wiped at his eyes. "I'm sorry to be so emotional. She's one of mine. She was part of the first group I sent in search of the lab a year ago." He grinned and released a pent-up breath. "Ah, I never gave up hope. She's my niece."

When he hung his head, Devon squeezed his shoulder. "She sounds like a fighter."

Remus turned so the other shifters wouldn't see his emotional state. Devon understood. He'd found himself in a similar situation when he'd learned of his parents' deaths and came home to find Lyra in a poor mental state. Then again, when Cressa had been kidnapped, and he'd thought she might have been killed. Family did that to a shifter as much as a vampire.

Remus took another moment before straightening and

running a hand through this hair, his emotions tucked away. "How do we get everyone out of here?"

"I sent a team to repair the road." Bella waved at someone, and they nodded before running down the hill. "We found shovels in the garage and expect the road to be passable in two hours."

"Have you called anyone?" Devon asked.

"I contacted Aramburu to advise of the situation. He's sending a plane to Brasov."

"We should contact the Sentinels and Eliminators," Devon suggested. He wanted Remus's opinion.

"Can you trust them?" Remus asked.

"I trust they'll find enough information to begin an inquiry. I don't trust the Council to do anything with it on its own merit." Devon wasn't fooled by what the Council would do. They would most likely see what happened here as Trelane's widening vengeance on Venizi with an unprovoked attack on House Larkin, a strong ally of Venizi's. And in retaliation, Venizi had the voice to sway the Council in his favor.

"If this is Larkin's lab, the Council won't be happy that it was destroyed." Bella tapped her hand in a quick staccato against her leg. "This was where the fertility testing was underway."

Devon grunted. "For a problem the Council created in the first place. But I understand your point. That's the avenue Venizi will likely take. He'll want them to believe this is one more example of House Trelane attacking him with no cause. One vial of Magic Poppy won't do anything to sway the Council today, not without showing our hand. And we're not ready for that." He glanced at Remus, who was listening, but The Wolf's expression hardened as he glanced at the battered shifters moving away from the building. "Sorry, Remus. While the success today lies at the feet of the shifters, I can't let you take all the heat. At some point, we'll have to contact the Sentinels."

Carlos, with Cadfael in tow, interrupted before Remus could

respond. "Cadfael has critical information to report. I think it might be timely."

They turned to the old Alpha, who stood tall, his gaze bright with inner strength. Devon guessed there was great wisdom behind those soulful eyes.

"For the last six years, I've only been known as shifter 272. I've witnessed many horrific experiments during my time here, but I'll wait for a more proper time to provide a full report. I heard the guards destroyed the labs and that the building is next." He dropped his gaze and gave them a reluctant smile. "Sergi and Alex both told me how important it was to find evidence of our mistreatment. The truth of what happened here." He looked Devon in the eye. "I need you to know Sergi and Alex didn't leave empty-handed. They had evidence with them."

Devon perked up. "What kind of evidence?"

The old shifter shrugged. "All I know is that Alex had several vials and a USB drive. She and Sergi were convinced it would reflect part of what the vampires had been working on."

"Get me a map of the backside of this facility." Devon needed to get to Sergi. He had to protect whatever they found.

A loud explosion shook the ground, and everyone fought to keep their footing. Devon glanced up, worried the entire mountain might collapse, but soon everything went quiet. All eyes turned toward the lab, and he wasn't the only one looking up.

A minute passed, then another.

"It appears the explosion didn't impact the overall structure of the facility," Remus said.

"It's best we don't take a chance. Who knows what impact the explosion might have in a volcanic area." Devon nodded for Bella to continue.

She placed her tablet on the hood of the Range Rover as everyone gathered around her. The red dot was clearly displayed and was currently stationary. "Sergi hasn't moved from this spot for the last thirty minutes. With it getting dark, I assume they've found shelter until morning."

"That would be for the best." Remus tapped the tablet. "This entire area is teeming with wild shifters. They wouldn't be safe out in the open. Alex knows this from her mission briefing."

Bella nodded. "Which might explain why Venizi selected this location all those years ago. The terrain on the other side of the mountain is difficult to navigate and has dozens of volcanic springs."

Devon glanced at Remus. "How do you feel about going after them?"

Remus stared at the map. "A team of six. I suggest the team be half vampire and half shifter. We need to be well-armed. Some of these packs are large."

"Bella, select four others to go with us. We'll move out as soon as the road is finished. Once we've loaded the shifters from the lab into Aramburu's plane and it's back in the air, contact the Sentinels. Let's not wait for them to interrogate the guards and lab staff. Record the discussions. I want names and faces."

"And the shifters from the cargo vans?" Bella asked.

Remus pointed to a spot on the map southwest of their location. "I'll call for my plane to arrive at our predesignated extraction point once we meet up with Sergi and Alex. The shifters taken from European locations should go to Aramburu's estate with the other shifters. Those from the States will come with us." Remus looked at Cadfael. "I'd like you to fly back to the States with us, at least for a short time."

"The Sentinels will want to question the shifters," Bella said. "Without that, they only have one side of the story."

"They can be questioned under Aramburu's presence once Remus gives his approval." Devon hoped he hadn't crossed a line with Remus, but the shifter was nodding along.

"There's a strong shifter presence in Spain. I'll contact the lead

Alpha. Perhaps he can be present to meet the plane. With Arambu-ru's agreement, of course."

"I don't think that will be a problem. We can call Gregor together."

They spent the next hour preparing the team for their trek into the woods. Neither Devon nor Remus wanted to wait until morning, but they understood the dangers of being out at night. Since the closest path to the other side of the mountain was near the village, they would follow the road and stop when they found the best trail to cross over. They'd find a place to rest, then begin their trek up the mountain an hour before dawn.

The two leaders gave Bella and Cadfael their final instructions.

"The guards and staff can go without food for now." Devon had no sympathy after seeing how thin the imprisoned shifters had been. He glanced over at them where they were now running as wolves through the parking lot, darting in and out of the forest. He couldn't blame them. If he'd been locked up for as long as they'd been, he'd want to sniff everything, stretch his legs, and hunt. Remus confirmed his thoughts.

"Don't worry," Remus said. "They're running in fresh air for the first time in a long time. They'll run as a pack to find food and return soon. I doubt the wild shifters will go near a pack their size."

"I'll call them back when it's time to leave." Cadfael looked to Bella.

She nodded. "We still have to finish repairing the road. Once the shifters are back, we'll leave for Bravos."

"It will be three or four days before we get back to the village," Remus added.

Bella, as usual, had the logistics already worked out. "Team One, the vans, and the drivers are still in the village. They'll wait for you, then you can meet us at the airstrip."

With the plan set, Devon let Remus round up the rest of their team while he found a spot next to a tree. He pulled out his burner phone and typed a text.

"I miss you."

It took a minute before the response came.

"Oh, thank god. I was worried. Miss you too."

"Sergi alive but haven't caught up yet. Hoping tomorrow or the next day."

It took a moment before Cressa responded. "Are you okay?"

"Lab destroyed but Sergi has evidence. There were captive shifters. Sending to Gregor for safety."

"That's horrible about the shifters. Gregor is a good idea. Are you okay?"

He grinned at her persistence to focus on him. "Today was a good day."

"I love you."

"I love you, too."

"Are you sure he's okay?"

She meant Sergi, and he could only shake his head at their strange relationship. "Can't be sure, but told he was fine before he escaped."

"Don't you dare tell him I asked."

For the first time since they started this mission, he laughed out loud. They would find Sergi, and everything would be okay.

# Chapter Thirty-One

I TRAILED after Sergi as he crossed a wide stream. One of my earliest training memories was of my uncle teaching me about river crossings, especially when it was impossible to determine its depth. There was one method when leading and a different one when following.

"Whenever you follow someone," my uncle said, "watch their path to the middle of the river before following in their same steps. If there are several in front of you, watch how others reach the center. Most won't follow the same path and end up falling into an unseen predicament. Always watch and learn."

He'd passed that wisdom on several times until one day, not long after that first time, I responded to his lesson rather than simply nodding. "You're not speaking of just the river, but life in general."

I never glanced away or flinched as he considered me. He lifted my chin with a finger, and when he spoke, the glow of his wolf held me still.

"You are wise for your age. Never let anyone make you doubt yourself."

When Sergi reached the center of the stream, he turned and

waited for me. He'd never questioned my actions since we'd left the cave at dawn. At times, I was barely a foot behind him, at others, I lagged several yards behind. Then there were moments like this when I paused before proceeding.

The distance between us had grown the last couple of miles. Soft footsteps from behind us came and went with the soft breeze and made it difficult to determine how far away they were. Sergi either understood my delays for what they were or assumed I grew tired.

After crossing the shallow stream, thankful my boots were waterproof, we walked in silence, each to our own thoughts, but I wasn't fooled by his focus on the landscape in front of us. He was vampire, and after listening to battle stories while we nibbled on nutrition bars for breakfast, there was no doubt he'd heard the same thing I did.

We were being followed. I couldn't determine their numbers, but it was more than two and probably less than ten. With wild shifters, it was impossible to guess their pack structure. Either way, Sergi didn't order me to stay close or request I take the lead to put himself in between me and the threat. He treated me like an equal. Like the wolf I was.

After another hour, as the sun dipped low, I found him waiting for me at the top of a small ridge.

"We should get rid of them before we find cover." He glanced behind me, his gaze following the tree line. "I sensed four, maybe five. What do you think?"

I wasn't surprised he was aware we were being followed or that he might have calculated the number of wolves, but I was pleased he wanted my opinion. Not because I was female but because I was a shifter. "Not more than ten, but I think some are closer than the others. These wild ones don't follow the same pack structures the rest of us do. They might not have an Alpha, and they will be unpredictable."

He considered it. "We can't kill ten, even with my daggers and your wolf. If it's less, maybe. But sometimes taking down one or two is enough to deter the others."

"Strike fast when they least expect it and hope we only have to deal with a handful of scouts. Leave them injured so they know we mean them no harm."

He nodded and jutted his chin toward the road ahead. "I noticed a couple of places we can wait for them."

I followed him to a thick stand of trees near a pool. When he told me his plan, I laughed. It wasn't because I thought it foolish. It was because I could picture my uncle doing the same thing, though not in wolf form. Our wolves don't like to get wet.

I took off my clothes and laid them at the base of a tree, out of sight of anyone approaching. It didn't surprise me to find Sergi watching me. This wasn't the first time. A shifter gets used to the naked body at an early age. Packs liked to run together so it was common to shift with others. Yet, when Sergi's gaze rolled over me, I was quite aware it was a male appraising me. And I liked it.

"What?" I couldn't help but ask. His expression was unreadable, and I found myself sinking into warm nut-brown eyes lit from behind with a soft red glow.

"It's not often I see a shifter change into their wolf. It's an amazing sight."

"I'll try not to bite you in the middle of battle."

The tips of his fangs showed when he flashed a wicked grin. "I'll try not to confuse you with the other wolves."

I was still laughing when the wolf came out, and it turned into a yip. The lust for a fight surged through me. Sergi wasn't an Alpha, but his proximity brought on my shift faster than normal. Maybe it was his beast. My wolf sensed it riding close to the surface. The primal instinct of our other selves preparing to do battle together.

Sergi took off his clothes and hid them. I watched every nuance of his muscled physique as he waded into the pool, a dagger in each hand.

The night was quiet, but they were out there. I yipped again as if I were injured, then made a couple of turns before nestling into the grass. With my snout on my paws, I lowered my lids and waited.

It was five minutes before I heard the first rustling along the trail. I listened for distinct sounds to determine how many were out there. We might have disturbed their hunt or simply crossed through their territory, and they didn't like trespassers. They would know something lurked beneath our human forms, so less likely on a hunt and more likely scouts not happy with our intrusion.

They didn't completely surround us. One was in the crop of trees to our left, and another approached along the pond's shore. One, maybe two, came down the path we'd walked.

Their footsteps were light, and if I wasn't in wolf form, it would have been difficult to hear them. That's what made the wild ones so dangerous. They spent most of their time as wolves, which heightened their senses. There was no doubt they'd picked up my scent. Did they know Sergi was vampire? I doubted they saw many in this area.

I kept my wolf still as I mentally prepared my attack. There wasn't time. The wolf to my left burst out of the trees as a howl pierced the silence. It was lean and smaller than me, but that didn't stop it as it leaped into the air.

My wolf rolled, and as the other landed where I'd once been, I grabbed the back of its neck. I shook it, my teeth sinking in, and blood filled my mouth. The wild, musky taste urged me on as the wolf howled in pain beneath me.

When it went limp, I dropped it and turned in time to see two things at once. One was the bared teeth of two wolves bearing down on me. The other was the warrior who rose out of the pond like Poseidon from the sea. His face was grim with determination, the water sluicing over his body in rivulets, emphasizing his bulging biceps and thick muscular thighs.

I wasn't the only one staring. The wolves, not expecting this new adversary, couldn't stop their trajectory or speed within such a short distance. The four of us met with claws, fangs, and daggers.

Sergi didn't hesitate, swinging his daggers as a wolf launched itself at him. I lost sight of him when the second wolf hit me in the side. We rolled, and though this wolf was larger than the first, it seemed dazed from seeing Sergi, who'd made a show of his bright white fangs.

Proof they hadn't known they'd invited a vampire to battle.

I bit at the wolf's neck, and it pulled away, but not before it took a huge bite of my shoulder. I yelped but didn't stop as I clamped down on a back leg as the wolf shifted position. Its cry of pain urged me on, and I used my size and weight to shove the wolf away before I grabbed the back of its front leg. Its snout whipped around, and it pulled away long enough to get a hold of my neck.

Fear gripped me, and putting all my strength into it, I yanked out of its teeth and scrambled back. I felt the blood seeping into my coat. It had gotten another bite of me.

We circled each other, which gave me a quick peek at Sergi and the wolf he battled. Blood smeared his torso, arms, and legs, but the wolf wasn't fairing any better. Sergi's daggers were stained red as he slashed at the wolf. He wasn't stabbing, which would produce deeper, harder-to-heal cuts, preferring to slice, which would still result in the rending of blood but heal easily after one or two shifts.

The wolf who I'd been sparring with lunged when he noticed my glance at Sergi, but I wasn't a foolish wolf. My uncle taught me as a pup to always keep an eye on the events around me while remaining focused on my enemy.

The wolf was surprised when I twisted as he hit, sending us both to the ground with me on top. Not what it was expecting as I grabbed it's neck and shook. If this were a lesser beast, a couple good shakes could break its neck, but wolves were made of tougher stuff, and all I wanted was a decent enough injury to make it stop.

Fighting to disarm or maim was always more difficult than fighting to kill. And it was made harder when the other side only wanted to see me dead. I held onto its neck as the blood filled my mouth, and when the wolf quieted, I stopped shaking it.

Keeping my paws firmly on the wolf, I looked up, blood dripping from my mouth, to find Sergi watching me. The wolf he'd been fighting lay at his feet, and the first one I'd fought had crawled over to it.

"You can release it." He nodded at the wolf under my feet. "They've given up."

I stared down at my prey and saw the defeat reflected in its gaze. I panted as my wolf calmed, then stepped back to release it. It got up, shook itself, then limped to where the other two lay.

I followed and stepped next to Sergi, who watched the wolves. My focus was on the fourth wolf, who was still out there but hadn't joined the fight.

Sergi turned with me as the fourth wolf, the one who'd been approaching from the pond, stepped out from behind a tree. It never joined the battle but simply watched and waited. I didn't think it was an Alpha, more likely the lead scout. It lifted its head and released one mournful howl.

Sergi dropped his daggers and spread out his arms as he faced it.

"We're not here to bother you. We just want to go home. You won't see us again."

The wolf stared, and while it didn't advance, it didn't appear impressed by Sergi's words of truce. Then Sergi spoke again in a language I didn't understand but recognized as the local Romanian tongue.

The wolf bowed its head, followed it with a whine, then barked. The three wolves near us slowly slipped away into the forest. Small drips of blood trailed after them.

"We'll continue so you can shift and heal your wounds. Don't follow us."

The wolf lifted its head and howled. Sergi glanced down at me, and I nodded. The fight was over, and while the wolves refused to take it as a loss, they wouldn't bother us anymore.

I trotted over to the trail that led down the mountain and waited while Sergi collected our clothes and backpack.

Without a glance back, which told the wolves we trusted them to honor their word, we continued our journey. One naked vampire and one limping wolf.

How quickly my life changed once again.

SERGI FOLLOWED the same trail for two miles, turning around every couple minutes to keep an eye on Alex. She remained in wolf form, and his first assumption was that she wanted to remain in her shifter form in case the wild ones decided revenge was better than prudence.

He didn't miss the increasing limp in her front leg. Blood stained her coat, and like him, much of it came from their opponents, but the stain on her shoulder gleamed wet, reflecting an open wound. They'd passed several pools and one creek where he refilled their water bottles. Alex drank deeply but still refused to shift back. After a few hundred yards, he selected a narrower path that bordered the mountainside as he searched for an appropriate cave.

He settled on the third one he found, which was the same size as the cave from the previous night but had an upper shelf ten feet long and two feet off the cave floor. It was tall enough for Alex to stand, though he'd have to hunch over, and space for both of them to sleep warmly with a nearby fire.

Alex laid down, head on her paws, and was still in that position when Sergi returned with firewood. Once the fire licked at the wood, he leaned against the rock wall that formed the shelf and watched her sleep. After a couple of minutes, she rose and limped toward the exit.

The limp was worse.

"Where are you going?"

The wolf stopped and paused a moment before looking back. When she took another step, he doubted she'd make it more than a few steps outside before collapsing.

"You're not leaving, and if you think you can outrun me with your injury, you're mistaken. Don't make me chase you."

She whined, and he shook his head.

"We're out of danger. Shift and heal your leg. You should have done that after the first mile."

When she held her ground, he stood and strolled toward her, leaving as much distance as the cave would allow until he positioned himself between her and the exit. He crossed his arms over his chest and stared her down. Rather than shift, she slowly lowered to the ground, her eyes closing as she once again rested her head on her front legs. Her movements confirmed what he already knew. Her injury was worse than she wanted him to believe.

After giving it some thought, he strolled over and squatted next to her. When she didn't appear bothered by his nearness, he sat. He wasn't sure why he made the next move because he wasn't an Alpha, and he was invading her space. Rather than worry if he was doing the right thing, he placed a hand on her back and stroked the surprisingly soft fur along her back. He stayed away from the matted blood that ran from midpoint on her neck, thickened in mass around her shoulder, then trailed down her leg.

They sat like that for several minutes. Her breathing turned to pants as he continued his gentle stroking. Then, without warning, she shifted back to human form.

At first, she yelped, but when it turned into a human cry, he knew it was bad. Her eyes were unfocused, and when he placed his hand on her forehead, he cursed under his breath.

He rolled her over. A bite on her shoulder, less than two hours old, was red, angry, and likely infected. Her shifter magic should have healed her, but it sometimes required more than one shift. He hadn't heard of shifters succumbing to infections after a fight, but these had been wild shifters. All the time he'd spent in the Carpathians, he'd never run across them before, and other than the warnings of how dangerous they were, he knew little else.

"Shift." He threw as much weight as he could into the command, but she didn't stir. If her wolf was awake, it didn't have any more luck in rousing her.

Her breathing became ragged, similar to her wolf's pants. He scanned the rest of her body but didn't find any other noticeable injuries until he pushed her hair up and found a second bite on her neck. This one wasn't as deep, but it also appeared infected.

An infection working as rapidly as it was could be deadly. He ran a hand over her hair, then left her side to pull the package of vials from her lab coat. He found what he wanted in the first package—the vials of the BP-X. The Blood Poppy had worked wonders for him, and it was vital to dreamwalkers, but what would it do to a shifter? Would it cure an infection? He could carry her the rest of the way, but they were a long way from a clinic, and when they reached it, it might be too late to save her, assuming she made it that far.

The vial was warm in his hand. Based on his experience with Blood Poppy, and what he'd seen from Remus's lab tests, she should only require a few drops, certainly no more than half the vial. He closed his eyes. It might not help, but would it hurt her? He stared at the flames, felt the warmth flush his face, and made a decision.

He lifted the top off the vial, opened her mouth, and dribbled a few drops on her tongue. One fell on her lips, and she instinctively licked it off. When she licked her lips again as if searching for more, he obliged her. He emptied a quarter of the vial before resealing it.

After a minute, and with no apparent change in her, he

decided on plan B. He left her long enough to put the vial back with the others and strip off his clothes, piling them next to the fire.

Alex didn't struggle when he lifted her into his arms. She was so cold. Not a good sign. She surprised him before he exited the cave when she curled into him, seeking his warmth.

He strode quickly through the dark forest, using his shoulder to push through the bushes and low-hanging limbs to protect her body. When he crossed the creek where they'd refreshed their water bottles, he turned right down a well-used trail that led to a small pool bordered by rocks and a small grassy area.

Without pausing, he waded into the warm water, a slight mineral scent tickling his nose. She startled when the water flowed over her but didn't attempt to leave his arms. The pool wasn't any deeper than a bathtub, and he sat in the middle, keeping her head above the water that reached his chest. Once he settled into a comfortable position, he held her tight as he lowered her deeper into the water, ensuring the water covered the injuries on her shoulder and the back of her neck.

The minerals in the water should clean out the wound, but he didn't think they would be enough to kill the infection. He rocked back and forth in a slow rhythm, keeping his senses alert for any other trouble, but he soon relaxed. They were safe for now.

After some time had passed, he sat her up so he could check her wounds. He pulled her wet hair aside and breathed a sigh of relief when the area around the bite was clean and the redness had faded to a dark pink. The most grievous wound on her shoulder had improved as well.

He remained in the water and carefully washed the blood off both their bodies. After checking the wounds once more, he was pleased enough to leave the pool. She was still unresponsive, but with any luck, her shifter blood, and perhaps the Blood Poppy, was healing her.

He stood and repositioned her in his arms once more before

striding for the path. If nothing else, her heart pounded strong against his chest. When he reached the cave, he settled in front of the fire with her still in his arms. He reached over and tossed two logs onto the fire. Once the flames burned brightly, he moved Alex so the heat would dry her skin.

The heat of the flames dried them quickly, and he gently dressed her and laid her on the shelf, where she curled into a fetal position. He didn't want to block her from the fire, but he refused to leave her the closest to the entrance, and as he expected, the air was warmer on the shelf. He stretched next to her and closed his eyes, allowing a hand to settle on her arm. Satisfied her skin radiated warmth, he relaxed into a satisfied sleep.

# Chapter Thirty-Two

I WOKE WITH A START, my eyes flashing open to darkness. Not complete darkness. From somewhere, a low, orange light flickered. I didn't move, trying to recall where I was.

The hard surface I lay on reminded me of my cell. Panic seized me. For a moment, my breath stuck in my throat. Then I remembered there had been a battle. When the fight with the wild shifters slammed into me, the air rushed out of me, and I reached for my shoulder.

The pain that had increased with each step as I followed Sergi through the dense forest was gone. I ran a hand over my right shoulder again, positive that was where the wolf had bitten me. I checked the left side. There wasn't a wound. Wait. There was a scab, thin and flaky. I scratched it off and tried to remember what happened after the fight.

Where was I?

Somehow, in my waking daze, I'd missed the strong scent of a wood fire. I lifted my head and looked toward the orange glow, but I couldn't see the source. A naked body blocked my view. Sergi lay flat, his eyes closed, and his chest rose and fell in a deep rhythm.

I immediately glanced down and was relieved to see I was wearing a guard's shirt. Nothing else, but at least my privates were covered. We were on a rock shelf, and I glanced up. Plenty of room to stand. I rose slowly, waiting for other signs of battle to make their presence known. Surprisingly, there was no pain. Not one ache. I pulled my knees to my chest and then stretched my legs, repeating the motion several times. I lifted my arms and bent my elbows. Not one single sore muscle.

In fact, now that I was fully awake, I felt good. Like, run laps good. My first thought was that Sergi had given me some of his blood, but unlike humans, vampire blood did nothing for a shifter. I must have shifted at least once since I was in human form.

The memory slammed into me like a bullet train.

Sergi had found a cave, and I'd limped in, agony twisting every nerve ending. I waited for him to settle so I could go outside to shift. I didn't want him to see my injury. Though, now that my mind was clearer than it had been in days, hell, months, that seemed idiotic. Like he wouldn't have noticed me limping.

I never left the cave. He stopped me and then sat by me. His rough hands were gentle as he stroked my wolf's back. She quieted quickly, enjoying the pleasure of his touch. My cheeks heated at the memory, as vague as it was. He'd calmed her as if he were an Alpha signaling she was safe. And then I'd shifted.

He'd carried me to a warm pool. My nose wrinkled, recalling the metallic smell of minerals, but beneath that was the light mix of freshly cut wood and musk. The scent of a male.

The water had been warm, and though we were both naked—and I clearly remembered the touch of his skin on mine—I didn't feel cold when he carried me back to the cave. Then I remembered nothing at all.

I stared into the low flames, and, without disturbing Sergi, I navigated around him and dropped to the floor. I added two logs to the fire then searched for the lab coat. I hadn't been wearing it during the fight, but I had to make sure nothing had been trampled when things got messy.

I spread out the vials and sighed when they were all accounted for. Then something caught my eye. Probably just a shadow from the sparking flames. I picked up the vial of BP-X and flipped it over and back. I picked up a second vial of BP-X and compared it to the first. Then I did it with the third vial. The first one was only three-quarters full. It had been full when I took it from the lab. I knew it to be true as well as I knew the sun rose in the morning.

I bit my lip. Drops of something on my tongue. I couldn't remember anything else. Had Sergi given me Blood Poppy? Why? All I needed were a couple of shifts to close the bite wounds. I touched the back of my neck. I'd forgotten I'd been bitten there, too, but there wasn't even a scab.

I don't know how long I stared at the vial, knowing I was missing part of the puzzle. Eventually, small bits returned. I must have been delirious with a fever. The pain had been increasing, as if my natural healing abilities had been nullified.

Had he saved my life again?

I'd never considered vampires would show such honor for shifters. And he hadn't just saved me. Once I'd freed him, he could have easily left the facility. He said he needed evidence. Was releasing all the shifters from their cells simply a diversionary tactic or mercy? Carlos had believed in his honor.

A flash of dark, mahogany-colored eyes touched with a red glow made my skin flush as a warm shiver ran through me. Soft skin behind the tribal tattoos of some long-ago culture. Lust ran through me as I remembered the soft curve of his lips when he smiled. The touch of his hands as he washed the blood from my body made the soft hairs on my arms buzz with energy.

Tomorrow, we'd reach civilization and a freedom I hadn't experienced for months. I'd go home to the pack. Sergi would go home to his House. That would be the end of anything between us. And there *was* something there, wasn't there? A spark of heat.

A shifter and a vampire had nothing in common. We'd been mortal enemies for centuries. Yet, my uncle didn't think all vampires were bad.

What was one night? Who would know?

It had been so long since anyone had held me. Since anyone had made me feel alive. Once I was home and the horrors of the experiments settled in, it could take months to overcome whatever post-traumatic memories would resurface. They were always close. And when I was alone, they pressed on me.

I placed the wrapped vials in the lab coat and laid them on my other clothes. The fire drew me to it, and as the flames heated my body, I stared up at the naked vampire.

He had turned on his side, resting on an elbow as he watched me. He'd awakened while I'd been lost in my thoughts. The red glow of his beast washed over me, inflicting emotions I didn't understand or chose not to.

He took my breath away.

Not a muscle twitched on his sculpted body as I walked toward him. The red glow intensified and stirred butterflies. I wasn't a shy female, and the way he devoured me with nothing more than a look made me shiver with anticipation.

At this moment, I didn't see him as vampire, even though the tips of his fangs showed when he licked his bottom lip. I grinned like a cat luring easy prey as I climbed onto the shelf.

All I could think was...mine.

I slipped the guard's shirt off my shoulders and let the garment slide to the floor. My wolf stirred with a deep hunger, and without memory of ever taking a step, my lips were on his, and his arms wrapped around me.

His own longing poured through me with that first touch of tongues. When I pushed closer, he gripped my waist and unleashed his passion.

He sat up and crushed me to him as he became the seducer. His fingers wove through my hair as his kiss grew deeper, and I ran my hands up his chest until I gripped his shoulders. I had to get closer. A bare inch separated us, and he was simply too far away.

His chest slid across my breasts as he lifted me up to straddle him. Better. He was hard, and I felt his manhood slide against my most sensitive areas. I moved against him until I was wet for him.

Though my thoughts were a jumble of emotions, I recognized this moment as something different than any male I'd been with.

I'd had my share of lovers. Some were tender and reverent in their touches but never ignited my passion. Others played rough, and while they released my wild side, they never took the time to go slow and explore.

This was different. His rough hands roamed my body as if memorizing parts of me. His strokes were as soft as when he'd ruffled my wolf's fur. Yet his kiss was demanding, thorough, and left me dizzy. I reached down to stroke the top of his thigh where our bodies met, and his shiver snaked through me with his low groan. For an instant, the red glow of his eyes flashed brighter before returning to the warmth of their natural color.

I'd been curious how the beast might react to Sergi's heightened senses. That red glow told me it was paying attention. I grinned as Sergi worked his lips down my neck. I hope the beast was enjoying these erotic sensations as much as my wolf was.

I rose to settle myself over him, knowing I was more than ready. When he slid inside, I closed my eyes and slowly rocked, seating myself deeper.

He rocked with me and returned to my lips. Our tongues collided, but as the waves of passion rolled over me, my head fell back. I stared up at the ceiling, and though there was nothing but rock touched with the orange tint from the fire, I swore I saw stars burst, their shining silver pieces falling like confetti around us.

Not wasting a moment, he took advantage of my exposed neck as his fangs traced a downward path until they scraped over my breasts. His teeth nipped, and I rocked faster.

Before I understood what happened, I was on my back. His

large frame loomed over me as he increased his strokes. The glow of the fire lit the sweat on his skin, and when he lifted my leg to let it settle in the crook of his arm, my head rolled back and forth as he moved deeper.

I gripped his hips and whispered, "Faster."

He obeyed my command.

Time evaporated. I faded into the scorching touch of hands and urgent nips of fangs. The stars I'd witnessed earlier returned in time to burst into orange fireballs as the building pressure released. Waves of pulsing sensations crashed over me. His shudder and long moan woke me from my stupor of sensory overload.

He rested on his elbows and trailed butterfly kisses down my neck and over my shoulder as my body shivered with delight. Then he pulled out and rolled next to me. His arm trapped my body, forcing me to roll with him until my head rested against his shoulder.

We slept for a short time as the fire died down. Based on the low light, we'd made love longer than I'd thought. I grinned and nestled closer to the hard body next to me. Funny. I'd always thought of vampires as a cold-blooded species, but there was nothing but heat radiating from him.

He shifted position and tugged me to him. "Are you cold?"

"No." I smiled but doubted he could see it with my head turned into his chest.

After a bit of silence, he asked the strangest of questions.

"What was the first thing you planned to do once you found your freedom?"

I snorted, then sobered at the thought. Or, more importantly, the lack of any thought toward that idea. I'd hoped to see my uncle again, but what happened after that never crossed my mind. Had I thought I'd die there?

I couldn't stop the shiver that coursed through me and silently cursed when Sergi squeezed me. I didn't deserve to be comforted if

KIM ALLRED

I hadn't considered a future. Sergi expected some form of answer, so I went with the one thing I knew to be true.

"Well, I hadn't expected it to be sex in a cave with a vampire."

I'd expected him to call me on my obvious evasion. Instead, he laughed. It was a deep belly laugh, and it made me smile. When I lifted my head to face him, I lost my train of thought. He was so beautiful in that moment. Not a classic beauty, but he had the magnetic allure of a warrior. His smile must have broken dozens of hearts during his long life. His was a beauty that touched my soul and stirred my wolf.

This was a caring male. A male willing to give up his freedom —his life—for shifters.

He ran a finger down my cheek and pulled my hair back, letting the straight strands run through his fingers. "This wasn't the first time I'd been captured and tortured. In fact, it was probably the shortest period of time that I'd been chained."

I sat up and leaned against an elbow so I could see his face as he told me his tale. And before he even started, it wasn't lost on me that he hadn't been satisfied with my answer.

"The first time was before I met Devon. I'd been young and stupid and hadn't been paying attention. I ended up as cargo with a group of slave traders." He chuckled. "They were human and had no idea what they'd captured. Still, it took two weeks in a dark cell crowded with other humans before I had an opportunity. I was hungry for blood. All I remember after that was the screaming of those I left behind as I escaped."

"They didn't go with you?"

He shrugged a shoulder and scratched his chin, his gaze seeming to replay the moment. "They were terrified of me. They might have eventually calmed down and followed once they realized I was long gone and the guard wasn't going to get back up."

"The other times were in the service of House Trelane?"

"It sounds strange when you ask it that way, though it's true enough. I never looked at Devon in that way, nor our Father

296

Guildford Trelane. Even with all the battles, life was simpler back then. The picture clearer of who was bad and who was good. And before you say it, I realize the answer depends on which side you're on. But either way, there was never a gray area. No collateral damage to worry about. Humanity has become complex."

I laughed and gave him a light pinch. "And here I thought vampires were rather two-dimensional. You sound a bit complex yourself."

He studied me, his gaze curious, but then he returned to the point he was trying to make. "The worst time was when the leader of a House in Italy had me beaten then tossed in a dark cell for three months without any food. Twice a day, they poured water from a grate above. I was given a single cup to catch what little water I could. I honestly didn't think I'd survive that one."

"Were you rescued?" I'd been locked in my cell as punishment for almost that long, but not in constant darkness. And I was fed, perhaps poorly, but I had food and water.

"That was the only way I was going to get out of there. It had taken Devon that long to find out who had taken me and where I was. They waited until the House leader traveled to a neighboring town and stormed the castle." He scratched his thigh, then turned and laid a hand on my hip.

"I'm not saying this right. I don't speak much about the past, and never the bad times. But you need to hear this whether you believe me now, sometime later, or maybe never."

I blew out a breath, knowing this had been his intent all along. If he was willing to share this much, I might as well let him finish.

"As arrogant as it might sound, I always knew I'd find a way out of a bad situation, yet, not once did I think of what I'd do when that day came. I focused on each day. Getting through it and watching for every opportunity. The only reason I asked the question of you was to see how you responded."

I ran a hand down his chest. It was as warm and hard as a brick wall on a summer day. When I rested my palm on his left breast, his heart pounded against it. "I guess I didn't pass the test."

His lips quirked. "No. You deflected."

"I never thought about getting out until you showed up." The words slipped out before I could pull them back. So, I let the rest go. "It makes me sound like a wolf giving up."

"Did it ever occur to you that maybe you were too busy surviving? And you did much more than that. You were witness to everything that happened, no matter how horrific. You memorized the floor plans, you learned, and you waited for your opportunity."

"I did think of my uncle and whether he thought I was dead. If he'd given up on me."

Sergi cupped my face, and I met his gaze. This time nothing but that warm mahogany waited for me. "Family never gives up. No matter how long they wait, until the day they die, they never give up hope. It's not the vampire way, and I know for a fact it's not the shifter way."

I ran my hand over the back of his neck and pulled his head down to kiss him.

His words might not heal me, or maybe they would. But they were what I needed to hear at this moment. All I wanted was to stay in his arms. To be one with him again.

He must have read my naughty thoughts because he pushed me onto my back and held his body over mine. He started with my breasts as he ran his tongue over my skin, forcing goose bumps to erupt. Then he moved down, tickling my belly before going farther. I arched when he reached the more sensitive spots, and my wolf howled with delight.

There was little talk the rest of the night.

THE FOLLOWING MORNING, I stretched, smiling when my elbow poked Sergi in the side and he grunted.

"Now that I'm free, I can tell you the first thing I could use right now is a strong cup of coffee."

"I'd prefer an espresso, but I wouldn't say no to a cup of French roast." He ran a hand down my side and grinned when I tried to squirm away.

I laughed. "That tickles. Stop it."

Sergi laughed as he pulled me close and, after giving me a searing kiss, strummed his fingers along my side, making me snort-laugh. My face heated when Sergi laughed harder, but the brief embarrassment was nothing compared to the mortification that rushed over me when a voice bellowed from the cave entrance.

"What's going on here?"

I rolled away from Sergi like he'd burst into flames, but he'd been faster. He stood in all his naked glory with his fists planted on his hips like some vampire Adonis. I looked around, searching for my clothing, and slapped my forehead. Every stitch had been left by the fire except for the guard's shirt, which was now lying at Sergi's feet.

A bit awkward to grab it now.

I glanced around him and fought the battling emotions of happiness and humiliation.

My uncle.

I gulped. He must have believed me dead after all this time. Then he finds me in a compromising position with a naked vampire. And whatever he thought was happening here...Well, in this case, it was exactly what was happening here. I stepped closer but stayed in the shadows near the wall.

The male standing next to my uncle was almost as tall as him but leaner. A handsome vampire. When I glanced at Sergi, his arms now folded across his chest, his expression was blank—the face he always wore for Gheata—but I caught the slight twitch of his lips.

This male had to be Devon Trelane. I could be wrong, but if my uncle was working with a vampire, it would be a House leader.

"Uncle." I didn't dare move into the light, and Sergi took a sidestep toward me. Both males would be able to see past the shadows, but that didn't mean I had to step into the dwindling firelight to show off my naked body. It was one thing to be naked after a shift, but it was quite another when it was pretty obvious this was an intimate setting.

Sergi turned his unbelieving gaze to me. "Remus is your uncle?"

I shrugged.

He shook his head as his lips quirked. "Now, it all makes sense." His eyes glittered with humor and a sudden heat that made my legs go weak.

He found this all amusing. Glad someone did.

"I take it my tracker is still working." Sergi faced the males, his tone smooth and respectful.

"Perhaps it's best if we give them time to get dressed." Devon held a hand out to guide my uncle out of the cave.

He gave Sergi a searing look before turning and marching out.

Devon grinned. "Take your time. The shifters are safe." Then he was gone.

Sergi held out his hand, but I remained where I was.

"I'm sorry I never mentioned my uncle by name. When you said your House leader would send another team, I had no idea my uncle would be part of it."

"Come here."

I took his hand, and he pulled me to him. "It doesn't change what happened last night." He breathed me in. "It doesn't change anything since you walked into my cell. You saved me. That's all that matters."

I wasn't sure what he meant. This had been a one-night thing. Comfort after a long incarceration. His kiss, slow and thorough, said something different. He held me tight for several minutes before he released me and jumped off the ledge. Instead of retrieving his clothes, he turned and gripped my waist. He slid my body over his as he lowered me.

If my uncle wasn't waiting outside, I would have leaped into Sergi's arms. I did the only thing I could think of to cool my hormones. I chuckled. We spent the rest of the time getting dressed, trying to hold back our laughter at the predicament we found ourselves in.

I followed Sergi toward the cave entrance, but he stopped me.

"Now that we don't have to worry about those we left behind, let's take the moment to say everything that needs to be said. You need time with Remus, and I have much to share with Devon."

I glanced at the door, eager to see my uncle but unsure of his acceptance or, more likely, disappointment in me.

Sergi rubbed my arm. "It will be alright. He's just had a bit of a shock."

"That's a bit of an understatement."

He chuckled, kissed the top of my head, then strode out. I moved back to the fire and picked up the lab coat. When I heard the soft footsteps behind me, I turned and let the coat drop to the ground.

His eyes were filled with unshed tears, and I raced to him. He wrapped me in his arms, his voice filled with emotion.

"Oh, Alex. I didn't think I'd ever see you again."

I hugged him tight, remembering this feeling when I was just a pup, orphaned and alone. He was the first shifter who'd shown kindness after the loss of my parents. And with that one action in front of his entire pack, I'd been accepted as one of them.

It was silly. I knew I was going home the minute I followed Sergi out the back door and into this wilderness. But having my uncle here? The fact that my nightmare was truly over hit me like a semi truck crashing into me, and it was my turn to cry.

We sat on the shelf, my feet dangling as I kicked my heels against the rock platform.

I described the events since discovering a vampire had been captured and was being tortured. I left out the experiments, how I'd been captured, and my year of captivity. There would be more than enough time to discuss that once I was ready. And most of it would come out in drips and drabs after I had time to come to terms with it all.

"Did shifter S-272, I mean Cadfael, make it out okay?"

Remus nodded. "As did Carlos and two others of my wolves."

"There were others?" I dropped my head. "I didn't know. They did their best to keep us from seeing or talking to each other. I only saw those whose cells I cleaned or who I worked with."

"Don't worry about that. Our priority is to get you off this mountain. The plane will be waiting for us."

I played with the rolled-up sleeve of my shirt. "Don't be mad at Sergi. I'm a grown female."

He stood and pushed dirt over the embers with a booted foot. "Let's not discuss that. We need to get moving."

I held back a sigh. He wasn't going to let it go. Whether his reaction was because he caught me with a vampire or that he'd caught me in such an intimate moment, I didn't know. My guess was that it was a bit of both as his fatherly instincts took over.

I picked up the lab coat and shrugged it on, reaching into the pockets to confirm the vials and USB drive were still there. My paranoia was on prime time. I could share the information with my uncle now, but he wasn't in the right mood.

Besides, it was important for Sergi and Devon Trelane to be involved in that conversation. If it hadn't been for Sergi, I would never have gotten out of the director's office alive to share the evidence.

I followed my uncle outside, eager to meet this House leader, who had found a way to befriend The Wolf. At least enough to run a joint mission.

Sergi was speaking with Devon, and it was easy to see the camaraderie between the two. Before we reached them, Devon grabbed Sergi's shoulder and bent his head. Sergi followed suit until their foreheads touched. I'd only seen the gesture once before, and I'd been told it was a sign of respect and close allegiance between vampires.

When we reached them, the two stepped back, and Devon turned to greet me with a warm smile. His gaze seemed to take in every inch of me, settling on my eyes.

"Thank you for saving Sergi. I owe you a great favor."

I was taken aback, knowing how much it meant to be given a favor. "The same could be said of him. I wouldn't be here without his aid."

"A testament to how well vampires and shifters work together in the face of adversity."

His words shocked me, though my uncle had been hoping for such an alliance. It appeared he found one.

I wasn't sure how to respond and glanced at Sergi.

"Let's get off this mountain." Sergi glanced at my uncle, who was conveniently surveying the area. "We can catch up on the plane."

Sergi stepped back and waited for Devon, but Devon merely held his hand out to my uncle. Sergi and I followed next, with Devon watching our backside. Or so I thought. It wasn't until then that I noticed two males and two wolves stepping out of the forest. They nodded to Devon before falling into line behind him.

When the trail grew wide enough, Sergi and I walked side by side. My uncle led us at a fast pace, and whenever he glanced back, a frown of disappointment or disapproval, it was hard to know which, was etched in every line of his face. Sergi and I waited until he refocused on the path before grinning at each other like school kids misbehaving. Every so often, his fingers would brush along mine and linger for the briefest of moments.

The action could be considered accidental touches on a trail barely wide enough for the two of us to pass. I knew the difference. Neither of us looked back to see what Devon was thinking. If Sergi didn't bother, I sure as hell wasn't. Then again, Sergi hadn't seemed bothered by Devon finding us naked and laughing. And I recalled Devon's quick grin before leaving us to dress. He didn't seem to have any issues with a dalliance between Sergi and a shifter.

Of course, I had to remind myself that it had been only one night. What happened didn't matter anymore.

Yet, when I glanced at Sergi, and he caught my gaze, the red glow of his beast said he wasn't quite done with me. Heat raced through me at the prospect. Suddenly, the idea didn't bother me one bit.

# Chapter Thirty-Three

WITH REMUS SETTING A FAST PACE, the last team walked out of the forest as dusk settled over the village where Team One and the van drivers waited. Though Devon had mentioned that everyone was assembling at the airstrip, Sergi wasn't surprised to see Rafael, Carlos, and Cadfael waiting for them. While Sergi greeted his team members, ensuring them he was fine and thankful for the bag of blood Rafael handed him, his gaze continued to stray toward Alex.

The shifters, especially Carlos, were eager to welcome Alex. Remus hovered over her as if she might disappear from his sight. And it didn't escape Sergi's notice that Remus glanced his way several times as if warning him to stay away.

Sergi half-listened as the team shared their adventurous journey to the facility and the limited defenses to their infiltration. He wasn't surprised to hear about the trucks of kidnapped shifters. It made sense based on Alex's information on the experiments.

It wasn't until the shifter group disbanded to load into a van that Alex glanced his way. She gave him a warm smile and a slight shrug. He understood she had to follow Remus's orders, whatever they were, at least for now.

He returned a soft smile and a nod of understanding, aware Devon was watching him, and that almost made him grimace. Devon wouldn't say anything with everyone around. He'd wait until the two of them were alone, and then Sergi would never hear the end of it.

It had been a long time since Sergi had shown an interest in a female, and even then, he'd remained aloof. Centuries couldn't break the wall he'd built, unwilling to fall for the charms of someone who could betray him. The same could be said of Devon, whose dalliances with females were rare until the day Cressa strolled into the manor.

Perhaps if he weren't so ancient, so disillusioned, he would have dared more meaningful relationships. But his experiences with the pain of loss—harsh losses—had taught him to avoid the pitfall altogether. The simplest thing to do would be to let this be the end with Alex. Easy enough with Remus acting like a guard dog around her.

"You seem distracted." Devon handed him a second blood bag. "Let's get in the van so you can feed. I need you clear-headed."

Sergi took the bag, the first one he'd been given still clutched in his other hand. "The energy from the Blood Poppy is finally wearing off." He held the bags up. "I appreciate this."

Devon gripped his shoulder. "I'm sorry we couldn't get to you sooner."

"It was a week by my calculation."

"Eight days if you count the time to find you in the cave."

Sergi grunted. "Then it's not nearly the longest I've had to wait for you."

They turned as one as they strode to the van.

"That's true enough." Devon stopped next to the van and waited as the others climbed in. "Thank the gods for modern transportation. It would have taken much longer by ship and horses."

Sergi chuckled, remembering the old days as he followed

Devon into the van. He was surprised when he was led to the last row, where blankets had been laid out across multiple seats for a makeshift bed.

"Drink the blood and rest. We have a two-hour ride to the airstrip."

When the vans pulled to a stop at their destination, vampires and shifters jumped out to grab the gear and stow it in the waiting plane. Sergi had woken when he felt the van slow, and he sat up, pleased to find his energy restored.

When he boarded the plane, he walked past Alex, Remus, Carlos, and Cadfael, who sat in a group of four seats that faced each other. Alex's back was to him, but Remus turned to nod at Devon, then ignored Sergi. He could only grin at The Wolf's easy dismissal. Soon enough, Remus would have to put his papa wolf's behavior aside for the success of their overall mission.

Devon led his team to another grouping of four seats. Before Sergi sat down, Bella handed him a small duffel.

"There's fresh clothes in there. I thought you might want to change once we level off." She carried a second bag to Alex before returning to her seat across from him.

They were wheels up five minutes later, and twenty minutes after that, Alex picked up the duffel and walked past him to the lavatory. She gave him a quick smile and a wink as she passed by, and he noted Remus tracking her movement toward the back of the plane.

Cadfael, now dressed in black combat clothing, rose several minutes later, and when he reached Sergi, he stopped long enough to say, "Walk with me."

Devon and Bella had their noses in their tablets, and Rafael slept, so Sergi picked up his duffel and followed. Cadfael led him through a curtained divider and stopped at a group of vacant seats by the bathroom. Remus's private jet could have carried a larger team, and he suspected Remus had a smaller one for more personal travel, leaving this one for missions.

The seats were just as comfortable as the front of the plane but were grouped in seats of eight rather than four. The divider between cabins would allow for team leaders to meet in front while letting the other team members relax and sleep without distraction.

The galley was located behind the seats, and a shifter and vampire were making coffee and pulling food out of the fridge. Everyone was in restoration mode.

Cadfael sat and waved a hand for Sergi to join him. "I assume Alex will take several minutes to clean up, and we haven't had a chance to speak since you left the facility."

"It's good to see you survived, as well as the other shifters. I wish we'd found the facility sooner than we did."

Cadfael waved his hand. "We can only learn from the past. We can't change it. To dwell on it only serves to deter one from looking toward the future."

Sergi couldn't argue the sentiment. It was something anyone with a long life ahead of them had to learn quickly if they didn't want to go mad. "What are your plans? You never said where your pack was located."

"My last pack was in upstate New York near the border of Vermont. I've been gone long enough that another Alpha would have taken over by now. Remus is checking their status, but unless they're in some form of disarray, I won't challenge the Alpha. Remus invited me to stay at his home while I reacclimate to current politics and learn more about this war House Trelane is leading."

"Your leadership will be essential in the weeks and months to come. I hope we'll see more of you once we're back in Santiga Bay."

Cadfael's eyes lit with humor. "I understand many shifters work for House Trelane now."

Sergi shrugged. "We're building strong defenses at all Trelane properties, and we'd be foolish not to work with partners who strive for the same outcome."

"Would it be possible to see how you integrated the shifters and vampires?"

"I think I'd like to see that myself."

The two males turned to Alex, who leaned on the back of a nearby chair. Her hair was damp, her face freshly washed, and from what he could see of her combat attire, it fit her well, outlining the body he fondly remembered lying beneath him.

He stood, pushing the intrusive thoughts away as he picked up his bundle. "The House is currently on lockdown, but I'm sure a tour could be arranged once everyone is back and settled." He lifted his bag. "I'll take a moment to change."

Sergi washed his face and armpits, then ran wet hands through his hair, which was sufficient until he got home. He'd always been one for cleanliness, but it wasn't lost on him that he'd become obsessed with it over the last few decades. It was his one way of controlling some small portion of his life when everything around him fell to chaos and, at times, despair.

He buttoned the black shirt and wondered if Bella had purposely brought clothes that would fit him. It would have been her way to maintain the belief they'd find him alive. Her own way of staying in control.

He shoved the guard clothes back in the bag. They'd be tossed once he was home. When he left the lavatory, he found Alex sitting next to Cadfael, and they were eating from a charcuterie board filled with sliced meats, cheese, crackers, grapes, and olives. His brow lifted when he saw three glasses of red wine.

"Have a seat, vampire." Alex pointed to the chair he'd been in earlier. "Now that you're free, you don't mind having a glass of wine with shifters, do you?"

He dropped the duffel next to Alex's then took a seat. He lifted his glass of wine in a toast before drinking half of it. "Does Remus always have an excellent selection of wine on his planes, or did he plan for a celebration?"

Alex laughed, and it warmed his belly. "With my uncle, there's always good wine and Scotch available, but I imagine he increased the number of bottles in hopes of something more."

"What can you tell us of the vampire Council?" Cadfael changed the topic, eager to catch up on all he'd missed. "Remus told us a bit, but I imagine you have more insight into the topic."

Sergi considered the question, and they spent the next twenty minutes discussing the divide that had been growing for years. He'd hesitated a moment regarding Devon's plan to stop Venizi, then decided Remus would keep them in his confidence, so he provided a high-level explanation of their joint mission. He didn't mention dreamwalkers, leaving that topic for Devon.

Cadfael stood after he set down an empty wineglass. "I probably shouldn't have had that second glass. I need to go slowly until my body resets to decent food again. And since Remus spoke of a meeting before we land, I think a small nap is in order to clear my head." He squeezed Alex's shoulder and strolled toward the front of the plane, stopping to speak with both vampires and shifters on his way. His Alpha nature to ask questions and listen came naturally to him, and Sergi was pleased that his years of captivity hadn't broken that.

Once he was alone with Alex, Sergi couldn't think of anything to say. They'd never had a chance to speak of what happened between them. And this wasn't the place to have that talk, assuming she hadn't already put their evening together behind her.

He should have anticipated her shifter boldness. She might not be an Alpha, but she thought like one under her uncle's tutelage. She'd make a good Beta for any pack, and his chest tightened at the thought of her leaving Santiga Bay.

"You look rested. You must have gotten fresh blood."

"I don't know how fresh it was, but it was enough to revive me." He glanced toward the divider between sections. The curtain was still closed, and Cadfael was engaged in conversation. "You must feel better in new clothes. How are you doing?"

She sighed and leaned back. "Well enough for now. I'm still riding high, but sooner or later, that Blood Poppy rush is going to drop like a hammer."

He chuckled, but they both knew they were avoiding saying it. Trauma. That would hit soon as well. He offered a suggestion that would help with either issue. "I find meditation and training helps."

Her head tilted to the side. "You meditate?"

He grinned. "Not something you expected of vampires or of me?"

Her smile made his gut clench. "I was aware that vampires prefer meditation to calm their minds."

When she didn't elaborate, he added, "Warriors find meditation effective before battle."

She leaned forward, clearly interested. "I would think mock battles would be more appropriate."

"Some, especially the younger ones who've seen little battle or it might be their first campaign, appreciate the practice. Those more experienced understand the importance of mind control during battle, and can be the difference between walking off the field or being carried."

She nodded. "Shifters like to play war games, but before a mission, they tend to party hardy."

"I'd be lying if I said vampires didn't do a bit of that. Devon always provided a banquet before a battle but let his army decide the best way to prepare for the following day."

"And didn't women play a part in that?"

"Both males and females fought in Devon's army, and he never discriminated over how they readied themselves."

"But you kept your preparation to just meditation?"

Sergi grinned. "It depended on the battle."

She laughed, finished her glass of wine, then reached out to touch his knee. "My uncle is feeling rather protective at the moment. I think it's mostly his own emotions he's trying to control. But you and I need to talk if we plan on working together in this coming war."

She stood and picked up her duffel before turning to stare down at him. The red glow of her wolf lit her hazel blue eyes, leaving an interesting shade of violet. She ran a finger up his arm then down his cheek. "Behave yourself."

She strode away with the confidence of a shifter, stopping to share words with Cadfael and a mixed group of shifters and vampires before they disappeared beyond the divider.

Between her words and her intimate gesture, Sergi couldn't decipher what Alex was thinking. At first, he'd thought she was saying their future would be nothing more than compatriots in war, but now he wasn't sure. The trail of her finger still burned his skin, leaving him more confused than before they spoke.

Now, he remembered why he'd stayed away from relationships.

I BURIED my grin as Cadfael and I returned to our seats in the front cabin. A year ago, I'm not sure I would have been able to hide it from my uncle, who seemed to read my expressions and hear my thoughts. A year of disguising my emotions from my captors gave me a skill I hadn't known I was missing or needed.

I gave my uncle a warm smile when he glanced up, and I swallowed a retort while he gave me a long perusal.

"You were gone a long time to change." His gaze became more studied. "Is everything alright?"

I waved him off as I dropped into my seat, holding back a stab of temper that surprised me. "Surely, you don't have to worry about my safety on your own plane. Cadfael and I stopped to talk to the other shifters. I met the two surviving wolves you sent in after us."

His expression became unreadable, and I closed my eyes and sighed. There wasn't anything I could tell him that would remove his guilt, but I tried anyway.

"It wasn't your fault. It was vital to find the lab. They were doing so much more than we suspected. If you hadn't teamed up with House Trelane, I would still be a captive. I can't say I didn't walk away without some trauma, and I can handle it, but not if I have to worry about you, too."

His gaze softened, but he looked away. "Let's discuss this when we get home."

I shrugged and picked up one of the magazines I grabbed from the rack by the door. Maybe I could catch up on what I'd missed this last year during the long flight home. I'd been nervous during the van ride, worried I might have a breakdown on the plane. There were still many hours left in the flight, so too soon to tell. It was more likely my subconscious was waiting for me to fall asleep and would greet me with nightmares.

My thoughts drifted to Sergi, and he'd said something that I couldn't shake. My captivity might have temporarily taken my freedom, but I'd been on a mission. Watching Sergi endure Gheata's torture and listening to him as he shared a previous captivity while on a mission—always searching for a way out and never giving up—somehow eased my burden.

My deepest fear wasn't of recalling what I'd endured but of falling asleep and seeing the faces of the shifters who didn't make it out. Those who died horrible, painful deaths at the whim of vampires. It was easy to hate all vampires until one saved my life—twice. When I walked through the cabin earlier, I'd expected to see shifters sitting with shifters and vampires sitting with vampires, and while that was partly true, I had to admit there were many more shifters than vampires on the plane. Still, I was amazed by how many were co-mingling and talking while sharing food and drink.

Had that much changed in the year I was gone? I'd never

paid attention to the work my uncle was doing or the secret meetings that Braden, his Beta, refused to speak of. If I had to guess, those sessions involved the groundwork he'd been building with Trelane. There was something rotten growing in the vampire Council, and I wondered if the evidence we'd gathered would have any impact or if it would quietly disappear. If there was a war coming that impacted shifters, I had some catching up to do.

I grinned as I flipped a page. There was one male who could help with that. It was difficult to look at him without remembering his hands on my skin or the wild sensations that spiked my passion when his fangs traced where his lips had been. The simple act of his laying a hand on my bare hip had sent shivers of excitement through me.

All I'd needed had been an amazing one-night stand to block out my year of loneliness. No matter how many times I told myself I should walk away, there was something about Sergi that spoke to my wolf. Calmed her anxieties. I wasn't ready to let go, not when every instinct said to follow where it went.

I closed the magazine and considered getting a cup of coffee when I noticed my uncle watching me, his brows furrowed in thought. Good grief. I'd spent years proving I was of value to the pack. I wasn't that little orphan pup anymore, yet it appeared we were back to that again. All those lonely nights in my cell, I imagined running into his arms so he could save me from all the bad things. It surprised even me that a vampire might heal me faster than family.

"I thought this might be a good time to review the results of the raid."

I glanced up to see Devon Trelane. He nodded to everyone before his gaze settled on my uncle. "Now that everyone has eaten, I'd like to review the raid before the lights are turned down for sleep."

"Excellent idea." My uncle stood and stretched. "I would like to hear more myself. Let's meet at the conference table." He turned to the three of us—Cadfael, Carlos, and me. "Join us."

He followed Trelane to the table, and the three vampires who'd been sitting with him, including Sergi, met us there. I sat to the left of my uncle at one end of the table, and Sergi took a seat at Trelane's left at the other end. Everyone else grabbed an available chair. I kept an eye on my uncle, curious how he would play this, and hoped he'd leave whatever issue he had with Sergi out of the discussion.

Everyone was already quiet, but I felt their eyes on me as I laid all the vials on the table. Trelane focused on the items, and his eyes glowed like silver ice before settling into his stunning baby blues. When I laid the USB drive next to them, I heard a harsh intake of breath, though I wasn't sure who it came from because my gaze slid to Sergi, who gave me the briefest of smiles to let me know he was there if I needed him.

"Let's get started."

I was surprised when it was Trelane who said the words. Then it dawned on me. House Trelane was preparing for war against another vampire House. It was his team who planned the incursion into the lab. And it had been Sergi who endured the torture until Trelane's team could arrive. This was his mission. My uncle partnered with him, but he'd succeeded leadership to Trelane. Interesting.

Bella passed a tablet down to Sergi, who placed it in front of him, nudging it until it sat squarely in front of him, but he didn't turn it on. Bella and Trelane both glanced at each other and then at the closed tablet. It was odd, but Sergi didn't seem to notice, his focus had turned to the vials.

After an uncomfortable silence, Trelane cleared his throat and turned to me. I tried not to squirm under his inquisitive smile. "Alex. Do you feel up to telling us about your time at the lab?" His tone was soft and pleasing, as if trying to calm a child or perhaps a traumatized person. At first, it rankled me, but then Sergi's stories returned, and I understood. Trelane had sent Family on many missions over the centuries, some who'd suffered in captivity. He didn't know me any better than I knew him, and he didn't want to push me.

"Of course, that's why we're here. Where would you like me to start?"

Trelane smile remained. "Perfect. I wouldn't have expected anything less. Let's start from the beginning."

It took an hour for me to tell my tale up to and including the first couple days cleaning Sergi's cell. I stopped frequently to answer questions ranging from how the shifters were housed, to the setup of the labs, to the security protocols.

The hardest part was describing the experiments I'd witnessed. When I had trouble holding my emotions in check, Cadfael filled in the gaps. I was touched when Devon stalled the questions at that point to request refreshments as he ran through more mundane questions. He sensed when I was ready to continue and redirected his questions back to the experiments.

Sergi joined in when the questions moved to his arrival at the facility. At that point, it became a dual report, succinct and almost synchronized in our telling until we reached the point where I'd stolen evidence.

I pushed the blood vials toward Trelane. "These empty vials contained human blood, and I gave those to Sergi before we escaped."

"The blood didn't taste any different," Sergi added. "I'm afraid I didn't leave much to test."

My uncle picked up the package. "No. Not much. But the lab might be able to scrape something out of it." He dropped the package on the table.

I pushed the next group forward. "These three are Magic Poppy, or so they're labeled." I held my grin when the vampires lifted brows of interest. "This other group is labeled BP-X. Sergi confirmed it was Blood Poppy, and he can also validate it has been modified from an earlier version that I'd obtained. We just don't know how." I pushed the last three to meet the other vials. "This last group is labeled with an S, and we assume it's one of the shifter serums they were testing. All I can say is it wasn't the same serums used in the last experiment. Those were a different color."

My uncle reviewed the vials and held one up. "There's a small amount missing from this one."

When all eyes turned to me, Sergi answered their unspoken question.

"We ran into trouble with a pack of wild shifters. Alex was injured during the fight and developed an infection. I tried cleaning it out, but without medical supplies, I worried it would be life-threatening." He looked to my uncle rather than Devon. "I was aware what Blood Poppy could do for a vampire and..." he hesitated for a moment, "...humans." I was pretty sure that hadn't been the word he was going to use.

"That's alright Sergi," Trelane interrupted. "I understand your hesitation. And while it might be jarring for those new at the table, we shouldn't shy away from it with our team." Devon glanced at the shifters. "Cadfael and Alex can be brought up to speed by Remus, but what Sergi is delicately working around is an old species, as long-lived as vampires and shifters, called dreamwalkers. They've been using Blood Poppy for some time and achieved the same health results. Go on, Sergi."

My uncle had spoken of dreamwalkers long ago, but no one truly believed they were real. I wanted to know everything, but Sergi brought us back to the topic at hand.

"I wasn't sure if it would hurt more than help, but I felt the situation dire enough that I gave Alex several drops of the Blood Poppy."

My uncle picked up the vials and gently shook them. "It appears there's a quarter of a vial missing."

Sergi shrugged again. "Maybe more than a few drops."

Trelane ignored them, his eyes on me. "How did you feel afterward?"

I grinned. "Great. I barely had a scar the following morning. and now it's completely gone. I still feel the increased energy." I'm not sure how I didn't blush, considering how I'd expended some of that energy, but I chalked it up to being a professional. "The rest of the trip down the mountain didn't exhaust me, though I was starving."

The others laughed, but all I noticed was Sergi's warm smile.

Devon got us back on track. "Remus, I'm sure you'll want to take the vials. How long for a report?"

My uncle pushed them to Carlos, who gathered them up. "A couple of days. Maybe three."

Trelane nodded. "Excellent. Thank you." His sharp gaze turned back to me. "And the USB drive."

My uncle had told me on the van ride to the airstrip that the lab had been destroyed, and all they'd found was one undamaged vial of Magic Poppy. He did find the director's destroyed laptop, and while he took the hard drive, he doubted they'd find anything usable. This single USB drive might mean more than I'd first thought.

"The data is from the director's laptop. There was already a file on the drive from a month ago with spreadsheets and data regarding shifter experiments. I found a file on the BP-X and was transferring it over when Gheata arrived." I didn't go into details since Sergi already covered the Gheata incident.

Devon grinned at me. "This is more valuable than you could know. In addition to the vials and the case we've already put together, this drive could be one of the last straws to break the Council and Venizi along with it."

# Chapter Thirty-Four

SERGI BRACED himself as he strode up the stairs behind Devon to the manor's front door, with Bella and Rafael trailing behind him. Mateo opened the door, and when Sergi reached him, the vampire held out his hand.

"It's good to have you back home with us." Mateo shut the door and handed Devon a note.

"It's good to be home." Sergi shook his friend's hand then glanced around, surprised Cressa wasn't lurking somewhere, eager to give him a hard time.

"Why don't you get some rest, maybe spend time in the training room." Devon patted Sergi on the back. "I have an engagement that will last through the evening." He turned to Bella. "Contact Lucas. I need him and Ginger here in the morning for a meeting. Double the security for the motorcades and all the properties. Something tells me Venizi is going to be a bit irritated with us. Oh, and tell Decker as well."

Bella nodded and strode down the hallway toward her office. Devon raced up the stairs without another word. Cressa must have made plans for his return.

Sergi was eager to get back to work, but at the same time,

taking the rest of the day to simply sleep was a treat he couldn't ignore. The Council would have been informed by now about the infiltration into the lab. They probably had their hands full restraining Venizi from calling for a complete sanction on House Trelane, but the evidence of shifters being held in captivity would complicate Venizi's revenge plans, at least for a short time. With any luck, Simone would be home soon, bringing the last piece of evidence Devon needed before declaring war.

Sergi's room was as immaculate as when he left it. No doubt Greta had been dusting regularly. He dropped the duffel on a nearby chair and opened the drapes to the afternoon sun. After placing a call for a blood donor, he fell across the bed and stared at the ceiling.

His typical routine after a mission usually involved checking messages and spending several hours in the training room, as Devon suggested, beating back the demons that always seemed to return home with him. It had been decades since he'd last been held captive. Perhaps in this enlightened age, it was time for new habits.

He put his hands behind his head and closed his eyes, not to sleep but to remember.

The way she trailed her fingers across his tattoos. The silky essence of her skin under his touch. The way she giggled when he ran a hand up her side and buried his face in her neck, leaving soft kisses behind. The way she rubbed her breasts along his chest as her hand stroked his cock.

If he laid perfectly still, he could smell her wild scent. What would it be like to run alongside her wolf? Would Remus let her come to the manor? She said they weren't done, but what did that mean? He thought of her coming to the manor and Cressa discovering their relationship. Then there was Ginger. He groaned.

Never-ending torture.

Remus didn't seem pleased she'd been intimate with him, but

was he like that with any male she was with, or was it only vampires? Or only him?

He ignored his thoughts and refocused on their one evening together until sleep took him. But it wasn't long before a knock woke him.

He rubbed his face and opened the door to find Felicia outside his door.

"That was quick." He stepped aside to let her in before sitting in one of the armchairs.

"We were told Devon was on his way home, so we were ready for the call." Felicia rolled up the sleeve of her linen blouse. It was a sign of trust that she wore such elegant clothing for a donation. Trust that Sergi was a gentleman and an expert at drawing blood without mishap. "If you don't mind me saying, you look better than I expected after hearing you'd been captured."

He settled back in the chair, turning slightly toward her. "Bella was kind enough to bring blood bags."

"Yes, several of us donated before they left, but we were all worried." She sat on the padded arm of the chair and gave him her hand. "Gerald sends his regards."

"You're still seeing him?" Sergi ran his thumb over her wrist, encouraging blood flow.

"You sound surprised." Her laugh held a soft melodic sound, similar to Lyra's. "He's faithful, fun to be around, and takes me to nice places. Well, he did before the lockdown. He still finds secret places for us to enjoy sunsets and passionate lovemaking."

Sergi lifted a brow. "They must be secluded spots since I haven't seen your name in a security report."

"High praise from a vampire."

They both grinned before he sunk his teeth into her veins. Bagged blood was sufficient to provide him the necessary nutrients, but fresh blood always tasted better. He didn't drink long, and soon he was healing her skin.

Felicia stood and pulled down her sleeve. "It's good to see you well." Then she gave him a long, uncomfortable look. "Something's different."

Torture would do that, but he didn't say it. It would only make her feel bad. "It was a long mission."

"Hmm. It's not that." Then she grinned. "Well, I didn't think I'd live to see it."

He tensed, unsure where this was going.

She pinched his cheek. "I'm so happy for you." Then she strode to the door.

He touched his cheek. Felicia had always been a tactile female, preferring hugs and light touches to show her friendship and affection. The pinch had been surprising.

"I'm not sure I know what you're talking about."

She laughed. "I can't wait to meet her."

Then she was out the door.

*Damn it all.*

If Felicia, who he only saw on occasion, had figured it out in ten short minutes, he wouldn't have a chance of hiding anything from Cressa.

WHEN THE LIMO arrived at my uncle's estate, the place I called home, I jumped out before the driver had a chance to come to a complete stop.

"Alex, where are you going?" Remus called from the limo.

I couldn't wait. Actually, my wolf couldn't wait. For the entire plane ride and the drive to the estate, my thoughts continually shifted between intimate moments with Sergi and my wolf straining to be released.

Once my wolf had gotten a taste of battle, all she wanted to do was run. I half stumbled, leaving a trail of clothes and shoes behind me as I raced for the back of the house. By the time I was dodging plants and flowerbeds in the lush backyard, I was fully naked and only stopped by the fountain long enough to shift. My transformation was faster than normal, and I wondered if it had anything to do with the Blood Poppy that was still flowing through my veins. It had been forty-eight hours since Sergi fed it to me, and I was still energized.

My wolf was running free. I stopped after a few minutes and lifted my nose to the air. The scent of grass and musk floated through the warm afternoon air and caught my wolf's interest. Soon, I was chasing a rabbit, but when I caught up to it and saw the terror in its eyes, I stopped. The rabbit scampered under a bush, and my wolf turned and ran.

After an hour of racing around hundreds of acres and panting hard, I found my favorite spot and dropped to the ground, my snout resting on my paws. My wolf had refused the rabbit as well as the others that had crossed our path. There hadn't been any qualms when I'd killed four rabbits in the Carpathians.

What was different?

One was for survival, and the other for fun. I whimpered when memories of shifters, their bodies exploding from the inside, leaving nothing but bits of bone, flesh, and too much blood flitted through my thoughts. The horror in their eyes when they understood what was happening.

Hunting for sport wasn't as fun as it used to be. Not after knowing what it was like to be prey.

I closed my eyes and woke as sunset approached. The manor was a good half-hour walk away, but it was worth shifting where I'd napped. There was a light coastal wind that made goose bumps erupt over my naked body. It felt good, but I picked up my pace to warm up.

The run had been exactly what I needed. It wasn't good to keep my wolf pent up for so long. I'd made a decision during our run. The past year was just that. The only thing I cared about was this day and the next. For now, that meant the upcoming war and the part I would play.

I reached the fountain, irritated that two wolves were still shadowing me. *Good grief.* My uncle had assigned me pup sitters. How embarrassing.

I shook my head at the fluffy robe and slippers waiting on a nearby patio chair. It didn't matter how many times I told my uncle I'd pick up my clothes when I returned, he had someone do it for me. The gesture had been appreciated before, but now it seemed stifling.

I understood my uncle's concern. He worried about my state of mind. His first instinct would drive him toward pack mentality, surrounding me with protection. It was his way of supporting my recovery, but his actions would be restrictive. My current opinion was that bodyguards weren't any different than the guards at the lab—constantly watching and reporting. What I needed was freedom. It was going to be a difficult pill for my uncle to swallow.

After a shower, I stood in my grand walk-in closet and grinned. Clothes were piled on top of a chair because I'd been too lazy to put them in their proper place. Purses lay scattered across another shelf, and my favorite shoes had been piled in a corner so they would be easy to find. Like the rest of my messy bedroom, everything was the way I'd left it. I slipped on a pair of jeans, rubbing my hands up and down my thighs. Oh, how I'd missed them. I pulled open several drawers that ran along the far wall until I found the older, well-worn, and softened-with-age, forest-green pullover sweater. Nothing better than comfort clothing. With a bit of prying, I managed to reopen my ear piercings to add a pair of silver earrings. There was a slight tingle from the silver, but not enough to be irritating. The initial jolt made me feel alive.

I found my uncle in the library with Cadfael, who looked dapper in a borrowed suit, Carlos, and Braden, my uncle's Beta. They were drinking Scotch by the looks of it, and I stopped at the bar and poured a glass of Burgundy wine.

Braden jumped out of his chair, and before I could replace the cork, he squeezed me in a bear hug. I laughed and hugged him back. He'd always been a big brother to me.

"I never gave up hope. Welcome home." He stepped back, his hands still gripping my shoulders as he looked me over. "You're too skinny. Paul will fatten you up in no time." He winked. "In fact, I hear it's steak, potatoes, stuffed mushrooms, and double-Dutch chocolate cake for dinner."

"Stop bothering her," Remus called from the seating area on the far side of the room. "She looks fine."

Braden pulled me in for another hug, but this time he whispered in my ear. "I'll try to keep him busy so he doesn't suffocate you. But give him some leeway." Then he said a bit louder, "You know where to find me if you need to brag about your amazing escape."

I punched him in the shoulder, but I was grateful for his words. He'd been with my uncle since I was a pup and knew him better than me. I could trust Braden to watch my back.

After dessert, brandy, and light conversation that avoided discussions about the raid, the packs, or the coming vampire war, everyone left for their rooms. I was partway down the hall when my uncle stopped me.

"Come with me to my office. This won't take long."

He dropped into his favorite chair in front of the fireplace where embers burned, looking tired for the first time since seeing him standing in the mouth of the cave. I slid into a matching plush leather chair and pulled my legs underneath me.

I spent most of my youth and then adulthood sitting in this chair, listening to my uncle's pack stories or sharing my problems as he handed down sage advice. Now, I waited, watching a spark create a low flame, as my uncle prepared for whatever was on his mind, though I had a good guess what it was.

"There have been many changes in the packs since you've been gone." He crossed a leg over his knee and tapped his fingers on the arm of his chair, his focus on the fire.

"Because of the coming war?" I asked, glancing at him to judge his mood. In addition to his fidgeting fingers, his brows lowered, and the corner of his eyes crinkled, but not from laughter. He was tense, and some of his Alpha mojo was leaking out, ruffling my wolf's fur.

"Yes. And before you ask, the local packs agreed with the decision to support House Trelane."

"What about the other packs?"

"I've only spoken with the Alphas of the larger packs and explained the situation and my trust in Trelane. They in turn spoke with like-minded House leaders who support Trelane. While the other packs might not be involved in the war itself, they have shown support."

I nodded. "They're tired of living under the boot of the vampire Council and see the benefit of a vampire civil war."

He gave me a grin, appreciating my ability to still see the big picture. I hadn't grown stupid over the last year, and I'd had a first-hand look at what House Trelane could accomplish. "We are placing a huge wager that Trelane can pull this off."

"And keeping with your gambling analogy, we're all in, but we still have to beat the house, where the odds are in their favor. The house being the Council, of course."

His smile widened. "I forgot how well you assimilate strategy."

I couldn't help but return his smile. "I learned from the best." I rubbed at a spot on the soft leather. "The raid on the lab. The search for evidence. This is information to take to the Council in hopes they'll lean a particular direction."

"It's more than that. I won't go into the details, you'll have plenty of time to catch up, but there are centuries of rot beneath the Council. Lies they've told their society to benefit a few at the risk of their entire species. Trelane is building a mountain of evidence in the hopes it will bury the Council."

We fell into silence as I thought back to lessons on the vampire Council. My uncle always preached to his Alphas that to beat your enemy, you had to know your enemy. The members of the Council were one of those lessons, and a couple of dots solidified in my head.

"Isn't Trelane on the Council?"

This time he laughed. "You remember."

I considered the events at the lab, the little details Sergi had shared about his House leader, and then watched and listened to Trelane in action. Not once had I remembered him being part of the Council. He didn't seem the type.

"I hadn't considered it before. Maybe because I was still coming down from the rush of the escape. I was surprised by how organized the rescue had been. The thought that a member of the Council did this never broached my thoughts."

"Devon took over as leader of his House after the untimely deaths of his parents. Deaths he attributes to Venizi though he has no proof. He joined the Council according to legacy rules, but he was soon censured. It was one of the reasons he turned to the shifters for business partnerships in addition to his human partnerships since he was cut off from doing business with other Houses.

"But his desire to bring peace among the species started with his father, Guildford, who I'd met a couple of times before his death. Devon, in preparation to someday become House leader, had spent years on his sojourn meeting with Houses and packs alike."

"He sounds like a Renaissance vampire."

"Quite true."

"So, how can I get involved with this war?"

Silence grew as I waited for my uncle to respond. History told me the longer he took to respond, the less likely I was going to like the answer.

"You have a lot to learn from being gone this last year. You need time to reacclimate. After a couple of months, we can assess what role suits you."

I held my breath and my tongue. Rash outbursts never worked

with my uncle. It was best to wear him down before yelling. "I understand why you'd think that. But I've stared at four walls for far too long to just sit around now. I have skills that can help. I want a more active role in this."

"There's much you don't understand. You've endured a long and dangerous mission. You kept your head. Cadfael was impressed with you from the start, but there are many things that can be done behind the scenes without putting yourself at risk. I can't expend the wolves to follow you all over the place. It's easier and safer if you remain on the estate, at least for a few weeks, then we can reassess."

Remain on the estate. The words slammed into me as if I could hear the locks on my cell engage. Was this about my safety or about Sergi? My wolf howled. My uncle was, to continue the gambling theme, hedging his bet. I'd be tucked in safe and sound, and with Trelane's lockdown, Sergi wouldn't seek me out. Not under my uncle's roof.

And I would slowly go mad.

It was one thing to know you were enslaved when you lived in a box and decisions were made for you. It was quite another to live on an estate with windows so you could see what was beyond the borders but were prevented from reaching it. Life in a gilded cage.

Not again. Not when I had the power to say no. He might be The Wolf, the Alpha to all the other Alphas, but he was still my uncle. And he was forcing me to play his niece and not a trained, highly skilled member of the pack.

I slowly stood and turned to him. He had to lean back to meet my eyes. His expression was blank, perhaps a bit curious, but there was deep concern in his gaze, and though it broke my heart to see it, I had to stand my ground now before he wore me down.

"You know I love you. That everything I am is because of you. It was a difficult year, but I survived. I heard your voice many times over that year, reminding me that I was wolf, and it gave me the strength I needed to persevere. But I'm not there anymore. I got out."

I wiped at my eyes then pushed back my hair. "I don't need protection, uncle. At least not the pup sitters who tracked me on my run, and I have no doubt will be positioned at the end of the hall, if not in front of my bedroom door.

"I've had too many eyes watching my every move for far too long. I need space. I need the freedom to choose. I know you're trying to do what's best for me, but you need to take a step back from being my uncle and instead look at me as the pack leader. I'm not a pup anymore. I have skills to help in this war, and they're not sitting behind a desk, locked away in this estate."

His face turned compassionate seconds before his Alpha persona took over. "I've made my decision."

Without a word, because it would be pointless, I spun around and marched out of the room.

I was so angry, and it soon became a hot rage as the two guards who'd been stationed along the hallway turned and followed me. Pup sitters in the house for Christ's sake. Would they pick my breakfast for me too?

I kept walking and pushed open the French doors leading to the back terrace hard enough that I feared they'd break.

Then I stopped in my tracks.

Braden was leaning against the wrought iron and stone railing, a beer in his hand. He lifted another one that had been sitting on one of the stone pillars.

I grinned as I walked toward him. He knew me so well.

"That's enough for tonight, boys. I think Alex remembers how to get to her room." After a couple of seconds, he stood straighter, and a red glow replaced his sea-green eyes. "I don't think her uncle meant for her to be treated like a prisoner. Try standing guard at the front doors if you must. And don't make me say it a second time."

I didn't turn around. Their retreating boot steps and the shutting of the French doors were enough.

Braden chuckled and opened the beer for me.

"Damn. This tastes really good."

"I told your uncle a barbecue on the terrace would have been just as good, but he wanted to show off for Cadfael."

I took in the landscape, lit with dozens of small lamps, and breathed in the mixed scent of blooms and fresh compost. "I have to admit, my uncle is right about acclimating. I forgot how peaceful it was here." I waited a beat, but Braden remained silent. I was curious if he felt the same way as my uncle. "I can't just sit around."

"Are you sure?"

I nodded enthusiastically. "In my last couple months at the facility, I'd been given more freedoms." I shuddered. "But it wasn't necessarily a good thing. I saw such horrendous experiments I don't think those images will ever go away." I took a long swig of the cold brew and turned toward him. "And maybe they shouldn't. Not while we're on the brink of war. If nothing else, I can be the reminder of why the shifters have to be in this war. This is quite literally our lives on the line. I cannot—no—I will not stand by while everyone else does the heavy lifting."

I wasn't sure what to expect from Braden. He was used to listening to my rants and petty grievances for years. What I didn't expect was the huge grin.

"Yeah, I know. I sound like I've been radicalized."

"And I have to say, little sister, it looks good on you."

I blushed. Not many could make me do that, but Braden was one of them. Then his words sunk in, and I squinted at him.

"What exactly does that mean?" I finally took the time to really assess him. He was up to something.

"I have a proposition for you."

# Chapter Thirty-Five

SERGI WOKE early but remained in bed, staring at the ceiling, a grin on his face. His dreams had been of Alex. Intimate dreams that turned erotic. It had been decades, maybe longer, since he'd been close with a female. Hell, in the last century in House Trelane, he'd dealt with more turmoil and tragedy than any House could bear. He'd had no time to think of females.

And in all that time, he hadn't forgotten how to pleasure a woman. His grin widened when he remembered how passionate Alex had been. He was curious whether her assertive nature came from her year of captivity or if it was her innate nature. When she'd come to his cell, her soft touches, while tentative, had been daring.

He jumped out of bed and showered, though it did little to erase the shifter from his thoughts. If he hurried, he would have time to catch up on reports before Devon's morning meeting. On the way to his office, he made a quick stop in the kitchen and ordered breakfast.

The first thing he noted when opening his office door was the scent of a woman.

He sighed. Cressa.

Was he disappointed it hadn't been Alex's scent?

He pushed the thought aside as he sat at his desk and immediately scowled. His chair was too high. He fiddled with the lever until it lowered to his preferred position. Then he surveyed his desk. Everything was out of place—even the mementos he kept at the corners.

A stack of folders sat to his left, and when he checked the labels, he released a long breath and maybe a small growl. There were dozens of multicolored sticky notes sticking out of all of them. He turned on his tablet and found forty-three messages waiting for him. Thirty-nine were from Cressa. The other four had arrived that morning from security team leaders welcoming him back and reporting all clear.

When he opened Cressa's first message, he assumed it would be a security report from that day.

It wasn't.

It was more of a diary of her daily activities, and each one was signed with the name Pandora and emojis of little hearts. He set the tablet aside and tried to open a desk drawer, but all the drawers were locked. He never locked his desk. No one was foolish enough to go into them. Cressa might have a need, but why lock them?

Because it was Cressa.

He sighed for the third time in less than a few minutes and reached for the tiny blown-glass bowl Lyra had given him where he kept his keys, but the bowl wasn't on his desk.

He scanned the room and spotted the bowl on a bookcase shelf. Letty interrupted his search of the room, where he found several items out of place. He thanked her as he took the tray from her and, after clearing off a portion of his desk, set it down and poured a cup of coffee from the urn.

He ate the spinach and egg-white omelet and sipped his coffee as he considered how to pay Cressa back. His games with her had begun out of irritation with her antics, but her ability to play the game had somehow defined their mutual respect for each other.

Devon had mentioned on the way home how worried Cressa

had been for him. He never mentioned it again, and Sergi knew Cressa would have been mortified to know Devon had told him. And he would never mention it either, but there were other ways to show he appreciated her concern.

After reviewing a couple of her official reports, he had to admit she had a knack for security, most likely learned during her criminal escapades as Pandora, which explained why she signed her messages with the moniker.

He glanced at a few more reports before setting them aside to read later and spent the last thirty minutes before Devon's meeting responding to each of Cressa's thirty-nine messages. Then he closed his tablet, finished his coffee, and strolled to Devon's office. The only thought in his head was how Alex was doing and how to locate her cell number.

He was the last one to join the meeting, and before taking his seat, he nodded to cadre members and Decker, then acknowledged Ginger but ignored Cressa. He laid his tablet on his lap but didn't bother opening it. Cressa's rebellious nature seemed to have triggered his own.

The meeting was long as they reviewed the mission at the lab, including the raid and the rehoming of the shifters. It was followed by individual reports from Lucas on the status of Oasis and Cressa on security at the manor and the two safe houses. The only concern was that no one had heard from Simone since her last email to Cressa five days earlier. Devon, who had agreed to her personal mission, said he would look into it.

Devon's next topic surprised Sergi.

"During our travel to Romania, Bella and I had a discussion with Remus regarding Venizi's aggressive attacks and constant drive-bys. After the raid and destruction of the lab, I expect we'll see more of this, possibly on grander scales. While the Sentinels and Eliminators weren't happy with the destruction of the lab or the discovery of shifter prisoners, I doubt the Council will see this as a win. As a result, I expect I'll once again be called to visit the Council."

Bella stood and began her pacing. "It's unfortunate for the Council that word has already leaked about the kidnapped shifters, and while nothing specific is being shared, the rumors of unlawful experiments are in the wind. There are concerns that this discovery could spark a war with the shifters."

"Remus has already filed a complaint with the Council." Decker munched on a handful of nuts from a container he'd grabbed from behind the bar. The shifter looked better than he had the last few months, and while Sergi sensed the slow-burning rage beneath his calm facade, he believed Decker had been energized by their progress against Venizi.

"That should keep the Council off our back for a bit." Lucas was scrolling through his tablet. "There's a lot of chatter this morning from various Houses asking what was being done about the raid. The smaller Houses tend to be located in large pack areas. They have to be feeling nervous about the situation."

"I had a discussion with Remus this morning." Devon picked up the white crystal on his desk and passed it back and forth between his hands. "Starting today, we're moving forward on the development of a counter-strike team."

Sergi sat up. "I wasn't aware of this."

Devon nodded and set the crystal down. "It was something Bella recommended. Remus and I were intrigued by the notion. I wanted to share it with you on our travel home, but it didn't seem the right time. Of course, I expect you to lead the initiative along with Bella."

"What's the directive?" Sergi asked. He liked the idea, but he wanted to know how far he'd be allowed to go.

"I want the Council to know I'm taking their concerns to heart. We can't proceed with making our war official until Simone returns. Until then, the lockdown will continue, and we'll fortify our positions, but we won't strike first. Venizi will have to make the first move, and when he does, we strike back hard and fast. Sometimes that will be with force, and other times, we might take a less direct approach."

Devon didn't go into details, and no one asked, but Sergi knew what he was thinking. Corporate espionage and hacking would be on the table. Finally. This strategic directive was exactly what he needed after the last mission.

"Sergi will have the last say regarding who the primary members of the team will be, but depending on the size of our response to each attack, we'll pull resources from the security detail and our partners as needed. I have a few names I'll request to be added, specifically Decker, who can coordinate strikes with Remus."

Devon glanced around the room, and with no further questions, he closed the meeting. When the group stood to leave, he said, "Sergi. Can you stay a moment?" The last person was barely out the door when he asked, "Are you alright?"

"Never felt better."

He nodded toward Sergi's lap. "You never opened your tablet."

Sergi laughed. "I've become too predictable."

"You seem different."

"If you think Alex has something to do with that," he shrugged, "I won't deny it. But it was the mission itself. You know how it is when you've been a captive, wondering if this time might be your last."

Devon leaned back, apparently satisfied with the answer. "I assume you're ready to get started on the counter-strike team."

"You couldn't have given me a better homecoming gift."

"Excellent. Will training start soon?"

"This afternoon. I've already sent messages."

"Are you planning payback?" Devon's grin was mischievous, and Sergi knew it had nothing to do with his training plan. Devon would be well aware that Cressa would take Sergi's absence to mess with him.

"Already started." Sergi stood. "Was that all?"

"For now."

Sergi returned to his office. Devon had wanted to ask about Alex, but it was a conversation better served with Scotch. He sat at his desk, ignored Bella's message about meeting to discuss the counter-strike team, and poured another cup of coffee from the urn Letty had left behind when she picked up his breakfast tray. It occurred to him he never got Alex's last name. He turned on his laptop and strummed his fingers. His job to locate her mobile number would be more difficult, but not impossible.

He wondered if Decker was still in the manor. It wasn't something he wanted to do, getting someone else involved in his personal matters, but who better to track down a shifter than another shifter?

I PULLED the pack car that Braden had finagled for me in front of the steps leading to the door of House Trelane. Butterflies played soccer in my gut, and I wasn't sure if it had to do with my meeting with Trelane or seeing Sergi. Would he be happy to see me, or was I pushing too hard?

My uncle had an all-day meeting at one of his downtown offices, so it would take a while before he blew his stack on finding me gone, and Braden took the shrapnel. My uncle always told me to trust my wolf. What would he say if I told him I was?

I stepped out of the car and stared across it to the historic manor. It was obvious it had been built ages ago, but I recognized the plaque from the local Historical Society mounted next to the front door. It must be a bitch to get any remodeling done.

I was halfway up the stairs when the front door opened at the same time someone yelled from behind me.

"I'm sorry, miss. If I can get your keys, I'll park the car until you're ready to leave."

At first, I thought I'd parked in the wrong spot, then I was worried I should have pulled around to the back like the staff. The guards at the front gate had waved me through with barely a glance when I gave them my name. Though I had to admit, I appreciated the security. Four armed guards and a wolf had been positioned at the gate.

I turned and took a couple of steps to meet the vampire.

When I plopped the keys into his hand, he winked. "Don't worry. I'll take good care of her."

He did know I wasn't a vampire, right? Hospitality and excellent security. Impressive.

My bad blood with vampires went a lot farther back than my incarceration at the lab, but somehow, within a few short days, Sergi made me look at vampires from a different perspective. I should have known there were good vampires and bad vampires, just like with shifters.

When I spun back to the front door, Bella waved. "I was pleased when Devon said you were coming for a meeting. You look good."

I glanced down at my jeans and black knee-high boots and shrugged with a slight grin. "It feels good to be in jeans again."

"And your blouse doesn't put too much focus on how much weight you must have lost."

I wasn't sure what to say to that.

"Sorry. Jacques says I can be too honest." She shrugged and waved me through the door. "I was captive for six months once. For some reason, the males always have to comment on how thin a female looks after being caged. You'd think they'd never looked in a mirror with an honest eye."

I laughed. "I got the impression they all believe they're god's gift."

"You're not wrong. We have training this afternoon, but maybe you can stay long enough for a drink after."

"We'll see how it goes."

Bella led me down a hallway and knocked on a door before sticking her head in. "Hey, boss. Alex's here."

"Excellent."

Bella stood back, waved me in, then marched away without another word. When I turned to close the door, a brown-haired female stared at me from down the hall. A second later, a dark-haired female with a pink scarf, who reminded me of a pixie, grabbed her arm and pulled her down the hall.

The first female turned back with a huge grin on her face. I couldn't help but smile back. How odd. I shut the door to find Trelane striding toward me with a smile.

"How are you acclimating?"

"Better than expected."

"Let's sit and be comfortable." He waved me to one of the armchairs by the fireplace, and he sat in the one across from me. I was grateful he didn't ask me to sit on the sofa. That would have put me at a disadvantage, and he seemed to know that. "Don't let the first couple of nights fool you. Sometimes the dreams don't come until later. I'm sure it comes as no surprise that I've experienced similar circumstances. My advice, if I might suggest, when they become so bad you avoid sleep, find someone to confide in. They won't be able to heal you. Only you can do that. But, as they say, sometimes talking about it helps."

"You sound like my uncle." I didn't want to admit the nightmares had already started. But before they took hold, Sergi was there, chasing them away in my dreams. It comforted me, as silly as that sounded.

Trelane laughed. "We are both wise leaders. So, what is it that I can do for you?"

Thank heavens the chit-chat was over, but that didn't mean I'd been ready for it. I thought Braden had told him why I was here. I relaxed against the chair. A maneuver my uncle told me would give me time to think. When I took a deep breath to halt the restless butterflies that had returned, I realized if I wanted something from him, I would need to ask.

"I was speaking with Braden about the coming war." I rubbed my hands on my thighs, and though Trelane flicked his gaze to the motion for the briefest of seconds, his expression never changed at my apparent nervousness. "I realize it's a vampire matter, but with my uncle taking a side, and..." My brain went blank. What should I call being held captive and watching vampires kill members of your own species in the most brutal ways possible? What the hell was I even doing here? I didn't have a chance to complete my thoughts.

Trelane leaned over and rested his elbows on his knees as he caught my gaze. Thank heavens mesmerizing didn't work on shifters, though his closeness didn't bother me. He acted as if he were taking me into his confidence. "You've survived a horrific experience at the hands of vampires, yet here you are, wanting to team with a species who you've seen as your enemy, possibly for your entire life."

Had my uncle told him something about my past, or was he just clairvoyant? I thought I'd learned how to school my emotions, yet there was something about the vampires in this House that constantly surprised me.

He gave me a moment to catch my breath and settle. I placed my arms on the chair, and while I gripped the fabric a bit too tightly, at least they remained still.

"My uncle kept me away from vampires, though all pups were taught about your species." When Trelane gave me a knowing smile, I relaxed and returned the grin. "I see you also follow the teachings of Sun Tzu in knowing your enemy. But I've only recently learned that one can't judge a species by their history."

"Well said. Though, as you know all too well, that can't be said of all of us. But I want you to feel comfortable and safe at all of the Trelane properties. And, since you've taken the first step, I'll make this easy on you." He sat back and winked. "This time."

My cheeks heated, but I appreciated him taking the lead.

"You're here about the counter-strike team, and your uncle is, as of yet, unaware of your request to join us. I have no biological children of my own, but my sister has always been dear to me. For a short time, I had to take care of her every need—until recently. It scared me to see her gain her independence, but when I witnessed her return to the strong woman she once was, I knew my fear was unwarranted." His smile returned. "Although I'd never admit it outside this room, I never want to be on the wrong side of her wrath."

I chuckled. "I assume Braden told you my uncle won't be happy about me being here."

He shrugged. "That will be up to you to sort out. But, if it helps, I'll ask Decker to intercede if Remus won't back down. Though, I won't risk our partnership over it."

"I understand." What a relief to have Decker on my side. I'd wondered if the old shifter was still around. I remembered him befriending vampires and shifters alike at his fight club. I glanced up to find Trelane staring at me. Had I missed a question? I replayed the conversation in my head.

"Wait. Does this mean I'm on the team?"

Trelane grinned just as a knock came. I didn't turn to look, but a woman's voice called out.

"I gave you as much time as I could."

"Just another minute," Trelane called out before he refocused on me, that smile still hovering. "I don't have the last word on the makeup of the team, but I have some influence. In fact, I'll ask Cressa to take you to the team leader. He'll make the final call."

"Who am I taking where?" The woman had entered the office, and when I turned, I found the brown-haired female I'd seen earlier in the hall.

"Cressa, this is Alex, Remus's niece." Before he could say anything else, the woman raced around the sofa and dropped onto it, her eyes lit with curiosity.

"I'd hug you, but I'll refrain since you don't know me well

enough yet. I can't tell you how thankful we are that you brought Sergi home."

That didn't take long for the gossip to get around.

"You'll have to excuse Cressa. She's human and filled in for Sergi while he was on mission. You might say they have a special relationship."

My stomach fell, and Cressa slapped Trelane's leg.

"Did you hear what you just said?" She turned to me. "It's not that type of relationship. It's more like big bully brother and misunderstood little sister." She grinned and chucked a thumb toward Trelane. "I'm with him."

Should I be concerned by how relieved I was?

"Come on. I assume I'm taking you to Sergi to get his approval to join the team."

Those butterflies returned. Sergi was the leader of the counter-strike team? I guess there was no question of seeing him before I left.

Cressa stood and strode to the door. She glanced back at Trelane. "Five minutes, and then I expect you on the widow's walk."

"Yes, ma'am." Trelane stood and took my hand. "I apologize for my insensitive wording. I didn't mean to give you a start."

My cheeks flamed. What had I expected? He'd seen me naked.

"Thank you, Mr. Trelane. I appreciate the opportunity. And I assume this satisfies the favor you owe me."

"It's Devon, and your participation on the team isn't up to me. I'm simply adding you to the list of candidates. I still owe you." He walked me to the door and handed me off to Cressa.

"Sergi is down this way." Cressa waved her arm down the hall to direct me but paused and made an odd motion with her head.

When I followed her gaze, the dark-haired female from earlier slapped a hand over her mouth before dashing around a corner.

"Sorry. That was my friend Ginger." She turned us down a

short hall and stopped. "Look, I'll be straight with you. I really don't know any other way."

My gut twisted again. I was going to need a whiskey before this day was over.

"Sergi has always been a bit uptight, and Ginger and I sometimes irritate the hell out of him. Not that he doesn't find creative ways to pay us back. But, well, we've never seen him with a woman before—vampire, shifter, or human. So—"

I crossed my arms over my chest and gave her a stern look. "So, you're busy-body females."

Cressa's eyes widened, but I wasn't expecting the nod and grin. "Exactly. I'm glad we got that out in the open." She continued down the hall and lowered her voice. "He doesn't know you're here." She stopped in front of a door and winked. "We'll make sure you have your privacy, but training starts in an hour. Just so you know."

She strode down the hall with an extra swing in her step, obviously having fun with this. I turned toward the door. It seemed everyone was privy to the evening she'd spent with Sergi. Well, shifters weren't shy, and I wasn't ashamed of my behavior. I wanted more nights with him.

I knocked, and when he gave the command to enter, my knees went weak. I closed my eyes, hoped I wasn't screwing this up, and pushed the door open.

Sergi was sitting behind his desk, typing into a laptop. His eyes bulged when he glanced up, and I almost took a step back. His warm mahogany eyes glowed red, and a slow smile stretched across his face.

# Chapter Thirty-Six

SERGI STARED at the vision in his doorway. The beast stirred at the sight, and he was momentarily speechless as his heart rate climbed. "Alex. What are you doing here?"

She had such a beautiful smile, but she didn't cross into the room. If she had been about to say something, she thought better of it. In fact, her smile faded, and he worried she'd leave.

He had the presence of mind to shut down the laptop, hiding the evidence that he'd been searching for her. Would she think he'd been stalking her? He stood, and as much as he wanted to race over to her, wrap her in his arms, and let her scent wash over him, he didn't want to spook her.

She'd said they needed to talk. Perhaps that was all this was. A way to close a chapter.

"Come in." He seemed at a loss to say anything else.

She took two steps in and fumbled with the handle as she shut the door behind her, but she didn't look at him. Instead, her gaze roamed his office, and a light smile hit her lips before her eyes captured his.

"I should have known you'd be a tidy vampire."

He grunted. "And what would I find if I walked into your

office? Stacks of files sprawled across your desk, books stacked on every available chair, and bookshelves overstuffed with tchotchkes?"

She slid farther into the room, taking small steps until she reached the chairs in front of his desk. "If I had an office, that would be a strong possibility."

"I'm surprised to see you." When doubt flitted across her face, he added, "I didn't think Remus would approve."

A breath slipped out, and her shoulders dropped. "He wouldn't. And for another few hours, he doesn't know I'm here, but I had to come."

"Why?"

Her shoulders tensed again. "I asked for a meeting with Devon."

Devon? He didn't understand and was disappointed she hadn't come to see him.

She wrung her hands and looked around. "You have a rather small office for being cadre. I was expecting a sitting area and a grand fireplace."

His lips twitched, and he stood, working his way in front of the desk to lean against it, his arms crossed over his chest as he considered her statement. She seemed to be dancing around the topic. "I don't like encouraging visitors while I'm working." When he realized how that sounded, he added, "But I make exceptions."

With only the guest chairs separating them, he picked up her light scent. She looked good in jeans and boots. Her turquoise-colored blouse brought out the blue of her hazel eyes, and the beast took notice.

"I'm surprised to see you in a suit, but I guess I shouldn't be. I mean, you look nice in it." She turned her head away, her gaze moving over the bookshelves as she wrung her hands again.

"This shouldn't be that difficult between us."

A myriad of emotions crossed her face—panic, sadness, hope, and humor. "I'm not even sure why I'm here."

"Let's start with your meeting with Devon." The words were automatic. The stoic Sergi, always staying on point, but he wanted to give her an out. A way to ease her into telling him the truth of why she was here.

A huge sigh escaped her, and she blurted it out. "I wanted to be considered for a spot on the counter-strike team."

His brows shot up. "How did you hear about that? Did Remus mention it?"

She shook her head and took a step closer. "Braden. My uncle wants me to stay on the estate and work behind the scenes." She locked eyes with him. "I want to do more."

He dropped his arms to his side. Remus was trying to protect her by keeping her locked up. "You want to fight."

She nodded.

"You want your freedom."

She nodded again, but this time he noted the spark in her eyes that were filled with unspent tears. He shoved a chair aside as he stepped in front of her and stared down at her upturned face.

"You want revenge."

The tears slipped, and he pulled her to him, crushing her to his chest as her arms wrapped around him. He couldn't remember the last time someone gave him such comfort.

Then his lips were on hers. They were salty from tears, but they parted without question as his tongue slipped inside. His passion, pent up for so long, overruled all other proprieties. Her arms tightened, then her hand roamed up his back. He broke the kiss to stare down at her again.

"I didn't know how to find you without contacting Remus."

"I wasn't sure if you wanted to see me again, but I had to try. At least once." She broke away from his arms and strolled around his desk, her fingers running over the smooth wood and dancing across the top of his laptop. "I don't want special treatment because of what we've shared. I want to compete with the other candidates on my own merits."

He grinned. "Is that the only reason you came?"

She pushed his laptop aside and turned her back to him as she perched on top of his desk. Her legs swung back and forth as he followed her path until he stood in front of her. She wore a mischievous grin, and her tears were long gone.

When he was directly in front of her, she grabbed his tie and tugged him closer until he stood between her legs. She reached up and grabbed his neck, pulling him down until their lips touched. Her tongue slid across his lips, and when his tongue met hers, he pushed his way past as the kiss deepened. He stroked a breast as her legs wrapped around his, locking him in place.

He did the only thing a male could do and devoured her with a heated kiss. Her immediate response was like a drug, and the beast roared with pleasure. Words weren't enough for what their bodies could say.

Her fingers were on his buckle, then on the button of his pants, the zipper moving down with practiced hands. The soft touch of her hands stroking him made his legs tremble.

"The door," he hissed as her fingers rolled over the tip of his cock.

"I locked it." He felt her smile under his lips, and with one wide sweep of his arm, he cleared the desk. Everything toppled to the carpeted floor—laptop, tablet, coffee urn, the stack of files Cressa had left for him, and who knew what else. He didn't care.

He pushed her arms away as he fumbled at her jeans, swearing as he tried to unbutton them. Her laughter only urged him on as she popped the button and let him slide the zipper down. Then she was holding on to the edge of the desk so she wouldn't slide off as he pulled her boots off and stripped her jeans and panties down her legs.

She sat up, pulled her blouse over her head, and unsnapped her bra in a single heartbeat.

Preambles were swept aside as he slipped a finger inside her and found her more than ready. When he slid inside, her nails pressed into his back. His strokes increased, and she laid back, bearing her breasts to him, and he obliged her, taking a nipple into his mouth.

Was this really happening? He closed his eyes and savored the moment, terrified he'd wake and find himself once again strapped to the wall with Gheata waiting for him. All of this nothing more than a wonderous and torturous dream.

He lifted one of her legs to drive deeper. Her throaty pants guided him. She was a wild creature, just as a wolf should be— brave and daring, but most of all, fierce and kind. It seemed odd that his beast had immediately formed an attachment to her from the first moment she'd walked into his cell. Had her wolf known?

Their moment was heated but brief. When her body squeezed down as the orgasm hit her, he covered her mouth with a demanding kiss, though most of the walls were soundproofed to block a vampire's exceptional hearing. He wanted her in his room, where the soundproofing was thicker. She could scream like a banshee, and most wouldn't hear it.

She stayed in rhythm with him until his own release came. Rather than fall over the top of her, he pulled her up and caught her in his arms as they tumbled to the floor.

Alex lifted her head and glanced around. She pulled a file folder from underneath her head and tossed it aside. "I've messed up your office." Her grin said she wasn't sorry for it.

"I can make Cressa reorganize the files."

"What's up with her?"

He grinned, though inside, he groaned at what new hell Cressa would put him through with this new development in his life. "She's bored with the lockdown and doesn't have enough to do. As irritating as she can be, she has excellent skills, most of them honed during her time as a thief, and she's deadly in a fight. She can be a general pain in the ass, and I'll reprimand you harshly if you ever tell her I said this, but she's good for this House."

"Reprimand? Exactly how harshly?" She teased, her eyes glowing with a hint of her wolf.

His eyes flashed with the beast. "I wish I had time to demonstrate, but we have training this afternoon. Perhaps you'd like to join us, and you can see what it takes to be on the counter-strike team."

She ran a finger down his cheek as her brows scrunched together, and her smile disappeared. "Is this the right thing to do?"

"What?"

"Us."

He didn't respond quickly, not wanting to blurt out platitudes. Not with her. "All I know is that this feels right. I don't take chances often. I've been burned rather severely in the past. But I'd be a fool not to give us a try. If we can survive a war, I think we can survive anything."

She kissed him hard and wrapped her arms around him. He felt her grin as she pressed her lips to his cheek and whispered, "Does this mean I'm on the team?"

"Is that what you were hoping to get out of this?" Sergi asked me as he settled on the floor, leaning on an elbow. His eyes were intense. Was he judging me?

I stared at him for a long moment, running a finger over his tattoo, following the curves down his arm and then back up to cross his chest. Goose bumps erupted over his skin.

If I'd met him during a business meeting or a social gathering, would this connection between us be this strong? There was a connection, wasn't there? I'd had my share of boyfriends. Most didn't last long. I'd either been too young to get tied down, or there was no substance to them. I was wolf, yet there were too many times I ignored that part of me when selecting a male.

One look in this vampire's eyes and my wolf stirred. If I'd seen him standing in a grocery store, my wolf would have taken notice. But there was no doubt that the situation we'd found ourselves in

—him pinned naked to a wall with blood dripping from dozens of wounds and me as much a captive as him—one would think it was a heat-of-the-moment thing.

I wanted to prove it wasn't. Something I wasn't sure my uncle would be willing to accept. Was it because this male next to me was vampire, that he was dangerous, or he simply thought I was being foolish? Perhaps he thought I liked this vampire for the simple fact that he saved my life.

Yet, my uncle would be the first to say the wolf doesn't lie.

"You're taking a long time to answer my question." He took my hand and kissed it. "I want honesty, if nothing else, between us."

I turned on my side and pushed up to lean my head in my hand. "I want the same. So, here it is. I haven't stopped thinking about you since I got home." I chuckled and glanced at his tattoos. In a strange way, they'd become my own talisman. That first physical connection to him. "To be honest, I still haven't gotten my head wrapped around the fact that I'm free. That I'm truly home. I knew my uncle would be overly protective. He thought I was dead." I grinned. "He left my bedroom as it was before I left for the mission."

I didn't add that the housekeeper hadn't bothered cleaning up the discarded clothes and books I'd left all over the place. He'd already guessed I might be messy.

"He never gave up hope."

Sergi broke me out of my wandering. I gave a half-shrug before glancing around the office, taking in the few knickknacks but noting there wasn't a single picture of him or anyone who might be dear to him. "When my uncle told me I was to stay at the estate and find a way to help the war that didn't require my leaving—" I struggled with the right words.

"It was like being locked up all over again."

I pushed hard to hold back the sting of tears. "I knew you wouldn't try coming to the estate, especially with your lockdown. I had the same problem with not knowing how to reach out to you, at least not without going through my uncle for a number. It never occurred to me that Braden would take my side." I shook my head, wanting Sergi to know everything. "That's not right. Braden has always had my back, but he was never so open in working around my uncle's wishes when it regarded me. I'd been orphaned young, and I think my uncle blamed himself for my parents' deaths, though it wasn't his fault."

"He couldn't protect them."

I nodded. "He's always so worried about everyone, even when he can't control everything. So, when Braden noticed the extra guards following me around, he knew I'd chafe with pup sitters." I blurted out a laugh. "And hell has no fury when Alex is on a bender. I think he was worried for his own self-preservation." I blew out a breath and looked at Sergi, whose warm gaze never seemed to leave me. It was more comforting than I cared to admit.

I glanced down at a file folder that lay between us and picked at an edge. "When Braden told me about this counter-strike team, it solved both my problems."

When too much silence followed, he lifted my chin. "Tell me."

That little red glow that burned deep in his brown eyes was a signal for the passion, or most likely, any strong emotion he kept buried inside. It made my insides turn to jelly and hammered at my boundaries, urging me to share all my deep, dark secrets.

"It gave me the chance to be a part of this war that is no longer just between vampires, not after what I experienced at the lab. You mentioned revenge. I call it vengeance, but I suppose the result will be the same."

I grasped his hand. "But that wasn't all. I needed to see you again. Be with you. See if the emotions we shared were deeper than just that single moment." I released his hand and rolled onto my back, rubbing my eyes before pushing my fingers through my hair. "This is so weird. I've never felt this strongly about anyone, and I can't believe I'm admitting this out loud."

Without warning, his lips were on mine, and I rolled into him, savoring every touch as his fingers trailed up and down my spine. The sensations sent small tremors through me as I breathed in the heady scent of male. When the kiss ended and he pulled back, he wrapped a long strand of my hair around his finger, rubbing a thumb over it before gently releasing it.

"I don't know whether we'll be the victor in our war with Venizi or what the outcome with the Council will be. All I know is that the beast wants you here, by my side, until you say otherwise."

"My wolf wouldn't have it any other way."

This time, his kiss was tender, and when he leaned back, I asked. "How long before your training starts?"

"Thirty minutes."

"Dressing will only take five. What should we do with the other twenty-five?"

He grinned as he claimed my lips and my body. There wasn't time for anything more than teasing nips, heated kisses, and long strokes that did nothing more than get our dander up without any sense of fulfillment. It would make for an interesting training session.

He broke off his last kiss after fifteen minutes and stood, pulling me up beside him. He made a quick phone call before we dressed, and once we were presentable, he stuck his head out the door. "The hallway is clear."

He took my hand, and we raced to the main hallway, where he stopped and quickly glanced around the corner. "Straight up the stairs. Stay close."

As if I had any other choice with his strong hand clenching mine, but I held back the giggles as we raced up the stairs and down the second-floor hallway. He pushed me inside a bedroom that could only be his, and I didn't come to that conclusion because he immediately stripped out of his suit.

There might not have been personal items in his office, but they were all over his bedroom. Ancient weapons that were polished to a shine, an old leather shield, and various trinkets that, at first glance, came from various parts of the world. This was the room of a warrior, and it turned me on.

I jumped when someone knocked, then was confused when no one entered or called out. Sergi stuck his head out of the walk-in closet.

"Can you check that? That should have been Greta leaving workout clothes for you. You seem close to Cressa's size."

I slowly pulled open the door, nervous that Devon might be on the other side, but there was nothing there but a stack of clothing and a pair of sneakers. I grabbed them and laid them on the bed.

"Hurry. We can't be late."

"Are these Cressa's?"

"No. We keep spares for the security teams."

I quickly changed, folding my jeans and blouse and leaving them on a chair. He grabbed my hand, and we were out the door, jogging back down to the first floor.

"It will be a full training session. Devon, Cressa, Lucas, and Ginger will be there. Are you prepared for that?"

"No. But I'll be fine."

"As the instructor, I won't be able to give you any special treatment."

"I wouldn't expect any. Besides, aren't the females human?"

He chuckled as he led me down the hall. "Two human females who are extremely dangerous. Don't let their looks or words fool you. It's their first line of defense against vampires who never take them seriously, to their own detriment. Although, I don't think they've trained with shifters. This will be interesting."

When we entered the room, I gave it a quick glance since there wasn't much to see. It was an expansive, rectangular room and was probably used as a ballroom at one time. Now, it was sparse, with the exception of a climbing wall that stretched across one long side of the room, a few tall posts of various heights, ropes that dangled from the ceiling, multiple mats, and a single bench.

Four sets of eyes watched our entrance. Devon and Cressa grinned while the other two appeared surprised, though the male's expression quickly became blank except for a hint of curiosity in his eyes. A vampire. The female next to him was the dark-haired female I'd seen earlier. Cressa's human friend.

This was definitely an unusual vampire House.

The dark-haired woman glanced at the others and then sighed. "So typical." She rushed over and held out her hand. "I'm Ginger. Welcome to House Trelane."

I took her hand, and she pumped it vigorously.

"This is so exciting." She winked at Sergi, and though we weren't touching, and I didn't dare glance his way, I sensed he was uncomfortable.

Now I understood him sneaking me through the manor. He was a male who protected his privacy. Unfortunately for him, I wasn't someone who could be hidden.

"I'm Alex."

She nodded. "A wolf. That's so exciting. I've never trained with a shifter before." She paused and glanced between Sergi and Devon. "Is she going to be allowed to train in wolf form? I mean, isn't the training meant to develop our own personal skills?"

Her question caught me off guard. Did she actually want to fight a wolf? I glanced at Cressa, who was grinning and bouncing on her toes, eager to get started.

"I think for our purpose here," Devon answered, "we need to ensure we have the skills to fight without the use of our fangs—shifter or vampire. Just like we don't let Cressa use her dreamwalker skills."

My gaze shot to Cressa. A dreamwalker? I just landed squarely in the middle of the Twilight Zone. My uncle had been busy while I was away.

"My wolf can handle herself, but my martial arts skills are a bit rusty. If you find yourself fighting against a wolf and you aren't vampire, my best suggestion would be a gun unless you excel with daggers."

The group glanced at each other, and the vampire called Lucas was the first to laugh out loud. "Well, I'd say Alex just set the tone for our training."

Sergi's grin was almost maniacal. "Agreed. Let's begin."

After an hour on the climbing wall and then martial arts bouts pitting two against each other, I was sweating like a leaky faucet, but my endorphins had me flying high. I was holding my own, but Cressa and Ginger had both taken me down several times. Sergi had been right. Their skills were impressive, and I had to admit, were better than mine.

On the last takedown, Cressa stood over me and held out her hand, which I took. Once I was back on my feet, she grinned. "You've got some good moves. After a couple weeks with Sergi, and you get your muscles and strength back, you'll be unstoppable."

"Thanks. I guess you surprised me."

"For being a human?" She never lost her grin, and she put an arm around me. "It fools the vamps when they first meet us. Most never get a second chance."

I laughed. "The human part would definitely surprise them, but seeing a female always makes them foolish."

Ginger rushed over. "This has been so fun. I think we should hit the hot tub and then the patio for some margaritas." She looked at me. "You are staying, right? You don't want to drive back and forth from Remus's estate to train every day." She tilted her head. "I don't actually know where his estate is, but still, if you're going to be on the counter-strike team, you should stay here. Oh, and I should see if Lyra can join us. That's Devon's sister. She doesn't train with us, but she's always up for margaritas."

"Enough, Ginger." Sergi joined us. "We're still working out the logistics." He turned and gave me an evil grin I'd only seen him use when readying for battle. "I'm sure Alex will enjoy the benefits of a hot tub and margaritas once she survives her last session of training."

Ginger and Cressa grinned at each other as they quietly backed up to join Devon and Lucas.

Sergi circled me, and I instinctively turned to keep him in my sights. His expression was downright menacing, but there was a twinkle in his eyes. This was so unfair. After watching his skills at taking down Gheata, I doubted there were many that could best him. On top of that, we'd been training for two hours, and he'd only joined a couple of bouts. Otherwise, he stood around and shouted orders.

While he was as fresh as a peach, I felt like an old mule after a hundred-mile hike through the desert. Every muscle in my body was waving for attention, and the thought of soaking them in the hot tub was nirvana. My legs were wobbly, and my arms felt like dead weights.

But the wolf paced—eager for mock battle. And while I had no chance of winning, I'd be damned if he'd take me down easy. I grinned, and I think he hesitated for a split second.

I crouched in my offensive stance, stuck out my arm, and wiggled my fingers in a come-hither gesture. Cressa and Ginger screeched and shouted out their support for me, and then Devon and Lucas joined in, leaving Sergi the odd male out. My grin grew wider.

His eyes glowed red with excitement at the coming bout. My thoughts moved beyond hot tubs and margaritas to an entire evening in Sergi's immense bed. Other than the heated conversation I was sure to have with my uncle, this was turning out to be the best day I'd had in a long time.

I gave Sergi a wink. "Come on, vampire. Let's see what you've got."

∾

## THANK YOU FOR READING!

But don't go! Keep reading for more of House Trelane.

*This is a temporary cover.*

The dreamwalker medallion.

Embossed on both sides are three objects that link both the vampire and dreamwalker species together: the Blood Poppy—The Ibis—The Dagger of Omar.

Simone, cadre to House Trelane, wasn't comfortable around dreamwalkers. She trusted Cressa with her life, which was an unexpected admission. But Colantha was a different story. She was royalty among dreamwalkers, and Simone would bet her life the female was hiding something.

Simone had almost disregarded Colantha's interpretation of the *De første dage* until she mentioned the Dagger of Omar. Her skin had itched at the name, and the universe had dropped away, leaving Simone in a black void so deep there weren't any stars.

She'd seen the Dagger of Omar. She'd thought it all a lie.

The same ancient blade Gaius took with him wherever he traveled.

Gaius.

Her lover. Her torturer.

Their last encounter...just months ago...had been a surprise. Gaius had seemed a different vampire. She had remembered the lover more than the torturer, and it had been centuries since that had been so.

Weeks had passed since she'd reached out to him. There had been no response. Dozens of reasons could explain why, but her gut told her something else.

Someone else might be searching for the Dagger of Omar. And Gaius could be in trouble. Or dead.

AND NOW A GLIMPSE...

# Simone

**Simone**
**Of Blood and Dreams - Book 8**

(This may or may not be the first chapter. Either way—Enjoy!)

I STOOD on the pier and watched the boat steer toward the south dock of Aetos Island. The calm waters of the Aegean Sea sparkled blue in the late afternoon sun. Did the Family not use the north side dock anymore? The satellite pictures hadn't shown any indication of there being more than one pier on the island, which was suspicious in itself. It was easy enough to dismantle a dock and pretend it never existed. Depending on when Gaius had it removed, centuries would have erased the remaining evidence hidden deep in the bay waters.

But it wasn't as easy to erase tunnels. Perhaps block the entrance with rubble from an explosion or cover it with the native bushes. But tunnels, once dug, wouldn't completely disappear. No ancient vampire would remove an escape route unless they'd completely lost their mind. And based on my recent visit with Gaius, he was far from senile.

"Miss. Will you be much longer?"

I ignored the cab driver as I considered my next move. The request for a meeting with the House leader had been denied. It wasn't completely unexpected. I hadn't presented myself as cadre to House Trelane. Still, while Gaius might not be getting his emails, he wouldn't turn me away from his home if he was in residence.

The cab driver didn't say anything more, but the constant shuffling of his feet over the gritty pier grated on my last nerve. With Cressa's constant admonishments floating around in my head, I turned and gave the man my most gracious smile, remembering to keep my fangs in check.

"Sorry. I'm ready to go." The fact that Cressa was in my head at all was annoying, and I did my best to cast her aside as I marched after the driver. I silently cursed as I squeezed into the back seat, my long legs forced to bend so tightly that the persistent pain in my right hip flared to life. Now, the reason why the dreamwalker had been in my head all morning made sense. I hadn't run through my Tai Chi program. If I had, there wouldn't have been a pain in my hip, regardless of being twisted up like a pretzel.

"Back to the hotel?" the driver asked.

"Yes." But he'd only driven a couple blocks when I asked, "Is the Emperor's Lair still open? It's been some time since I've been here."

The driver glanced at me through the rearview mirror with a concerned expression before making a quick sign of the cross. Well, at least he'd heard of the place.

He nodded his head. "I know it, but you don't want to go there."

"Do I need to call another cab?"

"No. No. It's just not safe. Bad neighborhood."

He was likely more concerned for his own safety than mine, but perhaps I should have more faith in humanity. I managed to hold back my snicker.

"I can take care of myself. If you don't want to take me all the way, get me as close as you can. I'll walk from there."

He didn't say another word, and I was surprised when the cab pulled down the dark alley that ended in a large circular driveway at the club's entrance. I glanced up at the building as the cab circled toward the front. It was still early, another couple hours until sunset, but the place was as foreboding in the daylight as it was at night.

The old castle, completed in the 15th century, just before the Ottoman Empire stormed Constantinople, appeared just as cold and dank as anything built during the Dark Ages. It wasn't easy to make a fortress look pleasing, and the vampire who owned this building, or perhaps his legacy now, wouldn't want it any other way. No human in their right mind would feel encouraged to knock on the front door.

When the cab stopped, I reached over the seat and handed the driver double the fare. "If you simply drive away once I'm out, you'll be fine. No harm will come to you."

I exited the cab but stopped to get a feel for the surroundings and gave a quick look over my shoulder to see if anyone had followed them. The cab hadn't sped away but maintained a respectable speed. He was braver than I'd given him credit. Sometimes, humanity surprised me.

I strode toward the doorway where two immense, frowning vampires stood as sentinels—and muscle. My sea blue caftan floated behind me, and my boots made a staccato, clicking sound on the flagstone walkway. When I reached the door, I flashed a full set of fangs and sneered.

The vampire on the right immediately opened the door. I didn't bother thanking him as I marched past. Vampire propriety reigned king in a vampire club. No one thanked the help.

The darkly imposing castle on the outside transformed into a brightly lit château on the inside. If I blinked and woke here, I might believe I was in a casino in Monte Carlo or Macau. I was greeted by white marble floors, alabaster walls, and high ceilings with sparkling crystal chandeliers finished off with just the right touch of burgundy and gold trimming. And I was only in the foyer. The rest of the rooms in the castle would be similar. At least on the first two floors. The other three floors belonged exclusively to the Family residents and were well-guarded.

The first two floors were open to club customers, with specific areas available only to VIP members. The rooms were divided to accommodate various preferences: gambling, private meetings, a social club with music and dancing, intimate settings to satisfy anyone's kink, and one darkly decorated to mirror an old English pub.

It was the pub that drew my attention. The highly intellectual, the philosophers who debated over their chess boards, and ancients who gathered to share old battle stories were the typical guests who found their way to this room. It was also the best place to make contacts for the more dangerous games. At least it used to be.

I stopped just past the entrance to survey the area but found very little had changed. The clientele appeared to be what I'd expected to see. The darker corners hid the individuals occupying them, but that was by design. With luck, I'd be in one of those booths before the night was over.

I turned toward the bar that ran along the far wall, ending at a hallway that led to the back offices. It was still early for most vampires, especially here in the old country, and several stools were open. I settled onto one a third of the way down and between two empty seats.

I tapped my fingers on the bar and perused the customers more slowly through the long mirror that hung behind the bar. Two vampires looked familiar though I couldn't recall their names. Perhaps I never knew them. But they sat at the same table, hunched over their chessboard, as they debated vampire politics.

They might be worth a quick chat if I didn't find what I was looking for. If they kept up with local politics, they might provide a clue as to why Gaius was ignoring me.

"What's your poison?"

The deep, sultry female voice instantly stopped my musings. I slowly turned toward the speaker, not ready for who I expected to find standing behind the bar. In a flash, memories from centuries ago hit me like a silver bullet had a couple of months ago.

"Are you still using that old line? It's nothing more than a cliché."

The blonde leaned over, the tip of her fangs showing, and in a low tone said, "Not if I'm the one who started it."

We stared at each other for several seconds before the blonde fell back and chuckled. "God damn, Simone, but it's good to see you." She grabbed a Boston shaker and poured alcohol into it, followed by ice.

"I could say the same of you, Edie. I would never believe you'd still be working behind a bar." When Edie only stared with a wicked grin, I shook my head. "Not Gianni." When the blonde nodded, I added, "After all this time?"

"You know the saying. The heart wants what the heart wants. And before you say anything, he's not the playboy he used to be. We both have our faults—and kinks." She winked and shook the container. "But we're as solid as the day he asked me to be his consort. Of course, we made it more official two decades ago." She poured the clear liquid into a martini glass, added a spear of olives, and placed it in front of me.

"I had no idea. Remaining in contact with friends isn't my specialty." I stared down at the drink before picking it up, anticipation swirling as I took a sip. I closed my eyes. My expectations had been perfectly met. I opened them to catch hers. "No one makes a dirty vodka martini like you."

"It's not your fault. You know vampires don't worry about personal relationships. Not unless there's a business transaction to be had. We live such long lives that sooner or later, we eventually end up in each other's path." She wiped down the bar and poured a dark beer from a tap, pushing it in front of a customer three seats to my left. "I hear you're in line for your own House."

Her words shocked me. "I didn't think it was common knowledge."

Edie laughed, but when she leaned over the bar again, her tone became serious. "You know Gaius has kept track of you through the centuries. Not stalking, or worried you might fall and stub your toe, but because he knew you'd be someone great. You're one of us. The lower born. The vampires who had no protection until a House needed servants or an army." She grabbed an empty glass from another vampire who was standing to leave. "Have a good evening, Simon." The male waved a hand as he turned away, but then he stopped and gave her a wink before putting his hat on and shuffling to the door. "I just adore that old male. Now, what was I saying?" She considered it for a second then continued, "I don't miss those old days. And here you are, soon to be a leader with your own House. That makes us all proud." When she noticed my discomfort, she added with a wink, "But not everyone is lucky enough to have their own Gianni."

I chuckled but was still uncomfortable until I remembered why I was there. Devon's words of strength and honor before I left Baywood came tumbling back, and I straightened in my chair, pushing Edie's words of praise away and taking the opening she'd given me.

"You said Gaius has been watching me?"

Her grin wouldn't go away, and I couldn't blame her. She'd always been a vivacious vampire. We weren't all morose and stubborn. "He was aware of your presence the last time you were here. How long has it been?"

"The Siege of Kastania in the late eighteenth century, if memory serves." That had been such a long time ago, yet, at the same time, only a blip for the long-lived. The haunting memories had hit hard after that trip, and Greece had been the last place I'd wanted to think about. I ignored the need to apologize for not reaching out. Communication hadn't been the most reliable back then. When Cressa's voice reached out to admonish me for the lame excuse, I pushed it aside. "If Gaius had known I was here, why didn't he reach out to me?"

"Why didn't you reach out to him?" She tilted her head. "Perhaps he wasn't sure you'd be receptive."

"He hadn't deserved it." Why had I made that past tense? Because he'd been a different vampire when I'd met him in San Francisco. And we'd parted on good terms. Hadn't we? If so, then why the ghosting?

"I was denied entrance to the island."

She frowned. "That doesn't make sense." She clicked her long, midnight-blue polished nails on the bar. "Though...Gianni mentioned something seemed off on the island."

"Like what?"

"He wasn't sure. It was little things he'd overheard. Some of the rumors were about business problems, but others claimed someone in the Family had the blood disease."

My chest clenched, and my stomach flip-flopped at the thought Gaius had contracted the blood disease.

"Nothing substantiated, of course. But something's going on that no one wants to talk about."

I glanced around and, assured no one was paying any attention to us, leaned in. "I'm only in town for a couple of days. I need someone good at infiltration. Know anyone like that?"

Her eyes glowed the soft blue of her beast for an instant before she grinned. "I know several. In fact, there's one in the back room as we speak."

The back room was for high-stake gamblers. Everything was legal within the club, but the gambling rooms were mostly for amateurs who didn't mind losing a few hundred dollars in an evening. The antes in the various back rooms started at ten grand. This would be a serious contact.

"Are they any good?"

"He thinks so. And I mean, he thinks he's good at everything. If you catch my drift."

"Great." The last thing I needed was a male who thought too highly of himself.

"But he truly is the best at his job. Take a seat at one of the open booths, and I'll have him come out as soon as he finishes his game."

"Send a martini over when you have a minute."

Thirty minutes and two martinis later, a tall male with curly dark hair, skin a couple shades lighter than mine, and filling out a dark-gray suit in all the right places plopped into the half-circle booth. He scooted close to me. "Simone, is it?"

I nodded.

"I'm Marco. Edie said I might be of assistance." He gave me a long, cool stare, and though I caught a flash of lust in his gaze, it disappeared quickly. He was a handsome vampire, but it was easy to tell he was cocky as hell. More than I wanted to deal with, even for one night.

"I need a thief. Preferably one who has expertise getting into difficult places."

He waved for a server, and the human brought him two shot glasses and a bottle of top-shelf tequila. The server filled both glasses and bowed before leaving them to their privacy.

I sighed. I would have to show fortitude in keeping up with him. It wasn't like the alcohol would impair either of us. It was more a show of respect. Though he'd have to prove his worthiness with more than a high-priced bottle of liquor.

I downed the shot and set the glass on the table. "Before we get much farther, I need to know you have what it takes to fulfill a one-time drop-off to a specific location protected by deadly security."

Marco swallowed his shot and refilled both glasses. "There's nothing we can't do for the right price." When I held my stare, he tossed back the second shot and continued. "We use the most current technology—computers, transportation, surveillance systems, drones, explosives, weapons, and spyware. If you're more interested in espionage, our hackers are the best in their field. We also have two professionally trained spies on our payroll."

He talked a good game, but anyone could run down a list and claim they had the best. Though his list had covered a broad range of all the right tools. I drained the second shot and gave him a tight smile that included the tips of my fangs.

"Give me the details on two of your most difficult infiltrations. Without names, locations, or time periods, of course."

His brows shot up. When I didn't blink, his gaze narrowed. I almost laughed. Did he think I was with the Eliminators, or perhaps the Sentinels, attempting to lure him into confessing deep, dark secrets?

I leaned close and placed a hand near his. "I'm not playing games. I have one mission I need to complete within the next couple of days, and I don't have time to screw around finding the services I require. Edie says there are several players who could help me with my problem. If you're not serious, I'll move on."

I held his stare, begging him to make some move that would tell me if I should stay or ask Edie for other contacts. He glanced at the room of clients and then back to me, scooting closer until our legs almost touched.

He told me of two jobs his team had recently run, and I listened intently, stopping him when I had a question about a certain detail. I didn't catch any fabrications. It was clear, whether he was boasting or not, his words weren't one of an amateur. In fact, if he proved to have the skilled resources and tech he promised, Devon might be interested in his services, depending on how far their war with Venizi went.

"If you like what you hear but are unforgiving on the time frame, I'll require double our normal fee."

I continued my stare. "If you can deliver what you promise,

then not a problem. Fifty percent once I've met your team and reviewed your plan. The final fifty at time of drop-off. Each payment will be transferred to the bank of your choosing."

"The fee is two hundred, not including any special equipment necessary to complete the job."

Two hundred thousand was a reasonable sum, considering how quickly I needed to complete the mission.

"I need the job completed no later than the morning of the day after tomorrow."

If he expected her to squabble about the amount, he didn't show it. "What's the mission?"

"I need you to drop me off, sight unseen, on Aetos Island."

His brows shot up, and then he grinned with sharp fangs. "Now, I remember where I heard the name Simone."

*Thank You for Reading*

*This is a temporary cover.*

**Simone,** Of Blood and Dreams - Book 8
Coming Fall 2025

**Make sure you never miss a new release!**

Join my FB Readers Group - Kim Allred's Heart Racing Romance
Join my newsletter...I'm pretty much unobtrusive.
Follow me at Amazon, Goodreads, or Bookbub
If you can't wait and want to check out my other series, visit my
website.

AS A SPECIAL TREAT, if you haven't already taken advantage of this **FREE** prequel to the Of Blood and Dreams series, this is the time. This novella is set one hundred years before the start of the series. Download your copy of Lyra today.

**The catalyst. The victim. The bridge.**

The Roaring Twenties. The time of flappers and Prohibition.

For Lyra, a young vampire and aspiring painter, the world is her canvas.

When she meets Hamilton, a sculptor and her family's gardener, time stops. He understands her like no one else.

But he's a human. And he's not the only one drawn to her. An ancient and powerful vampire has declared his desire to seduce her.

A perfect storm that sets the stage for all that is to come.

# *About the Author*

**Kim Allred** grew up in California but now enjoys the quiet life in an old

timber town in the Pacific Northwest where she raises alpacas, llamas, and an undetermined number of free-range chickens. Like her characters, Kim loves sharing stories while sipping a glass of wine or slurping a strong cup of brew.

Her spirit of adventure has taken her on a ten-day dogsledding trip in northern Alaska and found her sleeping under the stars on the savannas of eastern Africa.

Kim is currently making up stories while shooing cats and dogs away from her lap, and Willow, the parrot, from her keyboard. Willow can peel the keys from the board in fifteen seconds flat.

Kim's current works include her time travel romance series, the *Mórdha Stone Chronicles* and *The Swan Syndicate*, the urban fantasy romance series, *Of Blood & Dreams*, and a time travel sci-fi and fantasy adventure series, *Time Renegades*.